To



Wishing you good tennis, good reading, and, of course, good luck!

Lillian Duval

You Never Know

# you never know

*Tales of Tobias, an Accidental Lottery Winner*

LILIAN DUVAL

*You Never Know: Tales of Tobias, an Accidental Lottery Winner*



*Cover photo: Michel Hersen, www.Photographybymichel.net*

Published by Wheatmark®
610 East Delano Street, Suite 104
Tucson, Arizona 85705 U.S.A.
www.wheatmark.com

ISBN: 978-1-60494-520-1
LCCN: 2011922339

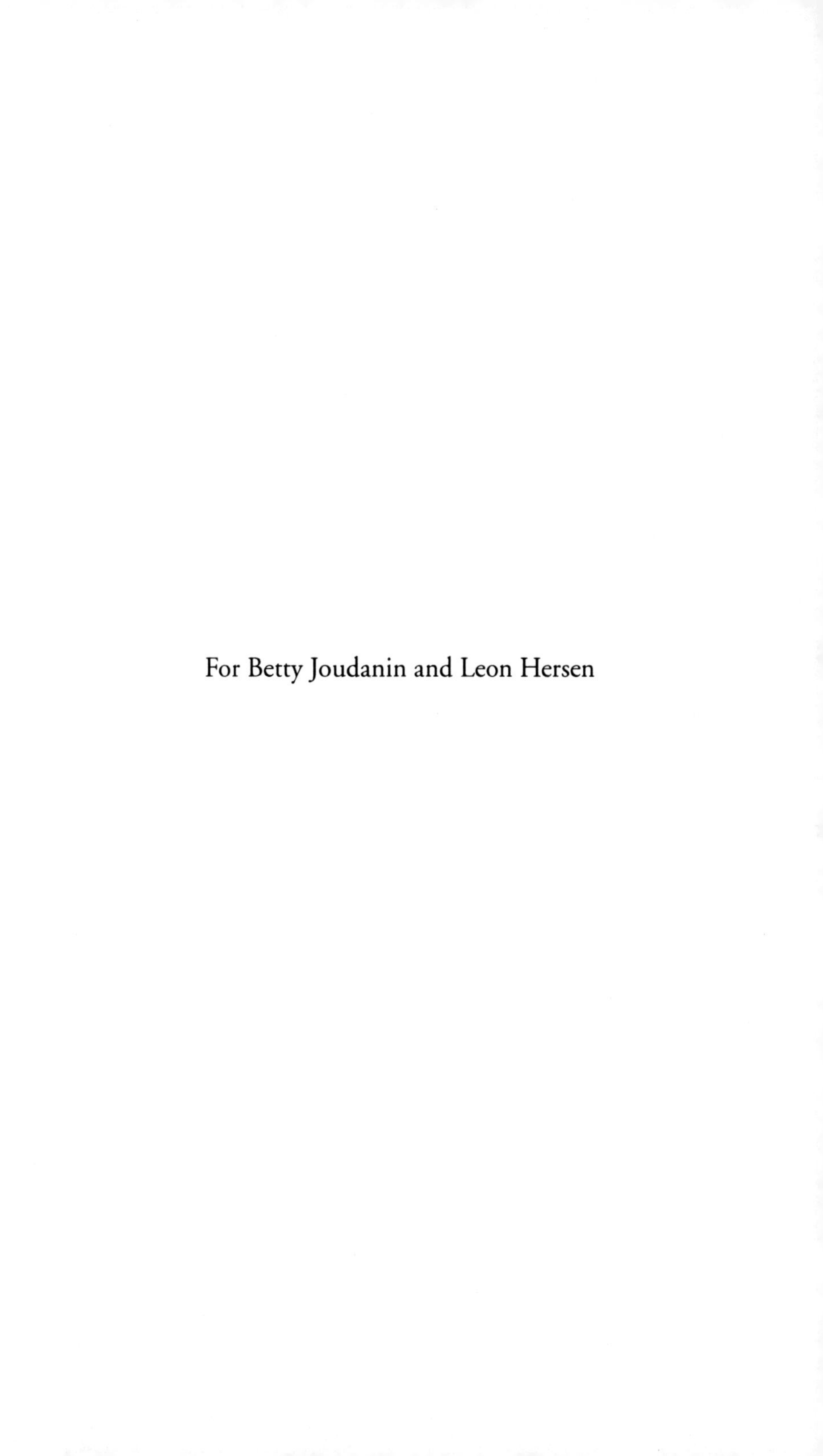

For Betty Joudanin and Leon Hersen

An optimist is a person who sees a green light everywhere, while a pessimist sees only the red stoplight. The truly wise person is colorblind.

*Albert Schweitzer*

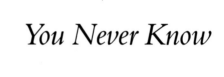

*You Never Know*

# *Prologue*

Tobias was a man who planned things out, who reflected on the way ahead. He organized his tools on a pegboard, his books on a shelf, his thoughts in his mind. He bought flashlights and batteries, canned goods, storm doors, and insurance.

Tobias avoided uncertainty. He was nevertheless compelled to live a life governed by coincidence.

Coincidence: a sequence of scattered events occurring together at random, yet seeming predestined. A constellation pitched into the galaxy of life, stars tossed every which way by a cosmic hand. A disordered collection whose stars, once mapped, seem to have been there for all eternity.

Coincidence: luck, fate, a good hand of cards. A life enhanced by a split-second decision made haphazardly—or not made at all.

Coincidence: tragedy, destruction, irreparable damage. A victim unjustifiably condemned by an unseen fortune-teller presiding over a kangaroo court.

Tobias didn't carry lucky pennies or make birthday wishes. He believed in good acts, not good fortune. Yet it was coincidence—both kinds—that defined him. This is his story.

# book one

# Chapter 1

Saturday, December 23, 1989, was the kind of tepid winter day that made people ask, "What winter?" Dark by four in the afternoon, but no wind, no bite, a gray curtain over the sky for most of the day, just barely cold enough to freeze the slush into a treacherous skin of black ice that coated the streets like slime in a dirty shower stall. Tobias skidded on it when he stepped off the New Jersey Transit bus from Port Authority.

He was to call home from the bus station as soon as he arrived. He would wait in Amy's Coffee House and pop out with his luggage when his father double-tapped the horn.

The bus had pulled into Woodrock, New Jersey, at four-thirty PM, half an hour late in Christmas traffic. Tobias slung his overstuffed book bag over his shoulder and dragged his valise into the crowded restaurant. He bought a giant latte and sat on a barstool at the end of the counter. Other college students were chatting about ski trips and courses and their current romances. Christmas carols played on an endless loop. The place smelled of cinnamon.

The location of home was debatable. The longer he stayed away, the more separate he became from the family still living in Woodrock, to the point where he could almost forget them. Home was where his life was: Abington College in Maryland and the off-campus apartment he shared with

Martin, his tennis partner, a math major planning on business school, who called Tobias a "liberal arts lefty." They got along fine, were evenly matched on the courts, and took turns abandoning their apartment for a few hours when one or the other had a girlfriend over. They were both twenty, going on twenty-one, seesawing between adolescence and adulthood.

Tobias took a gulp of coffee and scalded his tongue. His father would be sitting in front of the TV now, doing nothing, waiting for the phone to ring. His mother would be delaying dinner preparations, sneaking another glass of wine. His brother, Simeon, would be upstairs in his room, sketching or drawing.

He sipped half the coffee and folded his arms over his book bag. Simeon, age fifteen, was a cartoonist. His pictures had appeared in the high school newspaper, the town newspaper, and the state magazine. Their mother was an art teacher, but no one had taught him cartooning; he just drew all day long—in class, where he was warm in art and cold in every other subject; at home, where he holed up in his room, away from the fighting; and anyplace he went where he had to wait in line. He didn't talk much.

When Tobias was eleven, Simeon was six, and already attracting attention with his cartoons. He entered the school art contest with a drawing of his first-grade teacher, emphasizing her long earrings and long face, a caricature that was otherwise flattering. The school principal called and demanded to know who, in fact, had drawn a picture too advanced for a first-grader. Their mother huffed off to school, carrying a Grand Union bag crammed with Simeon's cartoons of the last year or so, mostly of family members, to back him up. Simeon won the prize: a drawing set containing colored pencils, chalk pastels, an eraser, a sharpener, and a blending stump, all in a tin box with compartments like a Swanson frozen dinner.

Watching him sketch at the kitchen table, Tobias told their mother, "He's talented because he practices so much. He never does anything else." Simeon went on drawing without seeming to listen.

"No," their mother said. "He practices so much because he's talented."

Tobias first saw his baby brother when he was two weeks old. He'd been sent alone at age five on a plane to his aunt Joyce in Encino, California, hovered over by flight attendants, at the time called stewardesses. Joyce, accustomed to covering for her alcoholic sister, took care of Tobias competently and joylessly for a month. On his return home, his father showed him the baby, asleep in a crib. "Here's your new brother," he said. "Just like you, only smaller."

By the time Tobias was twelve, his mother was drinking in the mornings, her coffee mug filled with wine, and couldn't get Simeon off to elementary school. Tobias packed his brother's lunch every day before he left for middle school, taught him to tell time, and made sure he got out the door on time, while their mother went back to bed.

Tobias finished his coffee and asked the girl next to him to watch his stuff while he went to the men's room. Someone was on the pay phone at the back of the restaurant. He ordered another coffee the same size. He wouldn't be able to sleep. But rather than making him jittery, the caffeine was calming him, and he cast around for something to look forward to after this visit. He was always thinking, *When this or that happens, then I'll be happy.* It was never now; it was always later. *Maybe happiness is forever anticipating being happy,* he thought. Getting what you want doesn't equal happiness. His was a life always heading somewhere but never arriving.

At the moment, he was looking forward to three things: One, seeing his brother, his only family member who was not stuck in time or moving backward. Two, perversely, for this visit to be over. And three, his undergraduate anthropology fellowship in the rainforests of the Peruvian Amazon and the Yanomami territories of Brazil and Venezuela.

His father had forbidden Simeon to draw or paint until he raised his grades in school, where he was making As in art and Cs and Ds in all his other tenth-grade subjects. Twice, Tobias had mediated on the phone long-distance, to no avail. Simeon could draw with a fingernail in the dirt, but missed his art supplies, which their father had confiscated for the semester.

The phone at the back was free. Tobias felt in the front zippered flap of his suitcase for his family's presents, all bought at the last minute from the campus store: an Abington College scarf for his mother, an Abington coffee mug for his father, and the book *Best Cartoonists of the 20th Century* for his brother. He lugged everything to the phone corner and started fishing for coins in his coat pocket, slowly. At the center table, students he had known in high school were staring at him. He turned his back and plunked a quarter into the phone.

"Toby!" a voice boomed from the open door. A man stepped into the coffee shop. "Tobias Hillyer." The thirty or so customers all stopped talking at once. "Holly Jolly Christmas" warbled on the soundtrack.

Tobias grabbed his backpack and valise, scattering the coins from the phone shelf onto the floor. "Dad, I just got here. I was just calling you." They hugged.

"An hour late," his father said, grinning under his winter hat, the kind with earflaps. He cuffed Tobias on the head—only playfully. It hurt anyway.

"Thanks for coming, Dad. Come on; let's go." Murmurs of conversation sprang up as they shuffled to the door.

"Your mother wants us to stop and get Chinese food. No time to cook." He put Tobias's bags in the trunk. "So she said."

"Dad, please don't put anything on top of the suitcase."

"How's school?"

"Good, fine, Dad. I got a work-study job tutoring. Doing

all right. So I'd like to invite you all out to dinner." Getting the family out in public would at least mitigate their initial meeting.

They got in the car. "You still going down there with those pygmies?"

"Dad, they're Yanomami. Brazilian Indians, some in Venezuela. It'll be all right."

"Yo Mama, that what you call them?" He laughed.

Tobias ignored him the rest of the way to the house. He started to unlock the front door, which gave way before he turned the key. Still broken.

"Hi, sweetie!" His mother embraced him. She reeked of wine, and her enthusiasm alarmed him. There would be a confrontation; he could sense it.

"Good to see you, Mom." He stepped into the kitchen, ostensibly to get a glass of water, but only to check the barrel of corks behind the kitchen door. The top of the barrel reached his waist, and it was full of corks, some still wet from the bottle.

His mother was following him. "Sorry, honey, I didn't have time to cook."

His father said, "Tobias has invited us out. He's into money now."

"Mom. Dad. Let's make this a good one, OK? How about in twenty minutes, we all go out and celebrate the Christmas season?" His head was hurting. If it weren't for Simeon, he would have stayed on campus with the foreign students who lived too far away to go home on a holiday. He went upstairs to the room he had shared with his brother, who still had not emerged to greet him. Their bedroom door was closed. He knocked and walked in without waiting for an answer.

"Toby!" Simeon grabbed him, laughing and jumping like a little kid.

Tobias hugged him hard and thumped him on the back. "What are you doing, kiddo?"

"Just goofing around." Simeon's desk was covered with cartoons drawn on notebook paper with pencil, his other materials still under lock and key. There were caricatures of school friends; drawings of girls he favored, endowed with plus-size breasts and deep cleavage; and one picture of their mother, wine glass in hand, and their father, apparently scolding her.

Simeon was tall and thin like Tobias, but nearsighted. His rectangular glasses were always slipping down his narrow nose. "Toby. I got you something special. For your trip." He opened his desk drawer. "Open it now."

"Today's only the twenty-third."

"No, I have a regular present for you for Christmas. This is extra."

"Aw, I feel bad, Simmy. All I have is one gift for you."

"Doesn't matter. This is for sticking up for me. Open it," Simeon said, handing him a wrapped box.

"Why now?"

"Hey, you never know."

The present was heavy and solid, the size of a book, but denser. Tobias undid the wrapping paper. "Oh, man, Simmy, these are expensive." It was a pair of Swarovski binoculars, 10 x 50 power, good enough for ornithologists in the jungle. "Oh, my God, Simmy, how could you do this?"

Simeon took the box from his brother and spilled the accessories out on the bed. "They're waterproof and fog-proof." He took out the lens covers, eyepiece covers, carrying case, and neck strap. "I won some art contests."

"Simmy. Thank you. Thank you so much. I need these." Tobias fingered the focusing knob. "These are great. Wow."

Simeon laughed. Someone was starting to climb the stairs. They packed up the binoculars, hid the box under the pillows, and hurried downstairs.

Their father wanted to go to Vinny's, their usual family restaurant. Tobias imagined the scene that would ensue. His mother would progress from tipsy to downright drunk. His parents would fight over how much she was drinking. Vinny's had low ceilings, and you could hear every word from table to table.

"Dad, in honor of this special occasion, I'd like to take you all somewhere fancy." The town's other Italian restaurant, the upscale one, had no liquor license and poor acoustics, where you could hardly hear a word across the table. "Come on, everybody. I'll drive."

His mother was carrying a bottle of wine in a canvas tote bag. "No, Toby, you never drive at school. Sit in the back." She opened the door of their Ford Escort.

"He can drive," his father barked and handed the keys to Tobias, and then sat in the front seat. Tobias wanted his brother to sit with him but didn't complain. One hurdle cleared, and ten more days to go. He didn't know how he was going to make it; his head was already throbbing. Simeon sat in the back behind Tobias and kicked the driver's seat three times. Tobias grinned at him in the rearview mirror.

All during dinner, Simeon drew. On a typewriter pad from his brother's book bag, he sketched a detailed cartoon of Tobias. In the drawing, Tobias was wearing a safari hat and hip boots and carrying a butterfly net. A pair of binoculars hung from a strap around his neck.

Their father scowled. "Simeon, quit scribbling, and join the family."

"He's not scribbling; he's drawing," his mother said.

"He's OK, Dad."

Simeon was exaggerating his brother's thick, dark hair in the cartoon, letting it droop over his forehead. In the picture, Tobias's nose was pointy and slightly bent, but his real-life nose, though aquiline, was fine and straight, its hook scarcely noticeable. His features were so symmetrical that you would have to compare his photo and its mirror image to spot any irregularities. Simeon's own nose was ineffective in holding up his glasses, which he poked upward every now and then. He printed *Toby* at the bottom of the picture, signed it *SIM*, and turned to a new page.

"The food here is great," Tobias said. He sprinkled some crushed red pepper on his spinach gnocchi in marinara sauce, which was delicious. He was ravenous, having skipped breakfast to catch the Greyhound bus from Baltimore to New York and having had nothing to eat all day but a bag of Fritos at a rest stop.

"Yeah, great," his father said. "Try this." He poked a meatball with his fork and dropped it onto Tobias's plate.

"No thanks, Dad. This is fine." Tobias returned the meatball and wiped his fork on the side of his plate.

"He's a vegetarian, remember?" his mother said.

"Oh, sure, I forgot. He's one of those tree huggers," his father said. "At least put some cheese on that."

Tobias was about to explain about being a vegan when he had another idea. He reached out his hands to his father opposite him and his mother on his left. "Mom. Dad. Simmy. I love you all." His mother clasped his left hand. "It's Christmastime. We're together. We're doing OK." His father clasped his right hand. "Let's enjoy this meal and stop bickering." Simeon stopped drawing and joined the circle of hands. Their mother's eyes teared.

Tobias paid the bill in cash over the objections of his father, who left a 20 percent tip. Simeon helped his mother with her coat. They got into the car in the same seats as before: Tobias in the driver's seat, his father next to him, his brother behind him, and their mother next to Simeon.

"Oh, rats! I forgot the sketch pad." He started to undo his seat belt to run back in for Simeon's cartoon, dreading the fight that might erupt among the other three at close range.

"I'll go, Toby. Stay there." Simeon jumped out and ran into the restaurant before Tobias could open the door.

On the way home, his father asked him about his fellowship and the trip to South America. Tobias, happy to break the tension, explained he'd be living among the Yanomami Indians and sleeping under nets, learning their language, taking notes for his research.

"You're distracting him," his mother complained. "It's icy."

"Goddamn it, stop interrupting," his father snarled. "This doesn't concern you."

Tobias approached the four-way intersection slowly and put on his left blinker. The light was red.

"Careful," his father said.

"Let him be," his mother said.

Tobias checked all the mirrors. The light turned green. In the back seat, his brother was smirking. As he went into the turn, out of nowhere, a larger vehicle ran the light, sped into the intersection, and skidded into the right side and back of the Hillyers' car. Tobias heard the deafening crack, like a thunderclap in the mountains, before registering the impact. The Ford spun around 180 degrees on the black ice. There were screams, splintering glass, scraping sounds, the sputtering motor. His hand turned the key and shut off the engine. His neck hurt.

He shouted, "Mom! Dad! Simmy!" No one answered. He jumped out of the car, tried to open the doors on the other side. The entire right side of the car was crushed. His parents weren't moving. In the street lights, he could see blood oozing out of their mouths. He ran back to the driver's side, opened the back door. "Simmy. Simeon. No, no!" he screamed. "Somebody help, please!"

Sirens, police cars, ambulances appeared as if in a nightmare. Paramedics brought something called the jaws of life. By the time his parents had been extricated, they were both dead. They were wheeled to ambulances on covered stretchers.

Simeon was unconscious but alive. No injuries were

apparent. They rushed him to the emergency room at Woodrock Hospital. A police officer drove Tobias to the hospital with sirens on and lights flashing.

The emergency room doctor came out of a white-curtained cubicle, holding a clipboard. "Mr. Hillyer?" he asked.

Tobias looked around. The doctor meant him. "Yes."

"Who's your next of kin?"

"My parents," Tobias said. "My brother. Where's my brother?"

"Your brother has a concussion and possibly some other head injuries. He's unconscious. Any other family members nearby?"

"My aunt in California. Grandparents in Florida. Can I see my brother?" The pad with Simeon's drawing was under his arm.

"We're testing him now. Any other relatives? Other grandparents?"

"One in a nursing home. One dead. That's all. Please take me to where my brother is. What's wrong with him?"

"He's in a coma. We suspect a diffuse axonal injury," the doctor said. "It's a type of traumatic brain damage." He looked behind Tobias, but no one was there besides the police officer who had brought him in. "How old is your brother? How old are you?" he asked.

"He's fifteen. I'm twenty. Twenty-one in March."

The doctor put his arm around Tobias. "I'm sorry, son," he said.

## *Chapter 2*

Tobias called his aunt Joyce in Encino, California, and she flew to Newark on Christmas Eve on a bereavement ticket. Joyce owned a recording studio in Burbank. She was pressed for time and unconditionally had to return after the funeral.

Tobias hadn't seen her in four years and squinted when she entered the Intensive Care Unit waiting room, where he had spent the night. She was wearing a tapered beige Max Mara blazer over gray stovepipe slacks with pressed creases. A white silk blouse, open at her throat, showcased a three-strand gold necklace. The raised collars of her blouse and jacket formed a backstop behind her platinum-streaked brown hair. With her vivid, fashionable clothes and perfect posture, she was a thinner, more alert version of the older sister who had once resembled her.

Tobias got off the chair where he'd been dozing for five minutes at a time, still in his jeans and sweatshirt from the day before. "Joyce. You got here so fast."

She hugged him, holding her head back to protect her hairdo. Relatives of other patients momentarily stared at them before returning to their magazines or the TV, always tuned to CNN.

She held him by his shoulders. "What happened?" she asked, in the tone of voice of someone inquiring about the weather. "Who was driving?"

"I was. A van went through the red light. Slipped on the ice. Plowed into us. So horribly sorry."

"It wasn't your fault." She looked around the room. Someone had taped red and green garlands to the walls and ceiling in a slapdash fashion. A five-foot artificial Christmas tree in the corner was draped in tinsel, with fake wrapped presents clustered at the bottom.

Tobias hadn't slept since the day before, on the bus from Baltimore. The fluorescent lights in the waiting room hurt his eyes, and he wanted to flick a switch to return things to the way they were, however uncomfortable the visit had been.

They spent ten minutes in Simeon's private room. His eyes were closed, and he wasn't moving at all. His glasses lay on the bedside table. There were no marks on his head or face, and he could simply have been sleeping—if not for all the charts, monitors, and electrodes. He was breathing on his own. An IV line dripped nutrients and medicine into his thin arm.

"Simmy. Simmy, it's me, Toby." Tobias squeezed his brother's hand, limp on top of the sheet.

"Let's get down to business." Joyce's Manolo Blahniks clacked on the hard floor as she walked out. She registered at the Ramada Inn and drove Tobias to his parents' house in a rented car. With her businesswoman's efficiency, she picked a funeral home from the Yellow Pages, phoned her parents in Miami, and booked their flights for the next day, which was Christmas. She spread out her papers on the kitchen table, untroubled by the ghosts that were already haunting Tobias.

"When's your birthday?" she asked him. "You'll be twenty-one, right?"

"March eighteenth."

She sipped the coffee she had made in his mother's kitchen. "We'll need to get you some kind of parental status in case you have to make a decision about your brother." She was sitting in his father's chair and drinking from his Yankees coffee mug. "To pull the plug if it comes to that."

"What?"

Joyce took off her reading glasses. "The doctors say his brain was damaged. He may never recover."

Tobias sat up straight. "No one's ever going to pull the plug on Simmy."

❁ ❁ ❁

Only Tobias, his maternal grandparents, and Aunt Joyce attended the funeral. Joyce picked her parents up at the airport, while he stayed with Simeon.

"Don't you think you'd better come along to see Grandma and Grandpa?" she asked. "The nurses will watch him."

"When he wakes up, I want him to be with someone he knows. So I can tell him about Mom and Dad if he asks."

In the funeral home chapel, his grandparents ignored Tobias, even when he went up to them and said, "Grandma, Grandpa, I'm sorry." Joyce said that they were shocked and grieving and not themselves. They visited Simeon for twenty minutes, slept at the Ramada Inn, and flew home to Florida the next day.

Tobias stayed in Simeon's hospital room as long as he was permitted, noon to eight PM every day. To keep track of passing days, he noted the date on his brother's charts. Simeon lay still most of the time, occasionally jerking his arms or legs like a marionette operated by a string. Sometimes, Tobias could see his brother's eyes moving behind their closed lids, as if he were watching action in his dreams or observing the lines of a figure to sketch in a cartoon. Nurses and attendants in cushioned white shoes padded in to adjust his IV or catheter or to change his linens, rolling him from side to side like a log. The neurologist visited every day and allowed Tobias to remain during the examination but deflected his questions like a politician bunting hardballs at a press conference.

"When do you think my brother will wake up?" he asked on December 27.

The neurologist, Dr. Mendicott, said it was impossible to predict, but that Simeon's eyes could be closed for a week or so. Then he would make some automatic muscular movements but not interact with his environment yet. The doctor nodded to two residents in the hall and started to walk out.

"Doctor, please wait." Tobias stepped forward. "When my brother opens his eyes, will he know who I am?"

Dr. Mendicott paused, waved away the two interns, and sat down in a visitor's chair, motioning Tobias to do the same. "Your brother probably wasn't wearing a seat belt. His frontal lobe was injured—that's the part of the brain most often damaged in car accidents. It's a traumatic brain injury caused by sudden deceleration." He picked up Tobias's empty paper coffee cup and shook it hard. "This is your head, and this is your brain inside, shifting around. Your head still looks normal."

Tobias glanced at Simeon, inert on his elevated bed, guard rails up on both sides. He had no trace of fuzz on his cheeks and looked younger than his fifteen years.

"Inside, your brain is disorganized." The doctor wiggled the cup from side to side. "Connections among the neurons were disrupted during the sudden stopping and twisting of your brain."

"Will he get better?" Tobias gripped the edge of his chair, needing to hear but not wanting to know.

"Time will tell. Every case is different."

At night, he returned to his parents' house and dug in his book bag. The travel guide for his fellowship semester listed supplies to bring: light-colored clothing, including long, tightly woven, lightweight cotton pants and long-sleeve, tightly woven cotton shirts. Sunblock lotion, a water bottle, a broad-brimmed hat that ties on, a neckerchief, waterproof hiking boots, a knee-length rain poncho. Insect repellent. Camera and batteries. Binoculars. "Do not overpack," the booklet advised.

He had to return to Maryland by January 3. The four fellowship students and their professor and advisor were leaving for South America on January 5 and would be gone for the entire semester, until the middle of May.

He called Grover Whitman, his fellowship advisor, a genial man who joked about having two last names. At Abington, students and faculty were on a first-name basis, so it didn't much matter. Grover, who lived near campus and might be in his office after a holiday, answered the phone on the first ring. "Tobias, I've been trying to reach you since Christmas. How are you? No answering machine?"

Tobias's parents had never bothered to install the answering machine he'd given them last Christmas; they didn't like to figure out new devices. "I'm OK, Grover."

"I wanted to share some wonderful news. We got a *tremendous* grant; just came in. Can you come back to campus a little early, say the first of the year, rather than January third?"

"Grover, I was in a car accident. My brother was hurt. I don't know when I'm coming back."

"Oh, I'm so sorry, Tobe. How are your parents?"

"They're both dead."

Tobias heard some muffled sounds and pictured Grover's spacious office in the anthropology department, a cluttered, homey place full of books, photos, and mementos of his field trips—tribal masks, rainbow-colored feathers, native paintings and sculptures, cooking pots. He had a lazy, striped cat named Edward who lay on his desk all day and went home with him at night in his bicycle basket in the summer, and on his Toyota's passenger seat in the winter.

"Tobias. I'm terribly sorry." His voice sounded darker, strained. "Oh my God. That's awful. Is anyone there with you?"

"Only my aunt. But she already flew back to the West Coast."

"Tobe. You want me to come up there? I can help you

with—I don't know, your brother, paperwork, anything you need—"

"Grover. Thank you. Thank you very much. No, no. I couldn't ask you to do that. No."

He promised to call again, and hung up. On the bulletin board next to his parents' phone were frequently called numbers, cards from local businesses, and cartoons by his brother. He hadn't moved or changed anything in the house since arriving. It was nine o'clock at night, fifteen hours before he could see his brother again. He called the nurses' station on Simeon's floor.

"He's doing fine," the head nurse said. "Comfortable. No change. We're watching him. Get some rest."

Tobias lay on the living room sofa where his father had last sat while waiting for him to call home. Exhausted, he couldn't sleep. He was too depleted to cry and had no one to cry with. A two-day-old newspaper on the coffee table didn't hold his attention. He unzipped his book bag and opened his fellowship guide booklet to a random page:

*We continue our journey with a visit to the Bora and Huitoto Indians. As you know, these tribes, formerly enemies, are now close allies. They will present traditional dances when we arrive in their village by Zodiac (inflatable boats). You will be invited to participate in some of their dances. Then you will have the opportunity to meet individuals and converse with them. Everybody speaks Spanish, so there will be no language barrier. They will be selling local handicrafts and paintings.*

*Note that the local people are suspicious of paper money that's less than perfect. Any tears or wrinkles in your bills might render your currency unacceptable. We advise you to bring some useful items for barter: T-shirts, dresses, and shorts in various sizes are good. These clothes can be used, but clean. School supplies are welcome: notebooks, pens, pencils, erasers, chalk. You can also bring colored thread for sewing.*

Tobias fell asleep with the pamphlet inverted on his chest.

At ten the next morning, he rolled off the couch, bathed in his parents' shower, dressed in clean clothes, and sat down in the hospital cafeteria, trying to eat until visiting hours resumed at noon. He was reading Grover's paper about the Tambopata Reserve in southern Peru, their first stop. They were going to stay at the Ese'eje Lodge and perform anthropological evaluations of the effects of tourism on the native Ese'ejas community.

*We will fly from Lima, Peru, on a small jet at 6:00 AM to Puerto Maldonado, where we'll ride in an open bus through the lively but primitive town for two miles. Then we'll ride a motorized canoe for half an hour on the Madre de Dios River, followed by a three-mile hike through the rainforest on a flat trail. We'll board human-powered canoes (you're all expected to row!) and paddle for twenty minutes through exquisite and narrow jungle streams until we reach the lush and untouched Sandoval Lake. There, we'll take a human-powered catamaran to Sandoval Lake Lodge, where you'll have lunch and, afterward, a siesta in your rooms, but first you'll have to climb about a hundred steps up to the lodge.*

A woman asked, "Interesting reading?" Tobias looked up. "Mind if I sit here?" It was Carmela Liston, a psychiatric nurse, one of the staff members he had met and then forgotten.

Tobias moved his pile of papers to make room for her tray, relieved to put aside his worries about what Simeon would be doing while he was paddling in the rainforest.

"I'm in the group that's working with your brother." They shook hands. "That's some injury."

"It's day-to-day. Thanks, I'm so worried." He searched her face for some clue about what doctors weren't saying. She had golden brown eyes, wavy auburn hair, and a round, pretty face. Carmela offered him some grapes, which he declined, and asked what he was reading.

"It's about a program I'm in at Abington College. Anthropology fellowship for undergraduates."

"Wow, awesome, fantastic! Lucky guy. Where are you going?"

He told her about the trip, already paid for by scholarships, loans, and his summer job in a local bookstore, and mentioned the Yanomami Indians.

She smiled, showing dimples, and swallowed a bite of chocolate layer cake. "They're amazing. I read a great book about them when I was an undergraduate."

He showed her his award letter, his maps, and the long list of items to bring. They laughed at the comment on the bottom about packing light. He checked his watch. Ten more minutes before visiting hours. "Carmela, if there's anything about my brother that you think I ought to know—"

"Absolutely. I'll tell you anything I hear." She was scraping up every last bit of crumbs and frosting with her fork.

"I mean, whether he's going to get better, if there's some place he'll have to go, or what—"

She laced her fingers together. "Tobias, there are things you can do right now to help him along." She asked him to bring in familiar objects from home—clothes, music, diaries, pictures—and put them in Simeon's room.

Tobias slid a folder out of his book bag and opened it to show Carmela the last cartoon Simeon had drawn. "This is my brother's artwork."

"This is brilliant." She looked up and down from Tobias to the cartoon. "He drew this? It looks exactly like you. What a talent."

Tobias covered his eyes for a moment, swallowed, took a breath.

She pressed her palms on the cafeteria table and leaned forward. "We can get him back. He's in there. Beautiful boy. Just have to find a way to unlock him."

❋ ❋ ❋

At his parents' house, Tobias was sleeping on the living

room sofa and dreading going upstairs to the bedrooms. That evening, he let the phone ring five times before he answered it.

"Tobias, this is Grover. How's your brother?"

"Grover, thanks, the same. He's in a coma."

"Look, I know this is a very bad time. I wish I could do something about it. As I was saying, we need everyone back on campus January first, New Year's Day. This gigantic grant came in—we weren't expecting it—and you and I and the four others have a lot of planning and writing to do before we leave."

"Grover, I have to wait for my brother to wake up."

"Call me?"

"Yes. I will."

For three more days, he sat with his brother for eight hours, went home alone, and waited. He ignored his parents' phone until December 30, when it rang eleven times after he returned from the hospital. It was Grover, pressing him about his return date. The expedition was a team project, and all team members had to be present, he said. If Tobias didn't return to campus on time, Grover would be in an awkward position. Other qualified candidates were eager to take his place. It was like a pyramid of gymnasts or cheerleaders—if one person falls, the entire structure collapses.

Tobias arranged for Simeon's eventual move to a rehabilitation center. His parents' insurance would pay the bills for now. He warned that he would be away until May, but the hospital administrator told him not to worry; this was a long-term case. "We're talking months, if not years," she said.

The morning of December 31, Tobias climbed the stairs to his brother's bedroom and collected a box full of his cartoons. There were caricatures of family members and self-portraits with pretty girls. Some pictures included talking dogs and cats. There were single-line drawings done with one pencil, and complicated New York City views in vivid colors.

With permission of the nurses, he taped some of the pictures around Simeon's hospital room, low enough so he would see them when he woke up. He pulled a chair close to the bedside and held the other pictures in front of his brother's face, one by one, telling him what each one depicted. One cartoon showed Simeon behind a girl, her blouse unbuttoned, his hands cupping her breasts, his fingers and thumbs caressing her erect nipples. The girl's face had an ecstatic expression. "This one shows Simmy the lover boy," he said. Then he stacked all the pictures neatly and put them in an accordion folder in his book bag. He leaned over the bed, pressed his cheek against his brother's hair, and turned to go.

"Toby."

He pivoted. Simeon was lying still, his eyes closed, mouth open but not moving.

"Simmy, Simmy, it's me, Toby. I'm here, Simmy."

No reaction. Visiting hours were over, and Carmela came by to cull the remaining visitors from the ward. "He talked," Tobias told her. "My brother said my name."

She came in, held Simeon's hand, stroked his face, spoke his name again and again. No reaction. Her eyes were kind, her expression sympathetic. She explained to Tobias that it was like looking for an absent loved one in a crowd, seeing that person's face, missing that person so desperately that your imagination plays tricks on you, and then coming closer and discovering that it was just another face in the crowd. Tobias went home and packed his suitcase.

On New Year's Day, there was a single morning bus to Port Authority. Tobias took a taxi to the Woodrock bus station and waited. The bus was late. He called the hospital from the pay phone, the number memorized, and asked for the nurses' station.

"Tobias, your brother!" The nurse's voice cut through the street noise like a brass instrument. His heart thumped. "Your brother's eyes are open!"

Forgetting his suitcase, he ran for the taxi, still idling at curbside, waiting for passengers from incoming buses, and then ran back to the pay phone to retrieve his suitcase.

"Short trip," the taxi driver said. "Hey, look, isn't that your bus coming?"

"I need to get to Woodrock Hospital as fast as possible. Please."

"You OK, man? What's going on?"

Tobias threw his valise into the back seat, got in, and shut the door. "I've changed my destination." The harsh winter sun bounced off the taxi's side mirror and made his eyes tear as the driver made a U-turn on the first day of the new year.

# *Chapter 3*

"Mastering Public Speaking" was a compulsory course at Abington College. Along with his reluctant classmates, Tobias had progressed from clammy hands to confident stance in his first semester. "Make eye contact," the speech professor stressed. This applied to speeches as well as interviews, dating, and anytime you had to connect with someone. By the end of that semester, eye contact had become ingrained.

Simeon's dark, cloudy eyes were open, but he wasn't making any eye contact at all. Tobias stood at his bedside, keeping his face within his brother's gazing range, which was unnerving, like looking a dog or a cat in the eye—they see you, but they don't look back. Dr. Mendicott assured him that this was normal for the early stages of emerging from a coma.

For Tobias, nothing was normal anymore. "Simmy, look at me," he pleaded, squeezing his brother's hand and hovering over his face. Simeon blinked. Tobias stopped talking and shifting. Nothing. "Simmy, I'm here. It's Toby." He wagged his head from side to side like a moviegoer sitting behind a tall person. Simeon blinked again. Tobias pressed his hand and felt a tremor. "Simmy, squeeze my hand." Another tremor. Still, his eyes roamed the ceiling, not focusing, not looking.

When his brother fell asleep, Tobias went outside to sit on

a cement bench near the hospital's front entrance. The wide automatic doors opened for a nurse pushing a young woman in a wheelchair, a new mother cradling her blue-swaddled newborn against her chest, her cheek grazing the baby's blue skullcap. Her husband, all smiles, walked backward, snapping photo after photo. He opened the door of his waiting car and helped his wife into the seat while the nurse held the infant. Click, click, more photos, and then they drove away.

There were no more buses to Port Authority or Baltimore until the next day. Tobias had to make a list of things to do, and then decide on priorities. It was too cold to write outside and he went back inside to the cafeteria. *January 1, 1990,* he printed in blue ink at the top of a blank page in a notebook from his anthropology seminar. *Look up bus schedules* was the first item. He skipped three lines and wrote *Get phone card,* and then *Bring music for Simmy* above that. *Find utility bills* was in the middle of the list, followed by *Fix front door* and *Look at help wanted ads.* Making lists forced him to be true to himself, and he admitted that this list was incomplete. He put his head in his hands and closed his eyes, and then wrote *Call Martin* and *Call Grover* at the bottom of the list, with *Make a decision* above their names.

He added an extra item: *Cancel newspaper.* The last issue of the local weekly dropped on his parents' driveway published a front-page story about the Hillyers' accident, with a picture of the wrecked vehicles above the fold. "Family Members Killed and Injured in Two-Car Crash" was the headline. *Longtime Woodrock residents Cheryl and Philip Hillyer were killed in a spectacular two-vehicle crash on December 23. The car, driven by their son Tobias, 20, a junior at Abington College, was crushed by a van driven by 17-year-old John Barring, also of Woodrock, who survived with minor injuries. Fifteen-year-old Simeon Hillyer was admitted to Woodrock Hospital, where he remains, with head injuries. Tobias was unharmed. The two talented brothers have been in the news for their achievements:*

*Tobias in tennis and academics, and Simeon in art. Philip Hillyer, 52, was a UPS truck driver. Cheryl Hillyer, 51, was a retired art teacher. The funeral was held on December 26.*

Tobias put the newspaper in his parents' bedroom, where he had set up a sort of shrine on his mother's dressing table, flanked by a three-panel mirror that showed all sides of the objects on it: His father's sole luxury, a Rolex watch. His mother's favorite photograph of the four of them, in which seven-year-old Tobias was holding two-year-old Simeon in his lap. Her favorite gold chain. His father's collection of company ID cards, in a year-by-year progression from thick, black hair to sparse gray.

Carmela was in Simeon's hospital room, writing on a clipboard, when Tobias returned. "Good morning—afternoon," she corrected herself. "Days go by so fast around here."

"Or so slowly." He resumed his futile head-shifting and hand-squeezing.

Carmela was planning Simeon's post-coma therapy and lining up the players: a neurologist, a physiatrist, a psychologist, and physical, occupational, and speech therapists. "We're going to use behavioral strategies to shape and reinforce appropriate behaviors," she said.

"That will be wonderful," Tobias said. "But he's not behaving at all or doing anything."

"Oh, he will. It's going to take love, patience, and a lot of work."

"I'm not sure I can handle it." He rested his hand on Simeon's arm.

"You can. You'll have lots of help, at least for the first six months, when it really matters." She had to continue her rounds and said she was free at three and could meet him in the cafeteria or go out for a short walk.

"What if he calls my name then, and I'm not here?" He watched his brother, who was rotating his head randomly while gazing at the ceiling.

"You don't have to be here every moment. He's in good hands."

When they met in the cafeteria, he realized he had forgotten to eat lunch. She loaded her tray with hamburger, fries, salad, pie, and soda. "I'm going on a diet next week, and I have to build up strength," she confided. He bought a sandwich and sat opposite her. She wanted to know when he was going back to school, and he said he didn't know yet.

"What about your fellowship, that trip?" she asked.

"It would kill me not to go." He didn't feel like eating. "It's everything I've worked for since I started college."

"Then why stay in Woodrock?" She shook a generous dribble of ketchup over her fries.

He put down his sandwich. "It was all my fault. I've ruined my brother's life and killed our parents, and he has nobody except me." He was going to cry and tried to drink some water instead. He told her about leaving Simmy's drawing pad in the restaurant, starting to get out of the car to retrieve it, and instead letting his brother go get it; then, not reminding him to fasten his seat belt when he returned. Any of those things could have made a difference, he told her: the seat belt, the trip back inside. If he'd remembered the drawing pad, that van wouldn't have hit them at that moment. If they'd gone to their usual family restaurant instead of the one he'd chosen, his mother would have gotten drunk, but she'd still be alive.

"Stop." Carmela thrust her hand forward like a crossing guard halting traffic. "You can't go through life this way, punishing yourself." She set down the ketchup container with a thump. "Let me tell you the truth: You didn't *want* to hurt your brother. You didn't *want* to kill your parents. You didn't *want* to total their car. These things happened. Your brother is in a modern hospital. You've got insurance. You absolutely have to pick yourself up and get your education."

❋ ❋ ❋

After visiting hours, he called his off-campus apartment in Maryland to leave a message for his roommate, Martin, who he assumed would still be away, visiting his parents. But Martin answered the phone, having arrived early to get his tennis in shape for spring tournaments, which Tobias would be missing because of his South American trip.

At Abington, typical college sports like football and basketball didn't get much attention, whereas sports like archery, gymnastics, fencing, and rowing were popular. And tennis—lots of tennis. The school had ten outdoor hard courts and a climate-controlled, six-court indoor tennis bubble, with traveling teams and display cases full of trophies. Expert coaching was provided to team members. It seemed like it was all free—all you had to do was qualify for the team. But nothing was free, and his sum of loans to repay grew year by year.

"We're gonna be missing you this season, man," Martin said. His substitute partner for men's intercollegiate doubles was a good player, but not like Tobias. He and Tobias had developed a seamless doubles strategy, and they knew each other's strokes so well that they communicated like brothers—like twin brothers, in fact.

"Actually, I'm going to have to take some time off." Tobias told his friend about the accident, omitting grisly details like identifying bodies and scattering his parents' ashes in the forest, off the trail where they once had hiked as a family in better times. He promised he'd pay his share of rent for their apartment as soon as he got hold of his finances.

"Oh my God, Tobe. Oh, I'm so sorry; that's awful." Martin would be raking his hair at this moment, a habit of his when things got tense. He had thick, unruly red hair that was always falling in his light blue eyes, even the day after a haircut, and freckles across his face and back, and he always hid under a hat on the courts, even on cloudy days. He said not to worry about the rent; he'd be fine for a month or two. "Give your brother my regards when he starts talking."

"I will, Martin. Good luck on the courts. Hit some for me." It was 10:00 PM, too late to reach Grover in his office.

❁ ❁ ❁

At three in the afternoon, shifts were changing: nurses and aides who worked from 7:00 AM to 3:00 PM were leaving, and the 3:00-to-11:00 staff members were coming in. There was a daily staff meeting to transfer information between the groups, and traffic in the hospital corridors was light. Tobias closed his brother's door, leaving a two-inch gap, and began a one-sided conversation.

"Hey, Simmy, I wish you'd talk." He peered through the crack in the door. It was quiet. "We never talked that much. I can understand that—the way Mom and Dad were, always fighting, they were hard to live with." He stopped, catching himself in the past tense. "I mean, the way they are. Dad picking on you, Mom standing up for you, and both of them arguing about it." Simeon's eyes were roving in the direction of his brother's face, and Tobias held his limp hand and rubbed his hair. Someone had washed and combed his hair, parting it on the wrong side. "We should have talked more. If you could talk now, I would just stand here for hours until we said everything we had to say, or until we both fell asleep."

Simeon closed his eyes for a few seconds, and then opened them again, letting them drift.

"If you could hear me, I would tell you what a great brother you were. You are." They had always shared a room, but had rarely fought. No chalk line on the floor ever divided one brother's possessions from the other's. "Something I never said, and I should have said, is that your cartoons are—they're amazing. I don't know anyone else who can draw like you."

Tobias searched his brother's eyes for recognition, for consciousness, for a spark of life. Simeon's vacant eyes passed back and forth across his brother's face and beyond, like a search beam radiating from a watchtower, illuminating everything but understanding nothing. Tobias leaned down over the guard rails, hugged his brother the best he could with the IV lines in the way, and said, "Oh, Simmy, I'm so sorry this happened to you. It was my fault. I love you so much." He straightened up and wiped his eyes with a tissue from Simeon's bedside cart, and then wiped the tears that he'd spilled onto his brother's face.

And then, just for an instant, Simeon looked straight at him, and their eyes connected. In the corners of his eyes were his own tears, real tears, and his regular breathing caught like a stifled sob.

"Simmy. Simmy, you heard everything, didn't you?"

The look was gone. The tears stopped, the vacant gazing resumed. But he knew, Tobias was sure. He had understood everything. He was struggling to come back.

❁ ❁ ❁

Grover's suitcases were packed, his students were prepared, and his plans were in place, except for the matter of Tobias Hillyer, who still had not shown up by January 2. Reluctant to complain to the dean about his best student, he could only wait. For the fifth time that evening, he dialed the number of Tobias's parents.

At 9:00 PM, Tobias answered, apologizing, saying he'd been about to call, and that he had decided not to go on the trip.

Grover paced around with the phone. Plans didn't get changed at such a late date. There were airline tickets, vaccination certificates, passports, departmental allocations, grants, a dean to answer to, and a waiting list of capable, disappointed students not chosen for the honor.

"Tobias. Listen to me. Are you there?"

"Yes."

"You made a promise. You made a commitment. I'm

depending on you. So is the department. We're all ready, except for you. We embark on January fourth. I expect you to be here."

"I can't leave, Grover."

Grover grasped for arguments to entice his student back to campus. "Tobe, you're the linchpin of this group. Without your analytical skills, the others won't do as well. Plus, I have a new title for you, and new responsibilities—I've put you in charge of assessing the costs of free education of Yanomami children and adults."

Tobias held his head with one hand and the phone with the other.

"You there?"

"Yes. I can't come back, Grover."

Grover was striding rhythmically now, as he did in front of a classroom when lecturing. It helped him to pace his words and shape his logic. "Tobias. I don't usually open up to students like this. I have to tell you something. You're a gifted young researcher. Do you appreciate what a trip like this represents for someone at your stage? It's like taking a ride on a shooting star. You go on this ride, and this trip will open up new worlds for you, now and forever."

"Grover, it's not just the trip. I'm not coming back to school."

The dropout rate at Abington was low, and was nearly nonexistent in Grover's department. He prided himself on it and scrambled for something to say. "Think about this: It's much easier to drop out than to drop back in. How many students wish they could be in your place?" No answer. "Studying unwritten languages by immersing yourself in the life of another culture? Going on to do humanitarian work after you graduate—the International Rescue Committee, the Peace Corps ... make a wrong decision now, and you will regret it for the rest of your life."

"Grover, the decision I have made is the right decision."

Grover felt his student slipping away. He lowered his voice and spoke deliberately. "Think about the other choice."

Tobias raised his voice as if addressing the last row in the public speaking class. "Grover, I have thought about it every day and every night, all night, when I can't sleep. This is my choice."

Grover stopped pacing and gestured futilely with his hand. "You can accomplish great things."

"It doesn't much matter what I accomplish if I abandon my brother. Now he's an orphan. And now I'm a parent."

Grover felt himself shaking and sat on his desk. "Tobe. Keep in touch. My best to you."

"Thank you, Grover." Tobias hung up the phone and checked off one more item on his to-do list.

# Chapter 4

The windy April morning was warm enough for a T-shirt and shorts. On an asphalt tennis court in the county park, Tobias was practicing his serves, hitting balls over the net again and again, pacing the hits, placing the ball accurately to an imaginary opponent. He hadn't touched a racket in five months. His former roommate, Martin, had shipped all his possessions to him in January, but Tobias had opened only the boxes of clothes and books, not being in the mood for sports.

For twenty minutes, he concentrated, and then the familiar strokes became automatic. Invigorated, he found his rhythm and let his mind wander. Martin was coming for five days at spring break, and Tobias hoped his car would make it to Port Authority in Manhattan in one piece. He couldn't ask Martin, a Maryland native, to navigate the cavernous bus terminal during rush hour after four and a half hours on the Greyhound from Baltimore and board yet another bus to Woodrock. His 1973 Volkswagen Beetle, painted apple-green, was all he could afford on his salary at the Book Trove, a sprawling independent bookstore in Woodrock that still attracted customers in spite of the enormous new Barnes & Noble on the highway.

Tobias served five more balls to his phantom opponent's backhand. Tired from insufficient sleep, he paused to mop his head with one of his mother's old dish towels. He hadn't been able to soothe himself back to sleep after lurching awake at 2:00 AM. In a nightmare, he was hunched over a desk in a windowless classroom at Abington College, taking an exam of all the important things in life, filling in little circles with his number 2 pencil, only to get a score of 46 percent correct. Rattled, he couldn't shake off the dream's condemnation, even though its premise was false: that you could master all the important things in life at any school and that you could qualify for some critical next step by acing a multiple-choice test.

Tobias hit the last ball wide at his invisible opponent's forehand to make him miss a shot almost out of reach or to force him to hit a weak return. He stepped around the court, scooping up balls with his hopper, and then took the opposite side of the net for another round of serves. Like a cat, he moved efficiently, compactly, getting the most out of each thrust and not lunging more than necessary. Keenly aware of his surroundings, he had a 180-degree sense of the court, was ready to pivot and return any unexpected attack. He was a natural, unlike Simeon, who had once demoted himself to eighth-grade untouchable by daydreaming on the basketball court during gym class and shooting a ball into the opposing team's basket.

After forty-five minutes, Tobias collected all his balls and hoisted his hopper into the dilapidated trunk of his VW Beetle. He changed into a button-down shirt, pulled on a pair of khakis over his tennis shorts, and drove eight miles to Pine Barrens Rehabilitation Institute, where Simeon was making slow progress and had a busy schedule. Tobias had set up a chart of his brother's appointments and sandwiched his visits into free periods. There was physical therapy, occupational therapy, counseling, and a daily session with the speech-language pathologist. Simeon was under the care of physicians, rehabilitation nurses, neuropsychologists, and a case manager. He attended group sessions with a handful of other teenage victims of traumatic brain injury.

The rehabilitation institute stood in a valley of pine-covered hills. Deciduous trees reached up to the hopeful April sun and enhanced the fresh, green smell that greeted Tobias. He walked across a bed of pine needles and entered the building. The receptionist knew him and waved him on; he'd been coming every morning at eleven for more than two months, ever since Simeon's discharge from Woodrock Hospital. Apprehension built as he climbed the three flights of stairs to his brother's room. Concerns about Simeon's treatment were not worrying him. It was his brother's future that was unpredictable, disquieting, and vexing.

This particular day was Simeon's sixteenth birthday, although no one at the rehab facility was paying much attention to this milestone. As on any other day, Simeon was being walked down the hall to his room by a physical therapist. Head down, he watched his feet as he trudged with the gait of a novice hiker on a rocky trail. Tobias waited until his brother was seated on his bed and then went in. Simeon stared at him, squinted, and then laughed and smiled a sunshiny smile. "Toe-toe-toe," he said.

"Right, Simmy. It's me, Toby. Hey, buddy." Tobias hugged his brother tightly. "Simmy, Simmy." They had told him that repetition was common among brain-damaged patients and that in time, his speech might become more normal.

Simeon leaned his head on his brother's shoulder. "Mom-Mom-Mom."

"Mom's not here." Tobias dreaded the day when, if ever, his brother would have enough presence of mind to understand that not only was Mom not here, but she would never be here, and neither would Dad.

The brothers ate lunch together seven days a week. When he could, Tobias brought lunch from home or from a deli. Usually they ate in the cafeteria. It was too early in Simeon's treatment for him to visit a restaurant in the outside world, and Tobias wanted to shield him from the stares that would certainly ensue.

"Happy birthday, Simeon!" someone called from the doorway. "Wow! Wow, are you looking great or what?" It was Carmela, dressed in her nurse's uniform for her 3:00-to-11:00 shift at Woodrock Hospital.

"Carmela!" Tobias jumped up and embraced her. "I can't believe you came all the way over here." It was a half-hour's drive from Woodrock.

"Not so far."

"And you remembered."

"How could I forget Simmy? I have his birth date and all his records, you know." She was the only one besides Tobias who used the nickname Simmy, other than their dead mother.

"Thank you so much for coming. I was feeling terrible, knowing it's his birthday, and nothing special happening, and I didn't know what to do to make it—"

"Don't even mention it." She hugged Simeon. "Remember me?" she asked him. "It hasn't been that long, right? A month or so?" She looked at Tobias.

"Two months."

"Simmy, it's me, Carmela." She was rocking him. "Say *Car-mel-ahh.*"

"Car…car…" Simeon was clinging to her.

"Good boy. I brought you a birthday present. Look!" She pulled a package out of her tote bag. He didn't have the manual dexterity to unwrap the colorful paper, which had cake and candles printed on it, such as one would give to a child. She tore off the wrapping and handed the gift to Simeon, closing his fingers around it. It was a book of full-color prints of paintings by Henri Matisse, with faithful reproductions on every page. "Book, Simmy. Say book."

"Book-book-book." Simeon held the book as she had

given it to him, seeming entranced by the colors. She showed him how to turn the pages and let him try it himself.

One Saturday when Tobias was ten, he had walked five-year-old Simeon to a new candy store that opened in town, one of those places where bin after bin was chockfull of chocolates, nuts, jelly beans, Gummy Bears—every variety of candy imaginable. Simeon couldn't decide which candy he wanted, instead letting his brother choose while he gobbled the display of shapes and colors with his eyes. At home, he spent the rest of the day drawing bins of candy in fantastical shapes, coloring them in with every crayon in the house, and still hungering for more when he finally went to bed.

"How are things?" Carmela asked. She was wearing dangling gold earrings and a touch of fruity perfume.

"OK, all right." His arm was around Simeon's shoulders. "So nice of you to come. It's really good to see you."

"What are you doing these days?"

"Working at the bookstore, 3:00 to 11:00, same as your schedule." He smiled at her. She was pretty. Her wavy auburn hair was braided in a rope behind her neck, out of the way of her nurse's cap. He could see the curve of her ample breasts under the thin fabric of her uniform. "My roommate from college is coming to visit. Getting my tennis in shape in case we play."

"Neat. That's wonderful. Where do you play?"

"Right near home, the county park. It's free."

"I'd love to watch that. Mind if I come?"

"Sure. I mean, of course not. But you might get bored. This could go on for an hour and a half or so."

"Oh, I wouldn't be bored," she said. "I played in high school until I got busy with other things—Future Nurses of America, dabbling in student theater."

"OK, I'll let you know when. We'll probably just hit around for a couple of days and then play an actual match." He sat on the bed next to Simeon, who had turned a group of pages instead of just one. "I come here as much as I can; still, he's left alone so much."

"What's on our side is that he's still young. With brain injuries, you never know." She sat on Simeon's other side. "Look how happy he is with this book." Simeon was absorbed in a copy of *Icarus*, cocking his head at the dancer who tempted the sun, turning the book this way and that, like the steering wheel of a toy car.

Tobias watched with tears in his eyes. Simeon was holding the picture upside down and seemed not to comprehend that the symbols on the page represented a human being dancing. "If only he could understand what he sees."

Carmela stroked Simeon's thick, dark hair. "That's just his way of looking. Maybe he sees things that we don't."

❁ ❁ ❁

Another kind of anxiety clutched Tobias as he drove into the Lincoln Tunnel. The roommate he'd left behind at college was now, inevitably, leaving him behind. While Tobias worked at the bookstore for twelve dollars per hour, Martin was wrapping up his junior year and thinking about MBA programs. This visit would probably mark the endpoint of their friendship. Meeting Martin again would be like looking in and out of a window at the same time.

His boss, Elsebeth, had given him five days off at the bookstore, even though he'd been working there full-time only since February. In high school, he had browsed the social sciences racks day after day, devouring one volume after another: sociology, psychology, anthropology. It was at the Book Trove that he decided his college major, and it was there that he selected the college he would attend. Elsebeth watched him standing at the racks or sitting cross-legged on the carpet. Business was good, and she offered him an after-school job, which evolved into a summer job opening cartons, shelving books, and taking inventory. Since then, she had extended her business hours to compete with the Barnes & Noble. She hired Tobias for the 3:00-to-11:00 slot and added responsibilities: reviewing, ordering, scheduling author visits, and working stints at the cash register.

Tobias waited for Martin's bus with butterflies in his stomach, as nervous as on the day of his first speech in the public speaking class at college. In the clump of passengers climbing down from the bus, he spotted his friend's carrot-top first, then his yellow polo shirt under his green Abington jacket. The man was a human traffic light. They shook hands, pounded each other on the back.

"Good, so good to see you, Tobe. Can't believe it's been three months." Martin looked taller.

"Martin, thanks for coming all the way out here. Sure need a friend at a time like this."

"Anything I can do. You talk, I'll listen. Whatever I can do to help—"

"No, no, no, Martin. We'll just hang out."

"I brought my racket." The W on the butt of his Wilson racket was poking through the zipper of his duffel bag. "If you want to play."

"Are you kidding? *If*? I just started hitting yesterday and can't wait to get back."

It was 7:00 PM, and they were both hungry. They decided against eating in the city, where dinner was expensive and there would be a big bill at the parking garage. Tobias drove uptown to the George Washington Bridge to show Martin its jeweled, electric necklace over the Hudson River.

"What a view. I've never been to New Jersey," Martin said. They parked in Woodrock and strolled past a row of restaurants. "How about this one? My treat."

"Anyplace but there," Tobias said. "That's where we were eating just before the accident."

At dinner, Martin avoided the topic of the accident until Tobias brought it up himself. His parents were snuffed out in a second, he told Martin, before he even had a chance to fix things at home.

Martin said that he couldn't have fixed things. "I wouldn't have been able to do it. No one else could have done it, either. You did absolutely nothing wrong."

❁ ❁ ❁

Martin slept on the living room sofa, and Tobias slept upstairs in his old bedroom, where all of Simeon's things remained untouched, except for his art supplies, which he had liberated from his father's locked filing cabinet and arranged neatly on his brother's desk: watercolors, tubes of oil paint, pencils, charcoal, brushes, erasers, paper, canvasses.

Early every morning and late every afternoon for three days, the friends practiced their strokes, both forehand and backhand, striking the ball deep to the baseline, proving that they could still gauge each other's timing. Martin added color to the court with his bright orange hair, blue eyes, green jacket, and Nike Air Ace 4 Plus shoes with red swooshes on the sides. Tobias was a study in black and white: dark hair and eyes; white shirt, shorts, socks, and shoes.

Nobody kept score. They didn't talk much during these sessions. On the second day, Tobias asked Martin which courses he was taking for the semester.

Martin scanned his friend's face for signs of hurt. "Oh, just the usual, nothing special." He took a swig from his water bottle.

"No, really, I want to know," Tobias said.

"Well, since you're out there in the real world now—I mean, working—let me tell you about something that came up in economics class: that the economy is getting worse and the Democratic Congress might force George Bush to raise taxes in spite of his 'Read my lips' promise about no new taxes. Remember the 1988 election?"

Tobias laughed. "Still coming after us Democrats? You'll never give up."

"Tax and spend, tax and spend," Martin chanted.

"Yeah, sure. Hit the ball," Tobias said, enjoying their familiar bickering.

At 10:30 every morning, they left the courts to visit Simeon. At first, Tobias excused himself, offering Martin alternate activities, but Martin insisted on accompanying his friend on the visits, did not mind the time spent. The three of them ate lunch together. Simeon seemed to recognize Martin after two days.

On the third afternoon, Tobias, out of a sense of obligation, suggested a best-of-three-sets match for the next morning.

Martin twirled his Wilson racket. "Now you're talking!"

"This is my weapon of choice." Tobias swung his Prince racket menacingly.

"I'll have to admit that so far, you haven't missed a beat in your timing," Martin said.

"I'm going to invite a lady to watch. Carmela."

"Girlfriend?"

"No, just a very nice person. She was one of Simmy's nurses in the ICU."

❁ ❁ ❁

Tobias dressed in tennis whites for their match and tied on his K-Swiss shoes, as worn by his idol Jim Courier, the Baseline and Grand Slam champion. He introduced Carmela and Martin. She was wearing a short yellow skirt that contrasted with her tan coloring, and she sat in a way that revealed her thighs, plump but shapely. She favored bright colors in unexpected combinations, and, except during working hours, dressed like a tropical bird. Tobias left them on the bench while he went to the men's room in the boathouse by the lake.

"Uh-oh, you must be getting nervous." Martin laughed at him.

"You wish!" Tobias said and walked away.

Carmela parked her sunglasses on top of her hair, done up in French braids. "What do you think; how's he been doing?"

Martin's racket was on his lap, and he was straightening its strings. "It's hard to tell. He doesn't talk much about the death of his parents."

"I can understand that," she said. "Mourning the dead is in the background because he's preoccupied with caring for the damaged living."

Martin nodded. "He's aged, you know. Maybe he's a little thinner, but it's not so much the way he looks. He seems resigned."

"It was a devastating tragedy. Anyone would have a hard time coping." A V-formation of Canadian geese flew over the tennis courts, stridently honking. "Is he religious at all?"

Martin, himself a lapsed Catholic, said, "No, not really. He doesn't believe in destiny or eternal life. He tries to value his present life."

She turned to face him. In the sunlight, there were spidery little worry filaments around her eyes. "I'm concerned that this long interruption of his education will make him lose sight of the person he wanted to become."

Martin jiggled his racket and shook his head. "That's one thing you don't have to worry about. Tobias—he's not one of those people who redefines himself every day of his life. In college, there are plenty of kids who can't decide what they want to become until they get pushed into one program or another. He isn't like that."

Carmela looked over at the boathouse. Tobias was trotting down the path, heading back to the courts. "I hope he can learn to be happy."

"Happiness, for him, is doing what he wants to do, not what someone tells him to do." Tobias was almost within earshot. Martin lowered his voice. "Tell me, do you think I should let him win?"

"No, *never*," she whispered. "Play for real."

As Tobias approached, Martin said to her, "Oh, definitely, in our apartment, he was always the neat one. I was the sloppy one."

On the court, Martin called out, "M or W?" He spun his racket and let it drop.

"M for money," Tobias yelled back.

The racket fell with the W on its butt inverted, awarding Tobias the choice of serve. He wiped his palms on his shorts. "I'll serve first."

Martin played a serve-and-volley strategy, forcing Tobias to be tentative and defend himself from the baseline. Having lost the first set 7–5, Tobias renewed his game with strong backhand passing shots mixed in with well-timed lobs. Martin, frustrated, made avoidable mistakes and lost to Tobias, 10–8, in a tiebreaker.

After a quick break during which no one spoke much, even Carmela, Martin said, "Let's bang it out like old times—a fight to the finish." Using the third-set strategy on which he'd been coached in college, Martin made a show of patience and spent more time at the baseline.

Tobias's strategy of lobs and backhand passing shots was now ineffective. Martin was no longer charging to the net, and Tobias couldn't come up with an alternate game plan.

Abruptly, on the final match point, Martin reversed tactics again by hitting deep to the center court and charging to the net like a sprinter. Tobias, nonplussed, answered with a short lob. Guiding his racket back, Martin hit a powerful overhead smash to put the game and the match on ice.

With Martin's victory of 6–4 in the final set, Tobias, exhausted, ran to the net to shake hands. "What a way to end our rivalry," he said. "You outlasted me. Congratulations—well done."

"Wow, that was close," Carmela said. She was standing and applauding. "You're both champs. What a match!"

Martin swabbed his red hair with a sopping towel and clapped Tobias on the back. "You still have it, buddy. No one else makes me run like that. And who said this is the end? I'll be back in the summer for a rematch!"

# *Chapter 5*

The late-evening customers at the Book Trove were the most eccentric and the most troubled. Like beauty salon patrons who need more than a hairdo, they came for sympathy, advice, or a listening ear.

They started at around 10:00 PM, one hour before closing. For every normal customer wanting a thriller or a book on taxes, there were two or three lost souls who weren't simply looking for something to read. They latched onto Tobias for his knowledge of the inventory and books in general, and they wouldn't let go until they had told their stories, or until the vacuum cleaners came out and chairs were stacked on tables.

There were familiar types: dumped lovers, anxious parents, binge eaters, and the chronically underemployed. Sensing empathy in Tobias, with his earnest good looks and deep, quiet voice, they tucked a book or two under their arms, and then spilled out details of curdled relationships, uncontrollable teenagers, or failed careers, while Tobias searched for the perfect book, squatting in front of a bookshelf or seated at the computer.

Then there were originals who never would have made it into the novels in the Literature section because their stories were too improbable, like the husband whose wife left him for another man, then cajoled him into attending her wedding, seduced him in a guest room while the reception was going on, returned to her party with smeared mascara, and ratted him out to her whole family as a crazed, obsessed stalker. That was some story—and maybe that was all it was, just a story.

The Book Trove prided itself on personal service, and Tobias always tried to give his customers their fair share. The owner, Elsebeth, valued those she termed "the forlorn few" as much as any other customers, and offered them extra attention, within reason.

❊ ❊ ❊

Carmela stood before her mirror, adjusting her outfit to make herself appear taller and thinner. The chain belt around her tunic top was all wrong, and she took it off. At five-feet-three and possessed by an unrelenting sweet tooth, she fought endlessly against her short and plump image, and would have paid, if such things could be bought, to be long and lean like Tobias, five-feet-eleven and with not more than a thirty-four-inch belt size. She slipped on a silky V-neck sweater with half sleeves, slimming in navy blue and cool enough for the July evening. Her short, slim linen skirt revealed legs still toned enough to resist the label "flabby." An eighteen-inch strand of pearls drew eyes to her round, curvy breasts. Her high-heeled, navy-blue sandals added two inches to her height and interest to her calves with their ribbon laces, intricately latticed around her ankles.

She puffed up her beautiful auburn hair, secured it on top with two pearl-studded combs, and let it trail down her back with a whiff of perfumed hair spray. While she did her coiffure, she considered how to make it seem natural for her to be in a bookstore at 10:00 PM on a Saturday night. She had weekends off because of seniority, even though, at twenty-four, she didn't feel much like a senior. Tobias was working, Saturday being a busy day at the Book Trove.

On the matter of frankly chasing him, she was perfectly

honest with herself, but unsure whether to be honest with him as well by confessing that she was there on a Saturday night in the hope of seeing him. What was alluring about him, besides his good looks and his feline grace on the tennis courts, was his maturity. Only twenty-one, he was years ahead of the boyfriends she was accustomed to—men who were recently boys. He had sacrificed his South American trip and his college education, at least for now, on behalf of his woebegone brother, still an outpatient at the rehab facility and with half a chance of ever recovering from his injuries.

As it turned out, she didn't have to justify her presence. She passed by the cash registers and displays of new arrivals at the front and started hunting around. He wasn't in Gardening, Photography, Current Events, or Political Science. A few kids were in Young Adult, snickering about something. She climbed the stairs to the second floor, where some businessmen and nerdy types were browsing in Computers and Technology. He wasn't in Classics or Literature or History.

When she found him, he was appeasing a demanding customer in Economics and Business, and she never got around to explaining her motive, nor did he ask. By the time she heard the commotion between two book racks, it was too late to plan her approach. He spotted her but couldn't escape from the confrontation to greet her. She sat in an armchair and leafed through a stack of art books while he answered one question after another. The customer, a tall guy with glasses and disheveled gray hair, wanted books advancing one specific kind of economic theory. She couldn't hear most of the words, only enough to know that this customer was always right but would never be satisfied. Carmela had patients like that, and she felt for Tobias, who suggested one book, then another, then a third.

The customer seemed to be enjoying the scene he was making. Their voices rose higher and higher until she heard Tobias say, "Well, really, that's not such a revolutionary theory.

You can watch experts analyzing that any Sunday morning on the political talk shows."

That was the last straw for the shopper, who drew himself up to look even taller, rolled his eyes, and turned on his heel, practically spitting at Tobias, "I don't *own* a television set."

Tobias strode toward Carmela with his hand extended. "Sorry, I was in the heavy-duty wash cycle and couldn't press the 'pause' button."

She laughed, got up, took his hand, and then, on impulse, hugged him. He hugged her back. "Or all the books would get flooded, right?" she said. He laughed. "What a curmudgeon, that guy."

"Oh, him, he wasn't so bad. You should have been here last night; I had one who was much worse. This woman, she—"

Another customer interrupted, and Tobias asked Carmela to meet him downstairs in the Book Trove Café at 11:00 PM, where they could sit for a while after closing. The café manager was his friend and wouldn't mind.

After dealing with the customer, Tobias gravitated toward Social Sciences to look through new works in anthropology, the field he was no longer pursuing. This activity caused him simultaneous pain and pleasure. His interest in the subject was almost keen enough to blunt his sadness in reading about great adventures that he would never have. Reading about them was not nearly as good as living them.

A customer came by to inquire about works on the Brazilian Indians, and Tobias advised him in detail. "You speak as if you've done all those things," the man said.

"I wish I had. I almost did."

On the public address system, Elsebeth announced that it was ten minutes until closing time. Tobias checked his watch. He was aware that Carmela was following him in a genial sort of way. This was her third appearance in his life since Simeon's discharge from Woodrock Hospital. In April, she came for Simeon's sixteenth birthday in the rehab facility, and the next week, she watched the tennis match with Martin. Occasionally she phoned for news about Simeon.

Tobias liked Carmela, who was kind, intelligent, and pretty, but there was no space in his life for romance because of three main concerns: his brother, his bills, and, worst of all, his guilt, which burdened him like a ball and chain.

His guilt was a swarm of gnats that fluttered around his head and would not be dispersed by a wave of the hand. Wherever he went, the swarm followed. If he was busy, it thrummed along in the background. If he stopped to think, it was his first thought. Clearing his mind was impossible, because it was always there. First thing in the morning, last thing in the evening, and in the middle of the night, it buzzed in his ears. He bargained with it. He ignored it. He attacked it, to no avail.

"I saved you a seat," Carmela joked in the empty café. They sat at a little round table next to a shelf of poetry books. Tobias's friend served them tall lemonades in skinny, frosted glasses, and then went around upending all the chairs except the ones they were sitting on.

"That was some customer you had back there, that no-TV guy." Carmela's silver charm bracelet clinked against the chilled glass. "Some of my patients are tough customers, too."

"Well, the difference is that your customers are patients," he said. "In retail, customers can be very *im*-patient."

She laughed. He liked having his jokes laughed at. They lingered over the lemonade until the ice melted and the store lights dimmed. "Sorry, I have to get home to my brother. The home nurse is leaving soon, and I can't leave him alone." He got up and inverted his chair onto the table.

Carmela did the same. "How's he doing?"

"When he's home, he mostly sleeps, eats, and sits in front of the TV. I can't get him interested in drawing or art. It's as if he never did these things before." They walked to the front door. "I take him outside walking, and he comes along sort of like a dog, just going where I go, but not initiating anything. It's so depressing."

"Doesn't he want to know what happened to your parents?" She tapped herself on the head. "Sorry for asking; it's completely none of my business."

"It's all right. You can ask me anything. I can tell he does want to know, but he doesn't have enough words to form the question, and I admit I'm taking advantage of that. I'm terrified of telling him the truth."

❁ ❁ ❁

A week went by, and Simeon was getting worse. He was moping in his parents' bedroom, where the shrine-like display on his mother's dressing table had accumulated a few more objects—his father's brass plaque from UPS for excellent service, two of his mother's miniature oil paintings from her student days, and knickknacks like key rings and foreign stamps. He asked for his mother, never his father, and always in the same plaintive way: "Mom-Mom-Mom." Whatever he was learning in speech therapy had not yet improved his primitive mode of communication.

Exasperated, Tobias always responded, "Mom's not here. Come on, Simmy, let's do something else; come with me."

One morning, he called Carmela to ask for advice. "You were prophetic," he said. "I'm going to have to tell him about our parents, and I don't know how to do it."

"What are they saying at the rehab?" she asked.

"Well, they're treating what they can see. They don't get to watch him pacing around in our parents' bedroom for hours." He glanced up the stairs to be sure his brother wasn't listening, on the outside chance that he could even understand. "Could you possibly come over to my house and find some way to tell him? That would be much more than a favor."

Professionally, that was inadvisable; in fact, it was unethical, and she knew it. It was equivalent to treating a patient without having the authority to do so. Worse, she would be getting involved with a patient's relative. "Professionally, I'm not allowed to intervene," she said. "Could I recommend someone?"

Desperate, he said, "The way I see it, you're the only one of all the people I've met since the accident who can get through to him. Please, Carmela, I'm begging you. Is there anything you might be able to do?"

Eager to help Simeon and Tobias at the same time, she hesitated. "We could act out the accident scene using toy cars and people."

"That would be great."

"But I'd be very reluctant to try that. It could backfire, and that would set back his therapy. And I'm concerned about you."

"Me?"

"Yes, all the burden of his care is on you, and the last thing I'd want would be to make things worse," she said.

"He's got to know," he said. "He's got to understand what happened so he can move on, grow, and learn. He's stuck now. I'm sure that's what's keeping him back." He persuaded her.

She came over on a Sunday morning, when they both had the day off, carrying a grocery bag with a towel covering its contents. On the verge of abandoning the idea, she warned that even if Simeon's memory returned, he would never be able to recall the accident itself. It would all be hearsay. "So why not leave well enough alone?"

"Please help," Tobias whispered. "It's haunting me, the way he keeps waiting for her to come home. If I tell him myself, he might not understand, or maybe he'll blame me."

"OK, we'll do our absolute best." She carried the bag into the living room. Simeon watched her from his seat on the couch. Kneeling on the carpet, she set out plastic roads to form a four-way intersection with a traffic light. She took a car and a van out of the bag. In the van, she placed one driver. Next to the car, she set out four occupational therapy figures to represent Tobias and their father in the front seat, and Simeon and their mother in the back seat.

Without being asked, Simeon came and crouched next to her on the floor. "Simmy, we're going to act out what happened the night you were hurt," she told him, as if he could understand everything she was saying. He sat on his tucked legs.

"You went out to dinner with your brother and your parents." She spoke slowly and deliberately. "After that, you all got in the car to go home. This is you in the back seat behind Toby." She had never before referred to Tobias as Toby. It was a nickname reserved for intimate family members. "Your dad sat here, and your mom sat back here next to you." He followed with his eyes as she seated the figures in the toy car.

"The traffic light was red." She turned the knob on the toy light to change it to red. "Your brother stopped the car. Then the light changed." She switched the light to green. "Toby looked left and right and behind, carefully. It was safe to turn left." She took the toy van and aimed it perpendicularly at the toy car in the intersection. "Then this van driver came along and saw the red light facing him. See? It's red for him, in this direction." Simeon nodded, something he hadn't done before. "The van driver should have stopped. Maybe he did try to stop, but he was going *way* too fast near an intersection. And then he skidded on the ice and hit your family's car hard, very hard."

Tobias was having second thoughts, torn between stopping her and letting the simulated accident play out. She rammed the van into the right side of the car, fast. He squeezed his eyes shut.

"You were in the back seat without a seat belt. Your head

hit something, and your brain got shaken up. And your parents, where they were sitting, they were directly in the path of the speeding van. They were hit." She held his hands and he didn't try to let go. "Simmy, I'm so sorry. They were both killed by the impact." She looked right into his eyes. "They didn't have time to suffer. They died right away. And that's why they're not here."

She put her arms around Simeon, but he broke away and climbed up the stairs with his halting gait. Carmela got up off the floor to go. "It's better if you have some privacy with him." She left the pretend accident scene on the carpet so that Simeon could return later and investigate.

Tobias was convinced they had done the right thing, but as the day progressed, he began to have doubts. All afternoon, Simeon refused to answer him or even look at him. Usually docile, he ignored his brother's simple requests. He wouldn't come downstairs for lunch. Tobias brought a sandwich up to his room, but Simeon refused to eat.

By evening, Tobias was panicking. He called Carmela, and she returned in a hurry, wearing jeans and no makeup. A mosquito flew in before he could shut the screen door, and he pounced on it in a forehand smash with a rolled-up newspaper.

She rested one hand on his shoulder, lightly. "Tobias, your brother is processing his emotions. It's natural for him to react with anger and blame." They sat on the couch with the accident setup at their feet, unchanged. Simeon remained in his bedroom.

"He's been home from rehab for six weeks now." Tobias watched the stairs. "Every day he goes back for therapy, but he's here all night, and I was just postponing what I had to do anyway. Not telling him was getting to be like lying to him."

"You made the right decision, and I think he'll recover faster because of it." She looked around the room. "I have an idea." It was a typical, middle-class New Jersey home, with quasi-modern furniture and a bay window overlooking a tree-lined street with similar houses. On one wall was a stereo cabinet. "Could you put on some music? Something Simmy really likes."

Ever since kindergarten, Simeon had liked only classical music, something that further distanced him from classmates, who already had him pegged as odd and different. He had specific tastes, preferring mostly baroque and romantic composers. Even stranger, he had no interest in playing an instrument himself but savored music in the background while he was drawing. All through grade school, teachers had tried to enlist him in the school chorus or sign him up for free lessons on band or orchestral instruments, but he was no more inclined to play music than to dribble a basketball.

Tobias shuffled the CDs. Some Bach would be good. Piano—Simeon always liked piano. He picked the Glenn Gould recording of the Goldberg Variations—not the one from 1955 that had made the pianist famous, but the 1981 recording, fitting and appropriate because it was the last that he would ever make. Only a few days after the recording was released, he suddenly died, his brilliant hands forever stilled at age fifty.

The Aria, the theme on which all the variations were based, filled the room. Unhurried, it was accompanied by Gould's guttural, idiosyncratic humming, which had never been expunged. This was not a sanitized recording made to sell a lot of copies or to convince anybody of anything. It was Gould's epitaph for himself. Music fit for a time capsule, it stood for the musical inspiration of all mankind, expressed in the work of two geniuses, two centuries apart, both gone forever. The music was so fine, and its execution so perfect, that it alone would have justified the existence of the human race to some far-off civilization, light-years away in another universe.

The second variation began. Tobias and Carmela stood

still under its spell. Only when the fourth variation started did they climb the carpeted stairs together, quietly.

Carmela entered the bedroom first. Simeon was sitting on the bed, his head tilted, straining to hear the next variation from the living room below. She took his hand in a firm clasp. "Come downstairs now, Simmy. Let's listen to the music."

Tobias stepped aside to let them walk down, Carmela always a step below Simeon, ready to break his fall. Simeon didn't look at his brother.

They sat on the couch, Carmela in the middle, until all thirty variations had finished. Except for the faint hum of the air conditioner, the room was quiet. A few backyards away, a firecracker left over from July Fourth sizzled and popped.

Carmela stood first, drawing Simeon in, pressing his head against her body. "You're going to be all right, Simmy."

"Mom," he said. Just once.

"Mom's not coming back. But she will always be in your mind. You will always remember her. You can see pictures of her, and movies of her, in your mind." She was crying silently. "It's like playing music you've heard before." She rocked him slightly. "Say Carmela."

"*Mel-a.*" He wrapped his arms around her.

Tobias stood, put his arm around Carmela, and stroked his brother's back. "This is one problem I'm afraid I can't solve," he said softly, as if to himself.

Carmela looked up at him, her tears flowing freely and no spare hand to wipe them away. "You're not alone," she said. "We're all going to work on this together."

# Chapter 6

Carmela started rounding everybody up that evening. The scene of this hurt boy clinging to her, and his brother's anguished face, chagrined her, and she was compelled to do something about it. Tobias was holding steady, at best, and on a slow, downward slide, at worst.

The way she saw it, they were struggling for air. On a plane, if you're travelling with a child and there's an emergency, you're supposed to put on your oxygen mask first, before the child's. Makes sense; if you're gasping for breath, how can you save anyone else? In her experience, a dependent patient like Simeon couldn't make much progress under a depressed caretaker.

On the way to her apartment on the other side of Woodrock, she jotted down ideas on her mental clipboard. As soon as she walked into the ground-floor apartment, her six-month-old kittens barged through their cat door from the courtyard, one after the other, complaining that their dinner was late. "Come on, you guys. Sorry, sorry." She opened a can. "Here you go, Flora. Here, Lynx, the tuna special."

She washed her hands and got busy hunting for Martin, which was easy, there being only one Martin A. Scanlon in the Abington College directory. "'A' for Agassi," Martin had joked about his middle initial after defeating Tobias in April. Not expecting Martin to be in his off-campus apartment in

July, she left a message and hoped he was checking. "Martin, this is Carmela Liston. How are you doing? Say, I hear you're coming for a little visit at the end of the summer, and I have an idea. Call me?"

The return call came within an hour. Martin had a summer undergraduate teaching assistantship in the math department at Abington. "Everything OK?" He sounded as if he'd been running. "How's Tobias? How's Simeon?"

"They're all right. Tobias is coping. Slow progress for Simmy—like one inch per month."

They laughed. Together, they planned a four-day visit at the beginning of September, culminating in the U.S. Open Men's Finals on Sunday, September 9, 1990, a week before the start of Martin's senior year. He was bringing his girlfriend, Valerie. He would tell Tobias he was coming for two days to play a rematch, but then would show up with Valerie and announce the weekend fun. She swore him to secrecy, and they agreed to split the cost of the four full-day tickets.

Then there was the matter of what to do about Simeon, who always spent Sundays with his brother. Tobias would be miserable all day, worrying about his brother alone at home with his attendant. Taking him along would be a burden, depending on how well Simmy was doing by then. She had to decide immediately before the tickets sold out.

The only way to prepare Simmy for a big day out was to get him accustomed to outings, gradually. She had to come up with a way to take him somewhere every Sunday until their date in Flushing Meadows. She got out her credit card, picked up the phone, and ordered five tickets at $120 each for the men's finals, having no idea who would still be standing by then.

❁ ❁ ❁

Elsebeth was a young-looking forty with an unwrinkled face. Her mother, who had named her, was Danish, and her father came from Trinidad. Both were engineers on government contracts. She had lived all over the United States with her four younger siblings, whom she entertained by telling stories late at night, wherever they lived.

Elsebeth's unusual heredity showed. She was five-feet-eight and of muscular build. Her graying hair was the lightest possible shade of brown before blond. Because it was kinky, a first view gave the false impression that she was an albino. But her coloring was also hybrid; she had a deep, year-round tan and blue-green eyes. Her full lips, naturally rose-colored, were lifted in a perpetual near-smile except for rare moments when she was annoyed about something.

Once, when a gaggle of women from the Junior League had assembled in the bookstore to attend a talk by an expert from the Orchid Society, one member approached Elsebeth from the side. "Pardon me." She tapped her on the elbow. "I was wondering about something. Hope you don't mind my asking."

Elsebeth cringed inwardly and smiled outwardly. "Go ahead."

"What are you, exactly?"

*Oh no, the species question*, she thought. "I'm the owner of the Book Trove. Pleased to meet you. And your name is?"

"Ramona Worthington. I mean, to clarify, where do you come from?"

Elsebeth said, "I moved here from Philadelphia, where I got my master's degree from UPenn."

"What I mean to say is ... could you explain ... what I'm trying to say is—"

Putting her tormentor out of her misery, Elsebeth excused herself to trot to the front door, where the guest author was entering with her entourage and armloads of flowers.

❁ ❁ ❁

Next on Carmela's agenda was a morning visit to the

Book Trove, where she asked to speak to the manager about a mutual friend. She extended her hand to Elsebeth. "I'm Carmela Liston, a nurse and a friend of Tobias." She explained her connection through Simeon and confided her plans for a four-day weekend two months off.

Elsebeth, aware of Tobias's grave problems, had treated him like any other employee from the first day of what she saw as his exile from higher education. Her approach was to keep him occupied, pay him a fair wage and benefits, watch him discreetly, and hope that in the end, he would thrive. She assigned him challenging work: finding authors to invite for book signings; scouting out unusual volumes unavailable in chain bookstores; designing workshops for customers.

Whenever she caught him in a reverie or a melancholy mood, she interrupted. She burst in on him one evening as he sat vacantly before the schedule book. "Tobias, I need your help, fast." Then she gave him a burdensome amount of busy work. True, there was always something to do, but the urgency was something she invented to break his mood, keep his hands busy, and relieve him from rumination.

Elsebeth agreed immediately to give him time off for the planned amusements. She marked the dates in her calendar and promised to keep the secret. Complicit in a nascent love affair, she smiled benignly at Carmela and privately wished her love.

❊ ❊ ❊

In Carmela's philosophy, peace of mind was the difference between getting dressed in the dark while hoping that everything matched and turning on the lights above a three-way mirror to see for sure. She proceeded as if everything would work out fine if she made all the right moves; everything would fall into place. It was like stacking dishes neatly in a cabinet, or piling clean towels on a shelf. She lived alone, and no one was there to disturb her orderly existence.

Arranging schedules for unpredictable people was a good deal trickier than housekeeping in a small apartment, and she worried every day that something would go awry. At stake was her little Project Happiness, as she called it, along with her chance to inspire Tobias to fall in love with her.

She was on an all vegetable, fruit, and whole grain diet these days, aiming for a sleek look in summer fashions, but allowed herself just three, then four, pieces of European chocolates as fortification before calling Tobias. His daily habit was to drop off his brother at the rehab facility for outpatient therapy, then practice his tennis serves in the county park until some other solitary player came along and offered to hit with him. After that, he would go home, shower, and get ready for work. The attendant he hired drove Simeon home from rehab every day and stayed with him until Tobias finished work at the Book Trove at 11:00 PM.

She called the next morning. "I enjoyed seeing you play last spring. Mind if I come watch you practice for a while before I go to work?" Simple as that. Surprised, he agreed. She came and watched for half an hour, then waved her hand and went home. A week later, she showed up near lunchtime with sandwiches from the deli, vegetarian for both of them. He tried to pay. She said, "You pay next time."

"When are you coming back?"

"Next Wednesday again?"

"And what if it's raining?" He smiled, toying with her.

"Thursday, then."

The following week, she came empty-handed and watched him hit balls against the wall until another player joined him for a while. She and Tobias went to Janet's Deli by the Woodrock commuter train station. They fell into a pattern of eating lunch together once a week, then twice a week. The third week, she asked if she could come by on Sunday to work with Simmy a bit. "Sundays must be hard, with no work and no therapy. It must be a very long day for you both."

"You got that exactly right," he said. "I try to get him to do things without stressing him out. He can walk fine and everything; it's just that he doesn't want to go unless you sort of push him. He's like a car with all its moving parts but no gas."

She tasted a spoonful of the spicy tomato soup between them, thinking how funny it was to be sharing soup with someone you had yet to kiss and, in fact, might never kiss. "With brain injuries like his, we don't know how much is organic and how much is behavioral."

"I can't figure that out, either."

"Do you think we could try something?" She tore off a corner of bread and dunked it in the soup. "There's an art exhibit at the Woodrock Historical Society. Some oil paintings of early town scenes and a few Hudson River views. I've heard there are around forty pictures. Do you want to try to bring Simmy over there on Sunday and see how it goes?"

That started another tradition. The first Sunday, they all met at the exhibit at two in the afternoon. They strolled from painting to painting. Simeon was passive as usual, but at least he was looking at the pictures. Not sure whether he was reading or even remembered how to read, Carmela and Tobias took turns reading the titles and artists' names to Simeon, asking him to repeat, which he usually did. They parted with hugs after an hour and made plans for the next Sunday.

The second outing was to the Montclair Art Museum for an exhibition of watercolors. They stayed slightly longer and went out to dinner. Tobias drove Carmela home and got out of the car to hug her good-bye.

On the third weekend, they began their exploration of art in New York City. The fastest way to New York on a Sunday was by car, only thirty minutes to midtown, and they took turns driving. They went to the Museum of Modern Art or the Metropolitan, Sunday after Sunday, exploring different collections. Alternatively, they went to the Guggenheim, the Frick Collection, the Whitney Museum, photography exhibits, galleries. Always passive and docile, Simeon seemed more alert on these visits. No one stared at this tall, thin, lost-looking teenager with glasses. In a city this size, there were odder people around than Simeon.

Famished after each museum outing, they ate in the city, and then drove home, with hugs all around. Simeon, their passive chaperone, was now hugging as well as being hugged.

On the last Sunday in August, Simeon was unusually attentive in the Picasso collection at MOMA. When it was time to go, for the first time, he protested instead of coming along willingly like a golden retriever on a leash. Tugging at his brother's sleeve, he said, "More."

"You want to stay?" Tobias asked.

Simeon looked side to side from his brother to Carmela. "More pictures," he said, making his first rudimentary sentence since the accident. In a spontaneous motion, Carmela and Tobias formed a little celebratory circle around him. They stayed another hour in the Picasso galleries, letting him gaze at each painting as long as he wanted.

While Simeon sat on the bench in front of "Three Musicians," Tobias and Carmela stood behind him. Tobias put his arm around her and drew her close. He pressed her head against his chest and grazed her perfumed auburn hair with his cheek. Moved by his brother's concentration on the picture, he closed his eyes and rocked her a little before trying to talk. "It's all thanks to you, Carmela. This is wonderful for him."

She squeezed him with both arms, keeping one eye on Simeon. "No, you're the one who's doing it all. I'm just here for company."

He kissed her, right there in the museum, a first kiss in the company of Picasso and a damaged adolescent. Guards were watching everything, and it was the shortest first kiss either had ever had. But it signaled a new connection. For the rest of the afternoon, Carmela couldn't tell if she was sitting or standing.

❁ ❁ ❁

In Carmela's presence, Tobias learned the meaning of "company." She watched his tennis practice twice a week, never interfering, just being a friendly presence. She arrived half an hour before he finished and went to lunch with him, not forcing herself on him, just enjoying his company. She seemed to understand everything he said, even partially formed thoughts.

Unlike his college girlfriends, she put his interests first, and he checked himself again and again to be sure he wasn't taking her for granted. Her concern for Simeon was warm and genuine. He had the impression that she would have cared about him even if she didn't love Tobias. She was like a relative.

He tried to hold himself back. It didn't seem fair for him to be living and loving when his parents were dead and his brother was like a hologram of his former self—three-dimensional, but lacking in depth. Even so, they were seeing each other more often.

She suggested bringing Simeon to her apartment for some modified pet therapy. "Did you have pets growing up?"

"No, we couldn't; our father was allergic."

On a Sunday morning before their weekly museum trip, the brothers knocked on Carmela's door. "We're going to visit her cats," Tobias told Simeon. They sat on the floor. Lynx and Flora, littermates aged seven months, were friendly and trusting. Curious, the cats slinked over to inspect the visitors.

"They're nice, see?" Carmela patted Lynx, a gregarious black-and-white tuxedo cat who stood on his hind legs and pushed his head against her hand. Flora, a tricolor with longish fur, put one two-toned paw on Simeon's knee.

At the corners of Simeon's lips was the foretaste of a smile. Carmela took a package of treats out of the drawer in her coffee table and showed them to Simeon. "Hold out your hands like this, and let them eat the treats. It's candy for them." She put multicolored fish-shaped treats in each of his hands, and the cats neatly picked them off his palms with rubbing and purring. Simeon's face lit up into a real smile.

They began to miss each other and to crave each other's company. The first time Tobias left a message for Carmela that wasn't about anything practical, she responded with a loving message of her own in an escalating game of phone tag. "Thanks for calling," she said. "It's not good strategy to say this, but I care more about you than about strategy." The line was silent, of course, but she went on. "I miss you most of the time. I'm happy to hear from you anytime." She inhaled sharply. "And I love you all the time."

Their first lovemaking had the furtive sense of two teenagers sneaking off and doing something they shouldn't, which made them enjoy it all the more. Her car was in the shop, and he picked her up outside Woodrock Hospital after he finished work at the Book Trove. She invited him over for a snack, but he had to relieve Simeon's attendant, Kenneth, and invited her to his house instead. After Kenneth left, Tobias went upstairs to check on his brother, who was sound asleep and breathing deeply. He closed Simeon's door, trotted downstairs, drew the drapes, and grabbed Carmela without a word. He shut off most of the lights, and they fell onto the couch together. Her light perfume and generous breasts intoxicated him, and his hunger possessed him. He managed one breathless "I love you so much, Carmela" before he couldn't say any more.

"I love you too, Toby." She unzipped her uniform while gazing at him with her round golden-brown eyes and slowly peeled off her white stockings. It was over before either of them had time to think. Afterward, a noise upstairs made Tobias sit up quickly and pull on his shorts, but it was only Simmy turning in his sleep.

Like all lovers, they began to think each other's thoughts or to imagine that they did. She joked that she would send him a bill for telepathic communications—a long-distance telepath bill.

What Tobias loved most about Carmela, he valued most highly in himself. Her qualities were those to which he himself aspired—to be altruistic, to help those who walked along his path. It wasn't that she was new and therefore exciting. She was exciting because she was always new to him, always bubbly and talking about something interesting. He didn't need road signs to drive around her world. "I'll never mind if you call right out of the blue and start in the middle of a sentence," he reassured her one day when she called before she left for work. "It's so easy to understand you, and to be understood by you, that I think we knew each other well in a previous life, if there ever were any previous lives."

With Carmela watching some of his morning practice, Tobias was gaining confidence on the courts. By the time Martin arrived in September, he felt prepared for the rematch. Valerie had just graduated with a degree in biology and was taking a break before graduate school. They were staying in Carmela's apartment, and Carmela was staying with Tobias. The two couples spent their first day catching up on things, and the men practiced hitting. The next day, Friday, they competed.

Martin was a bit nervous because the last match had gone three sets, and he'd won by the skin of his teeth in a tiebreaker. Tobias took to the courts and nonchalantly performed a few stretches before a brief warm-up practice with

Martin. Their first set went the full distance of 6–6 with a tiebreaker favoring Tobias, who ended with a 12–10 winning score.

During a three-minute break before the next set, Martin was unusually silent. Tobias, sensing his friend's tension, tried to heighten his anxiety by commenting on Martin's missed volleys. Martin, who usually won their first set, was now playing in the hole with no second chance in the next set, a must-win for him.

Tobias, smiling quickly at Carmela, looked relaxed, knowing that he could play more aggressively without fear of losing the match. Martin was playing defensively, slicing the ball often instead of hitting his offensive topspin and charging to the net. Tobias took advantage of Martin's tentative response by moving the ball from corner to corner.

Martin made a number of unforced errors and lost the set 6–4, giving the match to Tobias in only two sets. They ran to the net and shook hands.

"You always were a quick study," Martin complimented. "Wish you were still on my team at school."

"We would have been unbeatable in doubles," Tobias agreed. As they packed their bags, Tobias felt gleeful that he still had the right stuff in his tennis game.

Over dinner at the Hillyers' house, Valerie teased, "Now we have a gigantic surprise for you."

"You're getting married?" Tobias asked.

"No! Well, maybe… sometime." Martin laughed and Valerie blushed. "We don't know yet. It's something else. You tell him, Carmela."

Carmela opened her purse and took out a jumbo red envelope. Inside was a smaller blue envelope. She'd been saving up envelopes from greeting cards. And inside that one was the white, windowed ticket envelope from the U.S. Open Tennis Championships in Flushing Meadows, Queens. Watching Tobias's face, she very slowly removed the tickets one by one and spread them out on the table—all five of them.

Tobias couldn't believe what he was looking at. "The U.S. Open?" he said. "For all of us? This is fantastic. I thought you had to go home," he said to Martin and Valerie.

"Not till after the match on Sunday," Martin said. "We wouldn't miss that!"

Tobias looked again at the tickets, fanned out in front of his plate. "These are for the *finals*? I've never once gone to the U.S. Open. This is amazing. Carmela!" He got up and pulled her out of her chair, hugging her and swaying with her. She had never before seen a smile of pure joy on his face.

❊ ❊ ❊

Sunday was warm and sunny. The number-seven subway was the best way to get to the U.S.T.A. National Tennis Center in Flushing Meadows. Protecting Simeon on the subway was nothing compared to the hassle of long lines they would have faced in the parking lots. It was a short walk from the subway stop at Willets Point to the Louis Armstrong Stadium, which opened at eleven in the morning.

As they entered, they were delighted by the giant banners of Grand Slam winners hanging all around the stadium. It was a world of tennis. Stars like Jimmy Connors, Billie Jean King, Boris Becker, Steffi Graff, Ivan Lendl, Martina Navratilova, and John McEnroe looked down on the excited fans walking by. Martin and Tobias discussed the great matchups of the past and how the elite players were getting younger and stronger.

Enticed by the tennis racket shops, they marveled at the new rackets, shoes, and tennis duds on display. Martin splurged and bought matching 1990 U.S. Open sun visors for all five of them. The sun was pouring down, and only Tobias protested, but Martin said, "No big deal. I'll pay off all my school loans one month later." Carmela adjusted the Velcro on Simeon's visor and reached up to put it on his head. She thought he seemed pleased to have matching attire.

They bought lunch from the various food vendors and carried their trays to a round table under an umbrella. Tobias took his Swarovski binoculars out of his backpack and showed them to everybody. "We're all going to take turns using these." He watched his brother's face, but Simeon didn't seem to remember the Christmas gift he'd given his brother just before the accident.

By the time the match started at three, the suspense was electric. Pete Sampras was only nineteen years old and was not expected to win, although his fans were elated that he'd made it to the finals and were rooting for him fervently. It was an unusual match, with Sampras ranked fiftieth, and Agassi, himself only twenty years old, ranked fourth. Martin explained to Valerie, "Whoever gets the best of five sets is the winner."

"Who are you rooting for?" Valerie was peering through the binoculars to spy on celebrities in the stands, including singer Barbra Streisand, New York City Mayor David Dinkins, and other luminaries.

"Good question," Martin said. "They're very different players. Sampras is a serve-and-volley player like me, and Agassi is a baseline player like Tobias."

Carmela said, "So you're rooting for Sampras and Tobias is rooting for Agassi, right?" She was sitting next to Simeon, who was quietly observing the courts down below, where referees and other officials were setting up for the match.

"No, I'm for the underdog, Pete Sampras," Tobias said. "Andre Agassi is a hotshot, spoiled brat, very flashy and boastful. These guys are two very opposite characters."

Valerie handed the binoculars to Carmela, who adjusted the strap around Simeon's neck. He wasn't talking but seemed content and comfortable.

"Oh, come on," Martin said. "That brashness serves a purpose. Intimidating your opponent is part of the game."

"He's too confrontational for me," Tobias said. "Go, Pete!"

"Well, I like Agassi's in-your-face style. All the way, Andre," Martin said.

Everybody tried the binoculars, although the stadium was small enough that they could see every move without them. Tobias showed Simeon how to turn the focusing knob.

There was plenty of pre-match drama, but the match itself went in straight sets, increasingly favoring Sampras. They all applauded every point, even Simeon. In the end, Sampras defeated Agassi 6–4, 6–3, 6–2, becoming the U.S. Open's youngest ever male singles champion at the age of nineteen years and twenty-eight days. The stadium went wild.

❋ ❋ ❋

After Martin and Valerie had left, Carmela moved on to the next step in her Project Happiness. "There's a really good part-time master's degree program at Carlyle University," she told Tobias. "You could take one or two courses a semester and get your degree. They'd probably let you make up for the senior year you're missing."

"Oh, I wish I could," he said. "And I would, if not for two things: time and money." His insurance wouldn't pay for any more outpatient rehabilitation for Simeon, who was now attending a day program for mentally handicapped teenagers at Tobias's expense. "And the only thing I could give up to find more hours would be tennis. And if I did that, I'd go nuts!"

Even with Martin and Valerie gone, they continued to spend the night together. Carmela brought over Lynx and Flora so they wouldn't be lonely. Lying in bed one night after Simeon had gone to sleep, Tobias said, "If it hadn't been for the accident, I would have never met you."

"Bad luck can work both ways," she said.

"You know what I'd love to do?"

"No, what?" She was cuddled up in his arms on the fold-out sofa. Neither of them could sleep peacefully in his dead parents' bedroom.

"I'd love to ask you to move in with me. Along with your critters, of course."

"Then ask." She ran her fingers through his black hair. "I might even say yes. What's stopping you?"

"He goes where I go." He motioned to the stairway. "We'd never be alone. We'd never have any privacy."

She rolled over on her stomach and rested her chin on her folded arms. "That's no problem at all. He's my family, too."

# book two

# Chapter 7

After Carmela broke her lease, Tobias took out a second mortgage to refurbish his parents' bedroom and make it their own—new furniture, master bathroom, carpeting, blinds, paint, bedding, towels. Everything clean, everything new. Recessed lighting replaced the old ceiling fixture, changing the light as well as the atmosphere. The renovation was a small sacrifice compared with the cost of buying another house and moving out altogether.

They didn't neglect Simeon's room, still set up as a bedroom for two brothers. Tobias hired a contractor to knock down the wall between this bedroom and the adjoining one, his father's den. They outfitted the larger space with a tile floor, a new bed over a cozy area rug, a desk with a hutch, and floor-to-ceiling shelving on two walls. Some of Simeon's best cartoons from his pre-accident days were tacked up on an oversize bulletin board, the biggest they could find. On the walls were framed award certificates and citations.

Over the course of a month, they secretly hoarded art supplies, hiding them in closets and the garage, while Simeon attended classes at his special high school. When everything was ready, they both took the day off to frenetically stock the room with oil paints, pastels, pencils, pens, canvasses, sketch pads, charcoal, acrylics, drop cloths, brushes, a studio easel, all kinds of artists' paper, and, best of all, something called a Universal Design Creation Station, which had a spacious melamine top. You could adjust its height and also its tilt angle, from 0 degrees to 45 degrees. Two sets of three-drawer storage cabinets were built into it. The whole thing was on four casters, two of them lockable. It even had an adjustable pencil/paper ledge.

They set up artists' lamps on the easel and the Creation Station. On the shelves, they stacked books on art and art history from the Book Trove, where Tobias had an employee discount. A corner table held a compact CD player and a rack of Simeon's favorite CDs, brought upstairs from the living room. As a last-minute, humorous touch, Tobias placed a box of ninety-six Crayola crayons with a built-in sharpener on the desk.

When Simeon came home from school, he was surprised to have Tobias and Carmela escort him from his minibus to the door, telling him they had something new for him upstairs. He dropped his book bag in the living room and followed them up. In the expanded room, which had been nearly empty that morning, the art supplies were arrayed in the most enticing manner. If Tobias had the least bit of artistic talent, which he didn't, he would have dug in right away, drawing and painting until he dropped from exhaustion.

Simeon walked around the room in slow motion, touching everything, caressing objects in the manner that he petted Flora and Lynx, who often slept with him. He stroked the glossy covers of the new art books, patted the swiveling desk chair and the artist's stool, ran his fingers around the adjustable easel. Like a blind person feeling a statue, he handled the lamps, probing, exploring. He lifted a clump of assorted brushes from the little barrel in which they stood, feeling the bristles, replacing them as he had found them. And he fingered the pencils, charcoal, pastels, and tubes of paint, holding them one by one, putting them back in their assigned places. It was a spectacular wonderland of art and color.

Standing silently in the doorway, Carmela and Tobias let him explore his new workshop. No one spoke for half an hour. Simeon replaced a stack of canvas boards in a print rack and turned to them. "For me?" His eyes were shining.

"All for you," Carmela said. "From Toby and me."

He lunged for them, hugging them both at once. "Thank you. Thank you. Thank you."

Keeping their expectations low, Tobias and Carmela had decided on a strict policy of letting Simmy be. He stayed in the room all evening. Finally, at 11:00, Tobias checked on him, holding his breath. A CD was playing softly, music by Tchaikovsky. Simmy was sitting at the Creation Station with the Crayola crayons spilled out on the slightly tilted surface. He was rolling them in his hands, side to side, grouping them and regrouping them. None of the paper had been disturbed. The room was as neat and inviting as it had been eight hours before.

Within a span of three years, Tobias attended Martin's two graduations and his wedding, accompanied by Carmela and Simeon. Dreading each event, he tried to keep his negative feelings to himself. Martin always made efforts to maintain their friendship, no matter how crowded his schedule was getting to be. Their tennis matches sustained them from one visit to the next, and they remained equals in that respect, although Martin's climb up the ladder of credentials dwarfed his friend's position in the bookstore.

The most painful of these mileposts was Martin's 1991 graduation from Abington College near Baltimore, when they were both twenty-two years old. Tobias hadn't promised he'd be there and was ready to skip it until the last moment, but gritted his teeth and went anyway when Carmela pointed out that a good friend was for life, and furthermore, you never knew when you'd need each other. "Out of everyone you knew at school, who's still in touch?" she asked.

On campus, he avoided most of the people he didn't want to run into again. For one thing, he didn't want to explain why he'd dropped out when he'd been doing so well, had even distinguished himself with awards, scholarships, and academic honors. Another point, which he could barely admit to himself, was not exactly shame concerning his brother, but rather, the tiresome need to explain to curious strangers why this young man, now a lanky seventeen-year-old, had the vocabulary of a grade-school boy and didn't shake hands or look you in the eye like a normal person. Questions could be intrusive.

Relieved when the ceremony was almost over, he and Carmela enthusiastically applauded Martin as he strode across the stage, wayward plumes of red hair comically poking out from under his black mortarboard, to accept his bachelor of science in finance, summa cum laude. In a genuine burst of affection, Tobias dropped all inhibitions and rose to yell, "Way to go, Martin!" From the next section of folding chairs on the grassy field, Grover Whitman shielded his eyes and stared, and then ambled over to greet the student who had never returned. By the time Tobias saw him, there was no choice but to clasp his hand and exchange pleasantries.

"Grover, this is Carmela Liston, my girlfriend. Carmela, Grover Whitman, professor of anthropology." Tobias gently tugged his brother to turn and face Grover. "And this is my brother, Simeon."

A familiar cloud passed over Grover's face when he reached for Simeon's hand, which was tenuous and flimsy, as if Simmy needed lessons in performing this basic courtesy. It didn't matter on whose face the cloud appeared—a friend, a neighbor, a shopper in the supermarket—the reaction was always the same: staring, noticing something amiss, and then trying to look as if nothing was wrong.

Members of the class of 1991 filed by—his class. Tobias deflected Grover's curiosity and unspoken questions and excused himself to congratulate Martin as he stepped down from the stage.

❁ ❁ ❁

Between Martin's two graduations, Tobias and Carmela witnessed Simeon's low-key graduation in 1992 from Caerus Academy. After Simeon had spent some time at a workshop for mentally disabled teenagers, Tobias had enrolled him in a school that Carmela found, an actual high school with a varied program for students who were euphemistically labeled "exceptional." In Greek mythology, Caerus, the youngest child of Zeus, was the personification of opportunity, luck, and favorable moments. These qualities being in sparse supply in his life, Tobias struggled to pay the annual tuition of twenty thousand dollars, with help from Carmela's salary as a psychiatric nurse. Simeon aged out from the program at eighteen with nowhere to go.

Tobias couldn't complain about the curriculum, which was excellent, offering its handicapped students every high school subject plus what the school called technological arts, social arts, fine arts, performing arts, kinesthetic arts, and creative arts. Of these, Simeon responded, and then only slightly, to classes in painting and sculpting. His graduation project, a mural of mostly abstract splotches in acrylics, was nowhere near the quality of the sketch he'd drawn in pencil on a typewriter pad on the evening of the accident that crumpled his artistic future. That drawing, a cartoon of Tobias in safari gear, hung in their renovated master bedroom. Carmela had brought it to a professional framer and hung it on the wall with a little pull-cord lamp above it as a present for Tobias.

When he saw it, he slumped on their new bed, put his head in his hands, and cried like a motherless child.

Martin leaped over his next hurdle in 1993, graduating from Wharton College with an MBA in finance. This was really two milestones in one, Martin having accepted a full-time position at Lehman Brothers in New York, where he'd been an intern for the past two summers. He was formally hired as an assistant business analyst in commercial real estate with a starting salary of one hundred twenty thousand dollars. That was only the base; he would probably earn 30 percent of salary as a bonus, and that was only for the first year.

Tobias's career at the Book Trove had gone about as far as it was going to get. Elsebeth was very pleased with his work and had promoted him to evening manager. He was in charge of three other employees and had some autonomy in designing promotional sales campaigns and enjoyable activities to lure in customers. She paid him forty-five thousand dollars plus benefits, with a small bonus every Christmas.

The store was thriving in spite of the warehouse-size Barnes & Noble on the highway outside Woodrock. The Book Trove differed from commercial chains because it had a community atmosphere and attracted hordes of interesting speakers. Its staff was professional and courteous, and its clientele was devoted. Plus, there was an appealing café on the main floor with fifty varieties of upscale tea and scrumptious little cakes from the Filigree Gourmet Bakery.

Elsebeth had a benevolent attitude toward her employees and permitted them to read on the job, as long as their work was done and customers didn't need their help. She liked having an educated staff who could answer customers' questions from experience. This aspect of his work gave Tobias, an autodidact, a chance to compensate for his lost education to some degree but not in a form that would prove his accomplishment to the world.

❋ ❋ ❋

Valerie, now Martin's fiancée, was wearing a diamond ring. She was working on her PhD in biology at Princeton, and they were saving for a down payment on a house in New Jersey. "We'll be neighbors," Martin pointed out during one visit. "That means more tennis."

Martin and Valerie's wedding took place the following year, 1994, when Martin and Tobias were both twenty-five years old. Their engagement inspired Carmela, now twenty-eight, to prod Tobias into marriage as well. Reluctant to change anything while he was just holding on financially, Tobias procrastinated, offering the excuse that their finances were shaky, and any more commitments were impossible. They were still paying off their second mortgage and had just finished honoring their student loans.

The wedding was held at the Renaissance Harborplace Hotel in Martin's home state, Maryland, where rooms with two queen beds went for one hundred fifty dollars a night, even with the group discount. On the verge of sending a gift and his sincere regrets, Tobias caved in to Martin, who persuaded him that it was essential that he serve as best man, and offered to pay for the double room for two nights for Tobias, Carmela, and Simeon. He was already earning decent money, and it was the least he could do for such a good friend. Tobias, who hated handouts, would have refused if not for Carmela, who said simply, "Let's go. He's your best friend. He's like a brother."

Arriving the day before the wedding, Tobias was startled by the luxury of the place. In the sunken lobby were skylights, fountains, and marble floors, shiny enough that the reflected sunlight hurt his eyes. A uniformed host escorted them to the reception desk. "Scanlon wedding party," Tobias said, feeling underdressed in jeans and sneakers. Carmela guided Simeon to the waiting area, where plus-size goldfish swam in a trickling brook.

"Welcome to Renaissance Harborplace, sir." The clerk

gave Tobias a little folder containing key cards. "The elevators to your room are over there. Down at the other end is where you enter the Gallery—that's our four-story shopping mall in a glass atrium." Tobias felt in his hip pocket for his wallet. "You have access to our fitness center, pool, and spa. Across the street, you can shop to your heart's content at the Harborplace stores. The Inner Harbor is right there, too. That's where you rent boats, go sailing, and take tours. And the National Aquarium is three blocks that way. Anything you need, just ask, twenty-four hours a day. We wish you a pleasant stay."

Valerie had become good friends with Carmela over the years and invited her to be a bridesmaid. With Tobias as best man, this left the tricky problem of what to do about Simeon, who couldn't be counted on to behave appropriately when left unattended—he might wander off in the middle of the ceremony, or make comments during moments of silence, or converse with people who didn't know him, and not always comprehensibly. So Carmela didn't join the other bridesmaids, with Valerie's understanding, and looked at things from the bright side: She wouldn't have to buy a gown; she wouldn't have to worry about looking fat in spaghetti straps; and she wouldn't feel the stigma of "always a bridesmaid, never a bride."

It was the first wedding they had attended as a couple, and they were both moved by the simple, nondenominational service. Reluctant to appear hackneyed, Valerie and Martin were nevertheless spellbound by the poetry of Kahlil Gibran and, like thousands of other couples, chose his poem "You Were Born Together" for their inspirational reading before the minister united them. They both recited from memory.

Handsome in his white tuxedo, Martin began, his voice steady. Valerie took her turn, eyes glistening but voice well modulated. Then they entwined their arms and laced their fingers together, reciting in one voice the admonition to give each other their love, but not their souls, and to stand together, yet independently.

Sniffles and muffled sobs were heard among the guests in the chapel. Now it was time for the minister's formal ceremony. Colorful as always with his blue eyes and red hair, slicked in place, Martin blinked while the minister recited the familiar lines, and he repeated them with a catch in his voice. Valerie, ravishing and shapely in her strapless white gown, her light-brown hair blond for the occasion, repeated the phrases as if she'd written them herself.

"I now pronounce you husband and wife," the minister declared. Flashing cameras lit up Valerie's diamond tiara. The organist played the Mendelssohn Wedding March while the guests cheered. Simeon swayed, savoring the well-played music. Tobias stood still on the dais, letting the enormity of the ceremony permeate him. Carmela lost it altogether, sobbing into her handkerchief and smudging her mascara.

At the reception, the band played "Only You" in deference to Martin's parents. In a slow dance with Carmela, light on her feet in a gold silk gown, Tobias held her close and inhaled her floral perfume, keeping an eye on Simmy sitting at a table with Valerie's aunt and uncle. "I love you, darling," he said. "You look beautiful tonight."

"I love you, too." She leaned against him, following his moves. He was easy to follow, an untutored dancer with natural grace.

At his table, Simeon was turning his place card over and back when Valerie's younger sister came over to get him for the line dance that was forming for "La Macarena." He looked up at her smiling face. She was pretty in her sea-green bridesmaid's gown, with matching satin ribbons braided through her long brown hair. He took the hand she extended and felt its soft femininity. She pulled him along and he followed, taking his place next to her in the dance line.

Seeing his brother safe with Valerie's sister, Tobias led

Carmela away from the dance floor. "Let's talk." In a corner of the ballroom, he sat facing her and took her two hands, kissed them, and pulled his chair closer. "I've been thinking for a long time about what's good for us both."

She widened her eyes and stopped breathing. He had to phrase it right, find exactly the words they would remember. Carmela saw his eyes flicker in Simmy's direction, only for an instant, but she didn't change her expression.

The line dance began and Simeon tried to get the idea, but his feet wouldn't step the way the other dancers' feet did. When the pretty girl let go of his hand, he tripped out of the line and headed for his table. But with music playing, cameras flashing, and waiters carrying platters around, he lost his way.

In the center of the ballroom, the line dance was getting jumbled as more guests joined the group. Tobias lost sight of Simmy and squinted, scanning the dancers for his brother's tall, lean frame in a rented tuxedo. Then he saw him wandering away from the line and walking out of the ballroom. "Oh, shit." He gave Carmela's hands one last squeeze and jumped up. "Sorry, sorry, I've got to go get him." He raced for the door, rented shoes slowing him down and pinching his feet.

The wide corridor outside the ballroom was empty, and Tobias ran into the grand lobby. Simeon wasn't there. He panicked like a parent who's lost a child in a department store: One minute he's there, and the next minute he's gone. In the clumps of people in the lobby, he thought he saw Simmy entering the attached mall, and he ran for the entrance faster than he'd ever run to the net to return a drop shot from deep behind the baseline.

Desperate, he jogged from store to store, peering inside each window. People were staring at him. The second he jumped onto the escalator to the second floor, he spotted Simeon inside a necktie store down below. Shoppers were crowded all around him on the moving stairs, and he snaked his way up through them as fast as he could, trying not to bump anyone. He pivoted onto the down escalator, which was almost empty, and stomped down the steep steps, hands sliding along the grips.

Out of breath, he burst into the necktie store, heaving and sweating. A salesman with a curious expression was showing Simeon a rainbow display of ties—crimson, tangerine, chartreuse, salmon pink, indigo. There were ties with diagonal stripes, skinny lines, little stars, and subdued diamond patterns. Simeon, struck by the array, wasn't talking.

"Come on, buddy," Tobias told his brother. "We've got to get back to the party." The salesman smiled.

"Ties," Simmy said happily. "Lots of colors."

"They're pretty, aren't they?" Enormously relieved, Tobias put his arm around his little brother, now five-feet-eleven, as tall as he was, and steered him back to the ballroom.

❋ ❋ ❋

The next morning, Tobias left their luggage at the hotel desk and walked Carmela and Simeon to the Gallery. "Let's get a couple of little souvenirs." They strolled past the necktie shop on their way to the escalator. "But no ties."

Carmela laughed. The moment had passed, the proposal had not materialized, and life was going on. "Look, a hobby shop," she said. They went inside. Of all the interesting kits and models, Simeon was drawn only by a Rubik's cube, enticed by its six bright colors. The cashier cut it out of its plastic package and handed it to Simeon, who didn't let go of it for the rest of the day.

Tobias knew exactly where their next stop was. In Davenport Jewelry, while the astonished Carmela stood speechless, he told the proprietor that he wanted a diamond engagement ring. "The most beautiful ring you have in the store," he said. "For my beautiful fiancée."

She burst into tears. "You said little souvenirs!"

"This *is* a little souvenir," he said. "Little enough to fit on your finger."

The store owner, amused, unlocked two display cases of engagement rings. They were all masterpieces, and there were no bargains. This ring was for life, Tobias reasoned. The credit card that was always paid in full would now have a balance for many months to come, with interest on top of that. And, for once, he didn't care.

Carmela's choice wasn't the most expensive, but it suited her best: a platinum ring with a transparent, three-carat center stone, highly graded at VS2 clarity, surrounded by round diamonds on the bezel and down a split shank. They waited while the jeweler expertly resized it and fitted it to her finger. When he was finished, he placed the ring in an open box with a satin lining and handed it to Tobias.

No one else was in the store, and Tobias took the ring out of the box. "Will you wear my ring?"

"Yes," Carmela said, crying.

"Will you marry me?"

"Yes," she sobbed.

Touched by the heartfelt proposal, the owner disappeared into the back room and returned in a few minutes with a small velvet box from his estate sale collection. "This is another little souvenir. From me. For good luck." On a fine golden chain was a golden heart pendant with tiny diamond accents and the words "Love Luck Happiness" engraved on three lines. He undid its fine clasp and motioned for Carmela to turn around so he could fasten it around her neck. She held her thick auburn hair off her back. The dainty pendant was bursting with sparkle at every angle.

The only dry eyes in the store belonged to Simeon, standing in a corner, absorbed in his Rubik's Cube. He had twisted the cube so that each side held as many colors as possible, all mixed up.

On the way back to Woodrock, in the back seat of their

car, somewhere between Baltimore and Trenton, Simmy solved the puzzle. “Look, Carmela.” He handed her the cube.

“I can’t believe it.” She turned the cube over and around, verifying that each side held a single color. Not one tile was out of place.

Tobias shifted his eyes from the road for an instant. “No. Couldn’t be,” he said.

“He did it,” she said. “Simmy, I can’t believe it, that’s brilliant. How did you do that? You’re going to bring us all good luck now!”

# *Chapter 8*

Carmela fended off questions from some colleagues who wondered why a psychiatric nurse was engaged to marry a bookstore manager without a college degree. Not exactly putting it in those words, they implied that she could have done better. Surrounded by surgeons, researchers, and technicians, how could she end up with him? The brother of a former patient, no less, which raised eyebrows.

By contrast, Martin and Valerie invited them for an afternoon of swimming and celebration at their new house in the tony suburb of Berry Hill, where they had a backyard pool set off by custom landscaping and decorative boulders, and a deck with redwood lounge chairs.

Two things had caught Carmela's heart: Tobias's passion and his empathy. He devoted himself to his interests with a concentration rare among her colleagues with advanced degrees. On the tennis court, he was intense. At home, his library was growing—there were books on anthropology, of course, and a whole new section devoted to psychology, his latest interest. He could read all these free of charge at the Book Trove, but bought them at discount because he liked to write in his books as well as read them. When she came upon him reading, he sometimes jumped, so immersed was he in the subject matter. And then he would share—"Look, Carmela," he always began, and then offered some fascinating tidbit about indigenous cultures or a case history or a trend, whatever was captivating him.

His empathy extended beyond his devotion to Simeon. On a recent Sunday, Carmela was in the garage sorting out piles of papers for recycling. Tobias was trimming the shrubbery when a man stopped by with a boy around eight years old, both with bicycles and empty water bottles. It was a humid, sweltering July day. "Excuse me," the man called. "Do you have an outside faucet where we can refill these?" The entrance to the county park was at the end of the street.

Tobias started explaining that the garden faucet had been disconnected when the automatic sprinklers were installed (one of his father's imperfect home projects), and there was a fountain down in the park, when he noticed the child's flushed face and ran into the garage. "Just a minute," he told them and sliced open a new case of half-liter water bottles. He gave one each to the man and the boy.

"Thank you! I'd like to pay you back." The man took some singles out of his wallet.

"No, no, it's all right; just pay it forward," Tobias said.

As they wheeled their bikes away, the boy asked, "Dad, what did he mean, 'pay it forward'?" Carmela couldn't hear the answer, but threw her arms around Tobias and kissed him, sweat and all.

❋ ❋ ❋

They invited her parents from Westport, Connecticut, for the weekend to announce their engagement. It was August 1994, and the wedding was planned for early October. She'd been wearing her diamond ring since Martin and Valerie's wedding in June, but her parents didn't have to know that.

Her father, a retired ophthalmologist, couldn't see anything to worry about, but her mother, Irene, the headmistress of a private girls' school, saw plenty. She had the annoying habit of signaling her disapproval by taking off her glasses when anything unpleasant came up, clouding reality in a myopic haze.

Her glasses stayed on for their house tour. The living room looked good enough—intellectual, even, with its expanding book collection occupying most of the shelf space. Their master bedroom was modern, neat, and well organized, everything new. In Simeon's doorway, she held her glasses while surveying a workshop that lacked an artist. Simeon, now twenty, was perched on an artist's stool at his Creation Station, trying to trace squares around his Rubik's Cube onto a sheet of paper. He had to be prompted to rise and greet Carmela's parents.

Carmela had warned them about Simeon, making him sound worse than he actually was, hoping to inoculate them and ward off confrontations. At the dinner table, Simeon didn't talk and was busy arranging the olives in his salad in rows, like beads on an abacus. Irene leaned over the table and said, "That's a fine dish you're making, Simeon."

Conversation around the table stopped, while Simmy continued lining up his olives. He had one row of black ones and another row of green ones stuffed with pimientos.

Irene folded her glasses and set them next to her water glass. "Does he speak?"

Carmela assured her mother that, yes, he did talk, but was in his own world much of the time, that it was part of his recovery process. By the time Irene had put her glasses back on, and the couple had announced their engagement, the party mood, if there ever was one, was broken.

❁ ❁ ❁

Tobias didn't intend to overhear Carmela's phone conversation. He was in the storage closet under the stairs to the bedrooms and had closed the door to get a flashlight from behind the door when the hall phone rang and she answered.

"Mom, I know you're not in a good situation. We're not

asking for contributions." Pause. "No, Mom, a thousand dollars is way more than you should send. Especially since we'd have to pay you back. We're not planning that big of a wedding anyway."

Tobias was imagining what he couldn't hear. Irene had expected her daughter to marry a doctor. She could be saying, *You're with them every day at work. And you get engaged to a bookstore clerk.*

Carmela's voice was sharp. "I don't want a doctor. I want Tobias. He's brave and genuine." She paced with the phone.

Tobias imagined Irene saying, *Bravery. Bravery doesn't pay the bills. With his lack of credentials, you'll have no future.*

"Living with him is my future." Carmela's voice rose half an octave. "And how do you even know what makes me happy?"

The next pause was longer. Tobias held his breath. "His brother was a prodigy. An artist. A cartoonist like you could never imagine. He's going to recover," Carmela said. "The brain takes a long time. And one more thing: Simmy's part of my family now." Pause. "No, don't tell me any more." She hung up the phone and walked away.

Tobias stayed in the closet until he heard Carmela's footsteps overhead on the stairs. He never said a word about it to her.

❖ ❖ ❖

They were making love on a Sunday night, and everything was perfect. At the movies, Simeon had been tranquil and hadn't needed to be taken outside like a fidgety child. They'd gone to see *Forrest Gump* and guessed that Simeon identified with the Tom Hanks character, even though he'd been far from retarded before his accident.

Simeon went to bed, and Carmela took her time putting on a sexy nightgown and brushing her long hair over her shoulder. Tobias reclined on their bed, reading and watching her. She lit scented candles around the room, closed the door, and did a little belly dance for him. They both laughed. Tobias turned off his reading lamp and pulled her on top of him. She massaged him with her fragrant hair, and they fell into a rhythm of intense lovemaking.

In the heat of passion, he was quiet and she was vocal. The air conditioner was humming, her murmurs of pleasure rose, and he didn't hear or see anything until Simeon was standing right there next to the bed, gaping. The candlelight turned him into a giant whose shadow drifted side to side on the ceiling.

It was the moment just before the point of no return. Carmela gasped and yanked the sheet over her naked body. "Oh, no."

The next day, Tobias bought a locking doorknob and installed it on their bedroom door.

❋ ❋ ❋

Tobias's parents were Christian in name but had never bothered to attend church or give their sons a religious education. Carmela was an erstwhile Catholic who attended Mass once in a while. Neither drawn to religion nor repelled by it, Tobias pondered where to have the wedding. His boss, Elsebeth, suggested the Unitarian Society of Woodrock, where her girlfriend, Miriam Kahane, was the minister. "That way, you won't offend anybody," Elsebeth said. "All the trappings of religion, minus any dogma."

Tobias pointed out that they weren't members, but Elsebeth said that you didn't have to be members to be married in a Unitarian ceremony.

Carmela thought that a fine idea, reasoning that the inclusive atmosphere would make everybody happy—"everybody" being the thirty-odd guests they could barely afford to invite. These included her parents, her older sister, Delphine, and Delphine's husband, Theodore. Their eight-year-old son,

Gabriel, would be the ring bearer, and their six-year-old daughter, Beatrix, would be the flower girl. Tobias invited his grandparents from Florida and his aunt Joyce from California. Carmela invited both of her widowed grandmothers. Simeon's attendant Kenneth would come with his boyfriend.

That left room on the guest list for only their closest friends: Martin and Valerie, Elsebeth, and Miriam, who had the dual role of minister and guest. There were all three of Tobias's fellow employees from the evening shift at the bookstore, three of Carmela's colleagues from Woodrock Hospital, and two of her college friends. Each friend brought a spouse or partner and, counting Simeon, that added up to thirty-four.

❁ ❁ ❁

Tobias plunged into the wedding preparations with a sense of purpose that surprised Carmela and even himself. As he saw it, there were two kinds of *now*: the kind that matters immediately, and the kind that matters for the rest of your life.

First, there was a meeting at the Unitarian Society with Miriam and Elsebeth, who came along to introduce them. The A-frame building's cornerstone was dated 1898, and the sanctuary's main room was cool, with a high, vaulted ceiling and lots of natural light. Five of the floor-to-ceiling windows were Mondrian-like stained glass. The carpeted dais at the front had two steps up and served as a stage; wherever people sat, they could see what was going on. To the left of the dais was a grand piano, and just beyond that was a three-manual electronic organ. Behind the dais and all along the front wall was a wooden shelf carved from fallen trees, textured and stained in dark colors, on which vases of fresh flowers were placed.

Miriam was in her office at the computer. As they entered the cool hall, she came forward, dark-blond hair tied behind her back, welcoming them all with a hug even before Elsebeth said, "Miriam, this is Tobias, my evening manager, and his brother, Simeon. This is his fiancée, Carmela. She's a psychiatric nurse over at the hospital."

"Welcome to our sanctuary. It's hot outside; let me get you all some iced tea." Miriam explained that the ceremony was theirs to design and that they had great flexibility in making choices that would reflect their personalities. She described the components of the marriage ceremony, gave them readings on the subject, and turned it over to them. They were welcome to honor different religious backgrounds and cultural traditions. "We welcome every faith, plus atheists and agnostics." She was spiritual, warm, comforting, and hospitable.

Carmela offered to design the program and the invitations. Tobias put himself in charge of selecting guests to speak at the wedding, but left it entirely up to them what to say. Miriam was responsible for the opening words, address to family and friends, and address to the couple.

At home, Carmela brought up a subject they were both avoiding. "We'll have to involve Simmy in the ceremony."

"That's what I'm afraid of," Tobias said. "We'd better be careful, or we'll have a loose cannon with no one to chase after him."

Starting the next morning, Carmela worked with Simeon, trying to get him to draw something original, anything that they could include in the program as an illustration. She sat with him at the desk with the hutch and said, "Simmy, Toby and I are getting married. You know what that means?"

Simeon looked up from his sketch pad, on which he was rubbing a pencil back and forth in no discernible pattern. "Mom, Dad."

"Like Mom and Dad were. Yes. There's going to be a party, and you'll be there."

"Music," Simmy said without looking at her.

"Right, there'll be lots of music. Toby's working on that. And you can help, too. You know what we need?"

Simmy went on rubbing his pencil on the paper until its point was bald.

"We need a picture for the program. And we'd like you to draw something. So everyone there can get a copy." She had no idea if he understood any of what she was saying. Always hopeful, she stood by his shoulder and turned to a clean page. She gave him another pencil and, guiding his hand, drew a rudimentary man and woman holding hands. He laughed.

Every morning for two weeks, they worked on this patterning experiment. Nothing happened until the day Carmela started to draw big hearts with Simmy's hand in hers. After two hearts, he pushed her hand away. "I do it," he said, like a three-year-old wanting to tie his own shoelaces. In painfully slow motion on a new page, holding the pencil in his fist and perspiring from the effort, he drew two recognizable hearts side by side.

Trembling, Carmela creased the perforation, eased the page out of the book, and held back tears. "You can draw, Simmy!"

He smiled, wiped his damp forehead, and took the paper back from her. "Later."

"You want to draw more later?"

"More later."

She left him alone. After she and Tobias came home from work that night and Kenneth had left, they slipped into Simmy's room when he was asleep and found his hearts drawing on top of the Creation Station. Inside one heart was a pair of dark eyes that could have been Toby's. Inside the other heart, a pair of smiling eyes with long eyelashes might have been Carmela's. These were eyes that a small child could have drawn, but not the kind of child that Simmy had been.

Tobias wasn't sure about using the hearts picture in the

program. He worried that, years later, Simmy might resent them for displaying his early efforts.

Carmela insisted. "What's most important for Simmy is now, not later."

❁ ❁ ❁

The wedding took place on an October day made to order. The variegated colors of autumn were nearing their peak; it hadn't rained much, and glorious leaves were still on the trees. Tobias had made sure that all the guests would be staying nearby, and everybody was on time. Burning candles and bushels of flowers were all over the sanctuary, on tables, on windowsills, on the carved wooden shelf.

Carmela's older sister, Delphine, was married to a musician, Theodore. They had met while students, she at Boston University and he at the New England Conservatory, where he was now a faculty member. Theodore was one of those musicians who could sing and also play practically any instrument—in his case, anything that you didn't have to blow into. He was black, which had irked Irene, who finally accepted him, more or less, after the birth of their two children, who were exquisite.

At the Steinway grand piano to the left of the dais, Theodore played Bach while guests entered the sanctuary in twos and threes. First, the "March in D Major" from the Notebook for Anna Magdalena Bach filled the hall, hushing the little group of guests. He played "Jesu, Joy of Man's Desiring" while family members and those who would be speaking took their seats in their assigned places in the first row. Simeon, imbibing the music, kept his eyes on the piano.

Tobias's maternal grandparents, who had shunned him at his parents' funeral five years before, walked in on the arms of their daughter, his aunt Joyce, who was dressed to kill in black and gold. At the keyboard, Theodore dwelled lovingly on "Sheep May Safely Graze," smiling at his children, Gabriel and Beatrix, who sat on either side of Delphine in the front row. With everyone seated and holding programs, he concluded with "Sleepers, Awake!" and held the last chord an extra measure, his head bowed to discourage applause.

Miriam was draped in a gold silk robe with a Mandarin collar, flared sleeves, and a fitted waist. Around her neck was a rainbow-colored stole that reached the hem of the robe, decorated with Unitarian symbols on each side: a flaming chalice and a oneness symbol. She stood at the center of the dais. Tobias, nervous in his tuxedo, stood nearby with Martin at his side and his wife, Valerie, on the other side, waiting for Carmela. Theodore, dignified in coat and tails, softly walked a few steps to the organ to play the "Bridal Chorus" from *Lohengrin* by Wagner, the "Here Comes the Bride" song, at a stately tempo. From a door at the back, Carmela entered on the arm of her father, the ophthalmologist, his full head of white hair matching her flowing gown.

Tobias hadn't been allowed to see her since early morning. As she approached, he felt he could faint from her beauty. Her luxuriant auburn hair was highlighted in warm gold for the wedding and piled on top of her head to make her appear taller. Long cascades of waves spilled over her back in layers. She was crowned by the diamond tiara that Valerie had worn just a few months before; it was the "something borrowed" of the custom. Her ivory-colored gown had a sweetheart neckline, petal cap-sleeves, and a low, scooped back. Its lacy accents glimmered with crystals and beaded embellishments.

Delphine, the matron of honor, led the procession, followed by Gabriel with a velvet box of rings on a white silk cushion. Beatrix preceded Carmela, diligently strewing pink-and-white rose petals from a little basket before the bride as she walked down the aisle. Carmela reached the dais and stood beside Tobias. The children sat at the side while their mother watched anxiously, trusting them not to fight like cats and dogs in front of everybody.

When the organ music stopped and faded, Miriam reached out her arms in a grand, welcoming gesture. "Welcome all to our sanctuary, family and friends of Carmela and Tobias and witnesses to their vows." She looked around the room. Rays from the stained-glass windows played on everything white. Simeon gazed at one window after another, savoring all his favorite colors.

"Each of us has a story to our lives, and every couple has its own combined story. Like many couples, Carmela and Tobias met by accident, but this one was a tragic accident." Her face was calm, but her voice was full of tears. "Out of tragedy, these two young people have grown in love and devotion."

On the dais, bridesmaid Valerie wiped the corner of her eye and hoped she would be able to restrain her tears for the duration.

"In song and verse, in quotations, and in our own words, we, the friends and family of Carmela and Tobias, will tell their incomparable story and celebrate their union. This house of worship is open to all beliefs, and those who wish to pray, may pray. We begin with music to set the mood, again performed by the couple's brother-in-law, the great Theodore Highgate."

Theodore stepped forward and, this time accompanying himself on guitar, sang the Beatles' "Let It Be" in a fine tenor, channeling Paul McCartney, yet making it his own. Catching Irene's eye, he began. He sang all the verses, each of them its own way, no two alike. Looking at Simeon in the front row, he sang words that seemed written for him.

Watching his brother from the dais, Tobias relaxed a little. Simmy breathed through the song as if he were singing and playing it himself.

Martin stepped to the microphone with an athletic stride and removed it from its holder. "Tobias is my best friend, and I'm honored to be here for him on his and Carmela's day." He paced a little while speaking. "He's the best friend any guy would ever want to have." He spoke as if he were having a private conversation with only one person. "He's also the kind of guy who's always fun to be with, except when he's whipping me on the tennis court. And that's one issue that will never be resolved. We play as often as we can, and it's a coin toss about who's gonna win each time." The guests chuckled.

At the side of the dais, Gabriel grabbed his little sister's program. She poked him with her elbow and snatched it back. Delphine glared at them from the dais. Theodore frowned at them from the piano bench, and they froze, their small feet dangling from adult-size chairs.

Martin grew serious. "We were once college roommates. But while I went on with my education, tragedy interrupted his. His formal education, that is. Because I think that Tobias can teach us all something about life, even though he's only twenty-five. If his parents could have been here today, they would have been proud. Well, after I got my master's degree, he told me something." He gestured toward Tobias and then himself. "He said that he looked up to me. I want you to know that he was brilliant in his studies, absolutely brilliant. I don't know how many times he edited my papers, asking for nothing in return. So I told him that he's the one who deserves recognition, and he's the one that I look up to."

Martin stood still, paused, and looked at the audience. "You see, the path that I took was the easy way. Tobias made the great climb. And no matter what, he always took the high road. A faithful brother to Simeon, he's been just like a brother to me as well." He swept his arm in Carmela's direction. "So, our dear friend Carmela, beautiful bride, congratulations, and we joyously welcome you to our family."

Whoever was speaking, Miriam touched unobtrusively—a hand on a shoulder, on a back. She hugged Martin and took the microphone. "Before the next speaker, we have a treat for you."

Theodore rippled a few soft chords on the piano while Gabriel and Beatrix stepped up to the second level of the dais. Gabriel was dressed in a royal blue suit so perfectly fitted that it would have been too big a month ago and would be too small a month from now. His red bowtie and white shirt contrasted with his golden-brown complexion and deep-brown hair, natural in a modified Afro. Beatrix was dressed princess-style, in a rose-pink satin dress and white patent-leather shoes with ruffled anklets. Her hair was done up in two puffs at the back and tied with curled white-and-rose ribbons.

The guests quickly recognized the piano introduction to "Give Yourself to Love" by Kate Wolf. In a clear, high soprano that projected to the back of the hall, the little boy sang and swayed with his music.

In her own pure soprano, surprisingly powerful, the little girl sang. She was completely uninhibited. Theodore's accompaniment was subdued; the children's voices carried, and the guests could hear every word.

Then, in two-part harmony and impeccably in tune, brother and sister sang the chorus together. The well-taught children sang their parts confidently in the beautiful harmonies of their father's arrangement. Although they'd been arguing and jostling each other only minutes before, the siblings held hands and sang like angels.

Applause wasn't called for, but the guests couldn't hold back. Theodore bounded over from the piano and squatted behind his smiling children, one arm around each. Carmela cheered for the talented cousins of her future children.

With alarm, Tobias noticed his imminent mother-in-law, Irene, holding her glasses in one hand. But then he saw her wiping tears from both eyes.

Carmela's colleague Shanti, a cardiologist, and her husband recited a poem they'd read at their own wedding, a combined Eastern and Western ceremony, each reading two lines in turn. Miriam, sensing Shanti's shyness, moved the microphone stand closer to her and lowered it.

"This poem is by the Indian poet Sarojini Naidu, born in 1879," Shanti said. "She was an intellectual and a great humanitarian. Here is her poem 'Ecstasy.'"

"Cover mine eyes, O my Love!
Mine eyes that are weary of bliss
As of light that is poignant and strong
O silence my lips with a kiss,
My lips that are weary of song!
Shelter my soul, O my love!
My soul is bent low with the pain
And the burden of love, like the grace
Of a flower that's smitten with rain:
O shelter my soul from thy face!"

Shanti spoke of Carmela's character as a professional, how patients were always asking for her, and her thoughtfulness to her colleagues. Elsebeth talked about Tobias's work at the bookstore and his trustworthiness, dating back to his high school days. Delphine paid tribute to the loving kindness of her younger sister, Carmela.

The children stepped forward and sang "Wedding Song" by Bob Dylan, accompanied by their father at the piano. They left out the verse about having three babies, for which Tobias was grateful; that was a topic he wanted to avoid as long as possible, if not forever. He appreciated his new brother-in-law's selection of songs that were perfect for his situation.

The children sang alone and then, in harmonies so engaging that, for a moment, the song became the world itself, they sang lyrics that fit the couple like a custom-tailored suit.

Miriam stood and waited for the room to hush. "We are gathered here today to unite Carmela and Tobias in marriage before an intimate group of their closest relatives and friends. It is our privilege to witness their formal union in this ceremony, already touched by love in words, in music, and in your commitment to them.

"We affirm their lifetime partnership, a union that they have already proved by their dedication to each other and the guardianship of their cherished Simeon. Even before meeting the love of her life, our sister Carmela was already at work with Simeon in the hospital. One measure of how far he's come is in this wedding program." She held up her copy, on which Simeon's hearts drawing had been converted into a watermark on each page. The guests looked at their own programs. "Yes, that's Simeon's artwork, his first published picture since his accident." There were murmurs and quiet applause. "Simeon, we commend you for your courage. We're all rooting for you." In the front row next to his grandparents, Simeon smiled, seeming to understand that the applause was for him.

"Carmela and Tobias, come now and join me." She stretched out her hands. Carmela and Tobias stood up and solemnly walked to the center.

Miriam recited all her readings from memory. "From the New Testament, Mark 10, comes this passage:"

"But from the beginning of the creation God made them male and female.

For this cause shall a man leave his father and mother, and cleave to his wife;

And they twain shall be one flesh: so then they are no more twain, but one flesh.

What therefore God hath joined together, let not man put asunder."

"Carmela, will you take Tobias to be your husband; to love, honor, and cherish him now and forevermore?"

"I will," Carmela said.

"Tobias, will you take Carmela to be your wife; to love, honor, and cherish her now and forevermore?"

"I will," he said.

Carmela repeated after Miriam, "I, Carmela take you, Tobias, to be my husband; to have and to hold from this day forward, for better, for worse, for richer, for poorer, in sickness and in health, to love and cherish always, in sorrow and in joy, from this day forward." Tobias repeated his vow as well.

Miriam said, "As a token of mutual fidelity and affection, the rings are now given and received."

Gabriel came forward with the box of rings and stood between the couple. First, Tobias placed Carmela's ring on her finger, atop her diamond engagement ring. Then Carmela slipped his on. Each said, in turn, "With this ring, I wed you and pledge you my love now and forever."

"Let these rings ever be to you a symbol of the preciousness, the purity, and the permanence of wedded love," Miriam said. She placed one hand on each of them. "I now pronounce you husband and wife." As they kissed, Miriam could see Carmela's shoulders tremble.

"From the Old Testament, I recite the blessing from the Song of Solomon," Miriam said. "Place me like a seal over your heart, like a seal on your arm; for love is as strong as death, its jealousy unyielding as the grave. It burns like blazing fire, like a mighty flame. Many waters cannot quench love; rivers cannot wash it away. If one were to give all the wealth of his house for love, it would be utterly scorned."

In her wedding address, Miriam asked the couple to respect one another; to strive to improve themselves, but not each other; to give love freely, rather than demand it; to be courteous; to fight fairly; and never to stop touching.

For the recessional, Theodore played "Hornpipe" from the *Water Music* suite by Handel on the organ, while the couple and the wedding party filed to their seats at the back of the sanctuary. Beatrix scattered more flower petals after the bride, and then went to join her father and brother on the dais for one last song. Delicious smells were drifting in from the kitchen down the hall.

Flashing a party smile, Theodore announced, "In honor of the marriage of our sister, Carmela, and our brother, Tobias, we'd now like to perform our own special interpretation of 'Higher and Higher' by Jackie Wilson."

Everyone cheered while he strummed the opening chords on his guitar. Then, in daring dissonances that clashed and sliced the air in interlocking, three-part harmonies of musical fireworks, they sang all the verses of "Higher and Higher" with exhilaration and toe-tapping fervor, accompanied by Theodore's elegant guitar playing and the children's dance steps.

The audience was on its feet, clapping, singing, stepping, and believing. After a prolonged standing ovation, Theodore called out, "Thank you, thank you. The DJ is ready and waiting for us in the banquet room. All right, everybody, now let's party!"

# *Chapter 9*

The day after the wedding, Simeon stood peering at himself in the bathroom mirror with the door ajar. From the nick where he'd cut himself shaving, a crimson trickle was wending its way down his cheek to his jaw line. Entranced by the vivid, pure color in the morning sunshine, he froze, razor in hand, staring at the rivulet the way he gazed at pictures in a museum.

Passing by, Tobias stopped short at his brother's reflection. "Hey, Sim, you gotta be careful." He wiped off the blood with a hand towel. If this was the worst that would happen while he and Carmela were gone, Simmy was going to be fine. As it was, they weren't going too far, just a phone call away to another state. "You all right?"

"Red." Simeon held up the white towel to admire the stain.

Carmela, downstairs on the phone, reassured Valerie that Simeon wasn't coming along on the honeymoon. "But he's always there, you know," she said softly. "Even when he's not." She went upstairs to get a load of dirty laundry and added the bloodstained towel to her bin. "You can't save him from everything," she told Tobias, giving him a lover's pat.

"But he's bleeding," Tobias said. Shaving was a skill his brother had learned, rather than relearned, since his accident, when he had been too young to shave.

Simeon finished shaving and watched the couple pack their bags, pacing around the master bedroom, as he once did while waiting for his dead mother to come home. Since his injury, he had seldom gone anywhere besides the rehab facility, doctors' offices, his special high school, and now his day program for mentally challenged adults, where he worked on crafts projects at his own pace—very slowly. There were weekend jaunts now and then, but the suitcase he carried on those trips was in his closet, empty. He took it out and brought it to his brother, who was kneeling before his bureau drawers, sorting through jeans and khakis.

Tobias stood up, pushed his half-filled suitcase aside, and hugged his brother. "Simmy, let's talk, OK?" They both sat on the bed. "We're going away for a while. Not that long, eight days. It's called a honeymoon. Just Carmela and me."

"Carmela and me." Simeon still repeated, on occasion, and it was hard to know whether he meant what he said or was only practicing speech patterns.

"Kenneth will be here every day," Tobias said. "In fact, he's going to sleep right here, so you won't be alone." *This must be what it's like having a kid*, he thought. *Always worrying about him when you're traveling.*

"Clothes in suitcase." Simeon slid off the bed and picked up his empty valise.

"You want to help me? Here, you can put these in my suitcase." Tobias got up and handed Simeon a stack of folded pants to distract him from the inevitable shock. This was a ruse, and such deceptive actions made him feel sneaky. One day, if Simmy suddenly woke up and became his true self again, he would resent his older brother's trickery. No matter how Tobias tried to change the subject, Simeon was going to discover that he was being left behind. Emphatically wanting to start his marriage off on the right foot, Tobias didn't suggest to his wife that his brother might tag along once more.

Simeon wasn't taking the bait. At twenty, he had the body

of a man, the mind of a boy, and an unfocused memory of his life the way it used to be. Recalling events from his past, when he was a self-directed teenager with prodigious gifts, was like observing a scene reflected in a wrinkled sheet of aluminum foil.

Tobias raised his eyebrows at Carmela. This discussion couldn't wait, and they all sat on the bed with Simeon in the middle. In her nurse-therapist's voice, Carmela began, "Simmy, a honeymoon is a special kind of trip for just two people, to celebrate a marriage. We're going away for only about a week."

Simeon stared straight ahead, giving no sign that he was listening or even hearing. To his ears, sounds were often disorganized clusters, irrelevant bursts of unrelated words. Whenever they were intelligible, he wanted to delay them, hold onto them, take them apart, understand what they were made of. But like a train that leaves the station before you step onto the platform, these clusters rumbled by, out of reach, before he could ride with them. He clenched his fists in frustration as Carmela's words hurtled past.

"Kenneth is going to take you to all the fun places. No workshop this week—you're on vacation while we're gone. Tuesday, you're going to the Metropolitan. Wednesday, the Museum of Modern Art. And best of all, Thursday night, you're going to a concert at—"

Simeon spread his hands like a conductor trying to hush brass instruments. He looked around the room, searching for his words. "Where—where—"

"It's a symphony," Tobias said. "At Carnegie Hall, the visiting orchestra from—"

"No, no, he wants to know where *we're* going." Carmela got the tour pamphlet from her dressing table to show him.

"Don't do that," Tobias warned, but too late; she was already reading the highlights to Simmy.

"New England Fall Colors," she read from the brochure.

Simeon looked at the cover photos—a covered bridge in Vermont, the Boothbay Harbor in Maine, and the Kancamagus Highway in the White Mountains of New Hampshire. "Eight days, six states." She turned the pages, pointing. "This is Martha's Vineyard in Massachusetts, and this is the Nonantum Resort in Kennebunkport, Maine."

"Mel, that's not how we should approach this." Tobias wanted things to be calm before their departure the next morning.

"It's OK, Tobe." On the next page were four paintings from the Norman Rockwell Museum in Vermont. "Remember Norman Rockwell? You saw some of his pictures in New York. This is a museum that we're going to."

"Museum," Simeon said. "Want to go."

"I told you," Tobias said. He was sweating. Life was getting more difficult, now that his brother could express some of his wishes.

Carmela tried to engage Simeon's eyes. "We'll all keep going to museums together after we come back from our little trip." She was regretting her tour description. "Kenneth will take you to museums," she said hopefully.

"Want to come." Simeon's glasses were fogging up. "Tobe. Mela."

"Sorry," Carmela said to Tobias.

"Don't worry. Why don't you both go in there and draw for a while?" Tobias wagged his eyebrows at her, lifting his index finger as if to say, *I have an idea.* With his wife and brother tracing shapes in Simmy's art studio, Tobias called Kenneth. "I hate to bother you on a Sunday. We're having a small emergency."

"Hey Tobe, it's OK." Kenneth, soft-spoken and patient, was twenty-two, a part-time master's-degree student in psychology, working as Simeon's caretaker to pay his bills. He offered to take Simeon to the movies to get him away from the trip preparations.

While they were gone, Carmela and Tobias finished packing, straightened the house, watered the house plants, stacked up cans of cat food, left notes for Kenneth, and changed the linens in the master bedroom. They folded up their maps and hid all their suitcases in the trunk of the car. Ashamed of taking advantage of his brother's disability, Tobias nevertheless hoped that Simmy would conveniently forget what had been troubling him earlier, as he often did.

Kenneth stayed for dinner, and they assiduously avoided the topic of travel. Simeon was in good spirits and went to bed cheerfully. Kenneth moved into the master bedroom, and Carmela and Tobias made do with the fold-out couch in the living room.

At 5:00 the next morning, long before Simeon would awaken to find them gone, they fled in darkness without saying good-bye, getting a head start on their married life. Halfway to Boston, Tobias asked, "Do you think it's OK to call by now?" A rest stop beckoned at the next exit.

"It's not even eight," Carmela said. Not at all a morning person and bleary from lack of sleep, she was staying awake only to prevent Tobias from dozing off at the wheel.

But at the following rest stop, he pulled off the highway without asking. They zipped up their jackets and walked into the food court. As Carmela headed to the ladies' room, Tobias got out his phone card and called home. Kenneth answered on the fourth ring, just before the machine would have taken over. "Sorry," he said, "I was up here dealing with Simmy and couldn't get to the extension."

"How's he doing?" Tobias dreaded the answer. Sneaking out was a cowardly way to set necessary limits, and the news was disheartening: Simmy had walked into the master bedroom at 6:00 AM, waking Kenneth and asking for Tobias. Kenneth repeated the line about a honeymoon being for only two people, and promised him they'd have fun anyway. Simmy didn't say anything, but began to walk around the master bedroom, silently watching the door. After half an hour of compulsive pacing, he retreated to his own room and slumped over his desk, head in hands.

Carmela came out of the restroom and went to buy some coffee. There was a basket of fresh fruit on the counter, and in the self-serve case, croissants, Danishes, and muffins were on display. Slimmed down for the wedding, she tried to persuade herself to stick to her dessert-free diet, but the easy calories were calling her, and she piled two plump pastries on her cardboard tray.

On the phone, Tobias asked, “What’s he doing now? Can you get him to go downstairs?” Carmela watched his expression change from worried to deeply anxious. “OK, all right. All you can do is try your best.” He was combing his fingers through his hair. “Thank you. It’s OK. I’ll call later. Thanks, Ken. Bye.”

“He won’t come out of his room,” he told Carmela. “He won’t talk. He won’t eat.” He walked to the men’s room, still raking his hair.

Carmela went back to the car alone and sat in the driver’s seat. She set the cardboard tray on the armrest between the two bucket seats and inhaled the aroma of the two pastries. Tobias came trotting back to the car and got in the passenger seat. “I bought you some coffee and a Danish,” she said.

“Oh—thanks. Do you know if they have any fruit?” He swatted his hair out of his eyes. “Don’t want anything heavy first thing in the morning.” He jumped out and jogged back to the building.

She tugged the pecan Danish out of its wax paper sleeve, licked the glaze off her fingers, and devoured it in a few voracious bites, like a starving person. The warm, frosted pastry tasted so good; she hadn’t eaten any sweets at all in two months. She hurriedly tore the sticky paper off the cherry cheese Danish and gorged herself on that one too, wiping off her hands and mouth before Tobias came back to the car with an apple and a banana. They hardly spoke until they approached the Boston city limits and the beginning of their tour.

❋ ❋ ❋

It was their first fight, she admitted to herself, even though no harsh words had been exchanged. Hanging in the air was not what they said, but what remained unsaid. She avoided mentioning Simeon and was grateful that Tobias did the same. Whether he was calling home periodically to check on his brother, she couldn't say. Maybe he did it while she was shopping for souvenirs or taking a bath. Without discussing it outright, they both tried conscientiously to keep Simeon out of the trip and to concentrate on each other.

By the third day, things were going better. Congenial people were in the tour group, including some other young couples and even a pair of honeymooners from Florida who rarely got to see autumn foliage. Except for her wardrobe problems, Carmela was having the time of her life. Luckily she had packed clothes in two sizes—her wedding size and her pre-engagement size. Being a little too optimistic, she'd brought more slim clothes than fat clothes, but no one seemed to notice that she alternated between the only two pairs of pants that she could still zip up. Dieting was out of the question with the sumptuous buffets that greeted the travelers at every lunch and dinner.

The tour was very well organized around scenic sights in Vermont, Maine, Massachusetts, New Hampshire, Rhode Island, and Connecticut. On the itinerary were touristy places like Mystic Seaport, historic sites such as Plymouth Rock, and hundreds of miles of the most spectacular fall colors in the Northeast. Tobias had to stop himself from remarking that Simeon would have loved the colors. Carmela, thinking the same thing, also restrained herself.

The fifth day was devoted to the Franconia Notch region

of New Hampshire, which earned the most admiration from the tourists. Cameras stayed out while they rode and hiked the Covered Bridge Trail and the Waterfalls Trail. After viewing more than seventy waterfalls from the road, the travelers stopped counting. The Old Man of the Mountain, a glacial rock formation, looked down on them. According to their tour leader, all the rock formations were carved by Ice Age glaciations more than fifty thousand years ago. Dwarfed by this panorama, Tobias questioned whether his commonplace worries and temporal responsibilities had any significance in the great scheme of things, and took comfort in the beauty of his surroundings.

They stayed at the Fox Ridge Resort in North Conway, a perfect place for a honeymoon night. Holding hands, Carmela and Tobias took a romantic walk around the resort, with its lovingly tended pathways and rainbow-colored mountain views, orange and yellow trees in the distance framed by green lawns and aromatic pines. The resort staff served a candlelit dinner on damask tablecloths to all the tour members.

In their spacious hotel room, fresh flowers were on the table, the king-size bed was turned down, and plush snow-white bathrobes hung in a cedar-scented walk-in closet. It was the kind of night that could linger in memory for years to come.

Tobias tipped the bellboy and locked the door. "I love you so much," Carmela told him, burying her face in his chest.

He stroked her beautiful hair. "I love you too, darling."

The room phone rang. "Eleven o'clock at night," Carmela said. "Wonder if they have the wrong room?"

Tobias lurched for the phone. Kenneth said, "Sorry, sorry. I can't make him stop crying. He went to bed early and then woke up screaming, must be having some sort of nightmare. Keeps shouting your name. I don't know if I can get him to take the phone. I'm going to try."

In the background, Tobias could hear his brother calling

in a guttural, animalistic tone, "Toby, Toby." He sounded terrified, panicked, abandoned, and Kenneth was pleading with him to talk on the phone. Long seconds went by until Tobias heard loud breathing in the receiver.

"Simmy. It's me, Toby. Simmy, stop crying."

"Toby. Come back. Toby." He sounded like a boy with a man's voice.

"Simmy. Only three more days. Hang on, buddy, I'll come home. Go to sleep now, I'll be back. Be a good boy. Go back to bed now."

"Toby." A muffled sob.

"What, buddy?"

"Love you."

❋ ❋ ❋

They settled into married life, which was not much different from their previous routine, except that Elsebeth gave Tobias Saturdays off at the Book Trove, granting the newlyweds full weekends together for the first time. Carmela worked the 3:00-to-11:00 shift at Woodrock Hospital, and Tobias worked 3:00 to 11:00 at the bookstore. But in spite of all their work, they never managed to save any money, and it was all they could do to keep their bills paid and their credit card balances under control. The Woodrock municipal taxes alone were killing them.

Mornings, they took turns driving Simeon six miles to the Can-Do Workshop, a corny name for a worthwhile day program for young adults who didn't fit in anywhere else—not smart enough for regular employment or college, but too smart for make-work programs for the retarded. For fifteen thousand dollars per year, plus expenses, the eighteen participants were given lunch and snacks and were kept occupied with crafts, woodworking, and training in life skills such as reading labels and menus, counting change, and telling time. Kenneth picked him up at 5:00 PM and drove him home.

Tobias played tennis twice a week with Martin, now a business analyst in commercial real estate at Lehman Brothers in the World Financial Center. They usually played at the all-weather Upper Woodrock Tennis Club, situated on the fancy side of Woodrock and not far from Martin's home in upper-upper-middle-class Berry Hill.

On a late May day in 1995, the weather was very comfortable for both players, warm but not humid. A capricious wind took hold now and then, behaving like a third player who switched sides at will. Tobias, lacking confidence in his regular matchups with Martin, had shied away from competitive matches for months, preferring instead to work on practice drills. Martin egged him on now and then until Tobias finally agreed to play an actual match and test whether all that practice had paid off. He spun his racket and won the right to serve first. "OK, I won; now let's go home," he announced.

Martin shook his head. "Hey, man, where's your competitive fire?" His red hair flopped around his headband.

"Smoldering. I don't know. Fizzling. Let's play." After the first five games, Tobias was leading 3–2, with Martin still on serve. When Tobias shortened the rally because of the wind, he committed a flurry of unforced errors and ended up losing the first set 6–4. He sat on the bench to assess how to even the match in the next set.

Martin plopped down next to him and clapped him on the back. "Everything OK at home?"

"Sure, champ," Tobias said. Everything was OK, but nothing was easy, happy, or wonderful about the way he was living. Except for the change of seasons and the number of bills in his mailbox, he could hardly tell his weeks apart.

"Champ! I'm not a champ." Martin guzzled from his water bottle. "But soon there's going to be a new name for me."

"What name?"

Martin put down the water bottle and grinned like a new driver at the wheel for the first time. "Dad."

"No, really. You're kidding. You mean Valerie—"

"She's pregnant. She's expecting. Two months already. We'll get an ultrasound later to find out if it's a boy or a girl."

"Wow, I can't believe it. Congratulations!" Tobias grabbed Martin's hand and pumped it hard. "Dad. I can't imagine anyone calling you Dad. You still look so young to me."

"It's Valerie," Martin said. "She's already twenty-nine, and we were thinking, the best decade for motherhood, considering the mother and baby's health, is now."

"Carmela's thirty," Tobias said. By this point in his life, age twenty-seven, he thought he'd be sowing wild oats, exploring the world, doing things his way, making his mark. But instead of giving speeches, he was scheduling speakers at the Book Trove. Instead of forging ahead in anthropology, he was struggling with his brother, his bills, and his wife's expectations. She knew better than to talk about starting a family. Still, he sensed her yearning every time they passed a baby in a stroller, every time they saw a wooden stork yard sign in the neighborhood.

"Back on court; let's go," Martin said.

Tobias went up the service line, his focus on tennis now blurred, and immediately double-faulted on his first serve of the second set. Going through the motions, he played a defensive game, giving up all hope of striking winners.

Predictably, Martin took advantage of his opponent's defensive posture by attacking relentlessly and charging to the net to finish each point. Play ended quickly, with Martin taking the second set 6–2 and winning the match.

"Hey, man, the wind was tricky today," Martin offered, knowing that his friend's mind had not been on his game. This inequality between comrades who had started off as equals had long been eating at him, and there was nothing he could do about it. Talking about it outright would be risky;

Tobias might be hurt or insulted or could feel that his privacy was being invaded. This time, Martin guessed that Tobias was wishing that he, too, could become a father. Perhaps they had been trying, but failed to conceive. Or it could be that Carmela, having witnessed her share of scary deliveries at the hospital, was reluctant.

The two players made plans for their next meeting and left the club separately. On his way home, Tobias brooded over what would happen when his wife learned the news—or maybe she already knew and was deliberating how to approach the subject. He prepared his arguments for a battle that would test his marriage.

They already had a permanent child, one who would probably never grow up. Nothing could convince him that bringing another child into the world—his child, into his world—would be good for anybody: his wife, himself, his brother, or the child itself. It was a burden that he resolved to avoid at all costs.

# Chapter 10

When Carmela found out about Valerie's pregnancy, she congratulated her friend warmly, and then did nothing. Nothing, that is, to give Tobias the least hint that she knew, that she was affected by the news, that she wanted a child more than anything else in the world, or that her daily activities were relentlessly accompanied by the inane, internal lyrics, "Thirty, tick-tock, thirty, tick-tock," that shut off only when she went to sleep. She discreetly watched Tobias watching her, knowing that he knew that she knew, and these unspoken thoughts stalked them day after day.

No pregnancy is a secret for long, and the Scanlons announced theirs formally over dinner at their house. "You probably both already know," Valerie said. She had cut her dark-blond hair shorter than usual, just below her chin, and was wearing a loose blouse over stretch pants. Nothing about her figure revealed her condition, but her face was fuller, more mature-looking, and glowing, Carmela thought.

"We're having a baby," Martin said. "A girl!" Carmela and Tobias, feeling a little foolish, since both had been informed separately, lavishly congratulated them.

"What are you going to name her?" Carmela asked.

"Andrea Jane." Valerie smiled. "Nice and traditional."

"After Andre Agassi?" Tobias jumped to change the subject, if only slightly. "Or Andrea Jaeger?"

Martin laughed, looking even younger than his twenty-seven years. "No, not at all; we're not even thinking of tennis yet. Andrea is an old family name on Valerie's side, and my mother's name is Jane, so that's how we came up with it."

Valerie added, "And we already have nicknames picked out for her: Andie and A.J."

"Oh, that's so cute," Carmela said, surmising that Martin must have really wanted a boy instead, what with those masculine-sounding nicknames.

The idea of visitors in the delivery room was just coming into vogue in 1996, when Valerie was approaching her January due date. Her obstetrician practiced at Woodrock Hospital, and Carmela couldn't figure out how to meld her own roles of staff member and friend. While she pondered this delicate issue, Valerie invited her to attend the birth, which made Carmela squeamish, all things considered. She confided to Valerie that she would have to bring up the matter before the Internal Hospital Procedural Review Committee, some name that she made up, to see if such attendance was within the hospital's ethical guidelines.

In the end, she didn't have to decide at all. At five minutes past midnight and a week before her due date, Andrea Jane Scanlon made her debut in the back seat of Martin's car, half an hour after Valerie said it was time to go to the hospital. One minute, Martin was jumping up and down on the shoulder of the highway, waving down anyone who would stop, and the next minute he was catching his new daughter while Valerie screamed piercingly enough to stop all the traffic in New Jersey. A police car sent by a good Samaritan pulled over just in time to greet a grinning Valerie on a bloody car seat, cradling her slippery newborn, who was swaddled in Martin's Upper Woodrock Tennis Club sweatshirt.

The white-faced officer shone his flashlight on the nativity scene. "Is the baby breathing?" His own breath steamed in the January air.

The newborn, eyes wide open, had a pink face and a gooey thatch of dark hair. "Yes!" Valerie exclaimed. "I'm not wearing any pants," she added, almost apologetically.

An ambulance sped them to the hospital, where they were kept for four days, just to be sure that everybody was fine. They were. The infant's Apgar score was 9, almost perfect, and she had ten toes and ten fingers—long ones. Tobias commented on her hands the next day. "Are those long fingers going to play the piano?" he asked Valerie, radiant in her hospital smock and surrounded by bouquets of flowers.

"No, they're going to grip a tennis racket," Martin said.

"We'll see about that," Valerie said, snuggling the baby at her breast.

Tobias left it to his wife to buy the baby gifts, and she went all out, coming home with stuffed shopping bags from all three children's stores in Woodrock, for which he criticized her because everything in Woodrock was more expensive, and she could have bought the same for less out on the highway or in the mall. Carmela countered that this was not just any friend, but a special friend; and not just any baby, but a first baby; and that the fine quality of clothes in the local shops was worth the extra money, which added up to $548 for tiny garments in three different sizes, including a miniature pair of pink sneakers and matching anklet socks embroidered with tulips.

As she wrapped her packages, Carmela felt like a girl watching a jump rope turned by two other children, waiting her turn to make a move, hoping to get in on the game. Every mother in the stores had looked blissful, ecstatic, in her eyes. They all seemed younger than she was, and she feared that her fertility would decline, along with her chance to have a real child of her own, one who would grow, learn, need her, and love her.

❋ ❋ ❋

By 6:00 PM, lines were already forming for the express

elevator to Windows on the World at the top of World Trade Center #1, the north tower. The Scanlons, Hillyers, and Highgates waited between black velvet ropes at the end of a long line that snaked at a decent pace toward the high-speed elevators. These elevators were high-capacity, and the line would have moved along faster if not for the tightened security. Ever since the 1993 attack in the parking garage of the World Trade Center, everyone going up to the restaurant had to pass through a scanner and submit to a bag check—and this was after stepping around all the giant cement flowerpots erected around the buildings to ward off terrorist attacks by trucks and vans.

Valerie, slender in a slinky black dress six months after the birth of her daughter, opened a handbag containing Pampers, pacifiers, baby toys, a pocket photo album, and little else. "You're not much of a security threat," Carmela told her slim friend. By contrast, she was gaining weight, but not for the reason she wanted. European chocolates, which she stockpiled in a seldom-used kitchen cabinet, were her undoing. For this occasion, she was dressed in a flouncy, cover-up outfit that blurred her silhouette; it was a kind of burqa for imperfect figures. Next to Valerie and her sister, Delphine, she was self-conscious and uncomfortable. Delphine, five-feet-three like Carmela, had kept her figure to a T and was voluptuous in a low-cut, cream-colored dress and pearls, which set off her golden-brown hair.

They were going out to celebrate the concurrence of two events: the Theodore Highgate Trio was performing at the famous landmark, and Martin had just been promoted from business analyst to senior business analyst at Lehman, possibly leading to a salary of two hundred fifty thousand dollars, plus an annual bonus of five hundred thousand dollars. Carmela, happy to see her brother-in-law and Delphine, nevertheless felt ill at ease about Tobias, always standing still while Martin kept moving up.

They stepped into the elevator with a large crowd of expensively dressed people and started their climb to the 107th floor. For some reason, most of the conversations around them died down as soon as the elevator started up. There was a humming noise that muffled voices to some degree, but it was more than that: the car actually shimmied from side to side, a kind of swing low, sweet chariot type of motion, and the wind in the shaft made ghostly sounds. "Whooo whooo," Martin imitated in a low voice.

"Spooky, isn't it?" Tobias was wearing his only good suit. Not phobic, he nevertheless had distaste for elevators and took the stairs whenever possible. He had to swallow a few times to clear his ears.

It was July 1996 and still daylight, affording them a spectacular view from the table for five that Theodore had reserved for the two couples and his wife, Delphine. Tall columns spaced four feet apart spanned the full width of a windowed wall looking down on the north end of Manhattan, with the Hudson River to the left and the East River to the right. Incandescent pink rays highlighted the Empire State Building in the middle of the triangle demarcated by the two rivers. To the left were piers and boats, and beyond them, New Jersey. "Look, everybody, there's Woodrock," Martin joked. "And just wait till it gets dark. We'll be able to see the GW Bridge and everything all lit up."

A waiter served Cristal champagne to everybody except Valerie, still breast-feeding and always the designated driver. Theodore came out on stage with his drummer, a chunky white guy named Rolf Meadowlark, and his Chinese double-bass player, Kingston Cheng, at least six-feet-five and with arms long enough to wrap around the bass twice. They played a mixture of New Orleans, cool jazz, and progressive jazz, with a few dazzling numbers by Theodore himself, who smiled at his guests from the keyboard. When it was his turn to shine, he slipped in a riff on the Brahms Lullaby while winking at

Valerie, and then pivoted and improvised on a quote from "My Way" for Martin.

"He's playing your song, Martin," Tobias said.

Martin took a sip of his champagne. "Well, to my mind, slaving for a big corporation is definitely not doing things my way." His dream was to save his money, quit Lehman, and start his own business. He was already compiling lists of contacts, thanks to his connections in commercial real estate.

"Sounds risky," Tobias said.

"By the time I make the leap, it won't be." Martin would have the resources to provide financing for shopping malls and would even manage some of them himself, he declared.

❁ ❁ ❁

The worst time for a marital squabble is at the beginning of the work week, and that's when Tobias heard the question he'd long been dreading. It was 2:00 on a Monday afternoon. Simeon was away at his workshop, and Carmela had just put on her nurse's uniform. Tobias was winding up his monthly bill-paying when his wife came to him with a seductive smile and said simply, "Tobe, I have a small request."

Sensing conflict, he stood up. "What, sweetie?" He didn't have time for long discussions, even though it was only a ten-minute walk to the Book Trove. He had a lot of things to set up for the day's events and wasn't even properly dressed yet.

"I want a baby." She looked at him steadily, not smiling.

"Mel." He took her in his arms. "Sweetheart. We just can't do it. We don't have the money. We don't have the time. We don't have the space."

She pulled back a little and held his hands. "Tobe, I'm already thirty. I don't have much time left. It's now or never." Her eyes glistened.

It was seven minutes past two. He really needed to get going. "Mel. I just finished with all these bills." He pointed to the stack of envelopes. "We're just barely managing every month."

She dropped his hands. "I'm not talking about money. I'm talking about family."

"So am I." He raised his voice. "What if we have an emergency? What if something happens to Simmy?"

"You don't understand," she said, crying now. "The family I'm talking about is my real family, the *child* I want. Not your brother."

He shook his head. "You made me a promise. An implicit promise." He was breathing fast, the way he did when he played too hard without first warming up.

"I never promised you anything about children," she said, louder still.

"We can't afford it. Financially, emotionally, or any other way." He turned his back to go and get ready for work. This was a tirade, not a conversation.

She grabbed his arm, and he whirled around. "If you ever got yourself a real career instead of moping around over there in your bookstore, maybe we could have a real family instead of this." She waved her hand at the stairs leading to the bedrooms. "It's all your fault, and you know it." Without waiting for him to answer, she grabbed her purse and ran out, slamming the door behind her. Their two cats, frightened by the commotion, jumped out the cat door into the garden, one after the other.

Tobias grabbed the nearest breakable object and hurled it with all his force at the door as it banged shut. It shattered into a million pieces, which he hurriedly swept up before leaving for work. Only then did he realize what he had broken: an inscribed Steuben crystal wedding card with two hearts and the date of their marriage, specially ordered by Delphine and Theodore.

❀ ❀ ❀

They didn't speak to each other for nearly two weeks, that being their longest silence in two years of marriage. In spite of her remarks about Simeon, Carmela continued her early-morning sessions with him in his art studio, tracing shapes, guiding his hand, patterning his drawing motions. She drove him to workshop on days when it was her turn. Tobias chatted pleasantly with his wife's relatives on the phone. He brought her car to the shop for an oil change. She poured his orange juice. He stacked her mail on her desk.

For the first time, Martin cancelled one of their Saturday tennis matches. Valerie, now a researcher at Fairleigh Dickinson University, was conducting a weekend seminar, and Martin had full charge of their baby daughter, Andrea, who was turning out to be a real Daddy's girl.

Carmela noticed Tobias was staying home and, finally missing him enough to eat crow, apologized to him and held him tightly, crying and promising to behave like an adult.

Tobias, hating conflict and craving peace, promised to consider parenthood—eventually. Aware more than ever of her reproductive clock, Carmela suppressed her reply and smiled agreeably, at the same time resolving to become pregnant at all costs, even if she risked wrecking her marriage and severing ties to the father of the child she didn't yet have.

❁ ❁ ❁

The October ragweed season was as bad as it had ever been, sending Tobias to the medicine cabinet to find something that would appease his runny nose and itchy eyes long enough to survive his Wednesday morning tennis match with Martin. Methodically, he scrutinized the expiration dates on all the little boxes of various formulations of antihistamines, discarding the outdated ones and piling the others on the bathroom vanity.

A container of some sort fell out of the cluttered cabinet onto the tile floor, and he picked it up. It was Carmela's birth-control pill dispenser, three months outdated, with two of the pills still in their little plastic bubbles. He looked at the date again and again, feeling as betrayed as if his wife had left him for another man. He had trusted her. They had made an agreement, indefinitely postponing parenthood until further discussion. She had gone behind his back, exploiting his confidence in her, endangering their future.

It was too late to call Martin and cancel, so he went anyway, attributing his halfhearted attempt at volleying to allergic symptoms. Late at night, after Simeon was asleep and Carmela was home from work, he confronted her with the evidence. He sat on the living room sofa with a book in his lap and her birth-control dispenser in his pocket, still hoping that he was wrong.

She hung her raincoat in the hall closet, untied her white nurse's shoes, kicked them aside, and padded over to him in her white stockings. "Hi, sweetie." She plopped down on the couch next to him.

"Let's get it over with." He pulled the dispenser out of his pocket and held it up. "What's this?" He watched her expression change from everyday contentment to shock. Absorbed in the demands of his daily routine, he didn't often take time to really look at his wife anymore, as he used to do when they were falling in love and he would recall her features in her absence, struggling to reconstruct his mental image, redrawing the face of his loved one until the next time he would see her. She was different now, pretty still, but plumper, her frown lines deep enough to sketch in a cartoon, if a cartoonist were to sketch her. Her auburn hair, her best feature, flowed over her back and shoulders, having been liberated from the nurse's cap and net that she wore on the job.

"Why were you prowling through my things?" she asked.

"I was looking for allergy medicine, and this thing tumbled out." He shook the dispenser at her and narrowed his eyes. "Tell me something. Are you still on the pill?"

"Oh, birth control is my responsibility?"

He rolled his eyes at the ceiling and around the room and back to her. "It's *our* responsibility. Carmela. What's going on? How am I supposed to trust you anymore?"

Cornered, she leaned over, forehead almost touching her knees, and sobbed. "They were making me sick. I had to stop taking them."

She was crying for real, and he waited for her to stop. "Why didn't you tell me? This is not the time for us to be taking risks," he said. "We have to plan ahead, not just fall into things like this. Make an appointment. Get a different prescription."

She resumed crying, seeming not to hear him. He got some tissues and handed them to her. She mopped her face and straightened up, looking at him through red, swollen eyes. "It's already too late."

# Chapter 11

The afternoon when Simeon lost his virginity at age twenty-two, Tobias received a phone call at the Book Trove from his brother's workshop. Simeon had slipped away during recess after lunch at around the same time that a nineteen-year-old girl had failed to return from the ladies' room. The young woman, Glory, mildly retarded and a social butterfly, had been flirting with Simmy for weeks, but nobody thought anything of it until the pair was found in a storage room, lying on a carpet remnant, sharing a post-coital moment. Simeon was wriggling into his pants and Glory's shirt was still unbuttoned, her jeans on the floor. Her mother came to pick her up and withdrew her from the program.

Tobias called Kenneth to give him the day off. He told the truth to Elsebeth and left work for the day at 5:00 PM, having been there for only two hours. Simeon, surprised to see his brother instead of Kenneth coming to get him, looked the same as usual: handsome, slender, rectangular glasses slipping down his narrow nose, and behind the glasses, a not-quite-present look in his dark eyes. The workshop director took Tobias aside and gave him the best news he'd heard in many days: Glory's mother, admitting that this wasn't the girl's first sexual adventure, had ordered a tubal ligation performed on her daughter when she was only eighteen. Relieved beyond description, Tobias promised to have a talk with Simeon, and the director promised to keep an eagle eye on the young adults in his care.

Talking to Simeon was like having a conversation with a phone menu system. You could say whatever was on your mind, but the thing wasn't listening. To communicate, you had to press a button within its repertoire—2 to make an appointment, 3 to leave a message, 0 to speak to an actual human, and so forth. In Simmy's case, any statement that he couldn't easily classify was met with a pleasant but uncomprehending stare. You had to keep it simple.

"Hey, buddy, you met a girl, huh?" Tobias was throwing together an easy dinner for both of them. He handed his brother a package of prewashed salad greens and sat him down with two empty bowls.

"Glory." Simeon stopped pulling shreds of romaine out of the plastic bag and grinned broadly. Tobias could only guess that Simmy was recalling the encounter, maybe doing a bit of play-by-play.

"You know, you're not supposed to be doing that kind of thing at school." Tobias got a package of linguine and a jar of spaghetti sauce down from the cabinet.

"Twisters," Simmy said. He preferred the corkscrew shape. Tobias put back the linguine and took out a box of fusilli instead. He tried to get Simmy to look at him, but he was focused on the pasta twists. "Hot water."

"Right, you're going to get us all in hot water if you ever do that again," Tobias said, with no hope that his brother would understand the metaphor. He sat astride a chair facing Simmy and tried to connect. "Simmy, listen to me. What you did with Glory wasn't wrong, but you can't do that in workshop. Do you understand?"

"Yes." Simmy always answered "yes" when asked if he understood, as if he had empathy for the person trying to get him to understand something that he couldn't.

Frustrated to the point of dropping the subject altogether,

Tobias blathered on about that being something that people did in private, and how it wasn't appropriate in school, and if he really felt the urge, he could wait until he got home and just do it himself. "Know what I mean, buddy?"

"Yes."

Tobias held his brother's shoulders and told him that someday, when he got well, he would find a girl that he loved, and she would be his best friend for life. Simmy said he understood.

All of which made Tobias's impending fatherhood a little less staggering, three days after the shock that his wife was already two months pregnant and that there was no going back, as far as she was concerned. Her contrition was as intense as her single-mindedness. "I'm deeply sorry, grievously sorry," she had told him that night. "I lied to you, I sneaked behind your back, I told you one thing and did another." Crying nonstop, she said she knew he might leave her because of what she had done. The baby, however, was a fact of life. All this she blurted out before he could utter a word in response. He waited until she ran out of tears and apologies.

It was past midnight when he finally spoke. "Carmela. You've made a decision that changes my life forever, without even telling me." She covered her face with her hands. "But that baby is mine, too. I'm not going to lie to you: I didn't want it. We can't afford it. Still, I'm not going to leave you. You're my wife."

She sobbed and slid over to him, laying her head in his lap and her hand on his knee. "I'm sorry."

He smoothed her hair, damp and wild all over her face and back. "We have to agree on something."

She sat up, stopped sniffling, looked him in the eye.

"We need two incomes. We'll have to get baby-sitters and day care, that sort of thing."

"That's fine," she said. Many of her colleagues were

parents, and they made do. "It's my career. I want to keep working."

"And another thing. Promise. You have to promise."

"All right."

He spread his hands in a traffic-stopping gesture. "There will be no more after this one. Promise me this will be the only one. A real promise this time."

A small hesitation, a brief hiatus. An only child wouldn't be so bad. The important thing was to have one, to start the family. Maybe later, he would change his mind. "I promise," she said. "And I wish I could take back the horrible things I said to you. I didn't mean any of them."

"Then why did you say them?"

"I wanted a baby so much."

"You're getting your baby. I hope you don't destroy us all in the process."

They went to bed, exhausted, and made love anyway, at least not worrying about her getting pregnant.

❋ ❋ ❋

On a rainy October day in 1996, water was dripping into the indoor tennis court far behind the baseline, and big gray towels had been spread around to sop up the leaks. There was plenty of time to play before Martin had to hop on the commuter train to the city. He said that Tobias was lucky to be working 3:00 to 11:00 because he could go home, take a nap, and eat a leisurely lunch before going to work. They warmed up for ten minutes and Martin asked, "Game?"

Tobias, reeling from the way his life was changing beyond his control, could barely concentrate on hitting the ball. "Maybe Sunday," he said. "Let's do some drill work today. Too much on my mind."

Martin started slowly striking balls from his service line to Tobias's. "Everybody OK, I hope?"

Tobias tried to execute a light, topspin return. "Yes, if by 'everybody,' you mean the four of us."

Martin struck his return into the net. "No. You're kidding." He stopped hitting and stood his racket on its head, twirling it. He stuffed the ball that he'd been about to serve back in his pocket, where it poked out at his hip like a doorknob.

"I'm not kidding." Tobias walked to the net. "Wish I were. She just told me last week." He wasn't smiling. "We had a big fight about it."

They stopped hitting, and Martin tried to reassure his friend that everything would be all right and they would all be happy. Tobias asked him not to tell Valerie yet, so Carmela could make the announcement herself. Only half an hour remained before Martin had to leave for work. Nobody's mind was on tennis.

❊ ❊ ❊

He didn't accompany Carmela for her first ultrasound, being preoccupied with the speaker of the week at the Book Trove. The philosopher-historian Cornelius Atticus Hooper, descended from two generations of slaves, was giving a talk on racism and signing copies of his memoir, *Generation Forward: From Sharecropper's Grandson to Princeton Philosopher.*

It was not that he lacked curiosity. They had decided, together, to learn the baby's gender in advance, rather than waiting seven more months to find out. Boy or girl, he didn't lean sharply in either direction, although he supposed it would be nice to have a little son whom he could shape, who would succeed where he had failed, who would seize opportunities that he had wasted, who could be influenced to choose well, rather than just fall wherever life threw him.

Boy or girl, what alarmed Tobias was the possibility that his child might be imperfect. This, he admitted to no one. He could not find within himself the fortitude to face an infinite series of tomorrows with a child who, like his brother, might never achieve independence; for wasn't that the goal of raising a child? Even the word itself, raising, implied elevating, improving, nurturing, and then sending on its way. He imagined an endless array of birth defects: missing limbs, curved spine, blindness, deafness, retardation, damaged organs, or a flawed constitution that would condemn the poor child to a brief but painful existence.

While stacking hundreds of Professor Hooper's books optimistically on tables on either side of the podium, he went over risk factors in his mind. Drinking? Rarely, and that applied to Carmela as well. Smoking? Never. He wasn't aware of any grave hereditary diseases on either side of the family. Family. The family that he was starting, without having intended to start. His stack of books was crooked and too tall, and it started to fall over. He snapped himself back to the present, finished setting up the display, and conducted the book-signing event as best he could, afterward remembering little about the entire afternoon until he was called to the phone to speak to his wife. He jogged to the customer service desk, grabbed the receiver. "Mel? Everything OK?" He couldn't breathe.

"Tobe? It doesn't sound like you." Carmela sounded excited.

"Because I'm worried. Tell me." He paced back and forth as far as the coiled wire would let him, feeling like a dog constrained by a choke collar on a short leash.

"Guess." She laughed.

"I don't know—boy? Is he OK—or she?"

"Yes!" She laughed again.

"Healthy? Normal?" he gasped.

"Yes! My due date is May seventeenth."

"Boy or girl?"

"Both."

He was losing his mind. In his demented state, he imagined a hermaphrodite, a sexless child, confused by the appearance of both sexual organs; a child who was neither male nor female, but some malfunctioning compromise between the genders.

She asked him to sit down. There was nowhere to sit. Two of his colleagues were watching him, smirking convivially at each other.

"Tobe. We're having *twins.* They're twins! I couldn't believe it. There were two birth sacs on the ultrasound. They're sure. Sure beyond a shadow of a doubt. Twins! I'm so thrilled, it's so amazing that—"

"Twins? Two of them? Boys or girls?"

"One of each!" she exclaimed into the phone, practically shouting. "The grand prize. The pot of gold at the end of the rainbow."

He was getting dizzy and the phone cord was wrapping itself around him, snaring him like a cobra. He twirled himself the other way, uncoiling the wire, saying the nicest things he could think of to his wife, on automatic pilot, and detached himself from the phone call gracefully, and then slumped onto the carpeted floor in a moment that had no beginning and no end, like a wheel spinning in a perpetual motion machine, the machine that was now his life.

There was the matter of names. Every day, owing to his wife's euphoria, Tobias was bringing home more books for her on baby care, natural childbirth, healthy pregnancy, and names—lots of books on names, everything on the shelf, in fact. Elsebeth honored his employee discount and even threw in a couple of extra books free of charge. "This is my pre-gift to the baby," she said.

"Babies," he corrected.

Carmela devoured these books, finishing an average of one per day, as she had once devoured European chocolates, which for some reason didn't taste good anymore. She now favored fruit, Raisin Nut Bran cereal, and lots of pasta, which gave her something in common with Simeon. Over a pasta dinner at their house, the Hillyers announced her pregnancy, and now it was the Scanlons' turn to be surprised. When Carmela took an extra serving of rotini, she confided that it was for the next generation.

"Oh, how wonderful! I'm so happy for you!" Valerie squealed, and then jumped to scoop up Andrea, now ten months old and cruising along the coffee table, ready to grab a tiny fistful of two-tone leaves from a potted zebra plant. "Now you're eating for two."

"Three," Carmela said.

Martin and Valerie erupted into congratulations, hugs, and celebration, especially on hearing that they were boy-girl twins. "You've outdone us," Martin said. "What are you going to name them?"

"Names. That's the fun part," Carmela said.

As Tobias saw it, names were one more burden weighing on him, on top of money, time, and space. There was no baby's room upstairs in his house, that potential space having long ago been added to his brother's art studio. The babies could stay in the master bedroom to start, but eventually they would all have to move. The twins could share a bedroom for a while, but not for long; brother and sister would need their privacy. There was no way to afford a bigger house unless they moved to a lesser suburb, and that would increase commuting costs for both of them.

Names. His wife spent part of every morning before work, and large chunks of the weekend, poring over the baby-name books. The names she was coming up with did not agree with him, but he refrained from saying anything, reasoning that she needed time to browse and consider. Kaylee was one she had proposed for the girl, and then Kylie. For the boy, she suggested Tyler or Blake. He told her as tactfully as he could that those were made-up names and he would prefer something more traditional. But she said that all names had been made up at one time or another, and she had something there, so he kept quiet.

By Thanksgiving, she looked as if she had swallowed a whole turkey, and scraps of paper were sticking out of all her name books. He decided it was time to settle the matter, and suggested that they make lists of at least ten name pairs each. The names had to sound good together. It took her a week to draw up her list. He devoted himself to the task at work, coming up with his own list of ten favorites. On Sunday after his tennis match, they took turns reading names from their lists, and all hell broke loose.

"You start first," Tobias said. They decided that each would have veto power over the other's choices, leaving them with a manageable list of name pairs from which to choose. And they would save their top choices for last.

She started with Jordan and Morgan, and he wanted to know which was for the girl. Morgan, she told him, was a popular girl's name. He vetoed the names, saying they sounded like a law firm.

He offered Dominic and Marlene, which he thought sounded fine together. She vetoed that pair on the grounds that the names were too plain and old-fashioned. "Dakota and Sydney," she offered.

"Same problem," Tobias said. "How about Luther and Miranda?"

Carmela thought that sounded like a court case, and that Connor and Jordan would be much nicer and more modern.

"Connor for a girl?" he asked. "And just before, you said Jordan was a boy's name."

No, she said, Jordan could go either way, boy or girl.

"Why not Jordan and Jordan then?" His joke fell flat. He vetoed Connor and Jordan for two reasons: no last names used as first names, and no androgynous names.

"Androgynous?" she asked. "What do you mean?"

"Having both male and female characteristics. I want names that clearly indicate boy or girl." Lyle and Stephanie, he said, would be wonderful names. She vetoed that pair without stating a reason, and quickly suggested Dalton and Madison instead.

Tobias was losing patience, not believing that his wife could be drawn in by current fashions in naming, which he scorned. "That sounds like a school in Wisconsin," he complained.

"You don't have to be so nasty." Carmela drew her legs under her on the couch, or tried to.

"Marcus and Julianna," Tobias said, but, according to his wife, those names were from the middle ages. Tanner and Katie were more to her liking.

"Tanner? What's he tanning? And Katie, what's that short for?"

"It's not short for anything. Katie, just Katie. It's a cute name."

"It's a nickname," he said. "A nickname has to stand for something, for a real name, like Katherine."

"It's only a name. It doesn't have to *mean* anything."

"A name means everything," he said wearily. "Dwayne and Marjorie."

"Logan and Lindsey," she countered, not even bothering to veto his names.

"Emory and Stella," he shot back.

She wrinkled her nose at his choice. "Trevor and Paige."

"Gareth and Lavinia." There were only three name pairs remaining on his list.

"Cole and Caitlin," she said, thinking what a lovely pair of names those would be, up-to-date and fresh-sounding. "Or Garrett and Kelsey."

"Gregory and Lenora," he said. "Owen and Melanie." He was down to his first-choice pair of names, and so was she. "You didn't like any of my names at all?" he asked.

"Honestly, no. They're all so outdated." She rested one hand on her bulge. "The names I picked will be good for the kids. You know, I read a psychological study that concluded that kids with popular names are actually more popular in school."

"Popularity isn't everything," he said. "Tradition is more important. A name is for life. OK, what's your top choice?"

She put down her list and said slowly, enunciating the syllables as if to a person with a hearing problem, "Mason … and … Mackenzie." Anticipating his question, she identified Mackenzie as the girl's name.

"You're kidding. You want to call a girl Mackenzie?" he said. "First, that's a surname, not a first name. Second, the prefix 'Mac' means 'the son of.' The son of Kenzie. How the hell can a girl be the son of anybody?" He was yelling now.

Carmela sat up straight. This was going too far. "You can't fight against trends. That's in style these days. It's in the modern culture. There are lots of girls with 'Mac' names, like McKenna and—"

"Well, I don't live my life by trends. No 'Mac' anything. That's completely unacceptable."

"Anyway, how do you know what 'Mac' means? Could you ever possibly be wrong?" she asked.

"I actually learn something by working in a bookstore, you know, in spite of how you put me down for it. Those names are so … low-class."

"Oh, and you're so high-class?" She crossed her arms over her ample chest and glared at him, on the verge of exploding into either rage or hysteria. Restraining both impulses, she asked him to name his top choice.

"Lowell and Roxanne," he said. "Lowell means 'beloved.' Roxanne, from the Persian, means 'bright, star, dawn.' But none of that will matter to you." He tore his list in half, tossed the pieces into the recycling bin, and stomped out of the room.

They made up a few days later, more or less, and for the remainder of her pregnancy, he took care not to provoke her. She cried easily, and he sympathized with her exhaustion as she carried the growing twins on her five-feet-three frame. For the last two months, she took a leave of absence from nursing because her doctor ordered bed rest to ward off premature labor. With lots of free time, she played every CD from Simeon's collection to the babies, having read that hearing classical music in utero would make the babies more intelligent. They left the question of names unresolved.

Tobias could be objective about suffering that was not his own, and he felt that this was a character flaw. It pained him that he was not more disturbed than he was about war, famine, AIDS, earthquakes, tsunamis, and floods. The greater the number of victims, the less he felt for each individual.

This was not the case with his suffering wife in the delivery room. He felt every intense contraction in her unmedicated labor as if someone were shearing his own guts with a serrated carving knife. The hand he held, its nails digging into his palm, was his hand. His dry mouth thirsted for the ice chips he fed her from a blue bowl. Her groans and screams clutched him and propelled him in a panic to the nurses' station, begging for relief from her colleagues, who reminded him gently each time that Carmela had refused drugs on behalf of the babies, and that what was happening was a normal labor. How they could go on with their everyday nursing duties while such immense, unbearable suffering was taking place just down the hall was incomprehensible. He told them she was going to die, but they just sent him back to her room again and again for more hand-holding, ice-chip feeding, and comforting words that could do nothing to help her.

Her obstetrician, Dr. Marguerite Frank, said she could have an epidural anytime, since she was already dilated more than enough for the soul-saving anesthesia to be administered. Still, Carmela persisted in her heroism, or masochism, straining to cope with her violent contractions. She didn't want drugs or intervention of any kind. Tobias rubbed her back endlessly, held her hand, tried to alleviate her pain, begged her to take the epidural. Nauseated by the acuteness of her misery, he couldn't accept how a universe so sadistic could torture his loving wife beyond tolerance.

"*Aaarrgggh!*" she screamed, writhing, twisting, turning her head from one side to the other as another contraction, still more severe than the previous one, came upon her, seemingly right on top of the one before. He feared he would faint but held on, mesmerized by her horrible agony. Agatha, one of the nurses on duty, offered some Demerol. "No," Carmela replied, eyes rolling in oceans of unrelenting pain. She was untouchable, unreachable in her anguish, in a prison where she could neither talk nor think. He wanted to die, to kill himself there for having caused this abomination, all for one moment of pleasure. He was frustrated by his utter helplessness and shameless inadequacy.

After thirteen hours of this ordeal, the last four of which had yielded no progress, Dr. Frank advised Carmela to take the drugs so they could speed up her labor and get the babies out before they would be in danger of infection or complications. On hearing the word "danger," Carmela succumbed, saying a weak "yeah" before the next overpowering contraction seized her, distorting her features beyond recognition. Tobias watched as the anesthetic was injected into her spine, and the look of torment gradually evaporated from her face. "Better?" he asked, relieved that her pain had subsided.

"Yes," she said, holding his hand. Twenty minutes later, Dr. Frank said it was time to begin pushing. A nurse hoisted one of Carmela's legs over her shoulder and told Tobias to do the same. He was going to watch his children come into the world, in spite of a colleague's advice to stay by his wife's head and not to look "down below," as he put it. There was no backing out in front of the team: Dr. Frank, nurse Agatha, a burly nurse named Steven, and assorted other personnel were all in on it, rooting for Carmela like fans at the home game. The room was filling up with spectators from the hospital staff, coaxing, "Come on, Carmela. Go, Mel, you can do it."

After half an hour of pushing, a dark blotch appeared "down there," in the big hole that he had formerly known as her vagina. Dr. Frank gently turned the head, and almost immediately the shoulders followed, and then the body, shockingly and miraculously, and then the baby was crying, welcoming itself into the world and the pain of life, screaming, bloody, a living soul. "And we have a boy," Dr. Frank announced to applause.

Someone was taking pictures. Someone else told Tobias to lay his wife's leg down; it would be a while before the second twin came out. The baby stopped crying and was wrapped in something and placed on Carmela's chest. With the epidural in effect and her contractions temporarily at bay, they let Carmela have time with her new son. Tobias felt tears flowing down his face, and he let them roll. "Oh, Mel. He's beautiful."

Only ten minutes later, as Carmela grunted like a wrestler on the mat, the little girl baby made her entrance, crying even louder than her brother had. The room broke into cheers. Tobias looked around him, astonished. There must have been twenty people in there, dressed in scrubs, all staff members and friends of his wife.

Many pairs of hands got the babies weighed, cleaned up, and dressed, with a little pink skullcap for the girl and a little blue one for the boy. The family of four was brought to a private room so Carmela and Tobias could enjoy their babies quietly. Carmela, in a clean gown, lay in bed, exhausted, propped up by pillows, with one newborn tucked under each arm, wrapped up like little burritos. As she drifted in and out of sleep, he apologized to her for not helping, not knowing what to do, for letting her torture go on for so many hours.

"No, that's not how it was," she said. "I felt like you were there to protect me and to speak for me when I couldn't. I was amazed at how good you were. I couldn't have gotten through it without you. You made all the difference."

Men didn't cry, but he was crying again. He caressed her face, smoothed her damp hair off her forehead. "Thank you," he said, admiring the sleeping infants, wondering how he was going to support all these people, and then just letting go of all his fears and rejoicing in what to him was a blessing.

Agatha came in with a brisk step and a warm smile. She checked Carmela's vital signs and cooed over the babies. "They're absolutely gorgeous." She leaned over and whispered conspiratorially, "Some aren't, but yours are." As she removed the blood-pressure cuff from Carmela's arm, she asked, "What are you going to name them?"

"Mason and Mackenzie," Tobias answered immediately. Having witnessed his wife's journey through hell, he no longer minded the trendy names. She could call them whatever she liked, and he would adapt.

Carmela shook her head and smiled, a big smile with dimples. "No, no, we've decided on Lowell and Roxanne. Lowell Philip and Roxanne Cheryl," she said, adding middle names to honor her husband's dead parents.

"Mel! But you wanted modern names. It's OK, you can—"

In her last words before dropping into a dreamless sleep, Carmela said, "They're more than I ever longed for. Any names you give them will be beautiful to me."

Agatha left them, closing the door most of the way. Pale light showed through the pastel-colored curtains. It must have been early morning of the next day. Tobias pulled a chair close to his wife's bedside and touched his babies. He put a finger on his little girl's cheek, and he stroked his little boy's dark hair. "Lowell," he said to his son. "I love you." His little girl had long eyelashes and a button nose. "Roxanne, little Roxy. I love you."

Tobias stood up to kiss his sleeping wife. The three of them were the most beautiful sight he had ever seen. He had never felt happier in all his life. He would do anything for them. He slumped into the chair and slept hard until the twins awoke, crying for food, hungering for life.

# *Chapter 12*

Wanting his outsides to match his insides, Tobias put on a fancy new tennis shirt. These days, he was seeing life through the new eyes of his five-month-old twins, who already had distinct personalities: Lowell was tranquil and cheerful, while Roxanne was excitable and flirtatious. They looked like brother and sister, with dimpled smiles and large, wide-set eyes like Carmela and long arms and legs like Tobias, but their coloring was different. Lowell had wavy auburn hair like his mother's and dark eyes like his father's. Roxanne's hair was straight and almost black like her father's, but her eyes were golden brown like her mother's.

"Cool shirt," Martin said. "Snazzy." The shirt, a souvenir from the 1997 U.S. Open qualifiers, was tennis-white with an open collar and a dark-blue logo across the chest. On each sleeve were three bold horizontal stripes in red, white, and blue. The shirt was his only expense, Tobias said, since there had been no entry fee to watch the qualifiers. He'd even brought his own lunch. Martin said that was an advantage of his friend's job, that he could just take off and watch the elite players practice and still make it to work on time.

"Yeah, my fantastic career," Tobias said, but without bitterness. The joys of fatherhood eclipsed everything else. In spite of the growing pile of bills on his desk, the thrill of watching his babies grow made him smile and laugh every day. Their interaction with each other was the most amazing show he had ever seen. Too young to talk, they babbled at each other and played together in a fashion and were just learning to pass toys back and forth between them.

"Don't knock your career. If you're into self-punishment, try Lehman." Martin peeled off his jacket and tossed it on the bench. "It's a good day when I get home before 9:00 at night. I never get to see Andie on weeknights; she's always asleep by the time I get home. Valerie's getting upset about it. It feels like I'm living at the office. Go home, drop into bed, get back on the train at 6:30 the next morning, and do it all over again."

"Sounds awful." Tobias pulled his racket out of his tennis bag and opened a new can of balls, preempting Martin, who usually supplied the balls.

"How are the twins?"

"Great, wonderful," Tobias said. "One of us is always there with them. Carmela's on a half-time schedule. They gave her a break at the hospital."

Martin walked to his baseline slowly and methodically while Tobias jogged toward his. They warmed up with ten minutes of baseline hitting, volleying at the net, and overhead practice. Martin was out of energy, and Tobias easily won the first game, then took advantage of his opponent's lethargy and crushed him 6–1 in the first set.

During the changeover for the second set, there was less bantering than usual, and Tobias remained focused. The mental image of his beautiful family caressed him like a warm breeze, not distracting him, but leaving him light and loose as he darted around the court in high spirits. He played a still more aggressive attack game in the second set.

Martin's mind wandered to the relentless demands imposed on him at work. He found himself pushing the ball, retrieving aggressive drives, and throwing lobs just to stay in the game. On the final match point, Tobias banged a hard serve right down to the corner T for an ace, winning the second set 6–1.

Furious with himself, Martin pitched his racket into the net, something Tobias hadn't seen him do since their college days. "Breadsticks," he said, meaning the humiliating score of 6–1 in two consecutive sets. "Never thought I'd lose to you like that."

"Better than bagels," Tobias said, referring to a 6–0 score. "You know, even Sampras has bad days."

Martin stuffed his red hair under his cap and confided that his job was killing him. "You're supposed to work in order to live. In my case, I live in order to work." Even on vacation, he was always connected to business. He had grown to hate his pager, which insistently reminded him that he was not a free man.

❋ ❋ ❋

Two expenses were off Tobias's list: his brother's workshop and the baby nurse they'd hired because no relatives lived nearby, and Carmela had only two hands. But it was Simeon who provided the essential pair of arms when he came home from workshop every evening, beginning on the twins' first day at home, when the baby nurse walked Roxanne back and forth, offering the bottle, trying every known trick, but was unable to quell her.

Carmela was about to switch babies with her when Simmy said, "I hold her," and sat on the couch with his arms extended. The two women exchanged nearly imperceptible signs before the nurse transferred the wailing infant to Simmy, who held her close to his chest, murmuring to her. Roxanne let out one more whimper and fell asleep while Simmy rocked her with an instinctive rhythm. The same thing happened again and again over the first week. The twins relaxed in their uncle's arms, nursed from a bottle, and slept. After eight days, the baby nurse quit for another assignment.

They all decided to give Simeon an indefinite leave of absence from workshop. Kenneth's hours were reduced, but he was happy because graduate school left him little free time. On rare nights when the new parents went out, Kenneth served as baby-sitter for the baby-sitter—Simeon.

Carmela and the twins were the picture of happiness. Simeon sat on the sofa with a sketch pad and drew a primitive cartoon of them. In his sketch, Carmela was a pear-shaped figure in a rocking chair. Tobias could tell it was a rocking chair by the lines drawn under the figure; he deciphered it in the way that a mother alone understands her baby's first attempts at speech. On each side of the figure was a small lump representing a twin. At the bottom, Simmy signed the letter S. Tobias scanned the drawing for one small sign that the artist was still there, somewhere, learning to produce the details he had drawn before—the exquisite details, the telling lines that revealed depth, form, movement, emotion, and the illusion of life. This loss of his brother the artist was sadder than the loss of himself as a social scientist, because he, Tobias, was still there, if unfulfilled, but where his brother's spirit was, no one would ever know.

As Carmela's month-long maternity leave neared its end, Tobias couldn't imagine trusting his precious babies to some stranger, even a very kind and experienced stranger. Watching his wife breast-feed one twin while Simeon bottle-fed the other, he hit on the idea of split scheduling. Thanks to Carmela's seniority at the hospital, she was granted a half shift from 9:00 AM to 1:00 PM, leaving the twins in the care of their father and uncle, who learned to manage the bottles and diapers in her absence. It was a financial sacrifice, but worth it. For the first time in their married life, Tobias earned more than his wife. He kept his 3:00-to-11:00 shift, working overtime whenever he could, and took out a home equity loan on his second mortgage, with nagging doubts about his ability to repay it. Busier than ever before, he forced his financial worries out of his mind, saving them for another day.

Twins can be easier on parents than children of different ages because they tend to develop at the same pace. But Roxanne and Lowell, who burst into walking at eleven months of age, presented a "space challenge," as Carmela called it. The energetic babies were everywhere: climbing on everything, pulling books and knickknacks off shelves, and letting themselves out of their cribs in the middle of the night in the master bedroom, where they were still sleeping, in a manner of speaking. It was time to move.

In April 1998, they found a bigger house on the far side of Woodrock, bordering on a less desirable suburb, for six hundred fifty thousand dollars—way over budget, but the Hillyers gulped and snatched it anyway, before housing prices would rise still higher. They sold their old house and all its memories, but their home equity loan cut into their down payment, so they saddled themselves with an adjustable-rate mortgage, gambling that their future incomes might rise along with their interest payments.

For this, they finally escaped the ghosts of Tobias's dead parents, except for a box full of his mother's notebooks, pictures, and diaries that he had labeled "Mom's Personal Items." Probing his mother's inner life was one of those things he'd planned to do and had put off indefinitely. He stored the box in the attic of his new house and forgot about it.

They had four bedrooms: the master bedroom and three others, one each for Simeon, Lowell, and Roxanne. It was nice to have separate rooms for the twins, but they cried when separated, so for the moment, their cribs were kept in the same room. The main floor had a living room, kitchen, dining room, and, best of all, a family room, which they converted into an art studio for Simeon. Flora and Lynx, seven years old, were now mature and complacent house cats and had rights to every room.

Expenses were piling up: what their medical insurance didn't cover, baby clothes and equipment, car repairs, the new house, and household help for laundry and other endless tasks. Although fond of the Book Trove, Tobias searched for a better-paying job, leaving no stones unturned. Martin encouraged him, saying that these were the best of economic times: GDP was a healthy 4 percent, unemployment was below 5 percent, inflation was at 2 percent, the Dow had climbed from 4,000 to 9,000 in four years, and the country achieved its first surplus in ten years. Business at the Book Trove was booming, but the Hillyers' debt was growing month by month, and they could no longer pay off their ominous credit card bills on his salary there.

Landing interviews was not the toughest part of his job search. There were plenty of opportunities for experienced retail managers. But every management position required a college degree, except for the one at Global College Texts, a colossal textbook marketing company in Jersey City. The personnel manager invited Tobias into his office and shook his hand, saying, "Call me Everett." His thirtieth-floor picture window looked out on a tourist-worthy view of the Twin Towers, just across the Hudson on the Manhattan side of the river. Everett glanced at Tobias's resume and asked about college. Tobias told the truth, that he had dropped out in the middle of his junior year. Everett, muscular and blond, had a distracted look, as if he were trying to remember some important, elusive fact. He didn't seem concerned about the lack of a degree and motioned Tobias to sit down.

On Everett's desk was a framed photo of him and his wife with three boys, all under age seven, the youngest sitting on his mother's lap. Every member of the good-looking family had thick blond hair and sky-blue eyes. The photo could have been a perfect advertisement for the shop where it was taken.

"Nice family," Tobias said, and those were his last words until the end of the interview.

"The youngest one died ten months ago," Everett said, launching into a riveting narrative. If not for the man's intensity, Tobias would have thought that Everett was spinning a yarn. Speaking hurriedly in an uninterrupted monologue, he told his traumatic story, exposing details that only a person who had lived through it could relate. Everett was backing his car out of his suburban driveway on his way to work one morning and felt an obstacle under his wheel. He got out to investigate and found his youngest son, two years old, crushed underneath his BMW station wagon. "That was all," he said, staring at Tobias with piercing blue eyes rimmed with red lids. "Snuffed out, just like that. Didn't even see him. Wife didn't even know he could get outside by himself. Gone in one minute." He clapped his hands once.

The whole family was in therapy. Everett had kept working after it happened, could not stop going through his daily paces, or the two remaining boys would suffer even more than they already had. "They bonded so closely," he said, speaking of his wife and the dead baby. Then, he started in on evidence that the dead child was communicating with his earthly family. There were signs almost every day. Mysterious crayon marks on the wall. Falling objects. Inexplicable channel switching on the TV. Tapping sounds in the night. Dreams. Nightmares.

As Everett chronicled his misery, Tobias held on for as long as he could. He didn't have to answer a single question about his management experience at the Book Trove. After an hour and a half, he couldn't stand it anymore. He got up, shook the man's hand, and left, rattled. It was his last job interview. He resolved to stop searching, count his blessings, and be happy with what he had.

❋ ❋ ❋

For the first time in his life, Martin was losing his grip. At Lehman, an uncountable number of vice presidents on different levels were squeezing every drop of life from their jaded subordinates. He couldn't remember a night when he'd slept six hours in a row, and he had acquired the habit of stealing ten-minute naps in his office, hard to do with its glass walls. When he finally got to bed, he'd wake up in the middle of the night, worrying about some task he'd forgotten to do.

At the weekly status meeting, Clive, his boss, reprimanded him for falling asleep. "This is a world-class international corporation," he said in front of everyone.

"Sorry," Martin said. The others twiddled their pens and fidgeted in their wheeled chairs around the conference table. Clive's pink scalp gleamed through his comb-over. "I was on duty last night," Martin added. "My beeper went off at 1:30 in the morning."

"That's part of the job," Clive said.

A lot of torment was part of the job. Clive assigned Martin to an evening of entertaining clients, whom he called "friends," without warning. Sardonically. "Going out with our friends is an option tonight," he told Martin, as if he could actually refuse. That meant missing all the express trains and Andrea's performance.

"My little girl's school play is tonight," Martin said. Andie, age two and a quarter, was cast as a bunny rabbit in the spring play at her nursery school.

"No excuses," Clive said. "We all have lives to lead. It's your challenge to fit your activities around the job."

As the status meeting broke up, Martin complained to his colleague Neil, "Another morning shot to hell." They were the last to leave the conference room.

"Hey, what's your problem?" Neil asked. "You slept through the whole thing."

Martin poked him with his elbow. "Why should I stay

awake for his interminable, agenda-less meetings? They're nothing but a showcase for his ego."

"Ego?" Neil looked around him and behind the door. "Ego? Where did ego?"

Martin laughed. "He bores us to oblivion, then blames the audience when the show is no good."

"What you need to do is tell him off. In effigy, as it were. Come back in here. We'll have our own meeting." Neil shoved Martin back into the conference room and shut the door. "I'm Clive. You stand up and tell me off in front of the whole team."

"You're crazy," Martin said.

"Do it anyway."

Neil sat in Clive's chair at the head of the table and smirked. Martin put his hands on his hips and glared at him with the stare he reserved for loud talkers on the commuter train. "You asshole. You have no talent for management. You manage by emergency, not by plan." He paced in front of the whiteboard. "But do you know how a good manager is measured? By what his staff does when he's not around. When you're not here, everyone jokes about you and mimics the preposterous things you always say. Not one person in this whole group likes you even one little bit."

"Aw, nobody likes me." Neil pursed his lips and slumped in his chair.

Martin ignored him. "Your corporation is a dictatorship with a military chain of command." He raised his voice and stood up straighter. "But never forget that your pathetic little entity exists within the greatest democratic society the world has ever known. And the smallest unit of that society is not a cost center or a profit center. It is a *sentient human being*." He thumped the table.

Neil laughed and applauded. "Superb," he said.

Martin collected his papers, along with the magazine he'd

sneaked into the meeting for dull moments. "I've made up my mind to start my own business."

❋ ❋ ❋

By the time the twins were two years old, their favorite toys were not toys at all, and television didn't appeal to them. At home, unless they were sleeping or eating, they were always in Simmy's art studio, and he was in there with them. Crayons, pencils, markers, and even watercolors with brushes—these were their playthings, and Simeon was their playmate. They spent hours together in the studio, an airy, sunny room just off the living room, drawing, folding, tracing, and cutting shapes, accompanied by music from Simeon's CD player. If there were such an indicator as artistic age, the twins at two were more like three. Simeon at twenty-five had an artistic age of maybe six, but that was for a normal child, not the kind of child he had been.

They were good company for one another. The children conversed in that clairvoyant way that twins do, completing each other's sentences or sensing each other's wishes without having to speak much. Simeon, not at all a third wheel, complemented their efforts at speech as well as art. They didn't argue, nor did they compete for materials, which were bountiful. Tobias, touched by their familial closeness, spent what little free time he had building an art desk for the twins, which he furnished with two little matching chairs and placed in the center of the capacious studio.

By age two and a half, the children were talking a mile a minute, especially Roxanne, who had a lot to say about everything. Their toddler logic could be hilarious. Standing on a stool on tiptoes in the studio on a rainy day, Roxanne stared out the window and asked, "Hey, Lowey, you know why it's raining?"

Lowell paused in his coloring. "No, why?"

"'Cause there's puddles down the street!" Roxanne said.

Simeon laughed, and Tobias wondered if he understood the mistake or was just enjoying his nephew and niece. When the sun came out before the drizzle had ended, Tobias told his children that it was a sun shower. Lowell liked new words. "Sun shower, sun shower," he repeated over and over, practicing his new phrase while running around in the studio.

Bright and sociable, the twins had no trouble gaining admission to the prestigious First Years Nursery and Kindergarten in Woodrock. It was Carmela's idea. "That's the best school around," she told Tobias. "Montessori equipment, lots of great teachers, fabulous playground—"

"What's it going to cost?" Tobias asked. The twins were hopping all over the living room, dressed in identical First Years T-shirts with blue lettering on turquoise.

"Twelve thousand dollars," Carmela said, almost whispering.

"What? You don't mean it? For how long? This is for both of them together?"

"Each. Per year."

Tobias, trying his best not to reenact a childhood spent watching his parents fight and yell, spoke softly, in a quiet rage. The twins stopped playing and listened anyway. Where was the money to pay for it, he wanted to know. Why did they have to go to school now? Why couldn't they go to a cheaper school?

"Andie Scanlon goes there," Carmela said. She crossed her arms in front of her chest as if to protect herself from his anger.

Tobias raised his voice. "Andie Scanlon has rich parents. They can pay for anything they want. I'm doing the best I can. And my best is not good enough to send the kids to that kind of school."

"Daddy," Lowell said. "Daddy, at school, in that school, they have fire engines, you ride on them."

Roxy chimed in, "Yeah, I rode on—I rode on a spaceship." She zoomed away, making rocket noises.

"Tobe, please, it's so important for them." Carmela picked up Lowell and smoothed his hair.

Tobias stomped upstairs without answering and sat at his desk in their bedroom, trying to unearth money where there was none, furious that his wife had made all the arrangements without asking him, and frustrated by having to deny his children something that would be good for them. This last consideration ate at him until he thought he found enough ways to cut back on other expenses and still manage the tuition until the children were old enough for public school.

Which led again to the question of what to do about Simmy. The next day, Tobias took his brother for a walk in the park. Sitting him down for a private conversation wasn't the way to get through to Simmy; you had to approach him indirectly while walking or driving or listening to music. They strolled along the bike path, crunching September leaves underfoot. "You know, the twins are starting nursery school next week. They need to be with other children their age."

"Yeah. I know."

"The house is going to be pretty empty," Tobias said. "We need to find something for you to do so you won't be lonely while they're in school."

Simeon kept walking without looking at his brother.

"How would you like to go back to workshop, or to some other workshop?" That was a good idea, but he didn't know how he could pay for it now without taking out another loan. With the twins in nursery school five afternoons a week, Carmela would have to go back to work full time. Tobias dreaded asking her to increase her working hours, no matter how angry he was.

"Toby, no. No workshop."

"I thought you liked it."

Simeon stopped walking and stood there in the middle of the bike path, looking at his brother, unformed words on his lips. Bicycle riders and runners with dogs were swerving around them, and Tobias tugged Simmy to the side of the path.

Simeon looked around him, at the tops of trees, at the brook flowing beside the path. Just when Tobias feared that the moment was lost and he would have to find some other way into his brother's mind, Simeon looked him straight in the eye and said, in his most complex sentence since the accident, "Workshop is for retarded people." He shook his head. "I'm not retarded."

Tobias grabbed his brother's arm. They sat on a bench watching the runners, bikers, and Rollerbladers. "Simmy. It's true. You're not retarded." His heart raced, and blood rushed to his face.

"Toby. What's wrong with me?"

Tobias fumbled his explanation, struggling to avoid platitudes while reassuring his brother that he would be all right someday. What could he say to a man who had enough self-knowledge to sense that he was not himself?

❁ ❁ ❁

In all the years he'd worked for Elsebeth at the Book Trove, Tobias had asked her only one enormous favor: that she hire him full-time at age twenty, with no college degree, on the grounds that he'd been a good worker for her in high school and would do even better now. He had been desperate, and she acquiesced.

Nine years later, with nowhere to turn for Simeon, age twenty-five, he went to her again, still more desperate. There was no room in his budget for expensive, custom-tailored programs for a man like his brother, still dependent, unable to take public transportation on his own, who would never be able to navigate a world where not everybody was nice, and not everything happened according to plan. He knocked on her office door and pleaded.

"Tobe, no one's ever asked me anything like that," Elsebeth

said. "I could carve out a little job for him, I suppose. But how could he handle it? I'm running a business here."

Tobias persuaded her to give Simmy a two-week trial at minimum wage, provided that Tobias kept watch over him and still managed to get his own work done. Simeon's hours would be 1:00 PM to 5:00 PM, coinciding with the twins' school schedule and giving Tobias two hours to train Simmy before his own shift began at three. Tobias was grateful to the point of repeating his thanks four times, until Elsebeth finally told him that she had work to do, and his brother should show up on Monday.

"Good news," he told Simmy at home. "You've got a part-time job, buddy." The twins were sitting at their low table, filling in shapes that Simmy had made for them. He was kneeling on the floor and leaning on the table, drawing more shapes for them on colored paper.

Simeon stopped drawing and squinted. "Job."

"For when the twins start school. Starting Monday, every afternoon, not on weekends. You're going to go to work. Like me. Like Carmela. A real job."

Simmy's lips parted and his eyes flicked back and forth as if he were watching a tennis game. "Work."

"Simmy, you're going to work with me. At the bookstore. You're going to stack up books, push carts around, sharpen pencils, straighten shelves, do all sorts of things to help out, do stuff we need at the store. You're going to get paid."

Tobias didn't know what to expect, but what happened next was one of those theatrical family moments that no camera, no video recorder, could ever preserve. Tears formed at the corner of Simmy's eyes and flowed down his cheeks as a gigantic smile lit up his face. "A real job?" He took off his wet glasses and sniffed loudly. "Like a man?"

Tobias swallowed his own tears. "A real job, Sim."

The children, noticing their uncle's emotions, laughed together. "Uncle Simmy's laughing and crying," Lowell said.

"Look, Lowey and Roxy, it's the sun and the rain, together," Tobias said.

Roxanne, the chatty twin, said happily, "Uncle Simmy's doing a sun shower!"

# *Chapter 13*

On his thirty-first birthday, Carmela surprised her husband with a cell phone. It was March 2000, and the phones were popping up everywhere, like dandelions on suburban lawns. Customers in the bookstore had them. Staff members at the hospital clipped them onto their pockets. Parents organized carpools and visits with them.

This was a gift that kept on taking, in the form of a monthly statement, but Tobias liked the device and found more uses for it every day. For Carmela's thirty-fourth birthday in May, he gave her a still fancier model, with keys that lit up and a choice of ring tones. Sometimes their cell phone conversations were the only time they talked all day. She was back working full time from 7:00 AM to 3:00 PM, and Tobias was on from 3:00 PM to 11:00 PM, so they had a split-shift marriage; but the twins, almost three years old, had full-time parents.

The cell phone was a good way to stay in touch with Martin, deeply involved with Boutique Properties Inc., the small and successful commercial real estate company that he launched in November 1999 after quitting his job as one of hundreds of vice presidents at Lehman and six months after the birth of his son, Ethan. Martin couldn't tolerate a future that included no free time to enjoy his children. As he observed to Tobias, he wasn't doing something new; he was doing something that he knew. He knew the brokers, the lenders, and all the other players from his years at Lehman. The difference was that he was in charge of his business and his schedule. Sometimes he could fit in an extra tennis match. Occasionally, he had to cancel for meetings with promising clients. His entire staff consisted of one young MBA, Bruce, who had a couple of years of commercial real estate experience from his first job at Morgan Stanley.

Along with other small entrepreneurs, Martin was renting office space on the 79th floor of One World Trade Center. For that, he got a two-room office, secretarial service, cleaning service, a communal kitchen, and a famous corporate address on his business card, which had an image of the Twin Towers in the background.

Impressed by Martin's success, Tobias asked him what exactly he did all day. They had wound up their Sunday morning tennis match and were about to go their separate ways.

"I'm a matchmaker," Martin said. "I match up buyers and sellers in commercial real estate. One good thing that came from working in that sweatshop—a lot of my former clients and contacts are a source of deal-making activities." In a good year, he could gross two to three million dollars, which, after expenses, netted him one million dollars.

Tobias whistled. "Not bad for a two-man shop."

"Well, it's not risk-free," Martin said. "It's like fishing. I can wait a long time to close a big deal, and that's nerve-wracking."

* * *

Simeon was the perfect blue-collar worker at the Book Trove. His part-time job was just challenging enough to hold his attention, but not so challenging that he couldn't master it. He was jack-of-all-trades for any staff member who had some kind of repetitive work that he could handle. He was always available to shelve books, unpack boxes, deliver memos, sweep the entrance and sidewalk out front, or straighten window displays. In the Book Trove Café, he sponged off tables, pushed in chairs, and loaded the dishwasher.

Simeon worked Monday through Friday from 1:00 PM to 5:00 PM, while the twins were in school, and that was just long enough. As soon as he had passed his two weeks of probation, Elsebeth had awarded him two dark-green Book Trove polo shirts. He wore these with conspicuous pride. By June 2000, when he was twenty-six years old, everyone at the bookstore understood his limitations and assigned him work that he could do without much supervision. It was satisfying work, and he thrived on praise. "He'll get it," Elsebeth always told her staff. "Give him time."

Simeon was paid every Friday. Kenneth came to pick him up as usual at the end of his shift, and walked him to the bank to deposit his paycheck before driving him home. Except for what he spent on family gifts, Simeon was saving all his money—for what, he wouldn't tell anyone. Reunited with the twins at home, he amused them in his art studio while Carmela cooked dinner for everyone except Tobias, who was at work. They spent all their mornings in the studio, too, until it was time for Tobias to drop off his brother at the Book Trove on the way to the children's nursery school.

The twins, a month past their third birthday, were learning to draw recognizable people and objects. Roxanne's favorite subjects were the cats, Lynx and Flora, who lazed around the studio all day. Lowell drew pictures of cars and planes, and sometimes of his sister. Simeon, sitting at his desk or Creation Station, was obsessed with drawing the twins, but hadn't made much progress beyond two-dimensional blobs that were vaguely masculine or feminine. The outcome of his sketching and drawing didn't deter him, however, and he kept at it, day after day, page after page. Every few days, he dumped most of his nondescript sketches into the recycling bin.

Roxanne liked to bring the twins' finished pictures to her father or mother, depending on who was on duty: Tobias in the morning and Carmela in the evening. One morning, while Tobias was hunched over his desk, trying to make sense of his finances, she came bubbling into his room with a handful of drawings.

"Hey Roxy-Roxy, what you got there, sweetheart?" Tobias scooped her into his lap. She was cuddly in her pink velveteen corduroy overalls and flower-patterned T-shirt. The first picture clearly showed two cats sitting on a windowsill in the studio. One cat had patches in three pastel colors, and the other had big blotches of black and white, like a cow. "Did you draw this one?"

"Yeah." She pointed. "This is Lynx, and this is Flora."

"Wow, you did a really good job." In the next picture, a rocket ship was surrounded by stars. "Did you do this one, too, baby?" he asked, knowing the answer.

"No, you silly! Lowey drew it." She kicked her little legs in his lap.

The third picture showed the twins sitting together at their art table, bending over their work. The boy was holding a pencil and sketching what looked like a car. The girl was drawing another girl, who seemed to be wearing a party dress. What was arresting about the picture was its kinetic motion. It was a slice of a day in the twins' life. Although primitive, you could tell nevertheless that the children were male and female.

Not believing what he saw, Tobias asked his daughter, "Who did this one, honey, you or your brother?"

She laughed and called him silly again. "No, Daddy, it was Uncle Simmy!" Her dark ponytails brushed against his face.

Tobias took the picture to the studio, where Simeon was starting on a blank page depicting nothing; he was only sliding a pencil back and forth. "Simmy, Roxanne says you drew this." He waved the picture at his brother.

Simeon peered at it. “Yeah.”

“That’s great. That’s amazing, Simmy!” Tobias hugged him. “How’d you do that?”

Simeon looked around the room, at the art books on the shelves, at the tubes of paint, at his niece and nephew, at the cats on the windowsill. “I don’t know.” He shook his head. “I was at work. Thinking. The picture, the picture came into my head.”

❁ ❁ ❁

The day of the attack, they were all doing what they normally did on a Tuesday. Carmela was at the hospital for her morning shift. Tobias was home with the kids and his brother. It was the bluest of blue-sky days, and they all went walking in the county park after breakfast, tossing a toy soccer ball around. The twins, four years old, ran onto the playground, while their father and uncle strolled around its perimeter, never taking their eyes off the children. The eerie thing was that no one else was out there on such a beautiful day, except for a guy on a bicycle, who stopped and asked them if they had heard.

“Heard what?” Tobias asked him.

“There’s been an attack. World Trade Center. A 747 hit the first tower, and then another plane hit the second tower. Then the Pentagon. And somewhere in Pennsylvania. Terrorists. Better get the kids and go inside.” The man put one foot on his pedal to shove off.

Tobias took a good look at the man, who looked completely normal and believable, and then gathered the children and raced with them and his brother to their house, a good half-mile trot. “Daddy, why are we running?” Lowell wanted to know. Tobias told them it was a race to see who could touch the front door first.

The rest of the morning was a blur of panic as he tried to shield his children and his brother from the inconceivable truth, while at the same time trying to find out what happened to Martin. He called Carmela, who had to stay in the hospital and do a double shift on standby in case injured patients were brought in from the city. He called Valerie at her lab, but no one answered. He called Martin on his cell phone again and again, but there was no signal. He turned on the television with its sound muted until Roxanne asked him, "Daddy, why are those birds on fire?" On the TV screen were images of people leaping out of the burning towers. Tobias shut it off and kept it off. He called Elsebeth at the Book Trove, which had closed business for the day. The children's school was closed as well. The financial markets closed, and their employees fled. The world was closing down, but the bluest of blue skies glared on as if it were all utterly inconsequential.

Tobias paced and mourned his lost friend. Sickened and unable to do anything besides worry, he was shocked into reality when his children said they were hungry. Somehow, he was able to make lunch for them and his brother, who knew that something was amiss but could not say what. Tobias couldn't eat.

Not until one in the afternoon did the phone ring. It was Valerie.

"Oh, my God, Valerie, where's Martin?"

"He's safe." She was crying. "I just found out. He couldn't call before. No connection." Martin was upstairs in his office just before the first plane hit. He and Bruce, his assistant, were waiting for a visit from their client, who was running a few minutes late. Martin decided they would treat the client to breakfast, and they told him to meet them down in the concourse on the ground level. Luckily, he brought his laptop and all its irreplaceable data with him. Five more minutes, and they would have been trapped on the 79th floor, doomed.

"Right after they stepped out of the elevator, there was a gigantic crash, everything shaking like an earthquake,"

Valerie said, sobbing. "They thought it was a bomb and ran out of the building." They made their way through the debris to the New York Waterways ferry and waited for a long time until one of the boats carried them safely across the Hudson to New Jersey. Every boat in the fleet was out on the river, their dedicated crews working nonstop, saving everybody who wanted to ride, not charging any fares. Bruce walked to his apartment in Hoboken, and Martin was still riding on a slow, sad commuter train heading home, making all local stops to let out passengers who got only as far as the terminal that morning before being sent back by police and the FBI. Valerie's lab closed for the day, and she was staying home with the kids, waiting for Martin. By the time Tobias could talk to his best friend on the phone, it was already dark. Martin's voice was the best sound he had heard all day.

There was no hiding the truth from Simeon, who had to be told what happened, and who wanted to know why. Lacking an explanation, Tobias kept them all busy the best he could. But Simeon turned on the television and the twins saw the towers crumbling, and then he had to explain the inexplicable to them as well. There were innumerable calls to Mommy on the job at the hospital, helping with blood donations for the injured patients who never arrived. They were all dead, except for a handful of survivors who were brought to city hospitals.

At eight o'clock, Tobias rounded up the twins and got them ready for bed, but they were afraid, and he couldn't comfort them. As they clung together on one bed in Lowell's room, Simeon came to them and took their hands. "Let's build something," he said. They went downstairs to the art studio and draped sheets over the desk, the children's table, and the Creation Station.

"What are we building, Uncle Simmy?" Lowell wanted to know.

"It's a tent," Simmy said. "To keep you safe. You and Roxy."

Tobias watched while Simeon did all the work, giving the kids little jobs like making door flaps out of bath towels. When their nest was ready, they all crawled in, the children in their pajamas and Simeon in his jeans and Book Trove shirt. "Daddy, you come in, too," Lowell pleaded, and Tobias crept in on his hands and knees.

At 11:30 PM, Carmela unlocked the door and ran upstairs to check on the children. They weren't in their beds. She looked in Simeon's room and the master bedroom, and then came running back down the stairs.

"Mel, in here," Tobias called in a low voice.

She came in, panting, and he poked his head out of the makeshift tent, making a "shhh" noise, with his fingers on his lips. Inside the tent, on a bedspread on the floor, Simeon was lying on his back with Roxanne curled up inside one arm and Lowell inside the other, all huddled together and sound asleep. Tobias crept out from under a sheet inch by inch until he could finally straighten up. He took his wife in his arms, and they both cried for the dead that they didn't know, for the losses of strangers they would never meet, for stories that had ended before their time, and for the miracle of Martin's survival, thanks to a coincidence.

Carmela turned the dimmer switch to its lowest position and surveyed the room. Every good sheet in the house had been appropriated for the structure.

The desk lamp was still on. Roxanne had been afraid to go to sleep in the dark. On the desk was a picture of the twin towers crying. There was a human quality to the buildings; they were leaning on each other like broken soldiers. Oversize teardrops were spilling out of their windows. The only color was in the form of red splotches at the base of the stricken towers. Simple and stark, the sketch could have been drawn by a typical first-grader.

The next morning, Simeon asked his brother to give the picture to Martin, who had witnessed the catastrophe and escaped with his life.

❁ ❁ ❁

No one in the secretarial pool survived, nor did any of Martin's fellow tenants who were there that day. Martin took it hard and buried himself in his work. He bought new computers and relocated his office to midtown Manhattan, and he stopped playing tennis altogether, believing that survivors owed it to the memory of the victims to refrain from sports, parties, or celebrations. Tobias found other partners for his twice-weekly games, respecting Martin's need to grieve. After three months, the friends resumed their regular games, holding off on competitive matches until Martin felt strong enough to lose himself in the game once more.

One year after the disaster, Martin had recovered his sunny disposition and was reaping the benefits of his hard work. His staff grew to fourteen, and he moved his office again, to downtown Manhattan on Broad Street, near the Stock Exchange. "Back to the financial center of the world," he told Tobias on the phone. He was just leaving for a week at a commercial real estate conference in Bradenton, Florida. Without telling Tobias, he also signed up for a full weekend of rigorous professional instruction at Nick Bollettieri's IMG Tennis Academy. He flew home with a briefcase full of business cards, along with a killer forehand and the urge to try it out on his unsuspecting friend.

At their next match, Martin said that he'd been reading up on developing a better backhand. Falling into the trap, Tobias avoided hitting to Martin's backhand, and ended up mangled by his killer forehand, with a score of 6–2.

Switching tactics in the second set, Tobias hit to his opponent's backhand, to no avail because Martin constantly ran around the ball and positioned himself to hit winners with his fearsome forehand. The second set ended with a dismal score of 6–0 in Martin's favor, even though Tobias didn't make many errors.

Tobias wiped off his sweat. "Where'd you get that monstrous forehand?"

Martin grinned and twirled his racket. "Practice, practice, practice."

"Yeah, really? I thought you didn't have the time."

"It's not how *much* you practice," Martin said. "It's how *well*."

❊ ❊ ❊

Although the Hillyers both earned regular cost-of-living raises, there was an unbridgeable gap between their paychecks and their bills, with credit cards never paid in full. The twins, already five years old, had done so well at First Years Nursery and Kindergarten that Carmela said it would be a shame to trust them to public school kindergarten. First Years had an all-afternoon program and much better teachers than the public school. Andrea Scanlon had flourished there and was now at the top of her class in first grade. "Just one more year," Carmela pleaded, and Tobias gave in. But short of suddenly inheriting a fortune, he didn't know how they would manage if some emergency ever befell them.

The Book Trove was expanding its business, in spite of the recession that was looming. Elsebeth opened two new branches in nearby New Jersey suburbs. She offered Tobias, her most senior employee, full charge of the flagship Woodrock branch, freeing her to manage the new branches. "No one else could do this better than you," Elsebeth said. He jumped at the chance for more autonomy and a 10 percent raise. The change would take effect in a month, just in time to help him cope with his rising mortgage rate.

After his next Sunday match, he was about to talk about his promotion when Martin invited him out to lunch, which he usually had no time for. There was something important that he wanted to discuss. Mystified, Tobias followed Martin's car in his own. They stopped at the same restaurant where they had eaten twelve years earlier, on the occasion of Martin's first visit to his former college roommate.

Martin took his time ordering and making casual conversation about their children. And then, over big salads and baked stuffed potatoes, he made an offer that no responsible person could refuse. "Boutique Properties is really coming along," he began.

"I know; that's great." Tobias was a little miffed; Martin didn't usually show off or brag.

Martin folded his hands on the table. "I need someone to come on board with me. Someone who can supervise my staff and help me deal with clients. Someone that I know and trust. What I need is a vice president."

Tobias put down his fork and stopped breathing.

"The person that I need for Boutique Properties is you. For a hundred thousand a year, plus a share of the profits. I'll put it all down on paper with my accountant, everything in black and white." He leaned forward and nodded at his best friend. "What do you think?"

Carmela opposed the idea and pronounced it much too risky, and Tobias spent two sleepless nights worrying about diving into a three-year-old business headfirst, not even confident that he could do the job. But with his back against a wall of unpaid bills, he couldn't resist. He accepted the offer, took a day off, put on a jacket and tie, and went to visit Martin in his office suite at Boutique Properties Inc. for the first time. Martin introduced him to his staff, all of them eager and brilliant, including his former colleague, Neil. He showed Tobias the office that would be his, a small room right next to Martin's, with a desk, a computer, and a window overlooking Broad Street.

On his way back to the train station, Tobias splurged on a new attaché case, the first he had ever owned. In it, he placed his newspaper, a Boutique Properties pamphlet, and his signed contract.

The next day, he went to work at the Book Trove with a constricted feeling in his chest. His friends and colleagues looked at him in a different way. Maybe they knew, but how could they know? He hadn't told anyone besides Carmela, and she was as stunned as he was. It was only after his day was done, at 11:00 at night, that he learned what was afoot. As he approached the bookstore exit, the darkened Book Trove Café burst into a cacophony of cheers, with bright lights, balloons, and streamers waving all around. The twelve or so employees who worked the evening shift had all stayed to celebrate Tobias's promotion. On the counter was a frosted sheet cake bearing the words "Congratulations Tobias, 12 More Years." Elsebeth gave him a hug and a giant greeting card signed by everyone there.

Tobias put on a party smile and ate as much of his slice of cake as he could. The next day, he visited his boss in her private office. Trembling, he closed her door and sat down. "Elsebeth. This has to be the worst time for me to tell you this. My best friend, Martin—you met him at my wedding—he offered me a job at his company. Vice president. I'm going crazy trying to pay my bills. It's a great opportunity. I'll have to leave the Book Trove." He looked down. "I'm so sorry."

Elsebeth sat still at her desk as if she hadn't heard him. Her neutral expression didn't change. After what felt like minutes, she said, "And just last week you said that *this* was a great opportunity. You made a commitment. I was depending on you."

He squirmed and searched for the right words with which to slip away from a woman who had sustained his life and his family's for twelve years. His mouth was dry. "I had no choice. My family—"

"How long?" she asked.

"I'd like to leave in three weeks," he said.

She stood up, ending the meeting abruptly. "Concerning your brother. I'm giving you notice now. I want him out of here in three weeks."

❁ ❁ ❁

He said nothing to Simmy, and they carried on as usual. Of course, everyone else at the bookstore knew. Caught between their popular colleague and their well-loved boss, the other staff members kept quiet and didn't take sides at first. But after a few days, they set in motion a plan to keep Simeon on the job, giving him one task after another, making him appear indispensable. One of them helped him start arranging a colorful new window display, and then disappeared to get Elsebeth to check it out.

Simeon, unaware that his days were numbered, cheerfully accommodated their requests. A week before his dismissal, Tobias told him, keeping it as simple as possible. They were lingering at the breakfast table while the twins played in the living room. Unfazed, Simeon kept sipping his morning coffee. "Give her a present," he said.

"You want to give Elsebeth a present?" Tobias asked. "She's firing you."

Simeon smiled. "Go shopping."

Tobias would never be able to figure him out. "All right. What do you want to give her?"

Simeon stirred his coffee and held the spoon above the cup, watching it drip. "A watch."

A watch was as good a gift as any, although as Tobias saw it, no gift was called for. He took his brother and the twins to a jewelry store in town, the one next door to the bank where Simeon deposited his paychecks week after week, except for times when he needed money for family presents. His savings balance for three years of half-time work was more than twenty thousand dollars.

Simeon walked around the jewelry store looking at all the displays, rejecting everything the saleslady showed him. Attracted by the Tag Heuer collection, he selected one and only one ladies' watch, a magnificent quartz in 18-karat yellow gold with a butterfly folding buckle. It had a mother-of-pearl dial and a bezel set with tiny diamonds. Its numerals were diamond hour markers. The price tag was five thousand five hundred dollars. Tobias did his best to persuade Simeon to choose a much less expensive watch. "This adds up to almost one year's salary for you."

Simeon insisted. "It's beautiful."

"We'll be right back," Tobias told the saleslady, who didn't believe them and locked up the Tag Heuer case. When Tobias, his brother, and the twins reappeared fifteen minutes later with a cashier's check for the full amount, including tax, the saleslady blinked, unlocked the case, and gift-wrapped the luxurious watch in gold foil with red ribbons.

"Why do you want to give her a watch like this?" Tobias asked his brother on the way home.

Simeon thought about it and didn't answer until they pulled into their driveway. "She gave me a job."

On the brothers' last day at the Book Trove, Tobias stayed out of Elsebeth's way and concentrated on the staff member who was replacing him. In the middle of the afternoon, by himself, Simeon went to his boss's office and knocked on her open door.

"Come in." Elsebeth took off her reading glasses. "Sit down, Simeon."

Still standing, Simeon held the shiny package out to her with both hands. "For you."

Elsebeth didn't take the box. "Is this from your brother?"

"No. From me." He set the box on her desk and sat down, waiting.

She cut the curled ribbon, frowning, a frown that deepened when she saw the brand name Tag Heuer on the cover. Lifting out the watch, she shook her head. "No, no, Simeon. It's very nice of you and all that, but I cannot accept an expensive gift like this. You'll have to take it back to the store. I'm sure they'll give you a refund."

Simeon paused, finding his words. "It's for you. I picked it. I paid for it."

She put the watch back into its gift box. "This is just way out of bounds. I don't even deserve it. All it was, was a part-time job. Don't even—"

"You gave me—" He held out his palms.

She looked him in the eye, one hand still on the box.

He struggled again for words. "You gave me—*time*."

Elsebeth squinted, put her reading glasses back on, and picked up the beautiful watch. She had never owned a watch that was anything more than functional. She removed her Seiko and put it on her desk. She undid the clasp, put on the sparkling new watch, and stretched out her hand.

Simeon smiled.

Holding back tears, Elsebeth asked him, "Simeon. Would you like some more time?"

"Yes."

# book three

# *Chapter 14*

Tuesday, December 2, 2008. Three weeks before Christmas, and commuters are bumping into him, everybody rushing. He's in the Hoboken train terminal with ten minutes to spare before the 5:47, the last express to Woodrock. Another train to Woodrock is idling on one of the tracks, but it's a slow boat that stops in every port and takes twice as long to get there. The terminal is cold and damp. Tobias feels in his pocket for loose bills and gets in line at the snack bar to buy some hot tea.

It's been a day that he doesn't want to repeat. His phone rang nonstop all morning, he had meetings with demanding clients all afternoon, and Neil kept walking into his office to offer helpful advice that Tobias didn't need. On top of that, Martin is going to Chicago next week, leaving Tobias with the burden of running the office. Working for your best friend presents all kinds of challenges that Tobias never considered when he accepted the job.

The PA system announces, "Train number 1489, express to Woodrock, now boarding track number 12." He's tired and out of energy, is thinking of cancelling tomorrow's early-morning tennis match. These matches are not what they used to be. Playing all out against your boss is hard to do, but losing to him is even harder, since he's always on top, and you should at least get to even things out on the court. But cancelling matches can cause problems: tennis is Martin's safety valve, and Tobias, his preferred partner, doesn't want to deny him. Something that should be fun has become a chore.

Not that he doesn't enjoy his work; after a while, you tend to want what you're accustomed to. The staff at Boutique Properties Inc. has grown to twenty-three, mostly nice people, including Neil, Martin's former colleague from Lehman, who minds everyone else's business. Martin is like a relative to Tobias—a brother or a spouse, someone you live with day in and day out, whose flaws can be as endearing as his strengths. Their wives are close friends. Even their kids are friends, near enough in age to play together during all the inevitable visits.

The twins, eleven and a half and still as close as two peas in a pod, are waiting for him. He calls home, promising Roxanne that he's on his way.

Tobias is a pretty good father, although he never measures himself in that regard. He listens with love; he does things with his children, supporting them in whatever they like and choose to do. He may even be an inspiring father, sharing his joy as his children grow in creative ways. Roxanne draws and paints portraits of family members and all her friends, and she also belongs to the drama club. Lowell makes fanciful sculptures out of wood, clay, and castoff objects, and he also builds model rockets. They're both members of Future Artists of America at school. Tobias has taught them the fundamentals of tennis over the years, and they enjoy hitting together.

Carmela could just as well drive them to rehearsal, but Tobias loves to be with them whenever he can. He's looking forward to their dress rehearsal for the sixth-grade holiday play. The Woodrock public schools offer lots of activities for kids like the twins, who are popular and full of life. This year's play, "A Thousand Cranes" by Kathryn Schultz Miller, is based on the true story of a Japanese girl, Sadako Sasaki, who was two years old and living near the Misasa Bridge in Hiroshima when her home city was bombed. Nine years later, when she's in sixth grade, she develops radiation sickness and leukemia. Following a legend, she begins to fold a thousand origami cranes so that her wish for good health will be granted. But before she can finish her task, her grandmother appears in a mist and carries her away on the back of a giant crane to the land of a thousand, thousand spirits, where she meets her ancestors, and her wish comes true. Her friends and classmates finish folding her paper cranes after she departs the temporal world.

Lowell is one of eight boys supporting the framework of the giant crane that flies away with Sadako, all of them dressed in theatrical black from top to toe. He helped build and paint the backdrops for the stage. Roxanne is one of eight girls who take turns playing Sadako. They're all dressed exactly alike in royal blue kimonos printed with leaves and flowers and belted with cranberry sashes. Roxy has helped design the sashes and matching hair ribbons. Simeon, age thirty-four, volunteered to fold ten of the gigantic paper cranes hanging from the ceiling all around the middle school gym, where the play will be performed as theater in the round. It took him a week to figure out how to fold the first crane, and then he sped up. He's coming along to watch the rehearsal after work.

The line for beverages is too long, and Tobias is going to miss his train. He stuffs his money back in his pocket and jogs over to his track. In the middle of the terminal, a blind man with a red-tipped white cane is tapping his way through the crowd of commuters with their Christmas packages, red sweaters, and holly corsages. Tobias rushes on, and then turns for another look. The blind man is on a zigzag course. *What's he doing out here at rush hour with no one to help him?* Tobias wonders. The man is wearing sunglasses and a tan trench coat and looks to be about Tobias's age, thirty-nine. He's carrying a briefcase over one shoulder.

The PA system makes a last call for the Woodrock express, which means two minutes before they lock the gates. He turns to look again at the blind man, who's asking directions from another commuter wearing the same kind of trench coat. The guy shrugs, as if the blind man could see that, and moves on. The blind man stops a woman wearing a big glittering cross swinging from a golden chain. She's holding a red shopping bag from Macy's and a laptop case. Her lapel button reads "Jesus is the Reason." *Help him*, Tobias thinks to her. She shakes her head and hurries away, looking at her watch.

He runs to his platform just as a uniformed guard is tugging its heavy iron gate shut and yelling, "Last call, Woodrock, all aboard." One more time, Tobias looks over his shoulder at the blind man. Hundreds of commuters pass him by, unseeing. *He'll find his way*. The gate is swinging shut with Tobias on the inside. In the last fraction of a second, he grabs the iron bar, shoves the gate out far enough to slip through, and sprints toward the blind man before he gets lost in the crowd. The guard shouts after him, "Make up your mind."

Out of breath, he asks, "Can I help you?" The express train to Woodrock lurches out of the terminal.

The blind man turns in the direction of Tobias's voice. "Oh, thanks very much. I don't usually go this way." They're around the same height. "Track sixteen, please."

Tobias can see scars just below the rims of the dark glasses. He wonders what kind of horrible accident could have maimed the man, or whether the injury was intentional. The cruelty of the world appalls him sometimes, especially during the Christmas season. "It's this way." Tobias grips the man's elbow to guide him.

The blind man says it's easier for him to rest his hand on the sighted person's forearm instead, and Tobias complies. They walk to Track 16. "Local to Summit?" Tobias asks him.

"Right, thanks. I appreciate it." They edge their way through the multitude. "Is that where you're going, too?" He synchronizes his gait with Tobias's.

"Me? No, I live in Woodrock."

The blind man's facial muscles tighten around his temples.

Tobias wishes he could ask the man what kind of work he does, who lives with him, how he manages every day. "OK, here we are. The train door is right in front of you." He watches him climb up the three steps into the train, feeling his way into the car.

The man must sense that his guide is still there. Holding the handrail, he turns back toward Tobias and says, "God bless you."

Tobias sits on a bench in the waiting room. His own problems are nothing. He calls his wife, tells her he's sorry, he'll be late, he'll catch the kids later at the rehearsal; it's another twenty minutes before the next local train.

"Everything all right?" Carmela asks. The kids are chattering in the background.

He tells her about the blind man and the commuters who didn't see him.

"They saw him. They didn't *want* to see him." She's not angry; she knows he does things like this. "They're the ones who can't find the right track," she says. He adores her.

There are two long lines at the snack counter, and he goes to the end of one of them. By the time he gets home, it will be too late for dinner, but early enough to see the kids rehearse at school. He fingers the bills in his pocket. "Hot tea and a bag of Sun Chips," he tells the counter man.

"Where's your ticket?"

"What ticket?" Tobias asks.

A very tall man behind him says that this is the line for the lottery and points to the snack line parallel to it. Tobias excuses himself and steps out of line.

"Hey, don't you want to play?" the man asks. He hands Tobias a blank ticket for Mega Millions. He must play often; he's got a stack of maybe ten of them.

Tobias waves his hand. "No, that's OK, thanks."

The man is at least six-feet-five and has shocking white

hair; a lean, young face; and penetrating blue eyes. He is striking. He smiles and thrusts the ticket at Tobias anyway. "Here, take one, fill it out. Costs a buck. Hey, you never know." He laughs at the familiar slogan.

On a whim, Tobias changes his mind. He takes the ticket, thanks the tall man, and reads the rules on the back. You pick five different numbers, up to two digits each, in the top box and one number in the bottom box. It says that the odds of winning the top prize are one in a hundred seventy-six million.

It's fifteen minutes until his train leaves. He sits on a bench and looks up at the Departures board, where the display is being updated. The Woodrock express disappears from the top row, and the first three train numbers are now 2849, 3215, and 4537. He colors in six little rectangles accordingly: 28 49 32 15 45 37, and then returns to the lottery line and gives the cashier his ticket and a dollar. The man scans his ticket and returns it to him with a lottery receipt. Tobias drops them into his briefcase between a notepad and a magazine and forgets about them.

He sneaks backstage before the dress rehearsal to surprise his kids. Five or six of the girls sharing the role of Sadako are preening before a mirror and adjusting one another's sashes and hair ribbons. Roxanne is not among them, but Andrea Scanlon sees Tobias and takes him to where the twins are. Andie is twelve, going on thirteen, and in the seventh grade at nearby Berry Hill Middle School. She and Roxanne have seen so much of each other over the years that they're like cousins. Because Andie is spending the weekend at a junior tennis tournament and will miss the performance, she's here to watch her friends rehearse. Her nine-year-old brother, Ethan, is tagging along.

Lowell is making a last-minute fix to the tail of a paper

crane as big as he is, and Roxanne is holding up its body for him. His wavy auburn hair is cut short enough to look masculine, but long enough to show off its beautiful color and texture, just like his mother's. He's wearing a black turtleneck, black tights, and black shoes. His black gloves are on the floor while he folds and refolds the paper tail. Roxanne looks ravishing in her costume; her waist-length shiny hair, almost black, is intertwined with cranberry-colored ribbons. Her golden eyes reflect the floral designs on her blue silk kimono.

"Hey, Lowell, who's the lady?" Two other black-clad boys are snickering at him.

Lowell barely interrupts his work and doesn't bother looking at them. "Yeah, you wish you had a twin sister, too." Roxanne shoots them a dark look that shrivels. The boys stop teasing.

Carmela and Tobias have never gone along with the trend of separating twins to let them develop their individuality. They're always in the same classes at school. While they have their own friends, they are fundamentally inseparable. They might occasionally disagree, but they never fight. Tobias is perpetually amazed by their compatibility and closeness.

He hugs and kisses his children, wishes them good luck, and finds his wife, his brother, and Valerie among the parents in the gym watching the rehearsal. With their drama teacher encouraging them from a tall stool at the base of the central stage, the children perform earnestly and do an excellent job of conveying the message of peace. As the show begins, original background music floods the darkened room, while six barefoot boys and girls dressed in multicolored crane costumes dance across the stage, stretching out wings from which long white feathers are trailing. Their faces are serious and intense. The simple story engages even the youngest children in the rehearsal audience, watching, rapt, from their parents' arms.

At the end of the rehearsal, the stage manager lifts the

smallest cast member, a twelve-year-old girl with spina bifida, up to the platform that serves as a stage. She walks to the center, supported by leg braces, with flowing white wings tied onto her crutches, and solemnly recites from memory in a high, singsong voice: "In honor of Sadako, a Children's Peace Monument stands today in Peace Memorial Park in Hiroshima, Japan. Sadako's friends and classmates helped raise money for this memorial. Every year, children from all around the world send ten million paper cranes to a statue of Sadako holding a golden crane." Her wings flutter as she sweeps one thin arm at the cast and crew behind her. "And that's where we'll send all of our paper cranes after our performance this weekend. At the bottom of Sadako's statue, the wish of all the world's children is engraved: 'This is our cry. This is our prayer. Peace in the world.'" Leaning on her crutches, she bows deeply.

After the longest standing ovation he's ever seen for a dress rehearsal, Tobias collects his family and brings them home. They all go upstairs to bed, one by one, and Tobias checks his electronic bosses—his cell phone and his e-mail. On both are imperative messages from Martin, asking him to do this and commanding him to do that. There's an e-mail from Neil, too, who's always got his foot in the door. It never ends. Tobias sighs and shuts off both devices without replying to any of the messages.

He unrolls his yoga mat and clicks on the TV with the volume low, and turns it to the New Jersey Network to get the weather forecast. The news rattles on while he bends over in a downward-facing dog. He does a lunge, followed by a side-angle pose. He's starting to unwind, and he's getting sleepy.

The news anchor announces the Tuesday night live Mega Millions drawing. Tobias is stretching out in a triangle pose when the anchor says that a single winning ticket was bought this evening at the New Jersey Transit terminal in Hoboken. Tobias straightens up and peers at the screen. The TV man says that it was the jackpot—all five white balls matched, plus the one Mega Ball. The six winning numbers flash across the screen.

Tobias grabs a pencil and the phone pad and copies down the numbers. They look familiar, but this is crazy; he really should go to bed. He verifies that his penciled numbers agree with the ones on the screen and turns off the TV, starts climbing the stairs, but then comes down again just to check, gets his attaché case, tries to remember where he stuck his lottery papers, or even whether he still has them. He empties the case onto the floor and kneels there, rummaging through newspapers, magazines, business cards, and notepads. After sifting through the pile three times, he unearths the ticket and receipt and compares their numbers with what he's copied from the TV:

28. Check.

49. Check. His eyebrows go up.

32. Check. His heart thumps.

15. Check. Four numbers match; does that mean he's already won something? Maybe a thousand bucks or so; that would help.

45. Check. He is perspiring profusely.

37. Check. He's tired and he must have made a mistake.

Wide awake now, he goes through all six numbers again. They all match, every single one. He's certain. He fires up his computer and goes to the New Jersey Lottery page. The numbers all match. He is as quiet as a latecomer sneaking into a suspense movie that has just begun. The only sound in the room, apart from the whirring of the computer fan, is his own rapid breathing.

One Web site after another says the same thing: Someone holds a ticket matching all six winning numbers, for a jackpot of five hundred twenty-five million dollars. Ever the pragmatist, he digs deeper to investigate what that means to him after taxes. When he receives it as a lump sum, it will be three hundred forty million dollars. After a 25 percent withholding tax, he will be left with two hundred fifty-five million dollars. Two hundred fifty-five *million* dollars. In his head, he can hear Martin saying something like, *Poor guy; the government took your money to redistribute your wealth.* He compares the numbers over and over.

He looks at his ticket and receipt again. He surfs around the Web some more. It's true. He is a rich man. He is richer than he could have ever possibly hoped or imagined. He will never owe anybody anything ever again. He and his family can do whatever they want for the rest of their lives. All his worries are over. Hands shaking, he tucks the receipt and the ticket into his wallet. He's too stunned to shut down the computer.

It's past midnight. He lies flat on his back on the yoga mat in a dreamlike trance, neither asleep nor awake, a night prowler in a netherworld of possibilities. He's still there on the floor when Carmela pads down the stairs in the dark at six in the morning to get ready for her 7:00 AM shift.

"Oh, my God, Tobe, what's the matter?" She crouches beside him, cradling his head, alarmed.

He sits up straight, pulls her to him. She won't believe this. "We won," he tells her. "The Mega Millions jackpot. When I missed my train, I played the lottery. We won." He gets his wallet, takes out the tickets, taps the computer keyboard to wake up the screen, refreshes the display. By that time, the story is all over the Web: Someone has won the Mega Millions jackpot, and the authorities are just waiting for the mysterious, lucky recipient to come forward and claim the prize.

They sit on the hardwood floor together, laughing and crying in each other's arms, early in the morning on the first day of their new lives.

## *Chapter 15*

In their first week of trying to keep everything the same, it all comes out different.

Carmela is late for work for the first time in her nursing career. How can she not be? Her morning clockwork is disrupted by the news that she has abruptly become a multimillionaire. She gives Tobias a hurried kiss on her way out the door, agreeing to keep things quiet until they get their bearings. She has no time to run upstairs and say good-bye to the kids and her brother-in-law, all of whom are staggering out of bed in their typical morning confusion.

Tobias is running late for his Wednesday morning tennis match with Martin. Now he really wishes he'd cancelled. On top of that, he still hasn't reacted to yesterday's imperative e-mail and phone messages, nor has he planned his day at work. He's going to walk in cold, and Martin will shift seamlessly from tennis partner to irate boss.

Kenneth arrives on schedule to preside over the morning chaos and drive Simeon to the Book Trove, where he's working full-time. Kenneth is already a practicing therapist out on his own but has long been part of this family's pulse and assures them it's no trouble to pick up Simeon on his way to work every morning. He lets himself in with his key and smells change. "Hey, Tobe. What's going on?"

"Hey, Ken, nothing much." Tobias is zipping around in

his socks, trying to collect himself and find his keys, which are hiding behind his cell phone charger.

The twins clatter downstairs, dressed for school. They're old enough to get themselves to the bus stop on time, under strict orders to stay together, which they would do even without the orders. They notice their father running around, scooping items into his pockets, tennis bag, and attaché case. Masters of nonverbal communication, they know something is afoot but can't say what.

Even the cats sense a strange new energy in the air. Lynx and Flora, who died of old age and were respectfully mourned for months, have been replaced by two young cats from the shelter, Hamlet and Portia, who are tearing up and down the stairs and flying off the furniture. Roxanne stands on the couch in her pink socks and purple jeans and calmly unlatches Portia from the pleated drapes. "No, no, you're not allowed up here."

Lowell asks, "Uncle Simmy, do you know where my book bag is?"

"In the studio," Simeon says, looking distracted himself. "Under the desk."

Tobias waves good-bye to Simeon, Kenneth, and the twins, and rushes to the indoor courts at the Upper Woodrock Tennis Club, where Martin is practicing serves and frowning at his watch. He apologizes for being ten minutes late and they start to play, but he can't keep his mind on the game and makes one unforced error after another. They shower at the club, buy takeout breakfasts, and ride the train to the city together, each lost in his own newspaper. Martin is gripped by three problems at once as soon as he walks in the door, giving Tobias the opportunity to digest yesterday's messages. He wills himself into everyday competence, holding to his ordinary routine on the most extraordinary day of his life.

He and Carmela eat up half their lunch hour talking on the phone. Martin raps on his open office door twice and both times walks away when he sees Tobias still on the phone. The Hillyers decide that Carmela will keep her job, and so will Tobias—for now. The twins will stay in public school, where they are happy. Simeon will keep working at the bookstore, where his efforts are appreciated. They will continue living in the same house. They decide to hold a family meeting after dinner.

Carmela is satisfied and wants to leave it at that, but Tobias says they need to hire three people right away: an attorney, a tax accountant, and a topnotch financial advisor. "There are so many stories out there about people who win lotteries and then end up worse off than they were before," he says.

Tobias shuts his office door and makes a list: 1. Claim prize; 2. Open special, safe, FDIC bank account; 3. Hire attorney; 4. Hire accountant; 5. Hire investment advisor. Terrified of losing what he doesn't yet have, he vows to avoid anyone who will tempt him into turning his immense fortune into a still larger fortune.

In his entire universe, there is one person, and only one, whom he trusts to recommend three experts to help him grapple with this mammoth prize. That person is Martin, who is leaving for Chicago on Saturday morning. And Tobias is not yet ready to share his secret with anyone outside his family.

He calls the Lottery Headquarters in Lawrenceville, New Jersey, and tells them who he is. They want him to come to their bureau tomorrow morning with a boatload of identification. He opens his office door and plows through the rest of what feels like a very long day. At 4:30 PM, he walks into Martin's office and says he's under the weather, thinks he should take the next day off. He's telling the truth; he does have a pounding headache. He calls Carmela and asks her to do the same. With regret, Carmela requests a day off on short notice with no explanation, which she has never done before.

The infusion of so much cash into his life is shocking

his system. It's no different from drinking too much all at once, which he doesn't do, or from eating too much of a rich dessert too fast—he feels drugged, off his equilibrium. The worst thing he could possibly do would be to make a mistake and waste the money. He needs a reliable staff, and fast. On impulse, he knocks on Martin's open door.

"Come on in. You don't have to knock. Why are you knocking?" Martin's red hair is graying a little, and now he wears reading glasses. He takes them off and squints at Tobias, who looks different for some reason. "I thought you were going home early."

Tobias sits, looks his friend in the eye. "I know this isn't the right time to ask you something when you're getting ready for a trip. Something urgent came up. I need an attorney, an accountant, and a financial advisor."

"Close the door." Martin puts his phone on voice mail.

Neil peers into his boss's office as the door is closing. Tobias leans forward and says in a hushed voice, "I won the Mega Millions last night. First time I ever played. At the snack bar in the train station." His face is perfectly serious. "I'm not joking."

Martin blinks, freezes for a moment. "You mean it? How much?"

"Five hundred twenty-five million dollars. I figured out that after the present value of the upfront payment with taxes, it's two hundred fifty-five million dollars."

"You mean really. Really."

"Really. I mean really."

Martin breaks into a gleeful smile. He was never one to be jealous of anybody. Genuinely delighted by his friend's stupendous luck, he jumps up, slaps him on the back, and pumps his hand. Even while he's doing this, he's thinking ahead to the future of Tobias's job and who else could fulfill his responsibilities if he decides to take off. He flips through his files and makes copies of three business cards for his wealthy subordinate. They don't share the news with the office staff, who will all find out soon enough.

❋ ❋ ❋

At dinner, Tobias taps his spoon on his glass and announces, "OK, everybody, special family meeting." Family meetings, when they occur, are usually on Sunday evenings and concern mundane things like birthdays and outings.

"But today's Wednesday," Lowell says. He's grown two inches in the last half year and is on his second plate of ravioli.

"Well, it's a special occasion." Tobias stands up, and Carmela smiles at him. "We won a contest. It's called the lottery."

"Oh, I know what that is, the lottery, where you—" Roxanne cuts in.

"Sweetie, Dad is talking; don't interrupt."

"Nothing's going to change. You'll still go to the same school. We'll all go see you in the play on Saturday night." He nods at Simeon. "You'll keep working at the Book Trove." Simeon smiles.

"Well, if nothing is changing, why are we having a meeting?" Lowell asks.

Tobias warns his family, "You might see some reporters and photographers in days to come. Don't talk to any of them; just go about your business as usual. After a while, they'll lose interest and go away."

❋ ❋ ❋

The next morning, Tobias and Carmela find their way to Lawrenceville, two hours away, almost in Philadelphia. They surrender their signed ticket and dig out their passports, driver's licenses, marriage certificate, bank statements, utility bills, and all the other belt-and-suspenders documents Tobias has brought along to prove that he is who he says he is.

There's the traditional photo shoot, with the lucky couple

standing behind a podium bearing the seal of the state of New Jersey. Beside them is a grinning lottery official in a dark suit and a television-blue shirt, and next to him is a display stand holding a giant facsimile check made out to Tobias Hillyer for five hundred twenty-five million dollars. The funds will be wired to his joint investment bank account with Goldman Sachs in three weeks, the officials explain, and they wish him luck.

Luck. Tobias has thought about trying to hide from publicity, but there will be no way to deflect the curiosity seekers. Public information law requires the lottery to release the winner's name and hometown, and lists of previous Mega Millions winners are all over the Internet. A few invited members of the press are in the room with their video cameras, but they are all very quiet and respectful.

As soon as they step outside the building, it's pandemonium. What looks like hundreds of news organizations have already dispatched their legions to the scene, and there they are, snapping photos compulsively. Tobias takes his wife's hand, and they jog to their car as fast as they can and drive away. They feared this would happen, but they didn't know it would happen so fast. On the way home, they relax, having evaded their stalkers. They go inside, lock the door, kick off their shoes, and then it begins: the endless ringing of doorbells and telephones. Carmela walks to the bus stop to wait for the kids while Tobias mans the front door. At first, he answers questions briefly, and then not at all. The best he can do is to beg these people, whoever they are, to leave.

❊ ❊ ❊

The next day, Friday, commuters on the train are staring at him. One guy is holding a copy of the *New York Post,* and right on the front page is a picture of Tobias and Carmela with that supersize, made-for-TV check. The guy is comparing the photo with Tobias, who's wearing a baseball cap with the visor pulled down while he's hunched behind his *New York Times* in a window seat.

Of course, everyone in his office is buzzing about it, and they all congratulate him, especially Neil, who wants to know if he's going to retire now. Tobias says no and closes his office door to surf the Web and find a private security service to keep reporters away from his house and escort his children to and from their bus stop. He calls Carmela on her cell phone to tell her about it, but she's not answering. Then he remembers that today she is speaking at a seminar on psychiatric nursing at the local university. He tries her again during lunch hour, but evidently she has shut off her phone, is probably dining with the students. They promised they'd make all these decisions together, so he tries her again later, in vain.

Carmela is on the phone when he comes home. "No, we can't. No, we don't." She hangs up and the phone rings again. "Yes. No. How did you get our number?" It's only Friday, and the phone is ringing almost nonstop. She hangs up again, and he shuts off the ringers on all the extensions in the house. They order a new, unpublished number, and while they're waiting for that to be installed, they tell anyone they trust to call them only on their cell phones. The twins are not too happy about this, especially Roxanne, who likes to chat with her school friends in the evening, but they understand the reason and don't complain.

By Saturday morning, press vehicles are camped in force outside their house. The security guards can't chase them off the street, which is public property. Photographers dog the Hillyers as they make their way to the twins' middle school for the performance of their holiday play. The principal is standing in the schoolhouse door like George Wallace at the University of Alabama in 1963. She's not taking a stand against desegregation; she's barring entry to two photographers who have followed the Hillyers all the way to school. "No press," she warns them when they flash their badges.

"We're not here for the lottery winner. We're here for the show," one of them says. He's from the *North Jersey Record.* The guy from the *Woodrock News* says, "We're here to support the theme of the play, world peace."

The principal looks doubtful, but the photographers promise to stand in the back and not take any pictures until after the show. Parents and children are lining up behind them in the cold, and the principal relents and lets them in. The photographers keep their word as far as timing, but right after the curtain calls, they're all over the Hillyers. Cast members in full costume walk past the photo session, but if they appear in any of the shots, it's accidental, because they are not the targets. Roxanne and Lowell's friends stare at them and walk away, murmuring in low voices. Carmela attends the cast party with her children to make sure that no one else hounds them, but she feels the eyes of the other parents on her, and twenty minutes later, they all find one another and go home.

After the kids have gone to bed, Tobias shows Carmela the three business cards and tells her he's made appointments with the lawyer, the accountant, and the advisor. "It's such a relief," he says. "These guys are the best of the best. The Three Wise Men."

She stops brushing her hair and catches his eye in the mirror. "I thought we were going to make all these decisions together. And that applies to your security service, too."

"Mel, I tried. I kept calling you all day yesterday. Your phone was shut off."

She rolls her eyes. "Couldn't it wait till Monday?"

He has to make her understand that there's no time to waste. "Look, they're all out there already." He waves his arm at the darkened window. "We've got to protect ourselves."

❊ ❊ ❊

Sunday morning, Tobias erases most of the messages

on his home answering machine. The callers are people he's never met: Some say they're neighbors, others are soliciting for charities he's never heard of, and then there are people with scarcely believable hard-luck stories. But he replays the message from his aunt Joyce in California, who's calling for the first time since his wedding fourteen years ago. When his children were born eleven years ago, she sent a card and a much-needed check for one thousand dollars, but he hasn't heard from her since.

He listens to her message twice, and then plays it for Carmela. "Congratulations, I heard on the news," Joyce says. "It's so nice to know that a relative has hit it really big." She sends regards to his family and asks him to call her. Carmela makes a face but doesn't interfere.

Joyce answers on the first ring and makes small talk, as if they'd been keeping in touch all along. She repeats her congratulations.

"Thank you."

"I'm sure you're being inundated by calls," she says. "Unfortunately, you and I are at opposite ends of the spectrum of fate."

"Oh?"

She sighs. "You won't believe how hard I've been hit." She tells him that her recording company, which thrived for almost thirty years, has hit a rough patch and is sinking without a lifeboat. "It started in October," she says. "This year. 2008. After the crisis with Bear Stearns, I couldn't get loans for working capital from anywhere. All the banks were holding back." She says she limped along through November, drawing on savings to meet her payroll and pay her bills. By last week, she was running out of money and called her hedge fund manager to make a withdrawal.

The phone is silent. "And?" Tobias prompts.

"He said my contract requires three months' notice. The stock market is in freefall, and they're not releasing any funds." She says she has 1.75 million dollars in her hedge fund and can't get to any of it.

Gritting his teeth, Tobias tells her, "Well, I guess you'll just have to take a penalty for early withdrawal."

"No, even that's not possible. No early withdrawal. It's part of my hedge fund agreement. They demand three months' notice." She's talking louder and faster. "Let me cut to the chase. This is terrible; I absolutely *hate* to ask you. I'll put it in writing. Is there any way, please say yes, any way that you can *lend* me—just make me a bridge loan of five hundred thousand dollars, so I can keep my business above water? That will take me to March 2009. The financial crisis will blow over by then, and I'll be able to withdraw my money. And I'll pay you back immediately." She clears her throat. "In full."

Tobias tells her he has to discuss it with his wife, and says good-bye. Carmela has an idea of what's going on. When he gets to the amount of the loan, she raises her eyebrows and says, "Half a million dollars. And the prize money isn't even in our account yet."

"You want me to say no?" He's not going to remind her how few relatives he has left. "This is a loan, not a gift."

"Whatever you do is fine with me. But I wonder how she's made it all along without you. All of a sudden—what's this, three days after the news comes out?—she's calling her nephew and crying uncle, and you open your wallet."

❋ ❋ ❋

Monday, December 8, 2008. It's been almost one week. Tobias leaves most of their Christmas shopping to Carmela. They draw up a budget that's about twice its usual size and agree to splurge a little, but not enough to spoil the kids.

While Martin is in Chicago, Tobias comes up with a very good present for him: a day in a tennis resort that neither of them would ever belong to—it's too distant, too expensive, and too far above their social class, even Martin's. Tobias sets it for Saturday, December 20, a switch from their long-standing Sunday appointments, and sends Martin an e-mail invitation. *My treat, definitely,* he writes. *Merry Christmas! Can you come?*

*Yes, thanks, date fine, how come Saturday?* Martin replies.

Tobias writes back, *This club has special privileges for visitors on Saturdays.*

You can Google Martin, and hundreds of pages come up, but this has not been true for Tobias until now. Although he feels he did nothing to deserve such a gargantuan prize, he's going to taste the richer side of life for once. He needs a respite from all this unwelcome attention.

The Kensington Indoor Tennis Club is a fifty-mile ride from either of their homes. On December 20, while Carmela is Christmas shopping with the kids and Simeon, Tobias picks up Martin in his 2000 Honda Accord, a car that he just might trade in after his lottery check arrives.

The club is framed by pine trees and stands in a basin formed by evergreen hills. There's a wrought-iron gate at the entrance with a uniformed attendant sitting inside a little heated gatehouse under a peaked roof. Tobias flashes his bar-coded confirmation letter, and the guard tips his cap and presses a button to open the gates. They cruise along a circular drive to a parking lot populated by BMWs, Mercedeses, and Porsches. Martin whistles. They catch each other's eyes and laugh as they shoulder their tennis bags.

The grounds are landscaped like a palace. They pass under a wooden canopy covered with vines. At the door, a Maria Sharapova–lookalike hostess says, "Good morning, Mr. Hillyer," in a voice moistened with honey, with a vaguely European accent. She has long, straight, platinum-streaked hair; almond eyes; and perfect lips. Her leggy, V-shaped figure is clothed in a form-hugging yoga shirt and tight workout pants with a ribbon tie at the hip. She doesn't really shake hands; instead, she wraps her long fingers around his hand in a way that makes him forget all about tennis. Her azure eyes are deeper than the private lake shining through the picture window. "Mr. Hillyer, you have Court One today."

Martin feels small and out of place. He nods to the hostess to suggest that he's with Tobias.

Tobias lets his friend squirm for a moment and then introduces him. "This is my colleague, Martin Scanlon." Martin gets the hand-holding treatment, too, and Tobias is sure he can see him blushing.

The Sharapova-resembling hostess gives them each a thick, soft, monogrammed workout towel so pristinely white that it looks as if it's never been used. They each get a little canvas tote bag containing a bottle of fresh spring water and a container of some exotic sports concoction intended for serious athletes with lots of money. Included are wristbands, headbands, and key rings inscribed with the club's logo.

Martin is conjuring up all sorts of scenarios for what's going on here. It could be that "Mr. Hillyer" has been to this club several times since his lottery win and has been getting privileged coaching from the club pro. Martin thinks back, with shame, to the "killer forehand" stunt he once pulled on his unsuspecting friend. Maybe this is payback time for that humiliating episode eight years ago. "Hey, Tobe, have you ever been here before?"

Tobias laughs as they walk into a locker room plush enough for a five-star hotel. "Don't worry, I don't have a killer forehand."

Now Martin has a queasy feeling that this is a set-up match. They walk out on the courts to warm up on a Versacourt hard surface that feels like carpeting underfoot. It's a three-quarter-inch-thick, shock-absorbing, suspended surface designed to reduce playing fatigue and provide excellent ball rebound. Martin says, "Whoa, this is going to be like playing an unfamiliar piano."

Tobias laughs. "Well, it's new for me too, so we're even." He pulls out a coin, asks Martin to call heads or tails.

This is not the customary method of twirling the racket to determine who starts the serve. "What? How come?" Martin asks.

"Club rules," Tobias says solemnly, making Martin feel even more like a foreigner.

Their first set is a grueling one-hour contest. Martin senses he's going to have a tough fight, so he chases down every ball. His killer forehand is muted by Tobias's new reverse forehand, inspired by Rafael Nadal's signature shot.

When the first set ends, Tobias adjusts the score card for a 7–5 win over Martin. After the break between sets, Martin is tired and trudges to his baseline for the second set. Meanwhile, Tobias trots briskly to his baseline, casually bounces the ball a few times, and serves. After half an hour, Tobias is leading 5–2. Martin, totally exhausted, admits that his killer forehand has morphed into a meager forehand, and Tobias pounds the ball with four consecutive winning points to clinch the set 6–2.

Tobias runs and leaps over the net to shake Martin's hand, and then embraces his disgruntled opponent and slaps his back. "Come on, buddy," he says, fully aware that this is not the way to address your boss. "Let's get our massage and rest up in the steam room." They finish their outing with a sumptuous late lunch in the club's wood-paneled dining room. Martin falls asleep on the way home, while Tobias daydreams about new possibilities.

❋ ❋ ❋

It's practically their best Christmas Eve ever—low-key, nothing extravagant. Martin, who has recovered from their last tennis match, is there with Valerie and Andrea, almost thirteen, and Ethan, nine and a half, who have played with the twins, now eleven and a half, since they all can remember.

The kids have spent the entire evening in the studio with Simeon, who's often more comfortable with children than adults. They've temporarily wrecked the studio with acrylics and glitter, but everybody is happy, and no one cares about the mess.

The Scanlons have said nothing much about the lottery money, due to arrive in the Hillyer's new bank account the day after Christmas, which gives new meaning to the designation Boxing Day, as Tobias has told his wife; for them, it means that they're no longer boxed in. It's eleven at night by the time the Scanlons leave. "Merry Christmas!" Carmela calls after them. Ethan waves a glittery paper banner through the car window.

Tobias puts on a CD to set the mood while they clean up—the Boys' Choir of Harlem singing Christmas carols. He tells Carmela he'll be right back, he's going to give the security guard on duty a Christmas gift envelope. "And I think I'll tell him to just go home."

"Good idea," Carmela says. "Poor guy." She starts loading glasses into the dishwasher.

The guard thanks Tobias again and again, insisting that he can stay, it's no problem, but Tobias is firm and walks the man to his car, waving him off with a smile.

Not more than ten minutes later, the doorbell rings. Startled, Carmela dries her hands.

Tobias sets down a stack of plates. "I'll go."

Standing outside the door is a small, thin woman with a gray scarf tied around her head. The wind is making it flap around her weary-looking face. She's holding the handles of a child-size wheelchair, in which a skinny girl about ten years old is propped up by pillows. The child clearly has a damaged sense of balance and is lolling one way or the other as she tries to right herself.

"Oh, my God." Tobias holds open the door.

"I'm sorry. I'm so sorry," the woman says in a hoarse

voice, and starts to cry. "I'm Cindy. This is Angelica. I call her Angel."

"What's the matter?" Carmela runs over and looks. "Oh, my God, come in, come in." Together, the three adults lift the wheelchair with the child into the foyer. The mother and child are dressed cheaply and inadequately; the night has turned cold. Parked at the curb is an old car that looks ready for the junkyard. The little girl is shivering. On the stereo, the choir is singing "Silent Night."

Roxanne is standing on the stairs, halfway down. "Roxy, honey, run get two blankets from the closet, quick," Carmela tells her. She and Tobias wrap up Angel and give the other blanket to Cindy, who tells them the saddest story they have ever heard. Angel has a degenerative disease, which Cindy does not name, and her father blames Cindy for having a bad seed. He threw them out of the house three days before Christmas, and they're staying in a bare-bones motel. Tonight is the last night they can pay for, and they will end up sleeping in their jalopy.

Angel sobs and twists in her wheelchair. "She was doing real good in school," Cindy says. "Now I don't know how I'll get her back there with no place to live." Angel cries and covers her face.

Carmela, on the verge of tears herself, strokes Angel's stringy brown hair. It's coarse to the touch, as if it hasn't been washed in several days. "We can help you," she says, looking up at Tobias and holding his arm.

"How did you get my address?" Tobias asks Cindy.

Angel sits up for a moment to scratch her head, and then slumps again.

Cindy draws the blanket tighter around her thin frame. "Your sister," she says. "Your sister sent me here and told me you have a good heart, and you'll help a poor mother and her crippled daughter."

Carmela lets go of her husband's arm and grimaces.

"My sister." Tobias folds his arms across his chest. "I don't have a sister." He glares into Cindy's eyes.

Cindy hesitates, and then drops the blanket on the floor. "Run," she orders Angel, who bolts out of the wheelchair. She looks taller and older than when she was scrunched into the seat. They fold up the wheelchair, pillows, blanket, and all, with a practiced touch.

"Fuck this!" Angel screams. "I told you it wouldn't work." They push and drag the wheelchair down the walkway as fast as they can to the waiting car, which has just started up.

"Shut up, asshole," Cindy hisses.

Angel yells, "You shut up, bitch."

Someone peers through the Venetian blinds in the house across the street.

A man's arm reaches through the open car door and pulls the wheelchair inside. As Cindy and Angel jump into the back seat and flee, Tobias and Carmela watch through their locked storm door. They are only minutes away from their first Christmas as a rich family who can buy anything they want for the rest of their lives. Except privacy.

# *Chapter 16*

Moments of solitude in a family of five are rare. It's the day after Christmas, and everybody has the day off. Tobias has gone to Radio City with the twins and Simeon. Carmela, needing to take stock of things, is having a lazy day alone at home and enjoying it immensely. Over the weekend, they're all going to see "The Lion King," so she's not feeling guilty about skipping a family event. They're treating Martin and Valerie and their kids. Scaring up show tickets on short notice during school vacations is tough, but it's amazing what a lot of extra money does for ticket agents.

Bravely, she strips to her underwear and assesses herself, front and back, before the three-way, full-length mirror, with the shades open and the lights on. It's a good thing she's alone, because she gasps loudly enough to awaken Hamlet and Portia, curled up on her bed. The forty-two-year-old figure in the mirror is flabby enough for the "before" snapshot in a weight-loss advertisement. Five-feet-three, with puckered cushions of flesh puffed around her thighs, hips, waist, and arms like floatation devices, she makes up her mind to whittle herself down once and for all, now that she has the budget to do it.

Her hair, her crowning glory, is still as beautiful as ever—auburn, wavy, long, thick, sensual. It's her birthright. Her mother once had frizzy hair the color of tiger lilies in the morning sunshine. It fought for its brilliance and lost, as patch by patch was overtaken by an urban sprawl of gray, and now it's solid white. Her father's thick, straight hair was nearly black, and now it caps his head like a white football helmet. In Carmela, this hybrid appears as polished auburn waves, loose like the curves of a young woman's nude body. Even in middle age, she never cuts it shorter than the midpoint of her back, though she spends lavishly at the hairdresser to maintain its exquisite color. No gray ever smudges its deep mahogany gleam.

In this season of resolutions, Carmela embarks on a self-improvement program. She Googles around for upscale gyms, then has a better idea and calls a few personal trainers. At the Woodrock Fitness Emporium, there's a fellow named Jacques with a faintly Gallic accent and a warm, throaty voice. "Like 'jock,' he advises her on pronunciation. 'With a nice, soft G sound, as in *mirage*.'" She makes an appointment for the same day and washes her beautiful hair before going.

Jacques is tall, lean, and tan, with curly brown hair and the kind of exotic good looks typical of people of mixed parentage. He says he's part Creole and part Italian, with a little bit of Greek from somewhere back when; and he speaks Creole, French, Italian, and perfectly enunciated English with a continental inflection. He's thirtyish and well-muscled, but not in an aggressive manner. Jacques escorts Carmela into the Emporium's well-appointed private training room, where he tests her and outlines a training program.

Carmela, impressed by his credentials and experience, signs up for three months of personal training, two hours per session, three days per week. Out of habit, she pays with a debit card from her joint account with Tobias. It's how they've been earning airline fares all these years, and there's no sense dropping these frugal habits, even though they're multimillionaires. Pleased with herself, she shakes hands with soft-G Jacques and marks her training dates on her calendar.

The next day, after she's home from work at 3:30 in the afternoon, Tobias calls her from his office. She has overdrawn their joint checking account for the first time in their married life. "Honey, we have to be careful about things like this," he says. "It's not by a little bit. You overdrew by more than two thousand dollars. There are penalties."

"Oh, sorry." She didn't know the balance was low, and just figured that he'd moved some funds into their account. "I assumed you'd loosen the belt a bit."

"Don't assume anything." He sounds annoyed, but says only that their financial advisor recommends keeping their checking balance at its customary level for one year, and her spending was at an abnormal level.

"Abnormal? We have money. Why should we still be living paycheck to paycheck?"

"Mel. This is why I hired an advisor. He says it's best for us to live on a normal budget for a year so we can plan how to spend and allocate this huge amount of money." She doesn't answer him. "You can keep the gym membership. Just be careful in the future." She still isn't answering. He says good-bye and hangs up.

He hates when she sulks without clearing the air. They avoid each other all evening, and he ends up reading alone in the living room until he falls asleep on the couch with a book on his chest. The next day, the twins and Simeon know there's an unspoken argument going on, and they mostly keep to themselves in the art studio.

They patch things up by Sunday, in time for their date with the Scanlons to see "The Lion King." The Hillyers are dressed up in their new, striped Christmas clothes, fancy brand names for the entire family. Carmela gave the brothers V-neck cashmere sweaters in the same style, cordovan red for Tobias and gunmetal blue for Simeon, soft as a baby's blanket. Under the sweaters, they're wearing St. Croix shirts from Italy, very elegant with pencil-line stripes, at $225 each, almost as expensive as the sweaters. Slender Roxanne, just barely teetering on adolescence, is beautiful in a Juicy Couture hooded sweater dress in wide, multicolor stripes, with silky leggings in black, like her long hair. She's wearing knee-high Michael Kors boots, black with decorative metallic buttons. Lowell looks like a prep-school boy in his Jet Fuel shirt with gray and black stripes, a spread collar, and black satin cuffs over True Grit Billy jeans by True Religion. Carmela, not yet brave enough to wear stripes, looks elegant in a dark Burberry knit dress.

Before the show, they have reservations at the Union Square Café. Suspecting that Martin might sneak over to the headwaiter before they order and declare himself responsible for the bill, Tobias has already made preparations.

Valerie, always comfortable in her own skin, smiles and says, "You all look very festive."

"These are just the outsides." Tobias pulls out chairs for her and Carmela. "The insides are more important." The adults laugh a little self-consciously. Simeon, sitting between the twins and the Scanlon children, is quiet, observing from somewhere between childhood and adulthood in his perpetual adolescence.

They raise glasses of champagne, and Martin offers a toast: "To the Hillyers. Sometimes good things *do* happen to good people."

Half an hour before the show, Tobias retrieves all their coats and scarves from the coat check. Martin scurries over. "They told me you paid for everybody." He's frowning and blushing a little. Tobias can't tell whether it's from the small amount of alcohol or something else.

Martin, by tradition the one who treats others, protests. "That's not right. We didn't ask you to sponsor us."

Tobias says it's his pleasure to celebrate and paint the town red together. "It's only this once," he reassures his friend and claps him on the back. "Relax, buddy. This is the giving season."

❁ ❁ ❁

On the indoor tennis courts, their relationship is strained. Tobias senses that Martin is scrambling to redefine himself in relation to his best friend and employee, who's now wealthier than he will ever be, considering the current business environment and how hard Boutique Properties Inc. has been punched by the recession. After Martin faults on his serve a couple of times, Tobias suggests that they just practice hitting today, and Martin calms down.

At the office, the effects of the lottery win are still more obvious. As vice president and chief operating officer, Tobias supervises all of the others except for Martin and Neil, who's the personnel manager. They all speak to him politely, foregoing the joking and give-and-take that went on before. Tobias is beginning to feel like a rehabilitated ex-convict, rather than a lottery winner: no matter what he says, his backstory speaks more forcefully than he does. Conversation often stops when he walks into the coffee room, especially when Neil is there. The sudden silence is telling.

Still, he and Carmela aren't prepared to give up their careers. Tobias loves taking the train to the city every morning, slipping out of his quiet suburb into the chaos of downtown Manhattan, pulverizing one problem after another throughout his workday, smacking them like fast balls served by Andy Roddick.

In bed one night, near the beginning of the New Year, Carmela admits she wouldn't know what to do with herself without her career. "I've always loved nursing, especially the branch I'm in. It's the perfect mixture of therapy and medicine."

"Neither of us has to quit." Tobias is hugging her from behind, enjoying the smoothness of her new silk nightgown. The nightgown isn't all that's new. Her figure is shaping up, and he can wrap his arm all the way around her now. They agree to keep on working indefinitely, at least until they come up with other plans. "We'll just take our time and do what feels right," he says, which describes how they make love to seal their plan.

❁ ❁ ❁

The kids are taking it in stride, more or less. Their winter recess provided them a buffer zone; after twelve days away from school, other topics of interest seized their school friends and teachers. The security guard trailing them to and from the bus stop blends into the suburban environment almost as inconspicuously as the guy walking his dog on the other side of the street.

Now the twins are looking forward to something the Scanlons call Kids' Night, which takes place twice a year at their house in honor of their children's birthdays. The birthday child invites five or six friends, and the other sibling gets to invite one or two friends. Martin and Valerie go all out to make these occasions memorable. For Andrea's thirteenth-birthday sleepover in January, they've hired a fortune-teller, a magician, and a professional chef who's going to lead the children in a make-your-own-creative-snacks cook-fest. This will be followed by two movies in a row, allowing the children to get a few hours of rest in their sleeping bags before their parents come to collect them.

Carmela takes Roxanne shopping in the city for something really special for Andie's milestone birthday. She's made an appointment with a personal shopper at Bergdorf Goodman. Lowell doesn't want any part of this shopping trip. Roxanne doesn't like leaving her brother behind, but she goes along out of curiosity; all her life, she's had just enough clothes, and just good enough clothes, to fit in with the other kids at school.

They ride up to Room 4 on the fourth floor and enter a world of the privileged: This dressing room is larger than their living room. The personal shopper, Tina Patronelli, queries them, measures them, and brings them clothes by designers they've never heard of. In the room are two closets, each big enough to hold an entire wardrobe. The lighting is soft and flattering; you don't cringe while looking in the mirrors. Before Tina can empty out the store into their dressing room, Carmela explains that all she wants is one dressy dress for herself, one nice outfit for Roxanne, and something similar, one size bigger, for Andie. Tina smiles and closes the door softly, leaving them to themselves.

"Isn't this nice, Roxy?" Carmela is sipping a juice cocktail and nibbling on gourmet crudités.

"Mom, this is creepy. I feel like we don't belong here." Roxanne is hopping around the luxurious furniture like a toddler who needs to use the bathroom. "Can't we just go to Macy's and dig through the racks like everybody else?"

They try on a few more garments just for show, and then escape to Macy's, where they gratefully fold themselves into the post-holiday shopping throng.

❊ ❊ ❊

It's a sluggish January at Boutique Properties Inc. Tobias is alone in his office at the end of the day, looking over his forecasts, which are pessimistic because many of the company's commercial real estate deals have gone sour since Bear Stearns crashed in March 2008. He's pondering possibilities when Martin comes into his office, shuts the door, and sits in his visitor's chair. "Mind if I sit down?"

Tobias smiles. "You're already sitting. Anyway, everything here is yours."

Martin looks glum. "Not really. Not anymore. We're really at a low ebb, and I don't see things improving during the first half of 2009."

Tobias feels a premonition of something bad, like waking up in the morning with a sore, scratchy throat and knowing that you're in for a nasty flu that you won't shake off for weeks.

Martin closes his eyes and rubs his forehead as if to relieve an ache. "I'm afraid I have some bad news. I hate to tell you this. You're my best friend. I'm apologizing in advance."

In his mind, Tobias races through the last seven years, from his first days as one of three employees of Boutique Properties Inc., to the last four hectic but satisfying years, watching the staff and business grow, nurturing deals, bringing promises to fruition, and learning that business can be as enjoyable as a competitive game of tennis between well-matched players. He knows what Martin is going to say, and he knows it pains him to say it.

Tobias thrusts aside his initial reaction of panic, acknowledging that he has the means to support his family forever, including educating his children all the way through graduate school. He doesn't need this job. He never has to work another day in his life. What he does need, what he cannot relinquish, is the identity that this job confers on him. He came here as a bookstore clerk without a college degree. Now he's a well-regarded professional with clients, a title, a reputation, a prestigious corporate address, business cards, an attaché case, a Blackberry, scads of voice mail and e-mail messages, and a sense of purpose. The salary he earned was a measure of his worth. Without this career, he doesn't know who he will be. On his next birthday, he'll be forty, too young to become a nobody.

Martin grips the edge of Tobias's desk. "Tobe. The stock market is in freefall. Unemployment is on the rise. This recession is worse than I ever imagined, than any of us could have imagined." His voice is dry, and he coughs. Tobias gives him a bottle of water.

"Thanks. It's going to take a while, maybe a long while, before our business flow comes back. Could be months, I don't know."

Tobias tries to keep his expression steady. He is feeling as sorry for his friend as he is for himself. If he had to choose right now, he would not want to be the one on the other side of his desk.

Martin shakes his head. "We're laying off two programmers and two administrative assistants tomorrow. We've got to keep the staff lean. If we don't, we won't be in business much longer." He waits for Tobias to respond.

The way Tobias sees it, it's Martin's serve. He'll wait until his opponent is ready, but he's not going to toss him the ball.

"Tobe, please understand. You've done more for Boutique Properties than anyone else on staff. But people are starting to complain. They know you don't need the income. We're laying off employees, and they wonder why you're still working here when their jobs are threatened."

Tobias takes his time. He's sweating and feels like loosening his tie and unbuttoning his collar, but he sits still. It seems like minutes are going by, and someone has to break the stalemate. He clasps his hands together on the desk. "Martin. I've been with you all these years, in bad times and good times. I've stuck with you, no matter what," he says in a low voice. "Why can't you stick with me?"

Martin is sweating, too. "The economy is in bad shape, Tobe." Drops of perspiration form on his temples. "The staff won't understand. Morale will suffer."

"Oh, they'll suffer? And what about me, what if I suffer as a result of your senseless decision? A man's job equals his well-being. Did you give any thought to the effect on me?" Tobias stands up and leans toward his friend. "How can you fire me?" he shouts.

Martin stands up, too. "Sit down," he says. "People might still be here."

"I won't sit down. I've done nothing wrong." Tobias pounds the desk. "And everything right. And you know it."

Martin sits down and puts his elbows on the desk, his head in his hands. He looks up and says, "My back is against the wall. I've thought about it for weeks. I've tried to find a solution."

Tobias sits down and feels for an opening. "The economy is not my fault," he says slowly, in his normal speaking voice. "I have an idea. Money is not the issue—I won't draw a salary. I'll work for a dollar a year until business picks up. I can continue to contribute. No one has to know about our arrangement."

Martin's blue eyes are bloodshot, crisscrossed with thin red threads. "No, no, I couldn't even think of having you work for nothing." He shakes his head. His damp red hair, now half gray, falls into his eyes. "And sooner or later, everybody will find out. Even if they didn't, they would wonder why you were still here."

"What are you going to tell the others?"

"I'm going to say that you resigned or requested a leave of absence."

Tobias glares at him. "Who's going to take my place?"

Martin squirms. He looks as uncomfortable as on the day when Tobias hosted him for a day of defeat at the plush Kensington Indoor Tennis Club. "Neil," he answers, almost inaudibly.

Tobias folds his arms across his chest. "When do you want me to leave?"

Martin wishes he could say that he doesn't want him to leave, that they will continue to be friends, that he's never had a friend like Tobias and never will again, and that this is the saddest day of his life. But he knows that the game is over, and he has no more balls to serve. "Anytime you want. There's no deadline. Whenever you feel it's right. I'll ship anything home to you that you want to keep." He stands up to leave. "I haven't told any of the others yet. It's a private matter for now." He puts one hand on the doorknob, then turns back and offers Tobias his hand.

Tobias hesitates, then grasps his friend's hand and they shake, firmly, once.

"I'm terribly sorry," Martin says. "I wish I could turn

back the clock and make this economy right. This shouldn't be happening." He turns, steps out, and closes the door quietly.

Tobias can feel himself shaking. He could call his wife, but he needs to tell her face-to-face. Knowing the limits of privacy in a small company, he decides to leave now, rather than return for even a single day as a dead man walking. He stacks up the things that he wants to send home, and sticks notes on the piles. He leaves everything else the way it is and loads his briefcase with personal items. It's after 5:30, and most of the staff members have left already; there isn't much work to do, anyway. He flings his coat over his arm, picks up his attaché case, and walks out the door for the last time.

❋ ❋ ❋

"Just like that? He didn't even ask your opinion?" Carmela asks. She cried when he told her. "And you've done such a great job for him." They're alone in the living room, and the kids and Simeon are in the art studio, with Lowell's Christmas iPod hooked up to speakers and blasting an incongruous mixture of popular and classical music.

"What was there to ask about?" Tobias can't get a handle on his feelings and will just have to let them rise to the surface in their own time, like shipwrecked objects in a flooded basement. He's the one who should be humiliated, but she's the one who's grieving. He puts his arm around her.

"Valerie is just about my best friend. We talk all the time. I talk to her more than to my sister." She leans on his chest. "And what are we going to do about that party for the kids? Day after tomorrow."

"Why the past tense? She can still be your friend. The kids can still go to the party." Tobias admits it's going to be awkward bringing the twins over to the Scanlons'. Normally, one or both of the Hillyers would go inside with them, helping with their sleeping bags and adding to the merriment.

She's crying again. "I don't know how. Are you going to keep on playing tennis with him?"

The Wednesdays and Sundays have been a constant in his life since Martin moved to New Jersey after getting his MBA fifteen years ago. Tobias knows he will no longer be able to keep those appointments. It was something that he and Martin did not discuss, because they could not discuss it. This aspect of their rupture hurts Tobias as much as losing his title and his office. "No," he says. "I can't."

She holds him closer. They decide not to tell the kids, just yet. They hide their feelings, trying to keep things normal. Saturday evening, they both drop the kids off at the Scanlons' in Berry Hill, nine miles away. Lowell and Roxanne don't ask why their parents aren't coming inside with them. Once again, they sense that something isn't right, just as they know it's not for them to ask what.

❊ ❊ ❊

In recurring dreams, Tobias sees Martin on the tennis court, near the net. He's hitting a ball that's short into Tobias's court. Tobias runs up and smashes the ball, intentionally driving it straight at Martin's face. Then he wakes up and can't go back to sleep. This happens night after night for weeks.

He keeps his membership at the Upper Woodrock Tennis Club. It's the best club around, but he switches his days to Tuesday, Thursday, and Saturday. Finding other partners is no problem in a club this size. He's a skilled player and quickly sets up new appointments. The players here are serious about their sport and care more about his tennis game than his net worth. Playing with them is refreshing and good for his game.

But none of the other players can ever stand in for Martin. They've been playing together since age eighteen, when they became teammates and college roommates, and they know each other's moves like an old married couple. Tobias feels like an unfaithful spouse when he plays with new partners.

Missing Martin is inevitable, but out on the courts, he tries not to think about it, instead concentrating on his new opponents' strategies and analyzing their games.

While doing this, he comes up with a good idea: to take his family on a genuine getaway vacation. Two vacations, actually. The first will be during the children's February break at school, and the second during spring break in April. Liking this idea, he decides that Carmela will choose the first destination—anywhere in the world—and he will choose the second. He already knows where he wants to go. It won't be the same, but he'll have a chance to make up for what he sacrificed so many years ago.

Feeling better, he makes another decision: to pursue the advanced degrees that he never acquired. He's going to call all the universities within commuting range and find one that will accept someone like him into a master's program without a bachelor's degree—someone who's been tossed around in life by high waves and lacerated by sharp rocks on the ocean floor and is still swimming.

The guy on the other side of the net is waiting for him to serve. "Hey, Tobias, you OK?"

"Oh, sorry, sorry, I was just thinking." Tobias pulls a ball out of his left pocket, bounces it once, reaches his racket far back, and wallops his topspin serve as hard as he can into his new opponent's service box. He hasn't played with this guy before and doesn't know what to expect in return, but he bounces lightly on the balls of his feet, both hands on his racket, ready for anything that comes his way.

# *Chapter 17*

The kids are back in school, Carmela and Simeon are back at work, and Tobias has a blank page before him. He writes and mails formal letters to three universities, inquiring about graduate degree programs. He invites a remodeler over to measure the basement for a new home office, now that he's been thrown out of his Manhattan office. Violating his own rule about mutual decisions, he doesn't tell Carmela, but he'll get to it.

When Lowell and Roxanne come home from school, he gives them a snack, welcoming their noise and bustle. He's not sure how they feel about their father not working; they haven't said, and he hasn't asked. At 5:00, he leaves them doing their homework and drives to the Book Trove to pick up Simeon.

Elsebeth is happy to see him, as usual, having long ago forgiven him for abandoning her store for Boutique Properties. Still, there's an edge to her smile, a distance in her demeanor. Her words seem carefully chosen, as if she's applying for a job. Tobias asks her whether Simeon can take the next day off. He doesn't usually act on the spur of the moment, but his life is upside down, and he's not operating by pattern anymore. He hasn't even discussed a day off with Simeon, who's a creature of habit. Elsebeth grants his request; Simeon rarely uses up his yearly quota of vacation days.

Tobias tells his brother, who looks confused, "We'll spend the day together, just you and me. We'll go to the city and look at galleries."

"Museums?" Simeon asks. It's been a long time since anyone has had time for weekly visits to museums, as they did during the early months of his recovery.

"No, galleries, where they sell artwork. We'll browse, maybe buy something little. You'll like it." Tobias considers whether to tell Carmela about it in advance. She might object, but in any case, she leaves the house at 6:30 in the morning and won't know. He puts aside the question and decides to tell her after the fact.

The next day, they take the train to the city. Tobias has many unused squares remaining on his January train ticket, and the conductor punches holes in two of them. He opens his *New York Times* while Simeon alternates between gazing out the window and reading an art book from his studio, *Basic Skills of Drawing and Painting.* Still driven by art and obsessed by it, he is nowhere near the level of mastery that he'd acquired on his own by age ten or so. But if talent were gauged by intensity of interest, Simeon would be proficient enough for a one-man show.

They stroll up and down Prince Street, Mercer Street, and West Broadway, enjoying the works displayed there and liking most of them, but not preferring any in particular. In an inner room of the Lucia Gallantin Gallery on Vandam Street, Simeon takes a few steps, and then stops abruptly, entering a trance. Tobias has seen him in this state before, completely overtaken by the sweep of a picture, pinned to the floor by its emotional content, stunned by colors realer than real. He's standing in front of a signed and numbered serigraph by LeRoy Neiman, set in London and titled "Regents Park." In this peaceful, civilized park scene, a chorus of colors clamors for attention: green and yellow grass; a royal-blue pathway; a salmon-pink flower border; a black-and-white trellis supporting roses of various hues; happy people attired in summer clothes, lounging on forest-green deck chairs; trees in the distance reaching into a sky filled with white and purple clouds. So deep is Simeon's transfixion that it seems he would stand there motionless until exhausted.

There is no price plaque under the picture. The gallery owner, Lucia, assessing which brother is in charge, tells Tobias, "This is a limited-edition serigraph from 1984, published in only three hundred pieces. It's signed and numbered by the artist." She points to the signature. "Exquisitely framed and delivered to your door tomorrow morning. All for seven thousand dollars."

Tobias inhales sharply, as if dipping into a cold pool up to his chin.

"It's an investment piece," Lucia informs him. A Hermès scarf is draped stylishly around her slender shoulders. "The price will only go up. You can hold onto it for a few years, and then sell it for a profit."

Simeon breaks his reverie to note, "If I owned that picture, I would never sell it to anybody. For anything."

Lucia smiles approvingly at Simeon. "Another world, isn't it? Makes you want to step inside and never come out."

"That's how I would draw and paint," Simeon agrees. "If I could still draw and paint. That's how I would want to work." He can smell her expensive perfume.

"Are you an artist?" she asks in a personal tone of voice.

Simeon chews on this. "I was."

"We can give it to you for sixty-five hundred dollars," she tells Tobias. "I couldn't possibly go any lower. These editions are in great demand."

Tobias envisions the ridiculous sum of two hundred fifty-five million dollars, his take from the lottery. While Lucia is romancing his brother, he jots down figures on his notepad and calculates that the price of this print is less than three-hundredths of one percent of his total winnings, and that's not even considering the earnings his investments will bring him. He estimates that the dent in his budget would be equivalent to buying one newspaper every six months in his previous life.

Simeon seems unaffected by their windfall in any way; he's still living his usual life. In a flush of brotherly love, Tobias wants to do something extraordinary for him. "Simmy, would you like to bring this picture home?"

"You mean, keep it?" His eyes are shining like those of a man in love.

Lucia is on a roll. "Let me show you some other pieces by Neiman, just so you're sure you've picked the right one. We've got the best works in his collection."

Tobias doesn't want to see any more pictures, but his brother is already deliriously following the woman around. They pause here and there until Simeon stops in front of "Tavern on the Green," running his eyes around the picture. The tableau is a sumptuous carnival of colors, pointed roofs, and trees mixed with people, an irresistible blend of nature and architecture in the center of the biggest metropolis in the country. Tobias steps in for a closer look and waits for Simeon to move on, but he's mesmerized; he's fallen in love twice in one afternoon.

Next to the Tavern serigraph is "Love Story," depicting a doubles tennis match, perhaps at Wimbledon. The head umpire sits up high under an umbrella, and the crowds in the stands are sunlit cascades of reds, yellows, and summery hues. In the foreground, one player is caught in motion, lunging for the ball. Now Tobias is smitten. He's never seen anything like these pictures. This one is calling his name.

With precise and confident sleight of hand, Lucia adds up the prices of all three prints, for a grand total of nineteen thousand dollars. Before Tobias can say that he could not possibly find a logical reason to buy three signed-and-numbered serigraphs in one fell swoop, she lowers the price to seventeen thousand nine hundred dollars, displays the finely wrought frames in which they will be placed, unveils three parchment certificates of authenticity, promises free delivery the next day, and allows them a peek at her exclusive client list, for good measure. As if watching himself in a movie, Tobias pays in full with a credit card—not the one on his joint bank account. He's going to have to augment his home-owner's insurance.

Ruefully anticipating his wife's objections, in an episode of buyer's remorse, Tobias ducks into a travel agency to scoop up an armful of glossy brochures. After dinner, he gives them all to Carmela, awarding her carte blanche to plan the February vacation they'll all take. The kids will have all of Presidents' Week off school. They decide to go for eight days, and Tobias leaves the itinerary completely to her. She's already browsing the Web and making toll-free phone calls the same evening.

The next morning, the pictures arrive as promised in three oversize crates. Tobias signs for them and spends an hour unpacking the cumbersome boxes and gently liberating the artwork from its protective padding. In his sunny living room, they are still more beautiful than in the gallery, perhaps because now they are his. Before brooding about his wife's reaction, he allows himself a moment to gloat that something so high-class, artistic, and breathtaking belongs to him. He spends the next two hours choosing where to hang them and carefully hammering picture hooks, thoughtfully provided by the dealer, into his walls.

The tennis picture, "Love Story," goes in the upstairs hallway, where there's plenty of natural light from a side window. The divinely entertaining "Tavern on the Green" finds a new home in the art studio. Tobias repositions a bulletin board and a poster so as to showcase the masterpiece in the most favorable location in the room. Simeon will be ecstatic when he sees it there.

And the ravishing "Regents Park" will occupy a place

of honor in their foyer. Tobias takes down the dusty picture hanging there, a modest landscape in oil by some obscure artist, and replaces it with his new acquisition. He's running out of wall space, but finds a good spot for the old picture in their finished basement above the fake fireplace. The old painting depicts a humdrum American farm scene, and Tobias was never too fond of it anyway.

He has half an hour to drag the roomful of cartons, foam, and plastic peanuts down to the garage before the kids come home from school. They are the first to see the new pictures. "Wow, wow, wow," Roxanne exults. "Lowell, lookit, it's *awesome*. Where'd you get that, Daddy?"

Lowell, artistic like his twin sister, stops in his tracks and stares at "Regents Park." He drops his book bag on the hardwood floor. "Oh, just wait till Uncle Simmy sees this."

"He's already seen it," Tobias says. "I made him promise not to tell till I hung them up."

"Them? You mean there's more?" Lowell asks.

Tobias shows them the other two pictures. When Carmela comes home from work a few minutes later, she walks in on a party in full swing. Before she can ask what all the excitement is about, she sees "Regents Park" and stands in the foyer glowering, her coat still on.

"Wait till you see the other two, Mom," Roxanne says.

"What's going on here?" she asks Tobias. While he considers how to answer with his children listening, she tosses her coat on the mail table and clumps upstairs in her nurse's shoes, pausing for a moment to curse at "Love Story." She walks into their bedroom and closes the door, hard.

Tobias comes in quietly and sits on the bed near her, but she moves over as if he's carrying something contagious. "Mel, I took Simmy out yesterday to tour the galleries. You should have seen him light up when he saw—"

Glaring at him, she rants, "One. He's not a child. He's *thirty-four* years old." She's counting on her fingers. "Two.

You're sneaking around. *You* said we'd make decisions together." She's red in the face but too angry to cry.

"Mel, I meant to, but when—"

"I'm not done." She crescendos with each number. "Three. You're going shopping like a depraved housewife while I'm out there working, getting up in the dark every morning, helping people, lifting heavy patients—"

"Mel. Be reasonable. You were the one who said you wanted to keep working."

"Four." She's practically shouting now. "What kind of precedent are you setting for the kids? I see it, I want it, I buy it." She gets up and paces around, and then turns to him and lowers her voice. "Five," she says, barely audibly.

He's going to let her finish, and then take matters in his hands. No list of hers will ever be long enough to persuade him that she should control his life.

"That painting was a wedding gift." Her eyes tear. "From my parents. It was *their* wedding gift from my mother's parents. It's irreplaceable." She clamps her hands onto her shapely hips and hisses at him, "How could you throw away something like that?"

"That's enough." He stands up. "I didn't throw it away. It's hanging in the basement."

"And that's where you belong, down the basement. Put it back where it was," she orders him.

"No." He turns up the volume. "The kids like the pictures. Simmy likes them."

"I don't care what they like. This isn't even my house anymore."

Swallowing his pride, he tries to hug her, but she shoves him off hard enough to make him lose his balance. "You think you can push me around with your big money!" she screams. "Well, it's my money, too."

Appalled by her violence, he yells, "Who picked the numbers? Who bought the ticket? Who paid for all this? Who let you have kids when we couldn't afford any?" He catches his breath. "My biggest mistake was the day I said yes when you wanted to come watch me play tennis." He stomps out of the room, slams the door, and trots down the stairs. The kids are in the art studio with music playing at an ear-breaking level. He goes out, walking randomly until his hands, feet, and ears are too cold to feel. It's the middle of January and the coldest day he can remember in years.

❁ ❁ ❁

Late at night, Hamlet and Portia have a scuffle and scamper across Simeon's bed, scolding each other. He sees the light on in the living room and goes downstairs to investigate. Carmela is curled up on the couch with a magazine, but she's not reading.

"Don't you have to get up early for work?" he asks her.

Not wanting to lump Simeon and Tobias into a single target of her fury, she tries to be fair. "I just need to be alone to think things over." Her hair is a mess of tangles, and she's still wearing her nurse's uniform and white stockings with a run down her calf.

He sits at the other end of the couch and waits for her to say something or ask him to leave. After ten minutes or so, he offers to make her some tea.

"No, thanks. Why don't you just go back to bed?" she suggests.

This conversation is proceeding at the rate of drying paint. Not accustomed to taking the lead in anything, Simeon is stymied. He steals a sideways glance at his sister-in-law. She looks terrible. He waits another few minutes.

"Mel. It was my fault."

"No. How can it be your fault?" She whisks her hand as if to flick away his assertion.

"That picture. That picture, it's beautiful." He looks toward the foyer, where "Regents Park" is hanging, oblivious to the controversy it has provoked. "I saw it, and I..." He points to his chest with both hands. "It went into my heart. And then, you know what happened, and then, Toby—"

Carmela uncurls her legs and sits up, facing him, and raises her eyebrows, but Simeon doesn't go on. "Then what?"

"It's a secret." He's furrowing his brows.

She has never seen him look so pensive. "Tell me. Simmy, tell me."

He checks the stairs and listens. He looks down. "I *had* to say yes about the pictures." In a low voice, he explains, "Toby thinks it's his fault. What happened to me. In the accident."

Startled by his insight, and shocked that he knows things that no one would dare discuss with him, she shakes her head. "No, no."

What happens next surprises her more than anything Simeon has done since he replaced the baby nurse almost twelve years ago. He stoops before her, guides her head to his shoulder, and says, "Mel. You're going to be all right." He pats her on the back and whispers, "You've been a mom to me. I owe you."

He's murmuring so softly that she's not sure she heard him right. What does he owe her? Could he have said, *I know you*? His jaw is set; his dark eyes behind rectangular glasses reflect a wisdom and maturity she has not noticed before. He stands up and squares his shoulders, ending their private conversation and muting her unasked questions.

❁ ❁ ❁

The next day, Tobias leaves the house right after his children come home from school and before his wife returns from work. He runs errands, and then goes to the Book Trove to pick up his brother, who has to stay a little later to help with an author visit. Elsebeth invites him into her office. Fearing another firing, Tobias follows her and shuts the door.

"It's not about Simeon," she says, sensing his anxiety.

"He's the least of my worries." Her skin is lined, and her hair is grayer than he remembers it, even though he sees her often enough because of Simmy.

"How's business?" he asks obligingly.

"Not good. I had to let three staff members go, and I closed one of our new branches." She says that business has been declining since the middle of 2008, and her savings in the Primary Reserve Fund at Lehman have been frozen. "That was supposed to be a safe money-market fund; that's what they told me." When Lehman failed in September 2008, she tells him, the Primary Reserve Fund couldn't distribute its assets because of the credit crisis that's now raging.

His head is throbbing with the unpalatable details. Still in pain from the argument last night, he can only nod sympathetically.

"So yesterday, I tried to get a loan from my business banker, JPMorgan Chase. They're hoping for some TARP money from the Fed, but they're in no position to make any loans until the economy picks up."

"That's awful."

"It's worse than awful. It's going to be the death of the Book Trove. For the first time since I've been in business, I can't make payroll. Payday is next Friday, and I'm scraping the bottom of the barrel. I'm going to have to shut my doors and sell everything." She sweeps her hand around the room.

Tobias shoves his problems out of consciousness and listens to her request for nine hundred thousand dollars to tide her over. They dig into her audited financial statements of the last two quarters. He doesn't want to make her grovel, but he's learned enough at Boutique Properties to ask for her cash flow projection for the next two years. He pores over this alone at home, returns the next day, and offers to lend her seven hundred thousand dollars. She pleads for a low interest rate, and he requests 5 percent of the equity, which he will put into a trust fund for his children. He tells her he'll have his accountant draw up an agreement, and they shake hands. "Elsebeth, you're going to make it."

She throws her arms around him and smiles for the first time in a week. "Thanks to you."

Now he has one more transaction to hide from his wife.

❊ ❊ ❊

The Kiha Resort on Maui in Hawaii is the most opulent place Tobias and his family have ever seen. It's named for the goddess of Maui in Hawaiian mythology. All of the resort's clubs, restaurants, and gathering spots are named after other Hawaiian deities; in fact, this resort is too dazzling for mortals.

Carmela has kept most of her plans under wraps to surprise everybody. After their terrible fight blew over, and they both apologized, they agreed on an unlimited budget for this trip, and she has thrown herself into making this a vacation to remember. No detail has been neglected, including the empty suitcase they have brought along for toting home souvenirs.

Their private villa alone could keep them busy for the full eight days. Their personal butler and chef greet their arrival with floral leis and nonalcoholic mai tais. Tobias chokes on the word *butler*; moreover, a professionally upbeat person can be irritating, but this one is super polite and welcoming. He asks them a whole list of questions—their preferred room temperature, what kind of bottled water they favor, which of the zillion activities they're considering. He'll show them where everything is and make recommendations according to their interests, and he'll do anything from filling the bathtub to getting tennis rackets restrung. All they have to do is breathe and swallow, and he will take care of everything else, or he'll assign the task to someone else who will. There's even a guy who rakes the sand around their private beach daily at the crack of dawn to make sure it's nice and smooth and pebble-free.

Tobias, uneasy about being pampered, is about to ask if there's someone in charge of squeezing toothpaste onto brushes, but he keeps his mouth shut. Is upper class something that shows from the outside—something you put on, like a garment? Carmela stands aside with her arms folded, beaming. The twins are awestruck and silent. Simeon looks disoriented.

Kiha is a six-star resort. Tobias learns that some hoteliers have awarded themselves six stars for over-the-top amenities. Their fifty-five-hundred-square-foot suite has three bedrooms, a private swimming pool, and its own veranda with panoramic views of Haleakala Crater and the azure-blue Pacific.

"Rox, is that a volcano?" Lowell asks his sister, who was reading travel guides on the plane. The butler intercepts the question and says that it's an active volcano but not currently erupting. What's erupting internally is Tobias's culture shock. Not wanting to be a killjoy, he vows to make the best of an experience so far above his class that he needs a guide to navigate it.

Carmela signs up for a five-hour treatment series at a spa named for Koleamoku, the god of the art of healing. She's getting hydrotherapy, a salt scrub, a hot wrap, a cooling white clay cocoon, a private meditation session, and a volcanic ash purifying facial, all finished off with hairstyling and makeup application. Roxanne, suspicious of anything reminiscent of their aborted personal shopping adventure at Bergdorf Goodman, signs up for Camp Mooaleo, named after a gnome who lives on Lanai, and easily persuades Lowell to join her. The camp offers sand sculpting contests, reef exploration, scavenger hunts, craft-making with shells and wood, acting out Hawaiian legends, and private showings in the preteen movie theater.

There's still plenty of time left over for family activities. In Wailea Canyon, the activity pool is an amusement park of its own, in which rivers carry swimmers among nine free-form pools on six levels. There are jungle pools, water slides, a Tarzan pool with a rope swing, a water elevator, and a bar where you swim up to place your order for cocktails.

They take kayaking tours and scuba lessons. Carmela goes shopping for all sorts of beach souvenirs that Tobias thinks they don't need, but he doesn't complain. While she's shopping, he takes Simeon to see the local glassworks and pearls. In the Hiaka Gallery, they admire works of art by Andy Warhol, Fernand Leger, and Pablo Picasso, and buy nothing at all.

Tobias visits the fitness center and takes some private lessons with a pro on the Plexipave courts of the Ukanipo Tennis Pavilion of Maui, named for the Hawaiian shark god. While he's gone, Simeon totes a sketch pad around the resort, trying to render his impressions, filling page after page with designs that are neither abstract nor literal, expressing his vision stumblingly, like a stroke victim failing to speak eloquently—or even adequately.

Their personal chef cooks breakfast for them every morning, serving pancakes shaped like starfish and pineapples carved like volcanoes. At first, they take their other meals together in resort restaurants named after gods and goddesses, but the blatant snobbery of the other guests gets to them after a while, even Carmela, and they eat more of their meals on their private veranda overlooking their little beach.

By the end of the eight days, Carmela wishes she could stay for another week. "This place is magical," she says. The kids are missing their friends. Simeon, away from his routine, still looks lost. Tobias, disliking contrived magic, cannot wait to leave a paradise that he did not earn, populated by tourists who don't mingle, served by members of a working class trained to treat visitors like deities. He's not sure about the math, but he guesses that the total cost of goods and services for one day in this resort would be enough to pay for a hundred new schools in some impoverished country. He keeps this cliché to himself, gives generous tips to their butler and chef, and gratefully escorts his family to the airport.

They fly home in business class to dirty old New York, where the people are rude, the streets are crowded, the weather is atrocious, and magic arises of its own accord, from ordinary people doing small, unexpected things.

❋ ❋ ❋

From time to time, Tobias, when he was poor, thought that if he were rich, there wouldn't be any homeless people walking the streets. There wouldn't be any doomed pets locked up in tiny cages in shelters. Now that he's rich, he admits that he can't come near to solving all the world's problems. But he can help some people, and he needs to identify those. It's a project on his mental list of things to do.

As for dealing with the endless requests that come his way, legitimate and otherwise, Tobias makes the decisions, usually no, and deflects all the animosity to his advisor, who handles calls from strangers.

Calls from relatives are another matter. It's the middle of March, and he's home alone. At 9:00 in the morning, he gets a call from his aunt Joyce in California. "Did you hear?" she asks him.

"Hear what?" An opening like this from someone he rarely speaks to does not portend good news. "It's six in the morning for you, isn't it?"

Her voice is tremulous, like a singer with faulty vibrato. "It's all over, everywhere, the news about Bernard Madoff. He was running a Ponzi scheme. Everyone who invested with him is broke."

Tobias stands up and paces. "Actually, I saw it on the front page of today's *New York Times*."

She gets right to the point. "Well, my savings are in his asset management fund." These are the personal funds that she had to wait for three months to withdraw. Now it's three months later, and she cannot repay the bridge loan of five hundred thousand dollars that she took from Tobias in December.

Tobias goes beserk. "How much of your hedge fund is in Madoff's?"

"Most of it." She won't get a penny back from the fund. She'd had high hopes for repaying the bridge loan because she'd been getting a constant 10 percent to 11 percent return for years. It was too good to be true, and she was banking on it. Now it's all a fraud. She knows she owes Tobias, she won't forget it, and she will rebuild her business brick by brick until she pays it all back, she says. She's cutting back on expenses, she has enough cash flow to survive, and she doesn't need another loan. She even offers to mail him her P&L statement, but by this time, Tobias is too worried about Madoff to talk any longer.

Nearly hysterical and sweating like a prizefighter, he calls his financial advisor. There's no answer. He shouldn't have trusted the man. He might have lost everything—go to bed rich, wake up poor, owning nothing, owing everything. He leaves a message, then another message. He sends multiple e-mails.

While waiting for a response, he Googles every bit of information about the Madoff case, surfing all the financial Web sites, and his heart starts to pound. Even if only 10 percent of his fortune is in the Madoff fund, he will have lost twenty-five million dollars. He can neither sit nor stand for more than a minute straight. By the time his advisor calls at two in the afternoon, he has a giant headache and can't think.

"Calm down," the man says. "No Madoff. Your money is in the best place—Goldman Sachs. They rejected Madoff's fund for all their clients. Safer than Uncle Sam. I told you that you'd be in good hands."

Rejoicing at good news emerging from bad news, Tobias

thanks his advisor for a job well done and goes for a two-mile run to get it out of his system. He starts a ledger on Joyce's loan repayment, but says nothing about it to his wife.

Before he goes to bed, he checks his e-mail one more time, nervous about getting any more disturbing news on this frightening day. Startled, he sees a message from Martin, to whom he hasn't spoken since he was fired more than two months ago.

*Just saying hello,* the subject line reads. *Good evening, old friend,* the message begins cheerfully. *I hope you and Carmela, Simeon, and the kids are fine. We're doing all right over here. Just a line to wonder if you'd like to get together again for tennis one of these days. Hoping to hear from you, Martin.*

He goes to bed without replying, to sleep on it, but he can't sleep. He just manages to succumb to a tiring dream on a tennis court when his wife's alarm jangles him awake, worrying about what his old friend and former employer really wants from him.

## *Chapter 18*

Carmela wants to give Tobias something significant for his fortieth birthday, but the tennis shirts or show tickets that once made an impression are now commonplace. It's a challenge to buy a gift for a man who has four new tennis rackets, a personal tennis coach, a new BMW M6 convertible paid in cash, and an application for the graduate program at Elysian University, where the annual tuition is fifty thousand dollars.

A starting point is his home office being built in their basement. Instead of nagging about his unilateral decision, she tells him sweetly that she saw the blueprints in a folder on his desk, and she thinks it's a wonderful idea. When he grins, she knows she's hit pay dirt.

She commissions Simeon, Lowell, and Roxanne to create a one-of-a-kind of art object for the new home office. Liking the idea, they shut themselves in their art studio every night until two days before Tobias's birthday, when they unveil a triptych of stylized family portraits. On the center canvas is a painting of Tobias standing behind Carmela in a chair, her auburn hair flowing over his hands on her shoulders. The twins are in the canvas on the left, working together on a portrait of their uncle Simeon. Delightfully, the picture on the rightmost canvas is the same portrait of Simeon, larger and detailed. None of the artists will say who painted which picture, although the twins have long ago eclipsed their uncle in art. The finished product is good enough for a portrait studio.

Carmela hurries to a frame shop and greases the wheel generously to get the job done in one day. She selects an elegant, customized triple frame with gilt borders. Going out of her way like this, she assuages her guilt; weighing on her is the situation with her personal trainer, Jacques, which has been heating up. On her way home, she stops at the gym, ostensibly to rummage through her locker.

"Hello, darling," Jacques greets her on his way out of the weight room. He's the type of man who looks commanding in a club T-shirt with a towel hung around his neck. "Extra workout today?" He rubs her back and shoulder and fingers her hair, letting his eyes ride down her curves to her narrowing waist and tightening hips. "I don't say this to everyone," he confides in a low voice. "The change in your physique is just *dynamic* since you've been working out." He holds her at arm's length, studying her face and making her blush. "A beautiful face in a beautiful body." Before he rushes off to his next training session, they walk a few steps with their arms around each other's backs.

❋ ❋ ❋

On their father's birthday, the twins wake Simeon at 5:30 AM. Tobias, who usually rises right after his wife to avoid looking lazy, hears them scurrying around while he's shaving. When he's done, the three of them call out "Surprise!" and present him with a handmade birthday card.

Carmela appears in a bathrobe. "Happy birthday, sweetheart." She kisses him.

With a flourish, the twins remove the silk scarf draped over the triptych.

"Wow, this is amazing!" Tobias says. "Who did these?"

"We all did," Roxanne says. "And Mom got the frame."

Tobias hugs them all and proudly carries the triptych down to his home office, which is developing nicely with built-in cabinets and a custom-made L-shaped desk.

After dinner and birthday cake, they hold a family meeting to discuss their second major vacation of the year—a tour of the Amazon in Venezuela, starting with a visit to the Yanomami Indians. The twins are looking forward to such an exotic vacation at spring break. Simeon is neutral.

Carmela, who prefers glamorous and luxurious vacations, is dreading this trip intensely, and is just as forcefully concealing her emotions. Tobias reminds her more than once to pack very lightly, which rouses her suspicions. Moreover, her supervisor at the hospital is not pleased about her second prolonged absence this early in the year, but the shortage of expert nurses keeps him from complaining too loudly. Still, there's an unpleasant feeling at work these days, a kind of chilly politeness that can presage a deeper freeze.

❁ ❁ ❁

Tobias prepares his kids and his brother for their trip while Carmela is at the gym. Not that he doesn't want her to know, but she might overreact to certain aspects of roughing it in the jungle, and it will be better for everybody if she just adapts as she goes along. "First, we're going to visit the Yanomami Indians at the Casiquiare River," he tells them. "They're the last primitively living Indians in the entire world—real live, human, anthropological artifacts." He unfolds a colored map. "The Casiquiare connects the Orinoco and Amazon—they're the greatest river systems in South America."

"Oh, cool." Lowell traces the rivers with his finger while Simeon looks on with interest. "How primitive are they, Dad?"

"You'll be utterly amazed. So primitive that they don't have a counting system. So if you ask a man how many children he has, all he knows is one, two, or many."

"Incredible," Roxanne says. "Are we really going to get to hang out with them?"

Tobias outlines the trip, suggesting that they spare Carmela the details. They'll be forging the rivers in a small motorboat, even over strong rapids. Nights will be spent in a shapono with the natives.

"What's a shapono?" the twins ask together.

"A circular Indian dwelling made of palm leaves and wood. A whole bunch of families live in there together."

"How many?" Lowell asks.

"Oh, could be eighty to a hundred villagers under one roof. It's a communal home."

"Mom's not gonna like that," Roxanne predicts. "One bit."

"Well, she'll get used to it quickly. So let's not tell her about it now. This is a real learning tour."

The twins connect with nearly invisible peripheral glances.

The Yanomami visit is just for three days, he says, and then their tour will switch to a small, comfortably outfitted cruise ship on the upper Amazon with fifty-some anthropologists and ornithologists. He doesn't tell them that this trip is designed for experienced jungle explorers accustomed to intense heat, mosquitoes, uncomfortable conditions, and a limited choice of food.

It all sounds foreboding, even for Tobias, but the benefits for his whole family will far outweigh the sacrifices. He's game, and he's sure they'll all do just fine. They'll have a professional tour guide fluent in English, Spanish, and the Yanomami tribal language. What could possibly go wrong?

* * *

All their passports, sun hats, sunscreen, hiking boots, and waterproof ponchos are accumulating, ready to be packed. It's been two weeks since Martin reached out to him by e-mail, and Tobias finally responds, with ambivalent feelings. *I'd be happy to play with you again. When's good?*

Martin's reply pops right up, and they agree on Saturday morning. Tobias doesn't mention their meeting to his wife, who's still so incensed about Martin firing Tobias that she won't even talk to Valerie, and won't invite their children to the twins' twelfth birthday party coming up in May.

Tobias is nervous as he approaches Martin, already on the court, warming up and pretending not to see him. At a distance, Tobias pretends not to notice that he's been seen. As he draws closer, he's surprised that his friend can look so much older in only three months. They shake hands politely and skirt around a conversation, and then start hitting as soon as the basic, friendly phrases have been exchanged. They don't play a match, just hit for an hour or so, falling into their old rhythms as easily as jogging along a familiar path.

"Lunch?" Martin offers. They sit at a corner table in the club restaurant and eat salads and sandwiches, making small talk about their families.

When the bill arrives, there's an awkward pause. Tobias gives Martin a few seconds and then slips his credit card into the check holder. "How's business?" he asks.

Martin holds his reddish-gray hair off his face, revealing furrows on his forehead. "The truth is that I've fallen victim to this deep recession. It's the worst I've ever seen, and I frankly don't know how Boutique Properties will survive."

The busboy carries away their dishes. Tobias is cornered in a thicket of conflicting loyalties to his wife, his friend and former boss, and his sense of right and wrong in a life where everything has been upended. "How bad is it?"

Martin looks down while he talks. His chagrin is evident, and Tobias has to look away from him. The credit crisis is hitting his commercial real estate company especially hard, because Boutique Properties depends heavily on bridge financing from commercial and investment banks. The Dow has sunk to its lowest point, 6500. Now Martin can no longer rely on Morgan Stanley, Merrill Lynch, Bear Stearns, Lehman, or Black Rock.

Martin looks Tobias in the eye and admits in a hoarse voice, "Boutique Properties is going to fail unless I can get an outsize loan." His hands are shaking. "A *horrible* amount. Thirty million dollars." He's aware that Tobias's financial advisor, whom he recommended before firing him, will strongly advise his client against making this loan.

Tobias is nearly as shocked by this amount as he was when he won the lottery. He still can't wrap his head around such big figures. "There is simply no way I can extend you that kind of a loan."

Undaunted, Martin leans over the table to play his last card. "Would you consider a partnership?"

If Tobias has learned anything from his instant wealth, it's not to make any crucial decisions on the fly. He clasps his hands on the table and says, "We're leaving on vacation in a week or so. I'll tell you what I've decided just before that." They part politely.

Tobias gets on the phone with his financial advisor and tells him everything he knows about Boutique Properties Inc. The advisor launches a thorough and speedy due diligence process, poking into the company's debts, payroll, taxes, technology, market potential, business in the pipeline, and anything else he can see through the large and small ends of his telescope.

The afternoon before Tobias leaves for South America, he gets his advisor's report and recommendations and calls Martin. There's no time to meet in person. Tobias tells him, "I can help you if you agree to my terms." He feels awkward addressing his old friend so formally. "This is what I'll do. I'll become your financial partner. You give up a 30 percent stake in the business, and also put me on the board of directors. I'll see to it that Boutique Properties is funded until it springs back."

The other end of the phone is silent. Tobias waits, in pain for himself and his friend.

"Tobe. Thank you. You drive a hard bargain, but it's such a relief, you have no idea. Can I call you after you get back?"

Soothed to hear Martin calling him by his nickname, Tobias tells him to send an e-mail anytime. He'll bring his BlackBerry to South America. Who knows, maybe the Amazonians are wired?

❋ ❋ ❋

The Hillyers fly to Caracas, Venezuela, free of jet lag because Caracas clocks are only half an hour ahead of American Eastern time. They spend one night at the five-star Centro Lido Hotel, smack in the center of the city, just right for Carmela, whose only regret is that she can't go shopping because of the light-packing restriction.

Early the next morning, they board a small jet for Puerto Ayacucho, the capital of the state of Amazonas. The city is surrounded by rainforests and situated across the Orinoco River from the Colombian village of Casuarito. This isolated airport might as well be on a different planet from Caracas. Lowell, reading from his guide book, tells his family to keep an eye out for monkeys, tropical birds, tree frogs, and even jaguars.

Greeting them at the airport, their trilingual guide has the unlikely name Elvis Presley Gonzalez and the compact body and agile gait of a squirrel. "Just call me Elvis," he says, and hustles them all onto a rickety bus to the Orinoco River. Elvis helps them into his motorboat, which he navigates proficiently through little rapids and bigger ones. "Everyone put on your rain ponchos," he instructs. "Cameras under the ponchos." No one and nothing remains dry.

Tobias is in another world, finally savoring the adventure

that he missed so many years ago. He's got a field notebook ready for whatever anthropological observations he might be able to record in three days. The twins are excited, Simeon is speechless, and Carmela is clearly in distress but is not saying anything. Yet.

Elvis cuts the engine in a clearing, and they disembark into the heart of the remote jungle. With the motor off, they can hear birds calling and monkeys chattering. Instantly, fifteen or twenty naked Yanomami children swarm around them, laughing, pointing, all talking at the same time, arms wrapped around one another. The Hillyers are apparently the most bizarre objects of curiosity these children have ever seen. The stares they get at home for being lottery winners are nothing in comparison.

When Tobias climbs back into the boat to grab a suitcase, Elvis tells him to leave it for later.

"But all our things are in there," Carmela protests.

Elvis shakes his head. "No hotel check-in here. Anyway, they're not interested in your stuff," he reassures her. "This is what they want." He's lugging a heavy burlap sack crammed with useful items—machetes, axes, and aluminum pots, which he will give to the chief. "No photos," he orders. "I ask first." He guides Carmela, Tobias, Simeon, and the kids into the village, which comprises only a few huts and gardens and the shapono.

"There's going to be a dance tonight," Elvis announces. "For the hunt. You'll enjoy that."

Carmela isn't enjoying any of this, and would much rather attend a nice dinner–theater show than a tribal dance. Sweat is pouring from her forehead onto her plastic poncho, which she peels off. She glances anxiously at her children, on the verge of puberty at eleven going on twelve, and fascinated by the naked villagers. The women wear cotton strings tied between their nude, rounded breasts and around their backs, like pole dancers at a strip club. Lowell is riveted by their enormous brown nipples. Their pretty cotton waistbands are decorative, but barely cover the pubic area. Roxanne's eyes are drawn to the exposed penises of the men and adolescent boys, who have strings tied around their waists and attached to their stretched-out foreskins. This is a much more vivid sex education than Carmela had in mind.

If this isn't bad enough, Carmela, a health-conscious medical professional, is shocked that everyone here seems to be addicted to tobacco, even the children. They're all sucking it or chewing on it. She is nauseated by the smells, the heat, the humidity, and the cultural earthquake crashing in on her. If there were a bus going by in the jungle, she'd hop on it in no time, snatching her children away from these prehistoric savages and off to the nearest city.

Elvis walks them to one of the gardens, where some of the women are harvesting plantains, sweet potatoes, and corn. Others are in the shapono, roasting and preparing a variety of food yielding a strong mixture of odors—plantains, sugar cane, palm fruit, corn, wild honey, wild birds, crabs, and fish. "Wow, that's a lot of food," Lowell observes.

"That's not all," Elvis says. "They even eat insects and their larvae. And monkeys, armadillos, anteaters."

Carmela's nausea increases when they accompany some village men on a nearby fishing trip. The Yanomami drug their fish before catching them by soaking medicinal tree bark in the river until the fish get stoned. Then the women come along, scoop up the stupefied fish in baskets, and haul them home to smoke over the fire.

At nightfall, naked young girls perform a dance to promote a successful hunt the next day for the men. They have painted bodies and thin sticks like knitting needles poking through their faces. Tobias watches his brother ogling the shapely teenagers, wondering how Simeon has been coping with his sexual impulses all these years, and questioning whether his brother could somehow harbor secrets. Except for the incident at the workshop Simmy once attended, no other trysts have come to light.

"Where are we going to sleep?" Carmela wants to know. She sees the twins doing one of their imperceptible side glances.

"Right here." Elvis leads them inside the shapono, with its pungent odors of cooking and wet earth, and finds them a free area, where he hangs six coarse hammocks for all of them. Families group their hammocks anywhere they want within this circular shelter, he explains. They have no concept of privacy and don't build walls.

All family life goes on within the confines of this structure. Some scenes are heartwarming; Yanomami parents are very gentle and solicitous with their children. Tobias thought his twins were close, but they're American and have been brought up to respect boundaries. Yanomami siblings and playmates love one another and show it with affectionate, uninhibited gestures and hugs.

At a hearth not far from theirs, a newly betrothed couple is openly engaging in foreplay. The girl, no more than sixteen years old, is coyly smiling at the boy while vigorously jiggling his erect penis. The boy is lustily sucking on the girl's ripe breasts. Simeon watches with interest, his mouth slightly open. The twins are gaping at them, while everyone else in the shapono ignores them. Elvis confirms that the Yanomami don't try to hide their marital—or extramarital—relations.

It's midnight, and they're all exhausted. The Hillyers each lie down in a rickety hammock and try to sleep, but the Yanomami know nothing about keeping quiet so that others can sleep. In fact, they wake up and fall asleep as easily as house cats. Elvis says that you have to learn how to sleep through their talking, snoring, and crying babies.

At around one o'clock in the morning, a tribal elder stands in the center of the shapono and delivers a long, booming speech about hunting and fishing. No one hushes him. Maybe an hour later, a shaman under the influence of natural hallucinogens performs a prolonged mystical chant. Alarmed, Carmela stands between the children's hammocks. Elvis tells her not to worry and translates the speech and the chanting.

In spite of the never-ending conversations inside the shapono, they all doze off until about 3:00 AM, when a man at a nearby hearth leaps up, says a few words to anyone who might be listening, grabs an axe, and starts swinging it around overhead. Carmela screams and tries to cover her sleeping children with her body. Tobias jumps up and throws his arms around all of them.

"Go back to sleep," Elvis scolds. "He's only going out to chop some firewood." Indeed, percussive chopping sounds commence outside the shapono and continue for an hour or so. None of the Hillyers understand how anyone can sleep in this society.

Except for Tobias, who has filled only half a page in his field notebook, one night is all they can take. They thank Elvis Presley Gonzalez and give him a sizeable tip in American currency.

Carmela, hallucinating about a clean shower with soap, is counting the hours until she can return home. The rest of the family is looking forward to the next leg of their trip, as eco-tourists in the Amazon jungle.

"That was tough," Tobias admits. "But you're all going to love where we're going next," he promises.

## *Chapter 19*

They relax for two days at an international hotel in Lima, Peru. "Privacy! Running water! People wearing clothes!" Carmela exclaims on walking into their luxury suite.

Tobias shoots her a nasty look. "Don't rub it in. Other cultures are just as worthy as yours."

She ignores him and tells the kids to take showers. "Don't worry, Mom," Lowell says.

Aboard the Riverdream, an immaculate little cruise ship, Carmela greets other passengers with a hostess-worthy smile. The twins are thrilled to be sharing their own private cabin with Simeon. The ship's capacity is only seventy, staff and guests included, making for an intimate atmosphere.

Carmela unlatches her suitcase and stacks her clothes in the little bureau drawers. "This is perfect," she tells Tobias, who's busy with his new Nikon camera. She dips her hand into the suitcase pocket to grope around for anything left inside. "Ouch!" She whips her hand out. "Must be a safety pin in there or something."

Tobias is on his feet. That yelp of pain didn't sound right. He inspects her hand, and then shines a flashlight into the suitcase pocket. "Oh my God, a scorpion!" He throws open their cabin door to yell for help, knowing nothing about scorpions except that his wife might die from their venom.

One of the naturalists on board comes running and

scoops the scorpion into a bug cube. It's only an inch long, but dangerous enough to make Carmela's right thumb tingle. The poison is starting to do its work, and the captain barges into their room to rush her up the stairs to the ship's doctor.

"What's the matter with Mom?" Roxanne wants to know. No one has a good answer, so she follows the little group up the narrow steps, along with Lowell, Tobias, Simeon, and the naturalist. "Ew," she says, eying the bug cube.

The doctor examines Carmela's thumb, now visibly swollen, with the scorpion's stinger too deeply imbedded to extract. He applies a cold compress and checks her blood pressure and temperature, and then advises her to keep soaking her thumb in a glass of ice water for hours, until she goes to bed. He gives her anti-inflammatory medicine and pills for the pain, which he says will radiate from her thumb up to her elbow and beyond.

"The pain is not too bad," Carmela says, trying to be a good sport. She goes to dinner with her family, by which time she's become a celebrity. But between appetizers and the main course, the pain attacks her hand, crawls up her arm all the way to her shoulder, and doesn't let up. She swallows the pills. Back goes the thumb into the ice water. Not until midnight does the swelling go down some and the pain subside. She sleeps late the next morning, missing a canoe ride to admire turtles and giant river otters, but feeling much better.

It looks as if the vacation is saved. They take a bird-watching ride on an inflatable boat called a Zodiac, and they're all starting to recognize the most prevalent species. Parrots and parakeets fly far above in flocks so widespread and distant that they look like black pepper sprinkled in the clouds by a cosmic chef. Only when the birds fly near do they flaunt their iridescent green, gold, and blue.

Simeon's favorite birds are the hoatzins because they are big, comical-looking, and noisy. They gather on jungle tree limbs and call to their mates with a hissing screech that sounds like puffing bellows in a factory. Simmy can hear them long before he sees them. Their red eyes are framed by electric-blue skin, and their heads are crowned by four-inch crests of hot-pink spiky feathers that poke upward like a punk haircut.

Lowell looks them up in his bird book and tells Simeon, "When they're babies, they have claws on their wings. They can dive underwater before they learn to fly."

"Unbelievable," Simmy says. He's watching them hop clumsily from branch to branch like overweight, drunken, two-foot-long pigeons.

"They're smelly, too," Roxanne observes.

"That's because they use bacteria to digest plants in a special foregut chamber above their stomachs." Lowell is peering at them through the binoculars that his uncle gave to his father twenty years ago.

"Yuck," Roxanne comments on the hoatzins. Several oropendulas, her favorite birds, are hanging from trees inside long nests that look like sacks. They have pointed yellow bills, dark feathers, and bright yellow tails. They burble a complex song that sounds like drops of water dripping through the column of a long wooden flute and falling into the river.

Another day, while watching pink river dolphins on the Amazon tributaries, they're treated to an unexpected show. Five Dusky Tiki monkeys jump around on trees above their Zodiac. They have red markings on their backs, and all their underparts are red. A mother from a different monkey species passes by overhead with a cute little baby on her back. One by one, three of the Dusky Tikis cross the tributary above the Hillyers in the trees, cackling like a sitcom laugh track.

Their pilot says, "You're lucky—they're very rarely seen. They sleep in small groups all tangled by their tails, and untangle themselves in the morning." Carmela is about to compare them to the Yanomami natives, but decides not to, considering that this vacation is turning out fine after all.

They go on a nighttime outing with flashlights in a slow,

quiet motorboat, and spot a ladder-tailed nightjar, three great potoos, a caiman eighteen inches long, and a boa constrictor four feet long. The creatures' eyes shine back at them like pairs of headlights in the deep rainforest.

❁ ❁ ❁

The last day's featured activity is a leisurely afternoon jungle hike. Carmela wants to sit it out, but Tobias persuades her to come along. "It's our last day. Come on, Mel, it'll be fun."

About thirty hikers travel to the trailhead in Zodiacs, accompanied by three staff members, who promise an easy walk on a cleared trail. They disembark at a little cluster of jungle houses and trek up the slippery, muddy slope to the hiking path. Most of the tourists are wearing sturdy hiking boots, but a few have on little white sneakers with smooth soles. Looking back on the adventure a month later, Tobias has no idea how these people made it through the ensuing ordeal.

The original plan is to take an out-and-back route: one hour in, one hour out, and beat the tropical sunset at 6:00 PM. It's already ten minutes to four. But a few loud-mouthed tourists would much rather do a loop hike than double back on the same route, and their inexperienced leaders give in. The hikers will emerge from the jungle on the other end of the village from where they're starting. A local villager guiding them estimates that it will take less than two hours to cover the U-shaped course. But in contrast to the clumsy travelers, he glides through the dense jungle like a cat, making quick and skillful movements.

Carmela is sweating from more than the tropical steam. "What if we can't find our way out before dark? What if something happens to the kids?" Her fellow tourists laugh off her worries.

The hike is tough going from the beginning, with ascents and descents on the slimy, soaked, narrow trail. Often, the

Indian guide stops to chop vegetation out of the hikers' way with his machete. He speaks Spanish only, but it is very clear, and Tobias can understand all of it.

One of the leaders cautions the hikers not to hold onto trees in the jungle. Some are covered with zillions of sharp, spiny thorns; others are spiked with long jiggers like porcupine quills. And then there are trees of horror, infested with carnivorous ants. You do not want to have anything to do with those ants, the leader warns. You can't see them on the tree; they attack like bloodthirsty soldiers only if you touch the trunk.

The tourists arrive at a stream too wide and too deep to cross, and their leaders fashion a bridge from a fallen tree trunk. One by one, the hikers cross this log, while grasping dead branches stuck into the creek for support, like a fence made of stationary crutches.

At the next stream, the leaders craft another jagged fence from dead tree limbs, stabbing them into the creek bed next to the existing primitive bridge. The travelers slog on, but there are three more makeshift bridges to cross, each longer than the one before.

The group has begun disintegrating into clusters. Some people lag behind, apprehensive about crossing the streams. Others veer off the path to take pictures of every intricate leaf, every captivating flower. It's still daylight, and they feel that they have lots of time. Back home in the States or in Europe, the curtain of twilight falls gradually, as fading daylight gives way to urban electricity.

By now, Tobias fears that they're not going to emerge from the torrid jungle before nightfall. They're in too far to turn back, and he wonders whether their Indian guide really knows his way out. Only the leaders have flashlights. Tobias has never been in the rainforest before, but he knows that darkness in the jungle is black dark, the darkest dark in the world. Under the rainforest canopy, there's neither starlight, nor moonlight, nor the lights of civilization, now so far away as to be inconceivable. Darkness-loving predators will come out to stalk and attack their prey.

It's a quarter past five, only forty-five minutes until sunset. The hikers stop at a river at least thirty feet wide and way over their heads in depth. A six-inch-wide footbridge is completely submerged for its last eight feet on the opposite shore, where the water is above knee level and might harbor piranhas. Everybody is weighed down by backpacks, hiking boots, and long pants and shirts.

Abruptly, the leaders announce a decision for each hiker to make individually: either cross the perilous bridge at their own risk and wade through the water at the end, or wait for a Zodiac pilot to try to find them via directions on mobile phones.

The travelers consume some of the waning daylight deliberating over their decisions. In the end, no one stays behind, and no Zodiacs come to the rescue.

The handful of opinionated hikers who had been most opposed to doing an out-and-back, safe hike are now beginning to panic. A plump boy of eleven, the only child on the hike besides the twins, whimpers to his mother that he'll get an asthma attack and drop dead in the jungle. Many of the hikers procrastinate for long moments before getting the nerve to cross, wasting even more of the ebbing daylight.

The log that constitutes the bridge is slathered with mud the consistency of peanut butter from end to end. Worse still, it's not level with the ground; it's slanting downward. Bravely, Simeon steps onto the log, holding Roxanne firmly by the hand. She extends her other hand behind to Lowell, who holds his free hand out to balance. Not breathing, Tobias and Carmela watch their family edge across, feet sideways, inch by inch, and slog through the water on the other side, grasping at mud and roots to lug themselves up to the shore, filthy and drenched.

It's getting dark. The few who have crossed to the other side are hard to distinguish on the murky riverbank. Trembling, Carmela grips Tobias's hand, and they begin to cross. Halfway over, her foot slips, and she wavers, yanks his hand, and clutches a sapling growing in the river.

The tree is crawling with man-eating ants that tear into her hand, drawing blood, and she screams like someone undergoing an amputation without anesthesia, nearly toppling and pulling Tobias down with her. They're still holding hands and manage to right themselves on the slippery log by sheer force of will, exchanging a terrified glance of determination as they wave and wobble in opposite directions.

At the submerged end of the log, they plod through the water, slipping into holes in the bottom, and climb up the steep, sloshy bank. Groaning, Carmela grabs the towel from around her neck to wipe away the carnivorous ants that are picnicking on her flesh, but they latch onto the towel, too, and wherever she rubs, they find new places to transfer themselves to her skin. Tobias, two other hikers, and the native guide clean her off with three new towels, while blood trickles from her painful wounds.

It's too dark to see more than three feet ahead, and the path on the dim jungle floor has grown invisible. Their guide says that it's only five minutes back to the village, but it takes the longest half hour of the hike to come within shouting distance of the little houses. The hikers can scarcely see where they're going, and their surefooted guide keeps vanishing ahead into obscurity. Everyone's eyes sting from sweat; those wearing fogged-up glasses, like Simeon, might as well be blind. Tobias's towel is sopping and useless; Carmela's was abandoned in the jungle, swarming with carnivorous ants still feasting on her dried blood.

Now the leaders up ahead inexplicably disappear into the shadowy jungle; the hikers can neither see them nor hear them. They're no longer following a trail, but are flailing through a great many twists and turns, struggling through creeping vines to find their way out. Tobias shouts for those up ahead with flashlights to stop and wait, but they don't. Once or twice they call back, but the Hillyers can't see them.

At last, the native guide returns, promising that they'll reach the edge of the jungle in three minutes, which turns out to be fifteen minutes. Timekeeping is as meaningless to this man as counting is to the Yanomami. Trying a different approach, Tobias, in perfectly acceptable Spanish, asks the guide where their boats are. "Right nearby," he answers, and he sounds convinced; only then does Tobias believe that this nightmare will come to an end.

Saturated by perspiration and jungle steam, they lower themselves perilously down a slippery, muddy slope to the waiting Zodiacs. Back at the Riverdream, they hang their mud-soaked hiking clothes on rails outside their cabins. Their hiking boots are mud-coated beyond recognition.

❊ ❊ ❊

They leave for home the next day, weighed down by luggage made heavy by all those wet clothes and boots bundled into garbage bags. At the airport, two hours early, they slump into plastic chairs, sagging from exhaustion, except for Tobias, who's elated that his family had a great adventure, and they're all alive, and they have been forever altered by the experience, because they will never see the world the same way again.

Carmela is in a state of shock, comforted that everybody survived, but not sure that her marriage will. She has been tricked into this major episode of discomfort, to say the least, and into risking the lives of her whole family, to say the worst. She's talking as little as possible to Tobias, not wanting to start an argument on an international flight with nowhere to turn to get away from each other.

Tobias walks to the men's room with a silly smile on his face, leaving his backpack open on the seat next to his wife.

When his BlackBerry dings an e-mail announcement, she looks at it casually, but something catches her eye, and she lifts it out of the bag.

The new message is from Martin Scanlon, and its subject line reads *Accepting your terms.* She sits up, checks what her family is doing. The twins are slouching in adjacent chairs, Lowell reading and Roxanne writing in her journal. Simeon is trying to sketch a hoatzin on his drawing pad. Carmela watches Tobias come out of the men's room and head to the snack counter, where the line is long enough to give her time to open his e-mail message and read, *Tobe, how can I ever thank you enough. Hope you're all well and having a GREAT time. I accept all your terms for our financial partnership and appreciate your generous offer to keep B.P. Inc. alive for the duration. Will sign all your docs in person whenever good for you. Available any time. A million thanks. See you after you return, safe trip. Martin.*

She reads it again, then clicks Mark Unopened on the menu and replaces the BlackBerry in the backpack before Tobias returns with orange juice and muffins for all of them. She won't say anything about his deception until she's had time to stew over it.

Too angry to eat, she excuses herself and goes for a walk through the food court. Stopping at a gate with a lot of empty seats, she takes out her iPhone and calls Jacques at the gym. She needs someone to talk to about all this, or she will lose her mind, and why not him?

Jacques is warm and friendly as always, listening sympathetically to her jungle tales, and welcoming her back to civilization. They make an appointment for training for the next evening.

It's a long way home without talking. Tobias assumes that Carmela is processing everything that happened on the trip, and he lets her be. When they arrive home, they open their suitcases in the driveway, still not talking, and drag all the heavy plastic bags with wet clothes and boots into the garage, where they can wait until the next day.

Carmela listens to their voice mail while the others go out to finish unpacking the car. There's a message from Elsebeth, thanking Tobias for his generous loan, and giving him some statistics on how business is doing. Another message is from Aunt Joyce, who says there might be hope to recover some of her money from the Madoff assets, in which case she'll start paying back her loan even before her business picks up. Carmela leaves the messages undeleted and hangs up the phone before Tobias comes inside.

It's April, and the house is chilly, the thermostat set low while they were gone, but she is sweating as profusely as she was in the jungle. Ever since winning the lottery, Tobias has been careening completely out of control, and these latest secrets are infuriating. Carmela's iPhone is out of juice. She sets it in its charger and leaves a message for Jacques from the phone in her bedroom. "Be sure to call me back on my cell phone," she cautions.

The kids are in bed and Carmela is in the shower when the home phone rings. Lunging for it, Tobias sees the name of his wife's gym on the caller ID and lets the voice mail get it. Her coach seems to be taking his time with the message he's leaving. Something about his wife's preoccupation with her personal trainer doesn't feel right. She goes to the gym with makeup on, a nice hairstyle, and matching clothes.

When the call light shuts off, Tobias listens to the message: "Hi, Mel, darling. Nice of you to call again. Rough time you had there with those ants and scorpions, eh? A little massage will make those lovely arms and legs and other nice parts feel a lot better, no? That jungle monster husband of yours should be arrested for putting you through all that. Can't wait to see you tomorrow. Good-night, sweetheart." There's a kissing sound.

Furious enough to break everything in the room, Tobias

can't imagine how his wife could be so stupid as to let her affair break out in the open like this, when their children might pick up the phone. Putting two and two together, he guesses that Carmela sneaked a call from the home phone to Jacques, who returned it to the calling number instead of to her cell phone. On their unlisted home phone, the greeting, in Carmela's voice, simply asks callers to leave a message. Loverboy Jacques might well have thought he'd reached her private number. Tobias deletes the message and secludes himself in his basement office until his family has gone to sleep.

❋ ❋ ❋

It's sunny the next morning. The kids go to school, Simeon goes to work, and Tobias and Carmela hose off all the filthy hiking clothes in their driveway before loading them into the washing machine. They soak the five pairs of boots, rinse them in soapy water, and leave them to dry in the sun on the back porch.

His wife won't look him in the eye, and he's got to find out how far gone she is with this Jacques creep. "How are your hands and arms?" he asks, noting that her ant bites seem to have left no marks.

"Fine." She turns her back to drape a plastic poncho over the porch rail.

"Sorry about what happened to you," he offers. He'll approach slowly, and then cut to the chase.

"About which thing that happened to me?" She pulls her long hair away from her face and bundles it into a ponytail behind her neck, giving herself a severe look.

"The scorpion, the hike—"

"Oh, is that all? And what about the half million dollars you lent to Aunt Joyce that we're not getting back?" She crosses her arms and squints at him in the sunlight.

She's spying on him, and he has been violated. He grits his teeth and tries to keep his voice down. "It's not her fault that her funds were tied up with Madoff. She'll pay it all back as soon as she can."

"Oh, really? Then what about Elsebeth? Now you're supporting the Book Trove, too?"

This is too much, especially considering her infidelity, if she actually has been unfaithful. He holds the door open and tells her, "We'll finish this inside." The guy next door is taking out his recycling and staring at them over his fence. Tobias slams the door behind them. "Elsebeth provided our bread and butter for all those years. And she gave Simmy a job and a career. It's none of your business when I give her the help she needs."

She whirls to face him and yells, "*You* were the one who made the rules. The rules that we were going to do everything together, as a team. Not make decisions separately."

He clenches his jaw. "Don't push me around. You're so controlling that I knew, even if I told you the truth about the mess they were in—Elsebeth and Aunt Joyce—you still wouldn't see the need to help them. Even if it wasn't their fault at all. There's no reason both of us had to be concerned about what for us, in this situation, is such an insignificant amount."

"You're joking. Insignificant amount." It's a good thing no one else is at home. She shouts at full volume, "You call that an insignificant amount, what you're doing behind my back with Martin? Martin, who fired you, and now he comes crying, and you fall for it."

He slumps onto the steps that lead up to the living room and, for the first time, envisions a future with a broken-up family. There is no way he's going to continue to live with a woman who has become so corrupted by wealth that she is no longer the kind and loving person he fell in love with so many years ago.

She waits, arms crossed in front of her, in contempt for his lying and deception. He's going to sit there all day if she doesn't goad him on. "Secrets," she spits. "Ever since it happened..." They both know what "it" means. "Ever since it happened, we're not a couple anymore. You've been racking up secrets. Lies and secrets and—"

Tobias uncurls himself from the steps and stands, glowering down at her with the most hateful look she has ever seen on his face. "I'm not the only one keeping secrets."

Panicked, she steps back. "What do you mean?"

"That creep. That gym rat. Whatever his name is, Jack."

"Jacques," she corrects him.

He charges at her, stopping two inches in front of her. "I don't care what his fucking name is. You're having a fucking affair with him."

"No, I'm not," she protests, crying and shrinking back from him. "It's nothing but flirtation, an innocent release from all your lying and sneaking. You say these people will pay you back. How do I know that?"

Stepping up to her again, he screams, "You say you're not having an affair. How do I know that? How can I believe anything you say?"

She's crying now. "It's just a friendship," she says. "We never crossed the line."

"Oh, no? You know when a male-female friendship crosses the line? It's when that bastard knows more about *me* than I know about *him*."

"There's a good reason for that." She's hysterical now. "And there's one more thing that he's going to know about you. That you're an unfit husband. And an unfit father. I want a divorce."

# *Chapter 20*

It's the morning after the twins' twelfth birthday party, which the Scanlons' children didn't attend for the first time. The twins know only that their father bailed out Martin's company and their mother didn't want him to.

The party had a Hawaiian theme, every table with its own miniature hibachi—a celebration much fancier than Tobias had wanted, but he wasn't involved in the party planning. The invitations requested no gifts, which some guests brought anyway. Tobias suggested giving all the unopened presents to charity, but the kids pointed out that their friends would be upset if they did.

"Where's your mom?" Simeon is holding a carton of orange juice upside down and shaking it. "And Roxy?"

"Mom left already." Lowell sets a stack of four cereal bowls on the table. "Roxy's still fixing her hair." He listens at the basement stairs, and then puts one of the bowls back in the cabinet.

Roxanne comes into the kitchen dressed in her usual school outfit—tight jeans and layered shirts, a careless chic that Tobias calls "twelve going on sixteen." She slides her perfect little body into her chair, glances at her father's empty seat, looks at her twin brother, who shakes his head, and slumps. She shakes enough Raisin Nut Bran into her bowl to feed a robin.

Simeon eats his usual amount, but Lowell isn't hungry. "I don't feel so good," he says. He's pale and listless.

"Better go tell your dad," Simeon says.

Lowell tenses his eyebrows, opens the basement door, and descends into his father's home office, lately his apartment, where he's been sleeping on the sofa for two weeks.

"What hurts?" Tobias hugs Lowell, now up to his shoulder, and ruffles his wavy auburn hair.

"My head, my eyes, arms, legs. Mostly my head."

Tobias can list the same complaints, but they're not due to some virus. He walks Lowell up to his bedroom and does the nursey sorts of things that ordinarily Carmela would do. She's going to work earlier than usual these days. He leaves Lowell in bed with a slight fever and the novel he's reading for class, and offers to drive Roxanne to school in place of the security guard.

"Nah, Dad, it's OK. The kids will pick on me for that," she says.

Taking Roxy to school isn't simply driving there and letting her out of the car. It requires walking her out of the house, never leaving her side, parking the car a couple of blocks from school, and accompanying her all the way up to the schoolhouse door. This would be enough to brand his daughter a pariah for the remainder of sixth grade. The security guard, at least, is cool with his smart gray uniform and a cap with a badge on it, a sort of secret service agent for the progeny of lottery winners. The twins have favorites among the three or four guys who rotate in this job, and they like the latest one best, Tom Frost, a bouncy guy with blond hair who's built like a gymnast. He tells jokes and has funny nicknames for them.

Tobias drives Simeon to work at the Book Trove and returns home to stay with Lowell, who insists he doesn't need a baby-sitter, but worrying about Lowell all day would distract him from his classes, and one day won't make a difference. He'll read ahead and get his notes online.

Except for the chaos in his marriage, he's living by doing what he wants and becoming more and more precise about it, down to his PhD thesis, titled "Stories of Living and Losing: Dynamic Processes of Identification among the Yanomami of Venezuela."

Not having to earn his living, and away from the hubbub of the business world, he's proud that he's always done what he believed in, and still does. His credo is that people should live as they choose to, and not by accident.

❁ ❁ ❁

At a quarter to three, Tobias unlocks the front door and disarms the ADT system, ready for Roxanne to come hopping out of the security car and into the house. The service delivers the kids home like clockwork, because they have an early-dismissal arrangement to skip afternoon homeroom and get out the door before the mob of middle-schoolers makes it difficult to monitor them. And this vigilance is imperative, considering the handful of vague kidnapping threats they've received over the months since they won the lottery.

The security car is late, and it's never been late before. Tobias looks at his watch and cross-checks the time with his cell phone. It's not raining, it's not the day before a holiday, and there's no reason for the car to be late. Lowell, still pale, lopes downstairs with his hair disheveled. "Where's Roxy?"

"I don't know." Tobias starts pacing. He makes himself wait one full minute before calling the security company. The dispatcher says that he hasn't heard anything, that they should be there right now; he'll radio the car and check. He calls back to say that there's no answer from the car.

"What do you mean, no answer?" Tobias rasps into the phone. He can't control his voice. "Can't you trace it? That's my daughter in there."

Another attempted call to the car, another noncommittal reply from the security dispatcher.

"Dad, call the police. Dad." Lowell pleads.

Tobias calls 911. "What's your emergency?" a crisp female voice asks.

"My daughter. She didn't come home from school. The security service doesn't know where the car is."

"Sir? Please explain."

He starts over again, words falling on top of each other, wasting precious seconds explaining his crazy life. He tells the officer he's the lottery winner and his daughter is in danger. He's barely hung up the phone when two police officers appear on his front porch—walkie-talkies crackling, guns in their holsters—and come inside to get all the details: colors of clothing, what she was carrying, how tall, how much she weighs. "Long, straight black hair," Tobias says. "Golden-brown eyes. Blue jeans, a light jacket. Two or three shirts in layers. I don't remember the colors."

Lowell squints at the ceiling. "Lavender, teal blue, and rose pink," he lists.

Tobias and Lowell wrack their brains to provide every detail, down to the brand of purse Roxanne had slung over her shoulder. The description is so vivid that Tobias can see her standing in front of him as if she had come home as usual on any other weekday. But in his heart, he feels that he will never see his beautiful daughter again.

❋ ❋ ❋

At the end of her 7:00-to-3:00 shift, Carmela goes straight to the gym, rather than checking in at home first. Tobias is usually back from the university by the time the kids return from school. She takes off her coat and races up the steps to the women's locker room, pleased that she is barely winded at the top of two flights. Before turning the corner near the personal training suite, she hears his voice.

"Helene." He's calling to someone who answers in sweet tones. "Hello, darling. I don't say this to everyone," he confides in a low voice. "The change in your physique is just *dynamic* since you've been working out."

Against her judgment, Carmela peers around the corner. The plump woman, Helene, is about the size she was before starting her fitness regimen. Jacques is holding her at arm's length, studying her face and making her blush. "A beautiful face in a beautiful body."

Helene throws her arms around him, and they rotate enough for Jacques to see Carmela spying on him. Without stopping to put her coat back on, Carmela runs down the two flights of stairs to the parking lot, hot tears of shame coursing down her cheeks and neck and smudging her white uniform.

As she backs out of her parking space, her new Bluetooth device starts ringing. Fumbling to find the pickup switch for this technology that she hasn't yet mastered, she answers and hears a panicked Tobias, to whom she hasn't spoken in two weeks.

"It's Roxanne. She didn't come home from school. The police are here. Lowell stayed home sick. She went alone. She never came back."

❁ ❁ ❁

Simeon is working by himself in the Fine Arts section, shelving newly arrived books about painters of the twenty-first century, when Elsebeth comes to him with the terrifying news and offers to drive him home. "Roxanne?" he asks. "She's all right. I saw her this morning."

"She hasn't come home. Your brother called school, and they said she never got there. It was all a terrible mistake. Lowell called the attendance office in the morning to say he was sick and couldn't come to school. Whoever took his call put both Hillyer twins on the absentee list. So no one called home to report that Roxanne didn't show up. The security guard is missing. They can't reach him, and they can't track his car. There's an AMBER Alert out for Roxanne."

As they step up to the house, one of the police officers bars their way. "Names?" he asks. They have to show IDs before he lets them in. Three police cars are idling in the driveway, with blue lights flashing and the dire message barking over their speakers. Tobias identifies his brother and Elsebeth for the police and admits them to a real-life scene of a family in despair.

Carmela, who just arrived, is screaming, "You mean it's since this morning, and only now you call the police?"

"Mom, we didn't know." Lowell, crying uncontrollably, has never spent a day apart from his sister.

"Ma'am, we have a five-state alert out for her: New Jersey, New York, Pennsylvania, Connecticut, and Massachusetts. Plus the AMBER Alert that covers the whole country."

The phone rings, and Tobias dives for it. "I have Roxy here with me," an unctuous voice purrs. Tobias holds the phone out to one of the officers, who listens.

"It's a prank," the officer says, but he puts a trace on the caller anyway.

"We have an unlisted phone number," Tobias says.

"Those numbers have a way of getting around in spite of that."

A police detective comes inside to collect some of Roxy's personal items. He says "*belonged* to her," not "*belong*," which starts Carmela weeping. Lowell leads the detective to his sister's room and hands him clothes, a scarf, her favorite pen, her hairbrush, and her toothbrush. The detective packs them into separate Ziploc bags and stashes them in his satchel.

It's four in the afternoon. One of the officers turns on the local TV news to check whether the AMBER Alert is doing its work. A woman with a concerned expression reports, "Twelve-year-old Roxanne Hillyer was abducted this morning on her way to school in Woodrock by a professional security guard." At the top of the screen, Roxanne smiles in her sixth-grade school portrait. At the bottom, under the caption "Wanted," there's a photo of Tom Frost. "She has long black hair and light-brown eyes. Roxanne is four feet, ten inches tall and weighs eighty-six pounds. She was wearing blue jeans and a tangerine-colored jacket. Anyone with information, please call—"

"Dad, what if they can't find her?"

Tobias can't answer. Simeon says, "They'll find her. Come on, Lowey." They huddle together on the couch, Lowell crying into his uncle's chest, Simeon's arm around his nephew's shoulders.

"Does she have a phone?" an officer asks.

"Yes," Tobias answers. It went against the way he likes to do things, but he gave in when Carmela equipped both children with cell phones to use in case of emergency. Of course, the definition of "emergency" expanded to include calls and texts to their friends about anything at all, even the most humdrum activities.

Tobias would give anything to return to a humdrum life, where his greatest concern would be the commuter train arriving late at the station, or one of the kids needing eyeglasses, or imperfect school report cards. This horror cannot be real—now he understands the terrifying scenes on television when parents of kidnapped children scream "No!" as if saying the word would negate the tragedy.

Carmela gets on the phone, calling down through her list of sixth-grade parents, asking everybody who answers if they know anything, but one of the officers stops her. "We're on it," he reassures her. "We have to leave all lines open."

Dinnertime comes and goes. No one eats. In a speeding car, Roxanne could already be several states away. She could be out in the woods with the security guy, who's surely a child molester. She could be ruined, traumatized, lost forever. She could be on a plane with a forged passport. She could be dead. Tobias cannot contain himself. He paces around the room and out on the porch in endless circles, like a rabid, demented animal trying to escape the misery occupying its core.

Someone turns on the living room lights and draws the drapes. Police officers and detectives come and go. They discover that the missing security guard, Tom Frost, has police records in three states under a variety of pseudonyms corresponding to different hairstyles and hair colors. But now is not the time to ask how a security service could have hired a seasoned con man to escort children to school.

Tom Frost watches his victim through the sides of his eyes. He has tethered her to the door grip with a pair of handcuffs, even though she's a quiet one, polite even, who hasn't made any trouble. So far. The last girl was an annoying little whiner who didn't let up until he smothered her after he'd had his pleasure with her. He'd disposed of her body somewhere in the woods outside Wilkes-Barre.

There's no chance of this one jumping out in the middle of the PA Turnpike, where he's slogging through heavy morning traffic. He talks to her now and then, but she's not answering, just gazing out the window like a child on a family trip, holding her purse and her backpack full of school supplies, minus her cell phone, which he confiscated early on, as soon as they got on the highway, and hurled out the window into the bushes. At first, she'd wanted to know where they were going, and he said there was a traffic detour; by the time she'd caught on, it was too late.

The miles roll by while day turns into night. A three-car accident slows them down, and he stops once to let her pee by the side of the road behind the trees, holding her by the handcuffs all the time. While he's driving, he eats potato chips, but doesn't offer her anything. They cross the Pennsylvania border and continue west on the Turnpike until they finally get off at one of the Pittsburgh exits in a place called Monroeville.

Tired and bleary-eyed, Frost cruises along a hideous commercial highway that looks like any other road in the dreary megalopolis, pulling in at a motel that's missing lightbulbs in a sign reading "COMFOR EST Cable TV AC." He locks Roxanne's free wrist to the opposite door grip with a second pair of handcuffs and leaves her in the car while he checks in, and then drives around back to their room, where there's no outside light and apparently few other guests. Frost takes one cuff off Roxanne and pulls her to the door by the other. He unlocks the door and throws his jacket and duffel bag on the double bed, tethers her to the bedpost, and makes it into the bathroom just in time, slamming the door behind him.

In a passion to survive, Roxanne digs into the man's jacket pocket with her free hand, pulls out his cell phone, and sends a panicked text message to Lowell: *monroevill pa comfort rest mtl*

The man flushes the toilet and splashes his red eyes with cold water, rinses out his mouth, dries his face, throws the towel on the floor, and steps into the bedroom to claim his prize.

❁ ❁ ❁

In Woodrock, a text message flashes on Lowell's cell phone. "It's Roxy, she's alive!" he yells. The one policeman remaining in their house grabs the phone from Lowell, and the latest technology for tracking pedophiles lurches into action like a modern, well-equipped emergency room. Within ten minutes, the local police in Monroeville, Pennsylvania, are swarming around the motel with their headlights off. An officer shows the motel clerk a photo of Tom Frost, and the clerk points out the room he just rented to a man resembling the photo.

Four cops locate the room around back and force the door open. Three cops behind them jump in and tackle the guy, whatever his real name is, before he has time to take Roxanne hostage. He still has his pants on. They push and drag him out of the room and shove him into a waiting police car, which speeds away with sirens howling and lights flashing. The state police screech into the parking lot right behind the local police cars.

A policewoman named Leonora covers Roxanne, trembling in her underwear, in a bath towel, and bundles her like a baby, holding her and rocking her. She's so small and light. She's wearing a training bra, but the buds on her chest are nowhere near womanhood. For the first time today, Roxanne cries, a high-pitched, keening sound, like a dirge for a dead person, or a wail for her broken childhood. Leonora holds her tighter, stroking her tangled hair. "You're all right, now, baby. You're going home. Everything's gonna be all right now."

In the living room in Woodrock, more officers arrive. "They got her!" one of them shouts. No one dares to believe him until they hear Roxy's voice themselves.

Leonora takes Roxanne into the motel bathroom and sponges her face, helps her into her clothes, combs her hair. From the back seat of a police car, on the way to the Monroeville police station, Roxanne calls home. Carmela answers on the first half ring. "Mommy!" Roxanne cries.

Carmela can only ask, "Are you OK, baby?" and then presses the speaker-phone switch. The whole family is talking to her at once, savoring the sound of her little-girl's voice. She talks to them on the policewoman's cell phone until its batteries run low. Leonora sits in the back seat with Roxanne all the way home, holding her close.

When she arrives home at two in the morning, everyone is still in the living room, including Elsebeth. Leonora walks Roxanne out of the car, hand in hand, and the family converges on them. They're making a huge scene right in the front yard, but no one cares. Like a giant centipede, Roxanne and all her family step together into the house, where everyone is crying at the same time. Lowell and his twin sister wind their arms together as they did when they were toddlers and kindergartners, part of a unit, not letting go until they absolutely had to.

After all the forms are filled out and all the relatives called, the police officers leave. Roxanne hugs and kisses Leonora, who gives her a card with her phone number.

Simeon collapses on the couch with Roxanne next to him and Lowell on her other side. Lowell whispers, "Rox. Did he do anything?"

"He stuck his tongue in my mouth and swished it around my throat," she whispers back. "He was repulsive. Disgusting."

"Oh, Roxy." Simeon flings his arm around her and pulls her to his chest. Lowell links arms with her and leans back into the cushions. They all close their eyes and doze off, pressed together with no space between them.

Tobias gets a blanket from upstairs and spreads it over them. He lets them sleep while he goes around, turning off most of the lights. Carmela sits in a chair facing the couch, unable to take her eyes off her daughter. She pads over in her white stockings and kisses Roxy on the forehead. Simeon's rectangular glasses are slipping down his nose. Carmela gently removes them with both hands and sets them on the coffee table.

When she turns around in the semidarkness, Tobias is standing there in his socks with his arms open. She falls into them, and they cry together about how close they came to losing what no money can ever restore.

"I'm sorry," Carmela says.

"I'm sorry, too." Over his wife's shoulder, he watches his sleeping family. They stand there silently for five minutes, maybe more. "Mel. Where do we go from here?" he asks softly.

"Away. Far away."

"We start over," Tobias tells his wife.

"Yes. We start over."

# book four

# *Chapter 21*

Even though his daughter is safe, right there in the room with him, Tobias sits there replaying the rescue scene over and over, torturing himself about what almost happened. What if Tom Frost hadn't gone to the bathroom? Or what if he'd brought his cell phone into the bathroom with him, or what if its battery had died? What if Roxy hadn't been able to reach his jacket from where she was handcuffed to the bed frame? What if her text message hadn't come through? What if all these unpredictable events hadn't turned out exactly as they did, enabling her to escape from hell?

It's 8:00 on Tuesday morning, and none of them have slept in a bed since Sunday night. Carmela is dozing in an easy chair facing the sectional sofa, where the twins and Simeon remain bunched together. Tobias, in the L of the sofa, is drifting in and out of sleep and obsessing about their uncertain future. They've got to get out of this town, out of this state. With the Internet, there's no anonymity anymore, but changing the air would revive the whole family.

Hamlet and Portia, enjoying all this company, keep stepping over the four people on the couch until they all wake up. It goes without saying that no one is going to school or to work today. They all keep touching and hugging Roxanne, confirming that she's really there and not a phantom.

After they've all showered and eaten breakfast, they lie

down in their real beds. Tobias and Carmela are together after two weeks of silence, but their sense of relief is so overpowering that they're wide awake, and so is Simeon. Carmela checks on the twins, sleeping soundly in their own rooms. She closes their bedroom doors quietly and creeps downstairs. Tobias makes coffee, and the three of them sit around the kitchen table, drinking it.

"I think we should move away," Tobias begins.

"Definitely," Carmela says. "And get rid of that security service right now. I'll call them."

"Absolutely. Well, they're in the hands of the police now, anyway." Tobias sips. "Let's homeschool the kids until we move. Keep them safe at home. We can hire some tutors and—"

"No, that's not how it works." Sliding into her professional role, Carmela says that Roxanne needs therapy, the sooner the better. She could develop post-traumatic stress disorder, even though the symptoms might not show up immediately. "I know someone good who can work with her, a behavioral therapist who specializes in anxiety disorders; her name is—"

"No, no, you crazy? How can she go back to school? She'd be so scared."

The last thing Carmela wants is to start another quarrel, especially with Simeon there, just sipping and listening. You can never tell what's going on in his mind. "It's best to let her rest today and go back to school tomorrow," she says quietly. "If you don't do that, you reinforce phobic behaviors that might start up anytime. No homeschooling. She has to resume her daily activities as soon as possible. Any negative feelings she has, she can report to her therapist."

Tobias looks out the window, where bright-red cardinals and other birds of spring are flying. He hates the idea of kids going to psychiatrists, so quick to medicate them into zombies instead of really solving their problems. "Won't she do fine with all the love she's getting from the family?"

Calmly, Carmela explains that because Roxanne's kidnapping was so far outside the realm of normal human experience, the loving family circle won't suffice. "I'd like to call her now. Dr. Nadine Appleby. Get an appointment today, let her see Roxanne alone, and then later with Lowell."

"We should ask Roxy what she wants to do," Tobias says. "It's her life. And she's the one who would have to face all those kids gossiping about her."

Simeon puts down his coffee cup and snaps, "No. Don't ask her."

Surprised, Tobias asks his brother, "Well, what do you think we should do?"

"She just wants to be a normal kid." Simeon pushes his glasses up his nose. "Go to school. Be like before."

Tobias relents, feeling helpless, having no experience dealing with a prepubescent daughter who was kidnapped by a pedophile and one inch away from being raped and murdered.

❁ ❁ ❁

Because Dr. Appleby is her colleague, Carmela gets an appointment and takes Roxanne to her office the same afternoon, bringing Lowell along. He joins in the session after one hour, and both kids are in good spirits afterward. Without discussing what went on behind the closed door, Carmela takes them shopping for shoes. They're both having a growth spurt, and it's a good excuse to spend time doing something normal.

They come home after all this and hold a family meeting, sitting around the living room. "We've just been through a terrible ordeal," Tobias starts. "Mom and I have some ideas about what to do next. First, Roxy. How was Dr. Appleby?"

"She's really nice," Roxanne says. She looks well-rested, having slept most of the morning. "I'm going to see her twice a week. She said I can call her anytime. And that I need to go back to school."

"You OK about that?" Carmela asks.

"I guess so. The kids are gonna stare at me like crazy. They already do anyway."

Lowell nods his head. "It's like we have stripes or something. They're always watching us. Even if we can't hear what they're saying, we know they're talking about us."

"Dad and I are making plans for all of us to move away," Carmela says. "Far away. As soon as we can find a new home somewhere. A really, really nice place that we're all going to love. Where nobody knows us."

"But what about my job?" Simeon asks.

"There's something I haven't told you," Tobias admits. "The Book Trove is going bankrupt. Elsebeth is closing both stores in a few weeks and selling everything. She's going to retire." He throws his arm around his brother's shoulders. "Sorry, buddy. It's going to be rough on you; I know it."

Simeon doesn't say anything; he's staring at the corner of the room, in one of those moods where his eyes and ears aren't registering anything.

Roxanne grabs his hand and swings it. "Uncle Simmy, you'll get another job where we're going," she promises. "And Elsebeth can come and visit us over there."

"It's OK, Rox." Simeon gives her hand a little squeeze.

Carmela, taken aback, had no idea about that. This means that Elsebeth will never repay her loan and, worse, that Tobias has kept another secret from her.

Anticipating her reaction, Tobias adds, "I just found out about it last night when she was here with us, waiting for Roxy to come back."

"Well, that's the kind of thing that's been making me unhappy," Carmela says. "Your secrets."

*Oh, not in front of the kids*, Tobias thinks. "You've done your share of things to make me unhappy."

"I wish we'd never even won the lottery," Lowell interrupts. "I wish we could go back to before. We were fine. What's making us unhappy is all this money."

Simeon, who rarely says much at family meetings, stands up, and they all stop talking. "No. That's not what's making you unhappy. You're making *yourselves* unhappy. Roxy's here with us. Nothing else matters."

❀ ❀ ❀

Moving as far away as possible, but remaining in the United States, means going to the west coast. They both veto Alaska and Hawaii, and Tobias shies away from California, not wanting their immense wealth to attract attention in a state where movie-making is a major industry.

Carmela has her heart set on Oregon because Delphine and her family have been living there for a few years and love it. They moved there from Boston, tired of the frigid winters. Oregon's climate is temperate, its natural resources are beautiful, and Delphine's husband, Theodore, is on the faculty in the music department at Portland State University. There are good hospitals, where Carmela can continue her nursing career. There are good universities, where Tobias can pursue his graduate studies. There are fine opportunities for Simeon and the kids. Tobias agrees to take a closer look at the state.

Carmela requests yet another week of vacation and gets a warning from the hospital administrator. By this time, she's ready to give him her own warning, or simply to quit without notice, which she wouldn't do; she still loves her job, but not the people who are running things at Woodrock Hospital. Instead of appreciating her for staying on when she didn't need the money, they seem jealous of her luck.

To be sure that Roxanne is coping with everything, they wait for three weeks before traveling. Two or three times during the first week, she wakes up at night and comes into her parents' bedroom, as she did sometimes as a little girl when bad dreams frightened her. Twice, she calls Carmela from school, feeling jittery, and Carmela talks her through it.

But since then, she's had friends over a few times, working on school projects and chatting about whatever girls discuss in private. In most of her subjects, she gets As. She's already been to Dr. Appleby six times, and seems comfortable with her sessions. Tobias drives her to school every day, and Lowell walks her all the way to the school door. If he ever stays home sick again, Roxy won't go without him.

They leave Simeon behind with the twins. He's winding up his career at the Book Trove, occupying himself with familiar tasks, not giving much thought to his future, living in the present in the childlike way that he does. Elsebeth stays with them in the evening, and Kenneth, their trusted old friend, takes over before she leaves and spends the night.

Euphoric about how well Roxanne is doing, Tobias splurges on first-class plane tickets to Portland, Oregon, for him and Carmela.

"I used to feel like a low-lifer, lugging my carry-on past all those smug people in first class," Carmela confides as she settles into a seat wide enough for two of her. "Now I know that those people are nothing special. They have money, that's all."

"You're something special," Tobias compliments her, and orders savory appetizers for them to enjoy as they fly across the country. A taxi drops them off at The Nines, a five-star hotel near Pioneer Courthouse Square in Portland, an elegant, modern structure with spacious, luxurious rooms. They enter theirs and marvel at the beautiful city view. Right away, there's a knock, and a bellhop delivers a bouquet of long-stemmed red roses in a tall crystal vase.

"What's the occasion?" Carmela sets the vase on the desk.

"We're coming up on our fifteenth anniversary."

"But that's in October. This is only May!"

"The better to love you with," he says, and takes her to dinner at the Del Inti restaurant, which offers premium

Peruvian cuisine. Tobias has done his homework and advises his wife to save room for the dessert chef's specialty—molten chocolate cake with dulce de leche sauce, so rich it practically makes them drunk.

Free of hearing ears and seeing eyes for the first time since their honeymoon, they make love like twenty-somethings on a first date, and sleep as late as they can the next morning. Owing to the time difference, they're up at 7:00 AM anyway, well in time to greet Samantha Hsing, the real estate agent recommended by Delphine and Theodore. She'll be their hostess for three days, and comes to pick them up in a shiny new metallic-blue Toyota Prius. "We're a very green state," she explains.

Carmela can feel the once-over, even though Samantha is very subtle about it; a minor flick of her long, black eyelashes at the clothes they're wearing, the brands of shoes, Carmela's handbag. In spite of all their shopping, their wardrobes haven't quite caught up with their upper-class status, and might never do so. Thinking rich is hard to do.

"We'll start in Portland." Samantha drives into a community called Pacific Estates, where all the lawns are green, and every resident seems to have the same landscaper. She's doing about ten miles per hour. "These are your typical mid-price homes," she says. "Beautiful houses, all designed by—"

"But they're crammed so close together," Carmela notes. Even their ordinary suburban house in Woodrock has three times as much land as any of these. "We don't want to look right into our neighbors' windows."

*And we don't want them looking into ours*, Tobias thinks. "Let's move up in price a bit," he tells Samantha. She has no idea how much he's worth, and he's not going to give her any clues about that. Not yet.

"OK," Samantha agrees, and they drive to a prettier suburb, a little farther out from the city. "We'll have lots of fun. How many rooms are you thinking of?"

"Oh, I don't know, seven, eight," Carmela says, purposely vaguely.

"Large family?" Samantha asks. "Me, I have three kids, two of them girls, and you wouldn't believe the amount of stuff they generate." She has a warm smile and a friendly attitude, not at all like a pushy saleswoman.

Carmela likes her. "We have twelve-year-old twins, a boy and a girl, so they need their own rooms. And my brother-in-law."

"Oh, that's nice." Samantha pulls into a classy subdivision and parks in front of a model home. She unlocks the door, and they walk in. "How old is he?"

"Thirty-five," Tobias says. "He was injured in a car accident a long time ago."

"Oh, I'm so sorry," Samantha says. She looks him right in the eye and seems to mean it.

Carmela is surprised that Tobias would talk about his brother so openly; then again, Samantha has an engaging personality. She's the sort of person who would make a good therapist, or a good hairdresser—they're so often called upon to perform roles outside their occupation.

"Yeah, it was such a tragedy. He was a great cartoonist, an astonishing artist. He's OK now; it's not like he's helpless or anything. And the kids adore him; he's always been great with them. He has a job and all that. But he's not fully an adult, and it doesn't look like he'll ever be independent."

She asks if he has any family photos, and Carmela takes one out of her wallet, last year's Christmas shot with all five of them in front of the tree.

"Those kids are gorgeous. And that's your brother? Wow, does he ever look like you. Well, it's good you told me about them. We've got three days to find you the best possible environment for your wonderful family."

Samantha is a superb broker who makes them feel that they top her list of priorities. She keeps her cell phone silent, excusing herself now and then to respond to messages while Carmela and Tobias walk through gardens. For a day and a half, she shows them house after house in increasingly fancier suburbs, moving from middle-class neighborhoods with barbecue pits, basketball hoops, and cul-de-sacs, to more fortress-like subcommunities surrounded by iron fences, where you drive through a guarded entry gate to get in. They cover Beaverton, Aloha, and Cedar Mills. As they tour, the houses are getting nicer, but nothing plucks a chord on a harp.

While Samantha is in the ladies' room at the restaurant where they've had lunch, the Hillyers decide to upgrade their house-hunting, and they dig out their heavy artillery—their prequalification in the form of an asset/liability statement prepared especially for the occasion by their accountant. They hand this to Samantha after she pays their bill. She's writing off all these expenses and hopes they pay off, since she can't get a really good reading on the wealth of these clients. Her employer frowns on what he calls "real-estate tourists," whose mission is to go on fabulous house tours in exclusive neighborhoods by posing as buyers.

Samantha has to look twice at the document in her hand, which reveals that these unassuming, normal-looking people have a net worth above two hundred fifty million dollars. "Dessert, anybody?" she offers. They all laugh.

On the afternoon tour, the Hillyers fall in love with a house. Obeying her instinct, Samantha drives them along the shore of Oswego Lake, stopping at a sprawling, lakefront manor on Palisades Terrace Drive that could easily be converted into a Rockefeller-type museum or a luxury resort. "It belongs to an actor. I'm not allowed to say who," she says, enhancing the intrigue.

Mature pines hide the empty parking lot in back. There are no traffic sounds, only the calling of birds. On sculpted paths, they walk around to the main entrance, which takes time. The house, with several peaked roofs, is built like an extended ranch. Arriving at the front, they suck in their breaths, even Samantha, who has shown this property before, but the asking price of 4.1 million dollars was foreboding even for her wealthier clients. The house faces the lakefront, where nothing is disturbing the pristine blue water at the moment.

Tobias takes Carmela's hand and they walk a few steps to the shore and out on the dock, where a rowboat and two canoes are tied. "Lady Luck" is painted in royal blue script on one of them. There's a covered patio with an outdoor fireplace. Flowering bushes and annuals grace the surrounding gardens with a thousand colors. The lot is level, private, and secluded. They breathe deeply of the pine-scented air.

Samantha lets them admire the setting for a few minutes, then says, "There's even a dog run," and points out the long, fenced-in area near the dock.

"Oh, that's OK, we have cats." Carmela laughs.

"They'll love it here." Samantha unlocks the front door, disarms the security system, and invites them into the house, giving them a glimpse of a world they have never inhabited. "Everything you see here is new and ready to go. The owner had the whole house renovated, brilliantly. No old-house, lived-in smell in this one," she says. "If you like to cook, you're not going to believe these culinary appliances. And the wine cellar—wait till you see. You want to do informal entertaining, you go in here." They step into the three-room family suite, which includes a Dream Palace home theater with deep-red stage curtains and plush velour seats. "Movies, TV, music, anything you like. And here's the refreshments counter, with a new professional popcorn machine. Your kids can invite their friends and put on shows."

They take their time in the family suite, trying out the theater's reclining chairs, and then move on to the rest of the house. For formal entertaining, there's a lush sunken living room overlooking the lake, superbly decorated in a modern style, with a bluish, C-shaped sofa; matching paisley easy chairs and ottomans; varnished coffee tables built from natural tree stumps, showcasing their growth circles; and recessed shelving, with a few *objets d'art* and classical books placed randomly for an inviting look.

On the second floor, there are five bedrooms, each of which is bigger than their master bedroom in Woodrock. All of the rooms have hardwood floors, area carpets, and giant walk-in closets. Skylights illuminate the wide hallway. The enormous master bedroom makes them want to spend the night. They all stand there, gaping, even Samantha, who finally declares, "This is what I call move-in condition. Just sell your furniture, hop on a plane, and here you are. Five thousand two hundred fifty square feet, and all yours."

"It's a dream house," Carmela affirms.

"Welcome home," Samantha adds with a flourish. "You deserve it."

❁ ❁ ❁

The next morning, all they can think of is returning to that amazing house for another look, to walk through the gardens and along the shore, and to go inside and browse through all the rooms again. Like an instant dinner that needs only water, this house needs only a family—theirs.

Samantha happily picks them up to take them back. She has spent the previous evening Googling them and digging up everything she can about this wonderful piece of good luck that came across her desk only a week ago in the form of an e-mail inquiry from Tobias.

"We've made up our minds," he informs her.

"Congratulations!" She shakes his hand vigorously, but has to excuse herself to answer the phone. "Yes, don't worry about that," she tells the caller. "I'll tell them. They found a house they really love, so it's all right."

"Sorry," she tells them. "I always like to show my clients

one more house, just in case. You never can tell. Since you're here till tomorrow morning, I wanted to show you this one particular property this afternoon, but it seems that someone else is on the verge of making an offer. What a shame. It's very unusual."

Tobias is suspicious of well-worn sales tactics like this one, but Carmela is curious. "Where's the house?"

"It's in Lake Oswego, near yours," Samantha says. "Actually, it's on Oswego Lake, too. I should explain: The town is called Lake Oswego, and the lake is Oswego Lake. You'll get used to that." She's driving along the shore again, heading in the direction of "their" house. "Say, do you want to go have a look anyhow?" she asks.

"Sure," Tobias says, not minding an extra excursion. Although he feels put off by the notion of living well above the level he's accustomed to, he has to stash his money somewhere, and a fancy house is a great investment, as well as a nice place to live. Samantha has told them that they're at the bottom of the market, and she predicts that interest rates won't go any lower than they are now.

They drive past the street leading to their dream house. "Hello, future home." Samantha waves gaily as they drive on. "And here's the lake." She turns into a picturesque drive with flowering trees on both sides and no other cars. They're approaching a miniature causeway with a single-lane stone bridge across a narrow channel in the lake. "Private Drive," a sign greets them at the locked gate.

Samantha swipes an electronic key in the lock and says, "Welcome to Jantzen Island." The gate swings open. "The only island in the lake. And it's private. Five and a half acres."

"There are houses here?" Carmela asks. The place looks like a storybook illustration. Wood trolls could pop out from nooks in the trees and start dancing, and she wouldn't be surprised.

"One and only one house." Samantha parks the car just

off the road in a pine grove. They stroll along the well-maintained path while she recounts the island's history. In 1929, Carl Jantzen, the founder of Jantzen Knitting Mills, bought the island and had an English Tudor house constructed on it. In 1987, Jerry Stubblefield, the new owner, completely remodeled the main house and the guest house, which took two and a half years. "Do you know who he is?" she asks.

"No," Tobias replies. They sit on an old stone bench facing the lake. "Say, is that Mount Hood way over there?"

"Right, lucky it's clear today." Samantha explains that Stubblefield had been a classmate of Phil Knight, the founder of Nike. Stubblefield founded his own shoe company, Avia, and later made a fortune when he sold it to Reebok.

"There are thirteen thousand five hundred square feet of living space, divided between the main house and the guest house." They walk around, admiring the landscaped terraces, rose garden, waterfalls, boat house, sauna, and lakeside pool with a slate patio, all in immaculate condition. "There are hiking trails, too," Samantha says. "About a mile of them. You can get lost on your own property. If you want privacy and tranquility, this is the place."

"But you said it was taken," Carmela recalls, thinking that she'd like to tour the inside of the house even if another buyer has his eye on it.

"Let me call my office." Samantha dials. "Hi, I'm here now with the Hillyers…Jantzen Island. Any news?" She listens.

Tobias pats his wife's hand and points to a fir tree, where two eagles have perched. They link arms.

"Really? Well, that's encouraging. OK, all right then. We'll probably be here for a while." Samantha turns to them. "As far as we know, it's still on the market. The other people need time. Want to look around for an hour or so?"

An hour turns into two, and they've seen only the ground floor of the main house, which is built like a castle. On the second floor, there are five bedrooms and six bathrooms. Tobias is wondering who on earth would need six bathrooms, but this place is so miraculous that he doesn't ask.

Hungry after all that exploring, they leave the island to have lunch at an outdoor café with a patio overlooking the lake, and then return to the main house, where someone has hung a freshly etched wooden sign reading "Hillyers' Haven." Carmela's eyes open wide, and Samantha laughs. "I think I know who did that," she says.

They finish their tour of the ground floor, which has its own home theater down the hall from the formal living room. The eat-in kitchen features appliances that Carmela has never heard of. Upstairs, two of the bathrooms have high-speed jet tubs, and the décor in the bedrooms is distinctive, each with its own stylistic theme.

Samantha isn't pressuring them, but the Hillyers are warming to this island refuge. It has a beckoning character of its own. Not only does the new sign bear their name, but the air itself seems to be calling them. Still, Tobias ponders what it would cost to live in a house like this, imagining the total for taxes, utilities, designers, furniture, and insurance. The guest house alone, well removed from the main house, is bigger than some houses in their Woodrock neighborhood.

They spend the afternoon touring the house and grounds, finally stopping to rest on upholstered, wrought-iron chairs overlooking a broad fieldstone staircase leading down to the lake. Samantha hunts for something in her folder while Tobias catches his wife's eye. "Oh, I forgot to show you one last thing," Samantha tells them.

"There's more?" Carmela pictures herself swimming laps in the pool while the kids play water volleyball with their friends.

"You bet." They follow her down another pathway through the woods to a clearing, where, framed by tall firs on all four sides, there's a regulation-size red clay tennis court of professional quality. Better than professional quality.

"Holey moley." Tobias sprints ahead of them, lets himself into the court, stoops down, and fingers the crushed shale surface. *Very easy on the bones,* he thinks, considering his forty-year-old knees and ankles. What a fun surface this would be to play on, with a nice, slow bounce, like the courts at the French Open. He could have a Grand Slam court right in his own backyard. No court fees, no reservations. He kneels on the friendly surface and smoothes the clay with both hands, itching for a racket.

"Like it?" Samantha crouches beside him.

"Best clay court I've ever seen."

"Then come see this." They walk through the bushes to an enclosed shelter housing ball machines and surface rollers to preserve the court's perfect flatness. Surrounding the court are sprinklers specifically designed to maintain the clay's optimal water content.

"Look here." Carmela points to a spectator seating area—a small set of bleachers under an awning. And court-side, there's a player bench under a tent, for protection from the Pacific sunshine.

Tobias feels as if he has entered a church. Catching his breath, he asks Samantha the price.

"Nineteen five," she answers without hesitation. She means nineteen million five hundred thousand dollars. The only sound, apart from water lapping at the edge of the lake, comes from birds chattering in the fir trees. "That's for the house and all the other buildings, and the garden, the bridge, the private road, the entire island," she says. "*And* the tennis court." She smiles at him.

❊ ❊ ❊

Enjoying a quiet dinner at their hotel, they're both too

excited to finish their meal. "Do you think it's too much?" Carmela asks.

Tobias balances a forkful of salad. "No, we can manage it fine. The interest rates are so low. Let's figure a monthly payment under a hundred thousand dollars, and then the taxes are going to be around another hundred thousand a year, and maintenance—"

"No, I don't mean too much money. I mean too much, in the sense that people shouldn't live like that, so much wealth for so few." She slides her braised potato slices around on her plate.

"Well, maybe at one time I would have thought that way," Tobias admits. "But after what happened with Roxanne, all I want is privacy, safety. Elegance helps, too." He smiles.

"And tennis."

"Yes. And it's not showy or glitzy. It's quiet and personal."

"Like you." She smiles.

"Like us." He reaches for her hand.

They return to their room and call Samantha, who's been waiting all her working life for a sale like this. For nearly two years, this utopian estate has been on the market. When she sees Tobias's name on her phone, she tries not to sound too eager, but her heart rate must be up around 150. "Samantha Hsing." A commission like this is a career-maker.

"Samantha, this is Tobias Hillyer. We'd like to do business with you."

The only drawback, and it's a humdinger, is that the Hillyers won't sign anything or make a down payment until they return home, get their kids and his brother, and come back so they all can see where they'll be living. On this point, they're immovable.

Samantha respects their modern, democratic family approach, at the same time knowing that she won't be able to get Jantzen Island off her mind until their real signatures validate a promise made on the phone. Their return trip can't happen soon enough for her.

The Hillyers fly home to Woodrock via Newark, daydreaming about how their family will react on discovering their very own private island paradise.

# Chapter 22

Some things can't wait. Not that they're afraid another buyer will grab an island home costing almost twenty million dollars. But they're itching to show it to the rest of the family.

It's the end of May 2009, and school is still in session, but the Hillyers are off to Oregon again, a week after returning home, all five of them. They're crammed into economy class because Tobias doesn't want to spoil them. Simeon and the twins have no idea that their new home occupies an entire island. Carmela and Tobias are going to thrill them.

Samantha picks them up at the Nines Hotel, this time in an SUV with room for everybody. She's in on the surprise, too. "You'll enjoy the schools here," she tells the twins. "In middle school, they have core subjects like everywhere else, but you can also sign up for neat classes like Web design, marine biology, archaeology, art, lots of other interesting choices."

"Oh, cool." Lowell climbs into the rear seat with Roxanne next to him and Simeon on her other side. Since her kidnapping, they've formed human brackets around her whenever they can. They turn off the main road onto the private drive to Jantzen Island. Carmela sneaks a peek at the three of them from the middle seat. They're all looking out the windows at the sunny landscape.

"Dad, where does this lead?" Roxanne asks. She's got her

journal with her. Lowell has a digital camera, and Simeon brought his sketch pad.

Tobias turns around and smiles at her. "You'll see very soon, sweetie."

They get out of the car with the lake on one side of the path, the woods on the other side, and the grand stone mansion in the distance. "Tobe, is this an island?" Simeon asks.

"Yes." Tobias is seeing through their eyes.

"How many houses are on it?" Lowell wants to know. "Is it like a little village?"

Carmela says, "There's only one house on the whole island. It's very private."

"Oh." Roxanne says. "Mom, can we go look around?"

"Sure. Be careful."

"Come on, guys." Roxanne jogs ahead on the path with Lowell and Simeon.

"They won't get lost," Samantha reassures Tobias and Carmela, who watch them disappear behind the trees. "This will be a great place to celebrate their graduations," she notes.

"Oh, that's a long way off." Carmela smiles. "They're only starting seventh grade in September."

"And in the future, what a wonderful setting this will be for their weddings," Samantha adds.

Tobias laughs. "That's an even longer way off." He's not thinking of any such milestones for Simeon, but is already worrying what his brother will do once the kids grow up and branch out, as kids tend to do.

At the lakeside swimming pool an hour later, they catch up with Simeon and the twins, who have already discovered the two houses, the view of Mount Hood, the waterfalls, gardens, terraces, tennis court, sauna, boathouse, and hiking trails. A solitary Great Blue Heron dominates the lake, where Lowell has spotted a red-tailed hawk and two yellow-headed blackbirds.

"Ready to go inside?" Samantha asks them. "You all having fun?"

Roxanne answers yes. They're all smiling restrained, company smiles. Beside the front door of the house, the "Hillyers' Haven" sign greets them. Samantha unlocks the heavy front door, and Lowell gives a low whistle. "Wow, is this how rich we really are?"

Samantha guides them from room to room, sensing something amiss. Preteens are usually enthusiastic, even claiming rooms for their own. These twins are polite, well brought up, and quiet. As for the client's silent brother, she can't guess what he's thinking or whether he'll influence their decision. Anticipating their need for privacy, she excuses herself to sit on the patio with her phone and her laptop, agreeing to meet in an hour.

Tobias leads the way to the tennis court, where they admire the red clay surface, and then sit on the bleachers. "What do you all think?" He's trying to sound noncommittal, but guesses the verdict when the twins exchange one of their personal, sidelong glances. No one answers.

Carmela prompts, "How about you, Lowell?"

He rakes his hair, deep auburn like his mother's. "This is a beautiful place. I would feel like a prince living here." Canadian geese fly in a V above them.

"And?"

Lowell curls his feet under the bleachers. "Well, I'm not royalty. I'm just me." He looks at the court. "That's just how I feel."

"Roxy?"

She's twirling the ends of her long black hair. "In the house, the ceilings are so high, it feels like a museum. And I'd be sad that we were the only people on the whole island."

"Yeah, you know what, it's like having your own country," Lowell adds.

"No, your own *planet*," Roxanne says.

"It's so isolated," he says.

"It would be like telling everyone, look at us, we're super rich," she says.

Carmela feels her face falling, but she puts on a smile. Her husband's expression is darkening, too. "What about you, Simmy?"

Simeon looks around the tennis court. "This whole setup is amazing."

They're waiting for him to continue, but that's all.

"And?" Tobias asks.

"It's not up to me."

"But if it were?"

He gazes at the horizon above the lake. "Then I wouldn't want to live like this. You would have to import people to feel like you're part of the human race. Just us, out here on an island, alone."

Tobias turns away from the tennis court and toward his family. "We want to keep safe and have some privacy after everything that's happened since we won."

"You'll like it, I'm sure," Carmela insists. "Living surrounded by beauty; nothing could be better."

Listening to his family, Tobias is starting to have his own doubts about this island refuge. It won't take long for his new community to discover the truth about his wealth. When that happened in Woodrock, most of his social relationships grew strained. Some people shunned him to avoid the appearance of asking for money. Luck was a factor. He remembers that some people avoided him because of bad luck after his accident; maybe they were superstitious and feared it would rub off on them. He doesn't want this to happen because of showing off their good luck with ridiculously ostentatious real estate. *That's a valid reason not to buy your own island*, he thinks.

Lowell swivels on the bleacher and hugs his knees to his chest. "Mom, Dad. This island is fantastic, but it doesn't feel like home."

And he's right. They argue and discuss, tossing pros and cons back and forth, two against three, for another half hour. In the end, in spite of their net worth, they all agree not to live in a house so remote that it could qualify for its very own zip code.

❁ ❁ ❁

In the afternoon, Samantha, resigned, takes them to visit the lesser house, the lakefront manor on Palisades Terrace Drive in Lake Oswego. This magnificent estate feels ordinary in comparison to the castle on Jantzen Island. But Simeon and the kids fall in love with the house, the grounds, the lake, and the boats. Lowell takes a picture of his sister and his uncle standing in front of the boathouse, the "Lady Luck" canoe in a corner of the photo. They're thinking up names to paint on the other two boats. Roxanne jots down impressions in her journal. Simeon stops to sketch the outline of the spread-out house, with its charming peaked roofs and wide windows.

Inside, the adults talk business in the living room, while the other three tour the second floor, picking out bedrooms, deciding where they'd like the art studio to be. They come clattering down the stairs and explore the family suite, comprising a theater, a game room, and "his and hers" bathrooms with professional makeup lights above the vanities. Lowell finds ping pong balls and paddles on a shelf and plays against his sister. Simeon tries out the pool table, in between trotting around the game room, scooping up balls from their wild hits. All of them are laughing and shrieking.

In the hotel, after the decision has been made, Roxanne says warmly, "Daddy, you can just build the same kind of tennis court at our new house. There's a lot of space—we know because we ran all over everywhere. You can just copy the one from the island."

Tobias hugs her and smiles. "No, Roxy, you all got me

thinking. I need company, too. That court on the island is perfect, but I'd rather join a nice club and make some new friends."

"Dad?" Lowell asks. "Can we keep that sign?"

❊ ❊ ❊

Samantha was right about the house in Lake Oswego being in move-in condition. The Hillyers return to Woodrock and arrange for the sale of their house and furniture after they move. The kids finish school. Simeon helps Elsebeth pack up her inventory for auction. She's adjusting to her loss and even looking forward to retirement.

They host a dinner party for Elsebeth; her girlfriend, Miriam, who officiated at the Hillyers' wedding; and Kenneth and his boyfriend. Bygones having faded away, they invite the Scanlons, all four of them. The kids haven't seen each other for months, and Roxanne breaks the ice, running to hug Andrea and taking her up to her bedroom to talk for hours. Lowell leads Ethan into the art studio to assemble model rockets. Simeon stays with Elsebeth and Miriam. Carmela and Valerie pick up where they left off, as if their last conversation had been yesterday.

Martin and Tobias schedule one last tennis match before the Hillyers move to Oregon. They play in the county park, not at the club, and after their match, they stroll along the bike path and sit on a bench. "You've always amazed me, Tobe," Martin says. "The way you managed with your brother after losing your parents and having to quit college."

"Thanks. When tragedy hit, I lowered my expectations of how my life would turn out. As time went on, I tried to raise them."

"I admire how you coped with all of it—financial struggles, twins, the Book Trove."

Tobias twirls his racket. "Oh, I liked the Book Trove. I always had time to read and think."

"Sure, but not time to have the career you really deserved." Martin stuffs his hair, more gray than red, under his cap. "I felt bad about following my star when you couldn't follow yours. Which was why I was so happy for you when you won the lottery."

"Mixed blessing," Tobias confides. "In many ways. For one thing, Mel and I stopped appreciating small pleasures and victories in life. Winning changed our perspective on ordinary events. And the thrill of winning wore off." He flicks his hand.

"I guess it would," Martin says.

Tobias squints into the distance. "You know how people sometimes wonder what they would do if they won a huge prize—like I did? The weirdest thing is, ever since I won, I've always wondered what would have happened if I *hadn't.* Call me nuts."

"Really? How's that?"

"Simple," Tobias answers. "It's unearned wealth. I was in the right place at the right time, and I haven't done very much but consume and watch over my big fat nest egg. I haven't contributed much of anything to anyone through my achievements."

"No, I thought you gave away a lot to charity?"

"Oh, sure, we did—Katrina victims especially; they still haven't recovered in New Orleans. And the tsunami victims, and Alley Cat Allies, which the kids wanted. But it's not like—like *doing* something. Charity is so easy, you know? An easy way to justify wealth without work—one of Mohandas Gandhi's seven deadly sins."

Martin nods his head. "I'll have to say that the happiest I ever saw you was when you were working alongside me at Boutique Properties. You were so eager and intense, and a voracious learner, excelling and contributing. It was even more impressive because that's not the field you were aiming for."

Tobias agrees that it might have been the best time of his life. He had a sense of pride. "All of you were my mirror—you, the staff, our colleagues in the industry—and I liked what I saw. I've missed that experience."

"It was really something." Martin crosses his ankle over his knee and rests his chin in his hand.

"You know what, Martin? I still follow the news about lottery winners, hoping that some other sensational prize winner will push me off the horizon. The money's great, but not the notoriety."

"I can imagine," Martin says. He's fidgeting. "Want to walk for a while?" They walk silently for a few minutes. "Now it's my turn to admit something." He's looking down at the path, not at Tobias. "When you offered to stay on the job for a dollar a year and I asked for your resignation anyway, I was really afraid that—how can I say this—well, we've always been competitors. After you came into the money, I worried that you might compete against me and build an empire." He looks at Tobias for an instant. "In fact, I was really sweating it out."

"You're serious."

Martin nods. "Definitely. You had the knowledge, the drive, and the money. The economy was sinking. It was the perfect time to start a business and blow the hell out of the competition—me. So I showed you the door before you could steal my client list and my staff."

Tobias grins and shakes his head. "Well, didn't you think I'd do that anyway, out of retribution for getting fired?"

"Nah, I never suspected. Once off the court, you'd just take away your ball and go play somewhere else."

They laugh. "Hey, buddy, I could never have done that to you," Tobias says. They walk to the parking lot.

It's time to go. "You saved Boutique Properties. And me," Martin says.

"Don't even mention it," Tobias says. "I'll come back for

the next board meeting. And you'll all come and visit." They shake hands.

Martin claps his best friend on the back and looks him in the eye. "Don't say good-bye. Just say 'see ya.'"

# *Chapter 23*

The inner life of a child is hidden: from her parents, by definition; from her friends, who might label her "weird"; and from her teachers, who touch only the surface of her sense of self. Roxanne's inner life is hidden from her twin as well. He's part of who she is, but not all; because she is an individual, distinct, and outside of any other being.

Adults, not remembering, or not wanting to know, are oblivious to children's inner lives. Yet preadolescents, not fully formed, wrestle night and day with big ideas: the forces of life, love, loss, and death.

Ghosts preoccupy Roxanne in September 2009 as she walks from class to class in her new forward-thinking middle school in Oregon. In the four months since her kidnapping, she has pretty well recovered from her traumatic experience, having just missed becoming a ghost herself, a ghost who would have haunted all her family forevermore, making them wonder how she would have grown, what she would have become.

Her mother comes to her bedroom every morning at 6:30 before she leaves for work. Barely awake, Roxanne promises Carmela to be careful, to stay with her brother on the bus, to always look around her. Her father watches her go out the door with Lowell every day. She feels his eyes on her, keeping her in sight as long as he can. Her uncle looks for her as soon as he comes home from the university with Tobias. Lowell keeps an eye out for her when they part for gym class or electives. She worries about them worrying about her.

The ghosts that concern Roxanne are those of her dead grandparents. She isn't at all convinced that disembodied spirits really roam the earth, but whatever these things are, they're on her mind.

Not only that, and she won't say this to anyone, but she longs to find out why her Uncle Simmy is the way he is. A semi-sibling to her and Lowell, he's neither a child nor an adult. That's one aspect of her family life that no one ever addresses. Her dead grandparents and her uncle's history are bound together in an imaginary album of secret events that predated her birth.

In the twins' infancy, the ghosts moved with them from their cramped Woodrock home to a second Woodrock house, big enough to accommodate newborn twins. Their shrine migrated from their old bedroom to Tobias's study, where he arranged the photos and mementos neatly on a corner table. He dusted them when he thought about it, and as his children grew, he answered their questions about the grandparents they would never know. Carmela, having a healthy respect for the property of the dead, never disturbed their shrine.

Roxanne hasn't mentioned the ghosts to Lowell, who's in most of her classes. They're both in top-track English and math. For one of her electives, she chose Drawing and Painting Portraits. Lowell is taking Sculpting Natural Materials. Both selected Social Sciences Workshop, which makes their parents proud. It's a little bit of psychology, anthropology, economics, linguistics, and sociology. Something for everybody. It's the last period of the day, and the twins look forward to it all afternoon.

The social sciences teacher assigns his fourteen students a creative project for the semester. They can work alone or in pairs, and Lowell and Roxanne don't think twice before signing up together. Tossing ideas back and forth, Roxanne comes up with a genealogy project. More and more, she wonders who she is and where she comes from; she is curious about the grandparents she never met and about whom no one ever speaks much. Her grandmother's name, Cheryl, is her middle name, and Philip, her brother's middle name, was his grandfather's.

"Let's do our project about the ghosts," she suggests to Lowell after school.

"What ghosts?" Lowell looks around him.

"You can't see them," his sister says. "They hang around the shrine. And in our grandmother's suitcase. Maybe."

Once again, on moving to a new house, Tobias relocated the valise full of his mother's notebooks and pictures without looking inside. After the accident that took his parents' lives, he had gathered her diaries and photo albums and set them carefully in a clean suitcase. Without leafing through them, he added all her sketch pads from her student days. There was also an accordion-type folder, such as the kind used for paying bills or sorting coupons. Tobias labeled the suitcase "Mom's Personal Items" and stored it in the attic in Woodrock.

Prying into his dead mother's inner life was a task he'd had no time for when he was working to support his family. Now, twenty years later, there's still no reason to open it. This time, he placed the suitcase in the pleasant, airy attic of their new home. He carried it up a set of retractable stairs, climbed back down, released the folding stairs into the ceiling, and left the ghosts up there to rattle or mutter or do whatever they pleased.

Roxanne can think of plenty of reasons to pry into the suitcase, and she shares some of them with Lowell. "It's genealogy," she says. "We can look up what was going on in the world when they were young." Drawing on what she's learned in their stimulating class, she says that tracing your family tree can help you understand the history, economics, and culture of an era.

This all sounds fine to Lowell, who hasn't given as much thought to the assignment as his sister has. He applies himself to the tactile aspects: designing posters, drawing illustrations, and planning a book to assemble and print from the computer. Roxanne will interview their father, their far-off relatives, and the ghosts of their dead grandparents.

"How are you gonna do that?" Lowell challenges.

"Easy. Just ask Dad if we can go up there and look inside the suitcase."

❋ ❋ ❋

With her spotless references, Carmela finds a staff position as psychiatric nurse at a nearby hospital, Oregon Health & Science University, although she really doesn't need the salary. Tobias transfers to a graduate program at Portland State University, where he's working on his PhD in anthropology alongside students who are mostly under thirty.

Simeon wants to find a job, but Tobias tells him he doesn't have to. Armed with the negotiating skills he acquired while vice president of Boutique Properties, Tobias persuades the university administration to accept Simeon as a part-time freshman majoring in studio art practices.

This semester, Simeon has registered for Modern Art, an art history course covering romanticism, realism, impressionism, and twentieth-century art movements. For his studio course, he'll take Introduction to Drawing, which concentrates on techniques and strategies for transforming three-dimensional space into two-dimensional drawings. The syllabus calls for creating the illusion of depth and texture with the materials at hand. Next semester, he'll take two more courses, and they will see how it goes. At this rate, Tobias calculates, Simmy will take ten years to get his BFA degree. If he sticks to the program, that is.

The night before his first class, Simeon is like a kid on Christmas Eve. He can't sleep. He's mostly worried about keeping up with students much younger than he is. But Tobias has paved his way, meeting his two professors beforehand and explaining his brother's differences. "This is the work he did before," he says, showing the faculty members a folder of Simmy's cartoons from his teenage years. "And this is about where he is now," he says, showing one of his brother's inexpert sketches of their dock and boats in Oswego Lake.

The instructors don't seem to mind. "We'll help him. Recovering from a brain injury can be a lifelong process," one says.

The other professor remarks, "An artist's work does not have to be flawless in order to express something heartfelt." Tobias looks forward to the daily drive with his brother, nine miles to the university campus in Portland.

❁ ❁ ❁

Because Aunt Joyce is still struggling, Tobias extends her loan once again. And he stays in touch with Elsebeth, who's now on social security. Her girlfriend, Miriam, is still working, so they're doing all right. He never makes Elsebeth feel guilty about the loan that she can't repay. The loan was out of gratitude; Tobias hadn't expected to make a major return on his investment, knowing that the Book Trove might not survive the great recession of 2009.

But Martin's business is another story. The market has improved dramatically since its lowest point in March 2009; Boutique Properties is making a small profit, and certain sectors of the commercial real estate market are springing to life. Martin is putting out feelers to prospective buyers who want to expand their businesses, and he's received some bids competitive with Trump's commercial real estate enterprise. Tobias knows all this because he travels back to New York every quarter for regular board meetings.

Simeon misses his boss and talks to her on the phone once a week or so. During winter vacation from the university, he will travel with Tobias to go visit her. He's hard at work in drawing class on a picture of Elsebeth in her store. In his drawing, Simeon is peering through the store's display window with the sun shining on his face. He can hardly wait to deliver it personally to Elsebeth in December to commemorate his fond memories of the Book Trove.

❁ ❁ ❁

"OK, go ahead," Lowell says.

"No, you," Roxanne prods.

"Well, it was your idea—"

"Yeah, so now it's your turn."

The twins wait until after dinner. "Dad, we have something to ask you," Lowell says.

Tobias is in a relaxed frame of mind, enjoying his new home. Everything is going well, everybody is settled, Carmela likes her new job, and Simeon is holding up in college so far, in his own fashion.

"Go ahead." His son is growing, now finally a little taller than his sister. They're both excited about something.

"Can we go up in the attic and look in the suitcase?"

"Which suitcase?" He knows which suitcase. He could feel the children's eyes on the suitcase as he wrestled it up the attic stairs the day after they moved in, and he guessed that, sooner or later, their curiosity would surface. He's heard bits about their genealogy project.

Roxanne puts on the charm, smiling in her enchanting way. "The suitcase that belonged to our grandmother. For our social science project."

Tobias can't come up with a good excuse to deny them, and is gratified that they didn't simply sneak up to the attic when he wasn't home and dig into the suitcase on their own.

But he cannot admit to them that he's not yet ready to unpack its secrets, and might never be. They're watching him.

"All right. I'll go up and get it down for you."

"Thanks, Dad." They stand there, waiting for him to get up. Lowell steadies the folding staircase, and Tobias hauls down the suitcase, one step at a time. He sets it on the floor of the spacious bedroom hallway, where it kicks up a fluff of dust as the twins lug it to the art studio.

"Be careful with those old papers and stuff. Handle them gently."

"We will, Dad."

❋ ❋ ❋

He remembers her drawing sometimes, in the days before alcohol vanquished her nights, her days, and her mind. She made him colorful little picture books, in which she printed the first words that he learned to read. She taught him to draw, or tried to, but he was more interested in sports than in art. When Simmy came along, he proved to be a more apt pupil. Tobias didn't mind, because his mother's concentration on his younger brother meant more freedom for him.

In the faded drawing his children are showing him now, a little boy about five years old is sitting in an easy chair, his small hands curled around his infant brother, bundled in a baby blanket on his lap. "Is that you, Dad?" Lowell asks.

"Wow, yes, I guess it is." Tobias feels tears trying to rise to his eyes, but he won't let them. "Holding your uncle Simmy."

The twins exchange a private glance, but Tobias notices. "What else did you find in there?" He needs to know, but isn't prepared to see.

Another twin glance. "Oh, papers, diaries, drawings, a couple of paintings. Poems, baby pictures, things like that," Roxanne lists.

❋ ❋ ❋

"Do you think we should?" Lowell asks.

"I don't know. He might get upset," his sister answers. "What if it's something horrible?"

"What can be horrible? They're already dead." Lowell is sorting through the envelopes in his hands.

"I say we read ours first. And then give Uncle Simmy the one for him. And then think about it."

"OK." He slides a finger along the seal of an envelope addressed "To My Future Grandchildren." The glue, twice as old as the twins, gives way, and a two-page handwritten letter slides out. The twins are alone. Their mother, home from her 7:00-to-3:00 shift, is in their new kitchen, humming and sautéing something delicious. Their father and uncle are on their way home from the university. They kneel on the floor of the art studio, hunched over the letter, and read together:

*To my dear, precious future grandchildren,*

*Well, hi! I'm your Grandma. Cheryl. Or Grandma Cheryl. I don't know if you have another grandma, but if you're reading this letter, it means that I've passed away before I got to meet you. And I'm sad about that. Since you're old enough to read, I just want you to know that I made some mistakes, and if I hadn't, I would have been healthy enough to still be alive, to know your names, to hold you in my arms, to return your first smiles, to read you stories, to give you presents, and to talk to you on the phone.*

*Well, you're kids, and I don't want to burden you with a lot of details about silly grown-up problems. So the mistake I made was, I had a drinking problem. Wine. It made me feel better when I drank it. Then the happy feeling wore off, and I drank some more. And more. Until pretty soon, wine got to be my best friend, and later on, it became my only friend. Probably the reason we didn't get to meet in real life was because all that wine ended up making me too sick to live. I'm sorry, dear grandchildren.*

*I don't know if you're boys or girls, or how many of each, so I'll imagine you're one boy and one girl. Hi, sweeties! This is*

*Grandma Cheryl from the Great Hereafter. Now, I have to tell you the truth about how I deal with the hereafter. I don't know if there really is such a thing, but just in case there is, I'll always be there, thinking of my family—including you—and sending them good ideas. If there isn't, well, then, I'm doing it now, in this letter and the other letters, the ones for your father and your uncle. Either way, I'm always going to be a part of you.*

*What I want you to understand is that you come from good people. I figure your dad is my son, Tobias. Simeon probably won't have any kids. Tobias (Toby, we call him) is a strong man, only 19 as I write this letter, but already a man. He would have picked a strong woman for his wife—your mom, that is. Toby always tries to do the right thing, no matter how hard it is. In that respect, he's done way better than I have. And you know what? Having your kids outdo you is one of the blessings of life. So you two—or however many you are—must be 100 percent great. I love all of you.*

*Have a happy life. And do good work in school. I'll be up here watching over you.*

*Love forever from your Grandma Cheryl.*

Roxanne, kneeling on the floor, curls her head into her arms like someone in an air-raid drill would have done when Grandma Cheryl was a girl, and cries. Lowell, trying to soothe her, is crying, too. He gathers the other envelopes, addressed to Tobias, Simeon, and Philip. The one for their grandfather Philip is not a letter, but a greeting card in a matching envelope that had never been sealed. Without talking, Roxanne lifts its flap and tugs the card out. It's one of those museum cards, blank inside. Cheryl had written, *Dearest Phil, I am so sorry for ruining all of our lives. You deserved better. I always loved you. Cheryl.*

❋ ❋ ❋

It's eight in the evening. Carmela is still sorting out their possessions, happily rearranging the living room, kitchen, and family suite to her satisfaction. The cats are sociably following her around and getting in the way. Simeon is in the art studio, poring over his art history book for class, deciphering one sentence at a time. Tobias is in his new study, a spacious room upstairs with a view of the lake. Intent on his thesis, he jumps a little when the twins tap on his open door.

Roxanne gives her father the card addressed to her dead grandfather, Philip. "We found some notes in the bill box inside the suitcase." Then she hands him his own letter in its sealed envelope. "And some letters."

Tobias holds the envelope under his desk lamp, startled by his mother's familiar handwriting. He turns it around and over. "Thanks, Roxy, Lowell."

"Aren't you going to open it, Dad?" Lowell is holding the envelope for Simmy.

"I will. Later." He needs time. *How old was I when she wrote it? Why did she write letters to the family?* "Who else did she write to?"

"There's one for Simmy." Lowell shows him the envelope.

"And one for us," Roxanne says.

"For you? Really?"

"She said she was guessing she'd have one grandson and one granddaughter."

This letter from his dead mother feels like an intrusive house guest who arrives unannounced, moves in with all her baggage, and stays put. Tobias sets it on the top shelf of his credenza. It's been sealed for more than twenty years, and it can wait until he has the fortitude to read it. He has no room in his schedule for entertaining ghosts. "Better go give that one to Uncle Simmy."

Simeon is sitting at his desk in the art studio, head in hand, intently following the words in his textbook with one finger. Roxanne gives him the envelope, on which is written "To My Son Simeon."

"What's this, Roxy?"

"It's a letter for you. From your mom. From way back, a long time ago."

Simeon closes his textbook and stares at his name in his mother's handwriting. "Mom," he says to himself. He looks up at his niece and nephew.

"We found it in the suitcase in the attic."

"Thanks, guys." He slides a finger under the flap and unfolds the letter. Lowell and Roxanne leave the studio as he starts to read.

❁ ❁ ❁

The next morning, Tobias goes to his brother's room to awaken him; unusual, because Simmy is one of those people with a built-in alarm clock who always get up at the same time.

"My dream was just ending," Simeon says. "An amazing dream. Pictures, colors, sounds, music, people talking, like a movie."

"That's great, buddy. What was it about?"

Simeon looks up into the corners of his bedroom, trying to piece together the fragments of his dream. "Mom. She was here."

"In your dream."

"She was right here, in this house. In the art studio."

His brother looks different. Tobias hands him his glasses. Simeon puts them on, but his eyes are still focused on something he can see without them.

"Tobe. She was telling me what to draw. She drew a sketch for me. I can still see it. And she told me to copy it down."

After they return from a day of classes, Simeon goes up to the art studio with his new portfolio from the university. He sits down at the Creation Station and remains there for the rest of the evening.

"Go on up and get Uncle Simmy for dinner," Carmela tells Lowell.

"He's skipping dinner tonight," Lowell tells her. "He says he has a good idea for a drawing."

The next morning, without letting anyone see his sketch, Simeon places it carefully in his portfolio and takes it to his university drawing class.

❁ ❁ ❁

Another day passes, and another, and then the weekend. Tobias postpones reading the letter. Carmela doesn't interfere, but Roxanne is waiting, and her father knows it. On the fifth day, she asks if he would write a reply to his mother's letter. He demurs, but she says she needs it for her project. He tells her that he's busy, and he'll get to it when he can give it his proper attention.

"Dad." She's standing in the doorway of his study, her slender hands on the jambs, her long black hair framed by the bright hallway behind her, morning sun filtering down through the skylights. "Please, just a short little note. We already wrote ours. And Simmy wrote his. Mom even wrote one, too. You're the only missing link in our nuclear family tree."

He checks for the envelope, still on its shelf, untouched. It's early October 2009. In two months, it will be the twentieth anniversary of his mother's death by his hand in her car. He dreads going back two decades to confront her as if she were still alive, tasting his grief and guilt again, this time without the distraction of his brother's catastrophic injury. His daughter, a silhouette in the doorway, is standing still.

"Roxy, I'll read it. Now." He gets the envelope.

"Thanks, Dad." She steps out and shuts the door. He opens the door and goes to make himself a cup of coffee. He goes to the bathroom. He checks his e-mail and powers down his computer. He moves books around on his desk. Then he sighs and slits the envelope with a letter opener, even though its glue long ago lost its grip. He sits in his chair and reads:

*Dear Toby,*

*Oh, I hope you get to read this letter. You're 19 years old as I write. And I'm dead by now, dead by my own hand, so to speak.*

*You're probably wondering how I can manage to write a letter that makes sense, since I can't even get my act together well enough to write an acceptable absence note for you or Simmy when you miss school. Well, we drunks have our lucid moments. I'm taking advantage of one of mine to tell you the truth about some things that you should know.*

*When you left for college, that made me think. It was just me, alone with Dad, who long ago gave up on me. And Simmy, coping with school the best he could under the circumstances, which I'll explain. Then one day, between bottles of wine, it struck me how your life must have been unnecessarily hard, and how happy you must have been when you escaped to college.*

*The fact is, you were forced into a role you were too young to assume. Simeon was a little gift—we weren't planning any other children. I was already drinking heavily by then, and I could barely handle you. Don't get this wrong. You were a nice little kid, a typically active five-year-old. We sent you away to Aunt Joyce when it was near time for your brother to be born. I knew you didn't want to go. You cried enough to water all the lawns on our block. And that was a hell of a way to introduce you to your new brother—by shoving you out of the house for a few weeks.*

*Not that you resented him. You took care of him from the beginning. You did such a good job that I abandoned parenting more and more. My excuse at first was that I was still working, and you were the help I needed. But soon I was inflicting responsibilities on you that were far too weighty for your age—baby-sitting your brother while I got drunk. Feeding him. Watching him in the bathtub. Putting him to bed. Then when I got fired for being an unfit schoolteacher (you should know this), it just got worse. Dad was on the road for long hours, and you were Simmy's actual parent for most of the time, except when you were in school.*

*There's something else, Toby. I didn't drink while I was pregnant with you. But I did drink with Simmy, when I didn't even know I was pregnant. This was the first trimester, the most dangerous time. I stopped as soon as I knew, but it was too late.*

*And the alcohol got to him. There was a diagnosis. It took a few years to pinpoint, but here it is—fetal alcohol effects. It's less severe than fetal alcohol syndrome, where you can see the deformities, and the child is likely to be retarded. Not that it's any comfort, knowing that I damaged my own child. (Whatever killed me, I deserved it.)*

*The doctors warned me that he might have learning problems. Problems paying attention, problems socializing with other children, problems budgeting his time. Problems growing up.*

*Before I go on, one thing you have to know is that I hid this diagnosis from Dad, who was suffering like every other family member from my disease. And from you. And from Simmy's teachers. And from Simmy himself. I was so ashamed. And I wanted people to treat him like a normal boy. The harm that was done didn't show on the outside.*

*Another thing the doctors said was, we should take care that Simmy never gets a head injury of any kind. No concussions from playing football or falling off a bike, that sort of thing. Well, he wasn't athletically inclined anyway, which might have been because of the damage to his brain. I knew that you would always protect him, so that was the least of my worries.*

*But I do have to explain why I seemed to favor him, and I am so sorry, Toby. I loved you as much as I loved him, all along. How can I measure and weigh how much I loved my two sons? Toby, if I gave him more attention, it was my own selfish attempt to make it up to him for what I did. That, and nothing more.*

*Toby, I want you to know that I believe in you. You are a strong man, and a good man. Your gift to your brother, being a parent to him in my stead, I was grateful for until my dying day.*

*Oh, Toby. My wish for you is that you follow your heart,*

*but more important than that, follow your conscience. Always do what you think is right. I don't know how your life will turn out, because you are good at so many things. But I'm sure that you will do something to help people. Exciting things will happen in your life. You never know. Go for it, Toby!*

*All my love,*

*Mom*

Tobias sits there with the letter in his hands and rereads it, and then again, holding the pages away from his face so he won't smudge the old stationery. He folds the letter and feeds it into its envelope, which he places in his desk drawer.

He puts on his tennis clothes and shoes and goes to the local club, but not to meet anyone; he has no appointments today. In an empty court away from the sounds of play, he hits serves absently, not striving to improve his form, just keeping his body moving while his mind churns. Half an hour passes, then an hour.

Another man comes by with a tennis bag. He's wearing sandals, and it looks like he has socks on, but when he comes closer, Tobias sees that he has vivid suntan demarcation lines on both calves from wearing tennis socks. The man's skin is a deep tan, except for his wheat-colored ankles and feet. Tobias starts picking up his balls to let the other player have the court.

"Wait, don't go," the man says. He's Asian—could be Chinese or Hawaiian, with straight grayish-white hair and a lean, athletic build, a little shorter than Tobias, maybe five-feet-nine or ten. His body is young, and his face older, fifty or sixty, hard to tell.

"Are you waiting for someone?" Tobias asks.

"No, just came out to see who's here. Such a nice day." The man unzips his bag and takes out his white socks and tennis shoes. He's not in a hurry. "Though you never can tell with the rain in Portland," he jokes as the sun passes behind a cloud and the blue sky turns gray.

Tobias walks over and offers his hand. "I'm Tobias Hillyer. Just joined the club last month."

"Ezekiel Lim. I go by Zeke." He shakes firmly. "Zeke and ye shall find." He takes out his racket. "Want to hit some?"

"No, sorry, ordinarily I would. I'm working out my emotions. A sad event happened."

Zeke scans his face. There's a crease above one eyebrow, a nod. "I'm sorry."

Tobias asks for Zeke's number and saves it on his cell phone. "There was a death in my family," he explains, but makes no move to walk away.

Zeke clasps his racket in front of his thighs and inclines his head slightly. "My sympathy. And I hope that the years to come will wash away everything but the goodness." His voice is clear and quiet, his words distinct.

"Thank you," Tobias says to Zeke. "I'm thinking about that." He's rereading the letter in his mind again, replaying his brother's childhood, looking for clues he missed, reviewing his own youth, and stopping short at the accident.

Zeke waits for Tobias's drifting eyes to meet his own. "Pain is natural, but in the long run, your joys will be greater than your sorrows for having gone through this catharsis." He could be a priest, except that he has no doctrine to drill, no sermon to preach.

Tobias is startled by this congruity. He is hearing exactly what he needs to hear from another human being. "I've always thought that it was my fault," he says to himself and to Zeke.

Zeke opens his hands. "No, it is part of the motion of life. The tides ebb and flow, go in and out. You are not to blame."

Tobias shakes Zeke's hand again and turns to go. *You are not to blame.* The gray cloud floats away and the sun warms his face, drying his tears as they drop on the hard court like sprinkles from a fleeting rain shower.

## *Chapter 24*

"Take one every morning." Simeon's new psychiatrist is writing a prescription. "For not too long. Three months."

Knowing now that Simeon's brain damage predated the accident that worsened it, Tobias and Carmela have found a mental-health clinic that specializes in treating victims of substance abuse—even if the substance was abused many years ago. And even if the abuser and the patient were not the same person.

Simeon hasn't taken medicine of any kind since his accident twenty years ago. "Will I still be able to draw?" he asks.

The psychiatrist smiles. "We can't make you into an artist if you weren't one already. But nothing in our therapy will interfere with your artwork."

Tobias doubts that one pill a day, plus a program of therapy, will work miracles on Simeon. He doesn't expect an overnight transformation; in fact, he doesn't expect anything at all to change. "OK, buddy?" he asks his brother, who's sitting there, mulling it over.

Carmela prods, "You'll never know if you don't try."

"All right." Simeon takes the prescription form from the doctor and slips it into the portfolio that he's carried everywhere since entering the university.

"One pill a day for three months," Tobias repeats to his wife in the car. "What good is that going to do?" He looks in the back seat at Simeon, who's gazing out the window in his absent sort of way.

"It's not just one pill. Think about it. One pill can represent ten years of research. A hundred scientists experimenting in their labs day and night. A thousand frustrating blind alleys. Dozens of clinical trials. Piles of studies, papers, and reports. A lot of determined effort goes into just one pill."

❁ ❁ ❁

Zeke is making Tobias run all over the court. They're not keeping score, but if they were, Tobias would be down a few games. The last partner who kept him on his toes like this was Martin.

It's starting to drizzle and they pack up their rackets. "Good therapy, eh," Zeke comments.

"Oh, I'm OK," Tobias says. "Sorry about unloading my problems on you the other day. My family story is pretty complicated."

"Family stories are seldom comforting." Zeke unlatches the gate and holds it open. "And never simple."

Two days later, they play again. Tobias has to admit that Zeke, who must be at least sixty, is the better player. He soon discovers that Zeke is a staff member at the club and one of the coaches.

"What do you do?" Zeke asks him after polishing off their match, 6–4, 6–2.

"I guess you could say I'm retired. I'm a full-time student, going for my PhD in anthropology. Long delayed."

Zeke accepts his answer without inquiring further. Tobias feels the urge to unburden himself and tell the truth about his staggering wealth, which continues to overwhelm him when he assesses it almost two years later. "I won the Mega Millions in New Jersey in 2008."

"Congratulations. Wonderful!"

"Actually, I'm ashamed to admit it." Tobias hangs his sweat towel around his neck.

"How did you win?"

"I missed my train."

Zeke nods, as if accustomed to meeting instant multimillionaires. "Missing a train, simple as that. And why did you miss your train?"

They sit on a bench under the trees and Tobias tells his story.

"Beautiful," Zeke says. "Christmas, a blind man, nobody helps, and then you come along." He isn't being sarcastic. "It was bound to happen." He folds his hands in his lap.

"Oh, no, I don't believe in predestination." Tobias crisscrosses his hands back and forth.

"It is not essential to believe. The tides ebb and flow, go in and out, whether you believe or not."

❖ ❖ ❖

Months away from earning his PhD, Tobias watches Simeon work on his therapy and his college assignments, and comes up with a plan that makes his soul sing. Waking up at night, he paces the long bedroom hallway in his luxurious new house and resolves to open a mental health clinic that will serve rich and poor, old and young, and will operate on a principle of therapy through empathy. The latter being an expensive commodity, he's going to rely on his bottomless wallet to build and staff the clinic and establish an endowment. He's so inflamed by the idea that he cannot keep his brainchild from exploding and has to control himself to keep from waking Carmela before her alarm goes off.

As soon as she emerges from the shower, he spills it out to her, talking in uninterrupted paragraphs, pouring out everything that's been weighing on him since he won the lottery. He has half an hour before she has to leave for work, and he talks as fast as the disclaimer at the end of an investment ad on TV.

Carmela listens, gets into her uniform, puts on her makeup, combs her hair, and opens the Venetian blinds. They make the bed together while he continues unreeling his plans. She hasn't said a single word.

"We'll call it the Cheryl and Philip Hillyer Memorial Clinic. And we'll stress two alternative kinds of therapy I've been researching," he continues. "Art therapy and music therapy." She heads to the kitchen, and he follows. "You know how Simmy has a kind of intuition where he can look at anyone's drawing and read what's inside that person? We'll hire therapists who work that way. This is different from behavior therapy or drug-assisted therapy."

Carmela blows on her hot oatmeal while Tobias concludes, "You'll be in charge of designing every single program. I'll coordinate the location, construction, staffing, and financial underpinnings. And one more thing. We'll need a business manager. And someone to direct our research agenda."

She stops dunking her tea bag and looks at him. The morning light coming off the lake highlights her auburn waves, still thick and alluring. She smiles at him, marveling at the sparkle in his dark eyes when something inspires him. It's the look she used to see when he was reading something fascinating that he wanted to share.

"Martin," she says. "And Valerie."

"Yes."

"Oh, would I love to do that," she says with a wide grin. "But you're dreaming."

"Yes. I'm dreaming. And we *will* do it. Because we can." He lifts both hands in a sky's-the-limit gesture, and then clasps her hands in his. "We really can."

❊ ❊ ❊

Lowell rolls up his jeans and wades into the lake to steady

the rowboat while Simeon climbs in and takes the oars. Ethan Scanlon, visiting with his sister and parents, helps Simeon shove off. Roxanne and Andrea, giggling, get a head start in their canoe, the one named "Lady Luck." Ethan and Lowell nearly capsize their own canoe out of eagerness to beat their sisters in a race refereed by Simeon. They're all barrel-chested in bright-orange life vests, which Carmela insisted they buckle on.

It's the third day of their visit, and they're leaving tomorrow. On Oswego Lake, the October sun warms their frolics while their parents watch from the patio. The visit has gone so fast and so well that nobody feels like parting. Conversation turns to Boutique Properties, now a profitable corporation. Martin reports that, with the approval of the board, feelers have been floated in the market, just to see what the company might be worth. Always on the lookout for a more promising growth industry, Martin is toying with the idea of selling out and going into health care; specifically, electronic, digital data centers for medical information.

Tobias, a member of the corporation's board of directors, wants to know, "What are we worth, then?"

There are screams and cheers from the lake as the girls reach the shore in victory. The boys finish five canoe lengths behind them.

Martin laughs and applauds them, and then turns to Tobias. "There are strong indications that we could sell at a net profit between six and ten million dollars. If we sell the entire business, that means all of your equity investment will be returned in full—you'll get 30 percent of the profit, and I'll get 51 percent. Our senior executives and profit-sharing employees will divide up the remaining 19 percent."

"That's a fair return, considering the weakness in the industry," Tobias says.

Over the patio table, Carmela gives Tobias a little squint from both eyes, and he begins.

"We have a business proposition for both of you," he offers Martin and Valerie. Drawing imaginary charts in their outdoor boardroom, he outlines plans for the Cheryl and Philip Hillyer Memorial Clinic in more detail than the presentation he gave to his wife. Martin and Valerie, thoroughly surprised, listen intently.

Martin rakes his gray and red hair, watching the children climb out of their boats while weighing the prospect in his mind. Valerie waits.

"Martin. We need a business manager for our clinic. Valerie. We need a director of research."

Carmela smiles at both of them. "We'd like to invite you to move to this part of the country and join us."

Before they can react to this astonishing request, Tobias jumps in, "And I desperately need a tennis partner. This coach, Zeke, over here at the club, has been pulverizing me day after day for a month, and I can't take it anymore."

Martin and Valerie laugh. "We'll think about it," she promises. They have a lot to think about.

❋ ❋ ❋

One thing that hasn't changed about Simeon is the drawing he's been hiding. No one, not even the twins, has been allowed even a peek at it. It's hidden in his portfolio except for when he works on it during class. His drawing teacher is in on it, too. Tobias goes to see him for a kind of older-brother conference, but the professor says only that it's a good drawing and Simeon is making progress, is on his fourth version of the same picture.

There are unmistakable changes in Simeon's attitude and habits. Tobias and Carmela don't know whether it's the cross-country move, the university, the emotional upheaval of the kidnapping and rescue, the therapy he's taking, or the pills (unless they're placebos, and Tobias can't discount that). It could simply be the passage of time, which cures some ills.

It might even be a consequence of the letter Simeon received from his dead mother, another secret that he won't share with family members. "When all is said and done," Carmela notes, "the human brain remains a mystery."

Tobias can't put his finger on it, but his brother seems more engaged, for one thing. That blank look on his face—looking without seeing—isn't there anymore. When Simmy meets him for lunch at the university after his art history lecture, he pours two coffees from the spigot, caps them, and sets one on Tobias's tray. Not that he wasn't helpful before. But now he's acquired some indefinable presence of mind that was lacking.

The most curious development is that Simeon bought a cell phone and paid for it himself, using savings from all his years of work at the Book Trove. The whole family had gone shopping in town and dispersed on their various errands. When they met at the fountain in the center of town, Simmy was standing there with a big smile and the new phone clipped onto his belt. "It takes pictures and videos, too," he said, and assured Tobias that he could well afford to pay the monthly charges. He gave them all his new number.

Since then, he's been spotted more than once talking animatedly on his private phone while striding along the lakeshore next to their new home. Nobody knows who's on the other end of the conversation.

***

While waiting for the Scanlons' decision, Tobias calculates his ability to realize his dream, with the help of a few phone calls to his financial adviser in New York.

The state of his financial health is vibrant. 2009 was better than the year before; as of October, his investments of two hundred million dollars, deposited with Goldman Sachs, have netted a return of 20 percent on his balanced portfolio of high-quality stocks, bonds, and munis. Even after considering all of his outside investments, personal expenses, and everyday working capital of forty to fifty million dollars, his holdings at Goldman have increased to two hundred forty million dollars.

He can no longer in good conscience hold all this wealth to himself. Opening his books, he shows Carmela that they have enough to comfortably pay their mortgage, their children's college educations, his and Simeon's university expenses, their vacations, cars, entertainment, clothes, and anything else they might ever want. They will have enough to buy land for their new clinic, to hire an architect, and to build and staff the perfect home for Therapy Through Empathy. After that, much more than enough will be left over to make a huge difference to some worthwhile cause. Carmela, impressed by the thoroughness of his analysis, agrees.

"We're in a position to make a lasting contribution to a humanitarian cause by donating one-third of all our investment income every year for the next twelve years," he tells her. Since the expected return by the premier investment house averages 10 percent, their donation will amount to eight to nine million dollars each year, with a net contribution of one hundred million dollars over the entire term of twelve years. "This is a very generous contribution, and yet doesn't come near to denting our nest egg," he declares. "It will continue to grow from the two hundred forty million dollars we have right now, and we'll have an ample amount to invest in our clinic as well."

Together, they decide to evaluate a number of charities and begin their giving in a few months, at the start of the New Year, 2010.

"That will really make a difference," she marvels. "Good work."

"Oh, it's thanks to Martin's business acumen. He helped me frame the strategy for charitable donations. He says this is a way to make Wall Street part of the solution, for once."

His friend's proficiency at strategic financial planning gives Tobias full confidence that when Martin runs his clinic, he will keep it on a good financial footing. *If* he agrees to join them.

✿ ✿ ✿

It's time to go home after classes, but Simeon is late to their usual meeting place, the university library. Fretting about what could have possibly happened to his brother, Tobias remembers that now he has a cell phone and is just about to call him when Simmy arrives, panting, from around the corner.

"Sorry I'm late." His glasses are steamy, and his shirt is a little rumpled. The only thing that looks neat is his ever-present portfolio. "I can't go home yet. One of the teaching assistants has a few pictures in the faculty art exhibit that I have to go see."

Tobias checks his watch. "Well, OK, we can go for a little while, but then we have to get home because—"

"No, Tobe, I mean, you don't have to wait around for me. The TA is going to drive me home."

Tobias feels the way he did when his children learned to ride two-wheelers. He could run with them and shout encouragement, but they were the ones who had to balance and get up after a fall. His brother, thirty-five years old, has the demeanor of a five-year-old who has just cycled all the way around the pond by himself without falling.

"You're sure? He knows where you live? What's his name?"

Simeon laughs and claps Tobias on the shoulder. "I'll be fine." He laughs again and starts walking away, fast, clutching his portfolio under his arm.

"What time will you be home?"

Simeon turns around. "Oh, I don't know, after dinner. Don't worry."

"If you need me, just call," Tobias yells as Simeon rounds

the corner behind the library and disappears. He goes home alone and spends the next several hours worrying. Dinnertime comes and goes. Carmela, Lowell, and Roxanne are helping with the worrying, making it worse.

"Dad, can we call him now?" Lowell asks. "It's almost nine o'clock."

They all look at one another, not knowing what to do. Carmela offers, "I'll call him," and dials his cell phone while they all watch. "Simmy? Mel. You OK? Yeah . . . Oh, that's nice . . . Really? Great! Sure, yes, do. See you soon. Bye."

She thrusts the phone up in the air like a trophy and breaks into a room-illuminating smile. "He's on his way home. With a *woman*. Some teaching assistant in the art department. He sounds really happy."

"A girlfriend?" Roxanne has a gleeful expression on her face, like a cheerleader whose team has just scored a touchdown.

"He didn't say girlfriend," Carmela says.

They wait another half hour. No one can concentrate on anything, even the TV. When Simeon's key turns in the lock, they all jump up and rush to the door. Tobias gets there first.

Simeon steps in calmly with someone who appears to be a smaller, lighter, female version of himself, a young woman of maybe twenty-seven with dark-brown hair and big dark eyes behind rectangular glasses, similar to Simmy's. She's pretty, with an infectious, dimpled smile framed by colorful, dangling, asymmetrical earrings that look handmade. There's a matching pendant around her slender neck and multicolored bracelets on both wrists, contrasting with her simple and elegant black dress. Her complexion is light tan and she's wearing little makeup.

"Tobe, this is my friend, Cybele." Simeon pronounces the French name clearly and carefully, see-BELL. "She's a fantastic watercolor artist."

"Not true," Cybele protests, extending her delicate hand

to Tobias. Her fingers are lightly stained by a few spots of paint that resisted washing.

Simeon finishes his introductions. "This is my brother, Tobias. His wife, Carmela. My niece and nephew, Roxanne and Lowell."

Tobias is about to lose it. He cannot identify the conflicting emotions coursing through him all at once. This girl, this woman, this perfectly normal, beautiful, kind young woman with a friendly smile, is with his brother, who's resting one hand lightly on her elbow as if they were comfortably intimate. He cannot think of what to say. He feels like scooping her up and waltzing around the room with her in his arms. Instead, he takes her hand and says, "Cybele. So beautiful. Cybele. Welcome, come in."

## *Chapter 25*

"She's delightful," Carmela says. They're holding hands, walking on a trail around the lake. The kids are inside, doing their homework. Carmela took the day off to help Tobias plan the clinic. Tobias had one seminar for his PhD, and then came home without Simeon, who's staying late. Again. He practically has to make an appointment to see his own brother, who lives with him.

"I keep thinking—oh, this is a terrible thought." He zips up his jacket; it's getting windy around the lake, though not as raw as November on the east coast.

"No, say it." She twists her red and orange silk scarf at her neckline and looks at him.

"I keep thinking, maybe we'll find out there's something wrong with her."

Carmela laughs. "My thoughts exactly. But there isn't. We're just being parents."

"To Simmy?"

"Right." They shush through fallen leaves.

"That's not all." He pauses. "Does she really love him, or is she just hanging around for the money?"

"That didn't even occur to me. She seems so sincere. She—"

"What I mean is—this is horrible—can a woman love him, the way he is, you know, I mean the way he *was*, and—"

"Well, two things." Carmela stops walking. "First, she might not even know about the lottery."

"Yeah, well, she sees how we live, the house, the cars." He sweeps his arm in the direction of home as they resume walking.

"Oh, lots of people around here have nice houses. And for all we know, she might have rich parents. But women fall in love with men for their talents. And their looks. Simmy's cute. Like you. And his art is improving. More than that, maybe she admires him for overcoming adversity. There could be a lot of reasons."

Tobias raises his eyebrows and shrugs. "Maybe. And now he wants to take driving lessons."

"At a driving school?" Carmela imagines the dangers.

They're halfway around the lake, at a point where they can just make out their house and wharf in the rays of the setting sun. "No, with Cybele. She's already started teaching him."

In the evening, Simeon calls to say that he's staying overnight in Cybele's apartment near the university campus. It's his first night away from his family in twenty years.

Tobias wakes up at 2:30 in the morning and can't go back to sleep. Carmela is not in bed beside him. He finds her in the guest room with a book in her lap. "I couldn't sleep, either," she says.

❋ ❋ ❋

For Thanksgiving, they invite the Highgates, who moved to Oregon a few years ago—Carmela's sister, Delphine; her husband, Theodore; and their grown children, Gabriel and Beatrix, who sang like angels at their wedding when they were little. Theodore, a professor of music at Portland State University, is fascinated by music therapy, and offers to help Therapy Through Empathy get started.

Simeon has invited Cybele, who goes into the art studio

with the twins and admires Lowell's sculptures and Roxanne's portraits of her friends.

On the Monday after Thanksgiving, the Hillyers rent a floor of offices in downtown Portland as a temporary home for their clinic, until the architect they haven't yet hired presents his design for the land they haven't yet bought, and builders erect the structure that exists only in their minds.

University midterms are over, and Simeon surprises them with an A in his drawing class and a B on his art history exam. He's spending a lot of time studying and drawing, and he's been staying over at Cybele's more often these days.

Since Tobias doesn't have to drive his brother to campus every day, he flies to Los Angeles with Theodore for a week to try out art therapy and music therapy. Gamely, he offers himself as a subject at the Aphrodite Institute for Art Therapy. Theodore does likewise at Harmonia Music Therapy Services.

"It's an eye-opener," Theodore tells Tobias over dinner after his first session and interview. "Or an ear-opener. I thought I knew mostly everything about music. I didn't know that music therapy causes functional changes in behavior and the nonmusical brain. Studies prove that."

"Maybe that's why you're so well-balanced," Tobias says. "You're a musician."

Theodore laughs. "No, I'm as nutty as anyone else out there. Seriously, this is what happens: The patient's emotional response to music stimulates relaxation and leads to physiological changes in the brain and the body." He taps out an elegant rhythm with his fork on his glass. "These therapists help with all sorts of conditions—they reduce blood pressure and heart rate, they promote socialization, help with language development, control moods, treat depression and aggression—that's not even the whole list."

Tobias goes to meet the art therapist, Dr. Idan Katif, a kindly man with a soft yet penetrating voice and a faint Hebrew accent. Framed on his wall are his board certification and a number of degrees and titles, psychological as well as registered art therapist and licensed creative arts therapist.

His approach is intuitive, he explains, and fits itself to the patient like wet clay to a sculptor's hand. "Some people have been in therapy for years without overcoming their difficulties," he says. "Here, you're immersed in the experience. Once you break through an inner barrier, you won't have it anymore." He hands Tobias a blank sheet of off-white drawing paper and opens a tray of pastels in fifty different colors. "Right from the beginning, trust your sense of beauty and follow it, step by step, until it tells you to stop."

Tobias wonders how Simeon felt, confronted by a blank page, and not remembering how to draw. Out of his element, he fills the page with decidedly unartistic-looking, unrelated shapes. Some have colors inside of lines, as in a child's coloring book. A pink kite-like object flies in one corner. At the bottom is a yellow sun with purple rays that look like insect legs. There are two disconnected train tracks and a pair of eyes with long lashes. Tobias has no idea where these crazy objects are coming from, nor does he know why he stops at the precise moment when the drawing looks complete.

The therapist gives him a blank piece of writing paper and asks him to jot down words that describe this object, and then that object, and so on, until the whole strange picture has been annotated. He gives Tobias another sheet of drawing paper and asks him to draw what was omitted from the first picture: to fill in what was inside the blank spaces in the first drawing. "Go deeper," he encourages. And that is followed by another written page of descriptions, which Dr. Katif asks Tobias to read aloud. "I prefer that you call me Idan," he says. "So we're equals."

During an interview after the session, Idan explains that problems show up in patients' art when they're ready to be released. "It's a natural and pleasant process that penetrates deeper each session," he says. The patient needs courage to start the process of therapy. But entering a state of intuitive flow is surprisingly easy. Once there, the patient can accept what is exposed in his art.

The main benefit of art therapy is the ability to see the truth about what is going on inside, which is always missed and never approached through thinking and analyzing. "Healing is unencumbered by theoretical orthodoxies," Idan says. "Once you connect with intuition, you have a much wiser source than any mixture of psychological methods."

"Mel, what happened is almost indescribable," Tobias reports to his wife on the phone after his second session the next day. "Art therapy turns you inside out. You reveal secrets about yourself, *to* yourself—harmful thoughts that you didn't even know existed. You depict your inner workings without even trying. Poisonous notions come out in the sun, dry up, and blow away. Gone. For the first time, I woke up this morning without some unnamed worry hovering around, looking for a negative fact to latch onto."

"It's really that good?" Carmela asks.

"Yes. And music therapy—it brings the outsides in. Theodore says you hear the happiness of the world and absorb it. They're opposites, but they can work together. I'm starting to think we're onto something with Therapy Through Empathy."

The next day, Tobias asks about the popular tough love approach. Idan shakes his head and says that punishment never helps anybody. What does help is to enter a good state, where there is a sense of freedom and love. From there, patients conclude that what they thought was all right before was actually suffering. Only by entering a calmer state can a patient see the difference. "We're accustomed to the way we feel throughout our lives. Even a state of constant stress is our comfortable status quo. So we don't want to change it. But once we experience a better state, we can choose to change."

❋ ❋ ❋

At the beginning of December, Tobias receives the one gift he's been craving. Martin calls and says, simply, "Tobe? We're in." Then, in characteristic Martin style, he warns that this might not be a permanent venture because he still has his eye on more ambitious projects. Tobias, exhilarated that his friend is joining his dream, barely listens when Martin reminds him that leadership is in his DNA, and he'll want to strike out on his own again and build his fortune.

"Give me a date so I can mark my calendar," Tobias tells him.

"For when I can start at the clinic?"

"No. For when you're moving into your new house out here so I can get you a complimentary membership at the club. I signed us up for the men's doubles tournament."

Martin laughs. "As soon as I can, buddy."

❋ ❋ ❋

"Hey, Tobe. Want to go out for a walk?"

It's December 23, and the university is on winter break. There are no threatening rain clouds in the sulky, gray sky, and it's warm for December in Oregon, 50 degrees. Tobias has other things to do, but he says yes and puts on his jacket. Something in his brother's request commands attention.

Week by week since starting at the university, Simeon has been striving to recover his lost art, with a lot of hard work on his part. Occasionally, he shows a half-finished sketch or drawing to Tobias, but mostly, he keeps them in his portfolio because they're not yet polished. In his teenage years, he drew only cartoons, but now he's learning formal techniques of drawing and, next semester, painting.

They follow the smooth lakeside trail and then enter the woods on a rougher path, kicking up little rocks as they hike, and chatting about the university. Simeon has registered for three classes next semester instead of the planned two: one art history course and two studio classes. This time, he went to registration with Cybele instead of Tobias.

"Can you handle that OK?"

"Sure, I'm getting the hang of studying," Simeon says. "And the studio classes are fun."

Then, just like that, he changes the subject. "You know, Tobe, all those years when I was brain-damaged, that was a good time for me, a growing time, years not lost. The whole time, I always had pictures in my head, and now I'm drawing them."

Tobias stops still on the path, as if a deep gulch has suddenly opened in front of him and he has to brace himself to keep from tottering into it. "What are you talking about?" He has never heard such an expression of personal insight from his brother.

Seeming not to notice, Simeon veers left onto a divergent trail, and Tobias follows him. "Those were good years I spent with your family," he remarks.

Tobias stops again. "With my family? But it's your family, too!"

"Of course it is," Simeon says agreeably.

Now Tobias feels like the younger brother. If only his life would stand still for a moment so he could look ahead to where it's going before it rushes right on to the next unexpected byway.

"Well, someday, I'd like to start my own family," Simeon says calmly, as if discussing which good movies are coming out this weekend. He quickens his pace, and Tobias speeds up to stay with him. "And before that, you know what?"

The way this conversation is going, Tobias won't be astonished if Simeon announces that he is forming a political action committee in order to run for Congress. "I have no idea."

Simeon laughs. "Well, Cybele and I want to open a

gallery. A little, tiny shoebox, maybe in Portland or one of the towns. With pictures and sculptures by artists we know. And by us," he confides happily.

Tobias is struggling with what to say when Simeon plants his biggest surprise. "Tobe. After the holidays, I'll be moving in with Cybele. Her apartment is big enough for the two of us. We want to live together."

This time, Tobias stops and can't go on. He hasn't been paying attention to the trail marks, and if they go in any farther, they'll get lost in the woods.

Simeon is a few paces ahead when he sees that he's walking alone. He turns back and puts his arm around his brother's shoulders. "Want to go back?"

"Yeah, let's go." They turn together and find their way back to the main trail, the smooth, easy path that leads to home.

❀ ❀ ❀

It's Sunday, January 3, 2010, and Simeon is moving out. Carmela is poking around the art studio, checking for anything he might have missed. Tobias is sorting out the family's empty suitcases, picking two that are in good shape. Roxanne is alone in her room, crying. Lowell carries a box down the stairs and looks out the window at Simeon, who's setting another box out on the front porch while watching for Cybele's car. "Dad? Can Uncle Simmy just stay here with Cybele?" Lowell asks. "We have lots of space."

"That won't work, son." He ruffles Lowell's hair. "Lovers need privacy."

Cybele pulls into their circular driveway and waves through the open window. Tobias can hear music from the classical radio station. Simeon runs to meet her. They hug quickly and walk hand-in-hand to the house, talking and laughing.

This is all transpiring too fast for Tobias. "Roxy," he calls up the stairs. "Come on down and say good-bye to Uncle Simmy."

Cybele greets everybody, smiling and bubbly as usual. They're all doing a good job keeping their emotions under control, except for Roxanne, who trudges down the stairs with downcast red eyes.

Simeon hugs her, and she begins to sob. He holds her tighter. "Roxy," he says too softly for anyone else to hear. "Roxy. Don't cry. I'm not going far away." Her shoulders are shaking in his embrace. "We're coming right back next weekend for dinner. Will you show me your new drawings next time?"

"OK," Roxanne mumbles into his chest.

Cybele puts her arm around Roxanne from the other side. "Keep working on your portraits, OK, Roxy?" she asks gently. Tobias can see why his brother loves her.

"I will." Roxy sniffles.

"Next time I come, we'll draw together," Cybele promises her.

As the car drives away with Cybele, Simmy, and all of his possessions, each member of the family slinks away to a private spot to brood. A family of five has become a family of four, and the big house feels so empty.

Tobias goes upstairs to Simmy's bedroom, bare except for the furniture, some papers on the desk, and an easel in the corner with an old drop cloth tossed over it. He closes the door most of the way, so that all he can see is a crack of light coming from the window overlooking the lake.

Devastated, he goes to the tennis club, not to play or practice, just to watch other members playing and to hear the satisfying thwack of rackets connecting with tennis balls; the rhythm assures that the world is still turning. Zeke is inside one of the courts, coaching a high school player on his serves, and Tobias sits on a bench, watching them.

"Hey, Tobe." Zeke comes over after the kid leaves. "Haven't seen you in a few days. Want to hit?"

His head is hurting, his heart is sore, and his feet weigh two tons each. "I can't. Sorry. I lost my brother." He drops his head in his hands and his elbows on his knees.

"No. Oh, no, what happened?" Zeke squats next to the bench, looks up at Tobias's white face.

"No, not really lost. He's alive; he's fine. It's me. He moved out today. He's moving in with his girlfriend. He doesn't need us anymore."

Zeke sits next to him on the bench. They're silent for a few moments. "When someone leaves, you lose the caring," he says.

"Pardon?" Tobias lifts his head.

"The caring. You took care of him," Zeke says.

"Almost like he was my kid. But he was more than my kid." In a reverie, he reviews scenes from the past—Simmy in a hospital bed, learning to walk and talk again, going to physical therapy and occupational therapy, going to workshop, and working at the Book Trove. "Taking care of him all those years and looking out for him was my heart's mission."

"And he became independent," Zeke says.

"I always hoped he would. I hoped so hard that it was my deepest wish. Though I never expected him to leave."

"But you should rejoice." Zeke smiles at him, a fatherly kind of smile.

"I guess so." Tobias tries to sit up straight against the weight that's pulling him down.

"Yes, because it means your job was well done." Zeke clasps his hands in his lap. "And now your job is finished."

❊ ❊ ❊

On January 12, 2010, the earthquake in Haiti pushes sadness over Simeon and all other thoughts out of the way. Tobias and Carmela mourn for the children without homes, without limbs, and without parents. They agonize over images of panic, loss, pain, and destruction. In a fair world, the earth would not have swallowed the citizens of an impoverished island nation. In a just world, anyone who could spare anything would send help to Haiti, immediately.

"There must be something we can do. Now," Carmela says.

"There is," Tobias says. "Remember, we figured out how much we could contribute to a charity. We were supposed to start after the New Year."

Carmela remembers. After Simeon moved out, they busied themselves with preparations for the clinic, postponing the decision about charities.

"Now we have a reason to do it."

"How much? I forgot," Carmela asks.

"It's going to be eight to nine million dollars a year for twelve years, which adds up to one hundred million dollars."

"How are we going to supervise that?"

"We're not. We'll see if Elsebeth wants to do it."

Tobias calls Elsebeth and ends her retirement for as far into the future as they both can see. She agrees to manage his long-term assistance for the victims and for rebuilding Haiti and making it stronger. He flies to New Jersey to meet with her and her partner, Miriam, the Unitarian minister, who's going to help, along with volunteers from their sanctuary.

The old Book Trove no longer exists; the space it once filled has been cut up into two separate commercial properties. One is occupied by a tutoring service for students. The other office is vacant, and they rent it for their new foundation, named Haiti From the Ground Up, with Elsebeth as executive director.

As Tobias says good-bye to her until his next visit, Elsebeth declares, "Something good can always come out of something bad."

❋ ❋ ❋

Tobias still sees his brother on campus, and they eat lunch together on the days when they're both there. Sometimes Cybele joins them. Today, it's just Tobias and Simeon, who's excited about something. His rectangular glasses are a little foggy, perhaps from the sweat of happiness, if there is such a thing, because his work has been selected for a joint faculty-student exhibit in the art department. "They picked one of my drawings," he says. "And two of Cybele's watercolors. Friday night. Can you come?"

"Of course I can come." On Friday, Tobias drives home from the university, picks up Carmela and the kids, and drives back. It still feels lonely, just the four of them. There's a sensation of much more than one person missing.

At least fifty pictures are on display in the bright, high-ceilinged classroom that's serving as a gallery for the exhibition. Visitors are milling about with champagne flutes and little plates of finger sandwiches, just as at a regular art opening. The Hillyers spot Simeon and Cybele in a cluster of students and faculty members, and Simmy waves them over. He's dressed in a classy outfit that looks as if it might have been influenced by Cybele, who's all smiles in a short violet dress and long earrings.

His drawing teacher is making a little speech about Simeon's challenges and how far he's come, how he's been hiding his work from his family to surprise them. "He's made the most progress of any student this semester, and we're tremendously proud of him," he says. "Good work, Simeon." He claps him on the back.

Caught between embarrassment and elation, Simeon says, "It's all thanks to my brother and his wife."

"Not true!" Carmela protests.

Cybele leads them to the panel where their pictures are hanging. Her evocative watercolors include a view of Oswego Lake, with a flowering tree and hummingbirds in the foreground, and a painting of Simeon standing in profile, his rectangular glasses just slightly awry, as they often are.

"Oh, look, Lowell," Roxanne says. In the largest drawing on the panel, a striking study in perspective, the university art building towers in the distance at the upper left. A walkway, narrow at the back and wider at the front, leads diagonally from the door across green grass to the lower right, where Simeon and Cybele are gazing at each other through similar eyeglasses, each holding a portfolio. Under their feet is the signature *SIM* in block letters.

"Mom, look." Lowell turns his mother by the shoulder in the direction of Simeon's picture.

"Oh." Carmela inhales with an audible gasp, and then bursts into quiet tears. "It's amazing."

Tobias stands with his arm around his wife, mute from emotion. Could this be the trick of a sympathetic professor yearning for his charming but struggling student to succeed? But no, although it's a traditional drawing and not a cartoon, its lines are reminiscent of Simeon's early capacity to convey whimsy, to celebrate the commonplace, and to make an ordinary scene extraordinary. Tobias stands there taking it in, afraid that any words would sputter out in incoherent babbling.

"Do you like it, Tobe?" Simmy asks.

Tobias tries to arrange his features in a normal expression. "It's the most beautiful drawing I've ever seen." Beside him, his children are glowing.

Simeon sets his ever-present portfolio on the floor and unclasps it. "I have one more picture. Can I take it out?" he asks his professor.

"Sure!" The man is grinning. He knows something.

Simeon pulls out a cardboard folder and opens it to reveal a cartoon in black and white. Just to the right of center stands Cybele, smiling her sparkling smile, long dark hair trailing on her shoulders, big eyes behind her trademark rectangular glasses. She's wearing a floor-length gown with a single shoulder strap. Kneeling at her feet is Simeon, dressed in a dark suit, with monogrammed French cuffs peeping out from his coat sleeves. In one hand, he holds an open ring box containing an oversize diamond giving off flashes of light, as if generating its own electricity. He's holding the box up to Cybele, who's just about to reach for it.

Cybele stares at the cartoon, not trusting her eyes, which are tearing. She takes off her glasses to wipe them and puts them back on, looks up at Simeon standing in front of her with his cartoon.

"I didn't know your ring size, so all I have is the drawing for now. Will you marry me anyway, Cybele?"

"Yes!" she says and falls into his arms. The little group around them cheers, and others in the room walk over to see what all the fuss is about.

One of the professors congratulates Tobias. "How does it feel to be the brother of a celebrity?" she asks. Simeon and Cybele have drifted to the center of the room, surrounded by admiring guests.

"It feels fine. Just fine. A living dream."

While the party is going on, Tobias and Carmela prepare a check at a table in the back as an engagement present for the couple. "What do you think?" Tobias asks his wife. "Should a hundred thousand dollars be enough for them to start up their new art gallery?"

Carmela is already thinking of holding the wedding at their new house. The home theater could serve as a chapel, and guests could mingle in the family suite and living room. "Sounds great," she answers, wondering if Simmy even has a checking account.

One by one, the students and faculty members shake hands with Simeon and Cybele and slip away to their busy lives, until the Hillyers are the last ones in the room. With both hands, Carmela offers the check to the new couple.

Cybele looks at her fiancé. Simeon has a faraway look in his eye. Tobias thinks, *Oh, no, not that vacant wandering again.*

"Tobe. Mel." Simeon is looking directly at them. "Thank you so much. This would really help us get started. But you know what? We want to do it by ourselves, work on our little gallery until people come because it's good. It's not fair for us to get a head start."

Tobias puts the check in his pocket, awkwardly. "We understand," he tells them. "But we'll always be here if you need us."

❊ ❊ ❊

Lowell and Roxanne are first to discover the picture left in Simeon's bedroom. "Probably nothing under there," Lowell says.

"Then lift it up," Roxanne suggests. Their eyes meet.

He lifts the drop cloth and peeks, then lowers it. "Incredible," he says.

"Lift it off. Let me see."

They raise the heavy cloth together and drop it on the floor in a heap. "This is brilliant," Roxanne says.

"When did he do it?"

"No idea. I never saw him working on it. Something this big is hard to hide."

They stand before the 30 by 40–inch art board almost without breathing. There's a noise at the front door. "Better cover it up," Lowell says.

The next day, they tell their mother when their father is not at home. She hadn't thought of looking under an old drop cloth on the easel; in fact, she had stayed away from Simeon's old bedroom, not wanting to confront the mixture of feelings his absence was causing her. When the twins remove the cloth in the sunny bedroom, she holds her face in her hands and scans the wide drawing back and forth, again and again, as if watching the pendulum swing on a grandfather clock. "It's spectacular," she finally pronounces.

"Do you think we should tell Dad?" Roxanne asks.

"No. No. Don't say anything. He's not ready."

❁ ❁ ❁

Spring semester is under way, and Tobias has accepted his brother's departure, more or less. The two days a week when he's on campus, they meet for lunch at the student union. Sometimes Simeon brings Cybele. This time, he's alone.

Searching his brother's face, Simeon says, "I left a couple things for you when I moved out."

"You did?" Pretty much everything Simmy needed moved out the day he did, although he left practically all of the art supplies in the studio for the twins. "Where?"

"In my old bedroom."

"I haven't gone in there."

"It's OK to step in there. I cleaned it up," Simeon jokes.

"I'll look tonight," Tobias promises. He goes straight home after his seminar and enters the room, closing the door behind him. On the desk is an envelope addressed in his mother's handwriting, "To my son, Simeon." Tobias takes a deep breath and opens the envelope, unfolds the letter, and finds that it's a wordless message.

It's a drawing of a teenage Simeon smiling brilliantly, finishing a finely detailed cartoon of a youthful Tobias, who's smashing a tennis ball over the net, both feet off the ground, levitating with joy at pounding the winning ball. At the bottom right corner, Cheryl's right hand, holding a pencil, is wearing the birthstone ring that their father, Philip, gave her after Tobias was born. At the bottom left corner, an empty wine bottle lies on its side.

Tobias sits at the desk for long minutes, contemplating the picture and the people in it. Then, he lifts the cloth from the easel and stands before the most original and penetrating work of art he has ever seen.

In Simeon's secret drawing, an enormous pair of eyeglasses with rectangular frames occupies most of the forty-inch width of the art board. The glasses are upright, with their lenses facing the viewer and their legs pointing away. The lens on the left is a little farther away from the viewer, and the lens on the right is a little bigger because it's closer.

Simeon has drawn these eyeglasses as giant frames for two cartoons. Cartoons, Tobias always thought, are meant to be funny, and yet, it seems that the best humor in any art is flavored with a sprinkle of sadness.

In the lens on the left, Tobias is walking with Simeon on a trail in the woods, his arm loosely around Simeon's shoulders. Autumn leaves in glorious northeastern colors are scattered on the path. Tobias is looking straight ahead, his mouth forming words. Simeon is looking at his brother and fitting his feet to his stride. The brothers resemble each other closely, except for Simeon's glasses.

In the lens on the right, the two are walking away from the viewer, parting as the trail divides ahead. Their faces are fully visible as they turn to wave good-bye to each other. Spring wildflowers in pastel hues dot the trees and the undergrowth.

Tobias, his dark hair touched with gray, has the sculpted posture of a natural athlete. Simeon stands erect, but the slight slant of his shoulders suggests long hours practicing a meticulous art. Although they're the same height, Simeon appears a bit taller as he raises his hand high in a farewell gesture. His mouth is pursed in a pensive expression, but there's a bright light in his eyes.

Tobias is raising his hand in response, staring ahead to the path that his brother has chosen. His dark, shining cartoon eyes are focusing into the distance beyond the easel, and his brows are tensed in caution, but there's a hopeful light in those eyes—they're peering as far ahead as they can see into the forest. They dominate the picture.

Those eyes would see through trees, if they could. They would see around corners. They would survey every branch of the trail ahead, would inspect the unseen path, would look out for vines that might snag, for stones that might fall.

Those eyes, if they could, would see the future and make it safe. If only they could.

Standing alone in the room, Tobias turns away from his cartoon likeness, so true to life that it seizes him like a reflection in a mirror.

Instead, he connects with the smiling eyes of his cartoon brother, a figure caught in motion, like a high-speed snapshot. Those eyes, behind rectangular lenses, look ahead, but just far enough to live life frame by frame. *Come what may*, those eyes are saying. *You never know.*

# *Acknowledgments*

To Kat Gautreaux and Grael Norton of Wheatmark for championing my cause. My book is their book too.

To Michel Hersen and Victoria J. Hersen for their interest, involvement, and uncountable research contributions over the course of a year. A tall hurdle makes the runner jump high. And with deep gratitude to Michel for sharing his art.

To Béla Nagy for his astute advice on hair design.

To Ellen Extract for her incomparable taste and advice on jewelry, again and again.

To Debra DeYoung, who speaks for those who cannot speak for themselves.

To Sarah-Kate Maskin, Helen Orr, and the Van Buren Book Babes, with thanks for their hospitality and their allegiance to the written word.

To Giora Carmi, extraordinary art therapist, for sharing his insight and his empathetic and effective methods of therapy.

To exquisite classical guitarist Francisco Roldán, for teaching me not to be afraid.

To Chandler Fulton, PhD, and Elaine Lai Fulton, PhD, brilliant and distinguished Professors of Biology Emeritus, Brandeis University, for their early and steadfast support of an unknown writer.

To Barbara Liss Goldberg, a brave lady in a hat, always smiling, and an inspiration to the heartbroken. Many thanks for her warmth and encouragement. To Ivan Goldberg, fleet of mind, possessor of perfect page-number recall, with appreciation for his intuition and 2:00 a.m. e-mail.

To Beth Tulino for loving my characters as much as I do. Her involvement with *You Never Know* shaped and sharpened the climax. Her fidelity rendered a drawer full of rejection slips inconsequential. Her perceptive comments confirmed my resolve to tell this tale. My deep appreciation always, Beth.

To Deborah Urciuoli for her genuine goodness, vivid intelligence, clarity of mind, sense of humor, and uncanny insight into human nature. Her encouragement month after month made all the difference. As I wrote, she was always in the front row of the audience. My unbounded thanks forevermore, Debbie.

To George Cheah with love and appreciation for being my encyclopedia; and for reading, analyzing, diagnosing, telling the truth, and setting things straight – right on target, every single time. No one else could have taken your place.

Lilian Duval is the author of the forthcoming story collection *Random Acts of Kindness*. She is an amateur classical guitarist, and is a survivor of the 2001 terrorist attack on the World Trade Center. Lilian and her husband live in Ridgewood, New Jersey.

CPSIA information can be obtained at www.ICGtesting.com
260592BV00001B/2/P

9 781604 945201